Empire in Pine

Book Three

The Black Rose

Empire in Pine

Book Three

The Black Rose

By

Naomi Dawn Musch

Empire in Pine

Book One: The Green Veil
Book Two: The Red Fury
Book Three: The Black Rose

Desert Breeze Publishing, Inc.
27305 W. Live Oak Rd #424
Castaic, CA 91384

http://www.DesertBreezePublishing.com

ISBN 10: 1-61252-860-0
ISBN 13: 978-1-61252-860-1

Published in the United States of America
Electronic Publish Date: July 2012
Print Publish Date: July 2013

Editor-In-Chief: Gail R. Delaney
Content Editor: Melanie Noto
Marketing Director: Jenifer Ranieri
Cover Artist: Jenifer Ranieri

"Charm is deceitful, and beauty is vain, but a woman that fears the Lord, she shall be praised."

Proverbs 31:30

Chapter One

1893

In the playful dance of moonlight and shadow, Jesilyn knew it would be nearly impossible for Clayton to tell her apart from Corianne, her twin. Her eyes were cooler, more silvery than Cori's brilliant blue ones. But in the darkness of the rose garden, with the full moon turning all the world silver and black, Clay would never tell the difference.

This wouldn't be the first time she had fooled him. Her tricks had begun as something of a game, answering the door when he had first started courting her sister, pretending to be Cori, then laughing when he didn't catch on right away and blushing to the roots of his white-blond hair. She'd also intercepted a note or two -- well, all right; three, actually -- and had written replies copying her sister's curvaceous hand. Those letters had caused a stir for a few moments but no lasting harm, and he hadn't seemed to mind her jesting overly much.

The most fun had been the time he'd come to pick up Cori for church one Sunday in his rig. Cori was sick and couldn't attend. Jesi was supposed to give Clay the message, but instead, she'd donned her sister's bonnet and taken a seat beside him in the coach, allowing him to flirt with her the entire way to church. He didn't catch on until they stood side by side, singing from a hymnbook together, and she leaned over and told him who she was. If she could have captured his expression forever then, she would have. Well, in a way, she had. She'd stored it in her memory and played it over and over whenever it came to mind.

Jesilyn couldn't say just when she'd started enjoying her tricks a little too much, or when the pangs of jealousy had first set in. But before long, she wondered who she was really fooling.

Now, staring at Clay through the moonlit window as he waited for her sister out there in the rose garden, the pangs sharpened. Cori was spoiled. She got everything she wanted, whether she deserved it or not. Who was to say that, in fact, Jesi wasn't the one who deserved Clay?

She scowled. No, he'd never recognize her tonight, and she didn't need much time.

She let the curtain fall and slipped a shawl around her shoulders. Peeking out her bedroom door, she stepped into the hall and tiptoed down the stairs, anxious to get out the door before anyone stopped her. She slid her hand down the long banister, pausing at the bottom as she glanced around, certain the family housekeeper and Cori were nowhere in sight.

Quietly she slipped out the door onto the wide porch of her parents' two-and-a-half story home and pulled the door shut with hardly a click. A quick beam of light from the gas lamp in the hall cast a streak across the porch stairs and then disappeared.

Clay's head jerked up. He walked toward her. With only the barest backward glance, she hurried down the steps and met him in the moonlight.

"I didn't think you were going to come," he said, his voice deep and husky.

"Of course I'd come." She slipped her hands into his, and he kissed one of her knuckles. A shudder passed down to her toes.

"I don't want to get you in trouble. It is late."

She squeezed his fingers and smiled into his eyes, not in the least bit worried he might recognize her. "What trouble could you possibly get me into?"

His teeth shone white in the shadows of his face, and she stepped a little closer. Wisps of his breath skimmed her forehead as she leaned toward him.

She was going to kiss Clay Dalton.

Light flashed across the porch and onto the brick walk. Jesilyn dropped her hands from Clay's and stepped back just as Corianne appeared in the doorway.

"Clay? Is that you?"

Sensing his uncertainty, Jesi glanced at him.

"Y-Yes. Cori?"

Clay flashed Jesi a look, too hard to discern except he didn't appear pleased.

Cori came down the steps. She faltered. "Jesi? What are you doing out here?"

"I was just talking to Clay while he waited for you. We were... smelling the roses."

"In the dark?"

"The night dew makes their aroma more intoxicating."

"Intoxicating?" The smirk in Cori's voice sounded more amused than curious or suspicious. "Are you sure you aren't trying to steal Clay?"

Cori joked, but Jesi's chest burned. She toyed with a ringlet at her neck. She should just admit it. "Of course not. How do you know good old Clay wasn't trying to steal me?"

Cori laughed as she drew closer and hooked her arm in Clay's. "As if that would happen."

The burn drove deeper into Jesi as her sister smiled up into Clay's blue eyes, presuming he would never be interested in Jesi. If Cori only knew how close her beloved had come to compromising himself. Jesi swallowed.

"Well, I can say you're absolutely right, my darling," Clay said, gazing at Corianne. He sounded overly certain.

Jesi's palms sweated despite the chilly night air. She fidgeted, annoyed with both Clay and Cori. Moving off the path, she strode into the dark rose garden. She inhaled a sweet scent of dew, barely aware of the faint smell of the roses.

She forced her voice into nonchalance. "Will you be out here long?"

"What does it matter? With Papa gone on the railroad and Mama down in Chippewa Falls with Gran and Gramp, who's to care how long I stay out?"

"What about Evie?"

"Evie's gone to bed already, as I'm sure you know."

Jesi glanced up at the dark square of their housekeeper's window.

"Yes, I suppose she has. It is late. I feel like I have some sort of responsibility to chaperone the two of you." She let out a little laugh, forcing a humor she didn't feel.

"Why don't you go inside, Jesi? We won't stay out long. Clay has classes tomorrow morning, don't you?" Cori cast him another soft glance as she held both of his hands.

Jesi balled her hands at her sides. "All right, then. I'll leave you alone, but don't be long."

She strolled away, careful not to snag her silk gown on the rose bushes as she wandered off. Cori's soft giggle and Clay's playful murmurs carried through the dark night.

Then silence. Her chest burned.

He should be kissing *her.*

Cori didn't deserve him, but somehow she'd won him -- at least for now. Jesi strode up the front steps and into the house, shutting the door with a louder-than-necessary thud. She turned up the gas in the lamp on the staircase, but instead of going up to her room, she wandered into the parlor and plopped onto the settee in the dark. Turning around, she perched on her knees and peeked out the curtain, trying to see the dim forms of her sister and Clay beneath the moon's luminescence.

She breathed a sigh. At least some space existed between them. Resting her arms across the back of the settee, she propped her chin on them and watched the courting couple, grateful Cori wouldn't let Clay grow too amorous. Cori might talk about staying out unchaperoned, but in truth, nothing was too proper for Jesi's twin.

If you would only recognize what a real man Clay is, what you have, you wouldn't be so careless about him. You'd make sure he never looked the other way. Why, if Clay would look my way just once, I'd make sure he never turned his head in any other direction again.

She leaned forward so wisps of her breath formed a little fog on the window pane. With her fingertip she traced a heart in it. She looked again at Clay, framed inside the vapor center. Cori didn't fit.

Clay Dalton, you'd spin on your heel and march up to this door right now begging me to marry you if you knew how much I care about you.

Clay needed a doting wife, a wife who'd be his perfect ornament. He thought Cori would fill that role. Jesi knew better. Cori was perfectly groomed for it, surely, and she'd play the perfect wife for a while. But Cori was more than just a pretty face and a fawning sweetheart. She was smart, and eventually, after spending some time languishing in the role of doting wife, she'd get bored. She always did. Cori always had to be involved in a dozen things.

She taught the Sunday school children, played the piano, and sang passably well. Cori could also draw a little -- not as well as Mama or Gran -- but well enough for her attempts to be appreciated. She was skilled at knitting and crochet, too, making up for the fact that none of the Beaumont women were especially fine seamstresses. And she liked to arrange flowers and lead ladies' Bible studies and manage social events. She was always at the center in her circle of friends. Jesi couldn't imagine Clay's wife doing all those things and still having time for him.

What kind of woman in her sane mind wouldn't want to give Clay Dalton every little bit of herself she had to offer? One thing was vividly certain: Jesi had her sane mind.

If only she could win him. If she could help him see *she* was the one who could make him truly happy.

Jesi laid her head back on the sofa and for the hundredth time dreamed about being Clay's wife. Folks said Cori was accomplished. Was that really so important to Clay?

Voices echoed on the porch, and Jesi jolted upright. She smeared the breathy heart and looked out the window. Tilting her head, she strained to hear Clay and Cori's conversation.

"Will I see you tomorrow, before you parents come back?"

"You might. Maybe in the evening we can take a buggy ride."

"Not before then?"

"I promised Evie I'd help her cut out pieces for her new quilt."

"Can't you do it another time?"

Cori shook her head. Clay picked up Cori's hand and kissed it.

Jesi brushed her fingers over her lips remembering where his lips had barely touched her knuckles earlier, still recalling their softness and the feathery touch of his mustache against her skin.

"Tomorrow evening is a long time to wait."

"But aren't I worth it, darling?"

Jesi rolled her eyes and clenched her hands together. When she decided Clay was going to kiss Cori goodnight, she rose and moved deeper into the room.

Cori was so utterly self-confident. She had her worth all figured out.

Well, Clay had waited for Cori to spare him her time and attention long enough. He'd never have to wait another moment if he belonged to

Jesi instead. Had he really been displeased with her little ploy of pretending to be Cori earlier? She smiled to herself and wondered if he weren't more upset Cori had surprised them.

As Cori came inside and quietly shut the door, Jesi stepped back against the fireplace. Her sister drifted past the parlor door on her slow-motion stroll upstairs, turning down the gas lamp as she went and leaving Jesi in absolute darkness.

She chewed her fingernails. *He shouldn't have to wait forever for a woman's love. I don't believe he's the kind of man who will. If given more than a fleeting chance, he would probably be more than anxious to take hold of the love* I *have to offer him.*

Clay's buggy creaked as he drove away into the night. Maybe she would find out. Maybe it was time to stop her small attempts to capture his attention and instead prove her love. She might have one more impersonation left to make, but if Clay was ever going to realize they belonged together, then she must make her affection clear.

Then Clay's kiss -- and his heart -- would belong to her.

*****

Corianne yawned and rolled her head to loosen the muscles in her shoulders. Then she massaged the knuckles of her right hand. She'd gotten plenty of sleep last night, but she and Jesi had spent the morning with Mama cleaning and preparing the guest room for her grandparents' arrival. After that Corianne had filled the afternoon keeping her promise to help Evie cut out pieces for the quilt that would top her grandparents' bed this winter. Having worked the scissors through several yards of fabric squares, her fingers ached. She had also overtaxed her mind. She'd been too preoccupied with readying for her family's arrival to think much about her upcoming evening with Clay.

She glanced across the sewing table at Evie, who was still snipping away, her piles of brightly colored quilt squares stacked in front of her like little monuments to industry. How could the woman enjoy such a monotonous activity? At least that's how Corianne thought of the preparation work. Thankfully, Evie hadn't asked her to help stitch the squares together.

Cori's grandparents would share the empty bedroom at the end of the upstairs hall that had been a playroom for her and Jesilyn when they were little. Later, her parents had used it mostly for storage. Soon it would be a nice quiet room for Grandpa Nase and Grandma Colette. The way the afternoon shafts of soft sunlight brightened the flowered walls lent a peace to it.

Thinking of afternoon light, it was already close to dinner time. The day had flown by, despite the quilting project, and Cori could finally look forward to her evening buggy ride with Clay. She smiled, thinking of the way he'd grinned when she'd mentioned the idea last night. Why, if she were to crook her finger at him, he'd come running like a young buck. He was so sweet, and he certainly seemed intent on marrying her.

Cori stretched her fingers. Another dozen squares to go. She'd barely have time to finish cutting, eat supper, and change into a pretty dress before he arrived. She expected he'd get to the house plenty early, knowing how she felt about propriety and not being out too late.

Evie set down her scissors and rose suddenly. "If you don't mind finishing up these extra, I'd better get the stove lit downstairs. If I wait much longer, we won't have supper."

"Oh, no... I don't mind."

"Thank you, honey. That's sweet of you. I'll be sure and tell your grandpa how hard you worked on his quilt. He'll think of you when he's keeping nice and warm this winter." Evie gave her a rosy-cheeked grin and hummed her way out of the room.

Cori smiled, but once Evie was out of hearing, her enthusiasm fell flat. "Wonderful. Now I'll be here for another half hour."

She arched her back and plucked up another scrap of fabric. Holding it to her pattern piece, she cut. Where was Jesi when she could be making herself useful? How did her sister always manage to wheedle out of these tasks?

The answer was simple. Jesi didn't get herself embroiled in projects so easily because she didn't make herself readily available. That's how she was. Jesi was probably off doing something completely self-centered and carefree right now.

Cori tried to distract herself with other thoughts. What would she wear tonight to see Clay? Maybe the lemon yellow dress with the pink flowers on the sash, or the dark blue with the lavender ruffle on the sleeves. Considering a buggy ride with Clay after dark tantalized her. She had no doubt he'd come for her by dinnertime, because she didn't usually give in easily to them spending time alone, especially after nightfall.

A nagging doubt about what her parents would say if they were home spun through her thoughts, but she snipped it right out as if it were a fray in the fabric of her imagination. Clay had kissed her before, of course, and each time his kisses became more demanding.

She'd have to guard herself. No sense spoiling the adventure before they'd even had the chance to announce their engagement.

The clock kept ticking, and Cori kept cutting as she thought about her future as Mrs. Clay Dalton. The rays of sunlight moved lower and lower through the window, until the shadows made it hard to see her work. If she didn't finish soon, she'd be forced to light the gas or a candle.

The murmur of voices drifted to her from downstairs. Evie's and Jesi's voices. Maybe Jesi was helping Evie in the kitchen. She ought to be.

Then the front door closed. Had Clay arrived already? She hadn't even had a chance to change. Hurrying through the last two quilt squares, she tucked the scissors into Evie's sewing basket, brushed snippets of colored material off her lap, and hastened to her room.

The voices had stopped their murmuring.

She hummed as she changed into the dark blue dress. As quickly as she could, she twisted her hair into a loose bun, allowing wisps of red curls to frame her face. Funny, Evie still hadn't called to let her know of Clay's arrival. She must be feeding him.

She clasped a string of pearls around her neck before heading down. Then, with a pinch to her cheeks, she slowed her pace as she stepped around the corner into the kitchen, peeking first to see if he was in the parlor.

"Oh!" Evie jumped. "You startled me. Are you ready for some soup? It's simmering now. I fixed a nice big kettle, so we'll have something warm and delicious waiting when Lainey and her parents get here tomorrow."

Corianne frowned. "Where's Clay?"

"Clay?" Evie retrieved two bowls from the pantry.

"Yes, I told you this afternoon that he was coming to call, remember?"

"He's not here yet."

"Oh." Her shoulders fell. She'd imagined his arrival, then. She took a chair while Evie scooped her a bowl of chowder. "Where's Jesi?"

"She went out. I thought she was you at first, leaving without dinner. I haven't mixed the two of you up in a long time. Must have been your hat she had on."

Cori bit off a remark. Jesi always wore her things without asking. Didn't do her any good to complain to Evie about it.

"Where was she off to?"

"Said she was going to spend the evening at the Shipleys' home with Clara and her brother George."

"Oh." Cori sighed. "She never tells me what she's up to anymore. I guess I'll just eat with you and wait for Clay, then."

Cori spooned her soup, taking small nibbles and chatting with Evie. Still, she had a hard time concentrating on Evie's good cooking. She was surprised Clay hadn't arrived. Wasn't he as anxious to see her as she'd thought he'd be?

Every now and then she rose onto her toes to see if a noise she'd heard might be Clay coming up the road in his buggy. Unfortunately, only darkness covered the streets. Never did she see the lantern of his buggy swaying on its hook or parked at the end of the walk.

He'll be here. He's only running a bit late. Now, with the day spent and nothing left to do but wait, jitters claimed her, and her appetite dwindled. She'd never had to wait for Clay before. In fact, she usually found him in the parlor, waiting on her to make an entrance. By the time she'd half-heartedly eaten all she could and her conversation with Evie had worn thin, he still hadn't arrived.

Perplexity pulled her out of her chair. For two seconds more, she busied herself scraping her left-over soup into the scrap pail. What in the world could be keeping him?

Chapter Two

Clay reached across the buggy seat and enfolded Jesi's hand in his.

"You're warm."

"Yes."

Shadows hid his face, but his eyes still penetrated the darkness with every glance. Did he suspect? Would some subtle nuance reveal she wasn't Cori? He'd need to know eventually, once she helped him understand *she* was the girl he really wanted. Not yet, though. Not until he realized how much she loved him.

I love you, Clay.

She'd longed to whisper the words against his neck when she'd first run out of the house to meet him. He'd held her lightly for a moment, and she'd wanted to run her fingers through his hair and sing it, to throw her arms around him and shout it. But it wasn't the right time. They needed to get away before someone from the house saw them. She'd told Evie she was going to Clara's house, and if the housekeeper had caught Jesi in Clay's arms instead, that would've been the end of everything. And who knew what might have happened if Cori had seen them? So Jesi had reveled in that one hasty hug and urged Clay to hurry. He'd grinned at her enthusiasm, no doubt thinking it meant something entirely different.

He hadn't been far from the truth. She'd hardly been able to catch her breath for the sheer excitement of being with him. Every minute left her nerves quivering with anticipation and a frenetic fire of *what if?*

"You're sure about this? I don't want to get you into trouble."

"Just a ride... a few blocks."

In the buggy, he dashed a kiss on her cheek. It happened so quickly -- Clay's lips on her skin -- a flash that left her tingling all the way to her toes and her hands, warming even more.

Fingering the reins, he nickered at the horse and pulled away into the gathering twilight. Once the house was out of sight, Jesi's pulse slowed. So far he didn't seem to have any doubts about her being Cori. She took a breath, driving her thoughts into calm, willing herself into her role, and mostly, relishing his nearness.

They drove toward Lake Superior. The moonlight shimmered on the bay many yards beyond the tall grass. Lights twinkled on a ship in the harbor.

Clay pulled the buggy to a halt and turned in the seat to face her. Beneath the canopy of the buggy, his face stood shrouded in the deepening evening shadows. She knew hers must be also, yet she could see the desire in his eyes as he reached for her.

"Cori..." He leaned close, his outline disappearing. His lips softened against hers, forcing them apart just a little as their mouths caressed.

Her heart hammered afresh and she leaned away, gasping for breath. "Clay!"

"I'm sorry. I know it isn't the way you want it."

"No... No, it's okay."

"I don't know what came over me."

"Clay," she laid her hand on his arm, allowing herself a further thrill at the feel of his muscled forearm beneath his jacket. "It's okay. It -- it *is* what I want."

"You do?"

She nodded. "We've waited so long."

His hand came up around her neck, beneath her hair, and he pulled her to him again. This time she didn't break away from his kiss. When he leaned away, he picked up the reins.

"I don't want to go back home. Not yet."

Clay didn't say anything, but snapped the reins and steered the horse down the road. He drove at a leisurely pace. She tucked herself close to him, leaning back into the darkness of the buggy's cab.

"I'm glad you asked me to take you driving tonight. I rarely get to be alone with you."

Jesi's thoughts whirred. She had to think like Cori, act like Cori, respond like Cori -- for just a little while. "It's not that I don't want to be alone with you, Clay. I do. Very much. I'm just thinking about propriety."

"That's good to know." He smiled and held her hand, dangling the reins loosely in the other. "Sometimes I wonder if you love me."

"Oh, Clay." She wanted to say she loved him, but not while he thought she was Cori. "You shouldn't doubt it, not for a second."

They drove northwest along the harbor and passed a wagon loaded with crates. Clay flicked a wave at the other driver, whose outline flashed in the light of the swinging buggy lamp. Jesi nestled against his shoulder.

"Truth is, I can't wait for us to marry," he said, his voice deepening and growing tender. "I'll graduate with my business degree in the spring, but right after that..."

He rested his hand on her leg, and the pressure of his palm through her layers of skirting brought on that sensational tingle.

"I wish we didn't have to wait. I don't want to either, Clay."

He turned his head to look at her, and she studied him back. Even in the darkness, the outline of his jaw was just as handsome and perfect. The glitter in his eyes pulled her in.

He blinked and a frown curved his brow. "Are you cold?"

Had he felt her trembling? She nodded.

"I have a friend who lives behind the bank in the west end." His voice grew husky. "He's out of town."

His words held suggestion and promise without saying a thing.

"All right."

They rode in silence, but she held onto his arm. Slowly she realized how cold the night had turned, even though it was late August. That was typical of the night air coming off Lake Superior in the summertime. Goose bumps rolled up her arms beneath the sleeves of her dress. She tugged the edge of her crocheted wrap close and melded herself to Clay for added warmth.

At the home of his friend, he let them inside. Thick darkness wrapped around them, but he held onto her hand. "Are you all right?"

The timber of his voice brought her back to reality. A *wonderful* reality. "Yes, I'm more than all right."

She touched his face and felt his smile.

"I'll light a candle."

He fumbled in the darkness for a minute before striking a match. A burst of light made his face glow. His blond hair shimmered. Holding the candle aloft with one hand, he looked at her again. His gaze flickered over her face, and he paused.

Jesi held her breath and smiled. Finally, his look settled and he took her by the hand, leading her upstairs into a bedroom.

He set the candle on a dresser and turned to her. "I must admit, I didn't expect so much of this evening."

Jesi flushed and glanced at her feet. How very Cori-like of her. What if he suspected she wasn't Cori at all? Might he be willing to see how much Jesi cared?

"It's not too late. I can take you home." His words were more of a formality, but not like he really wanted her to change her mind.

"No. I want to stay."

Then she looked at him. *Really* looked at him. She studied his face in the light of the candle's burn, giving him every chance to recognize her, to realize she wasn't Corianne, but Jesi, the woman who really loved him. Daring him to recognize her.

His gaze roved from her eyes to her lips. Then it continued to travel until she no longer felt cold.

*****

Cori dried the last dish and hung the flour sack towel over the rack by the sideboard. "I guess I thought he'd be here a lot earlier than this."

Evie covered the butter dish. "Didn't Clay say when he was coming?"

"In the evening. I just thought--"

"That he couldn't stay away until then?" Evie chuckled. She reached across the table to turn down the extra oil lamp. "He's a busy boy,

Corianne. He can't spend all his time pining after you, like it or not."

She flushed. "I know that." Was she really so obvious about believing Clay was smitten? "Well, I guess I'll go wait for him in the parlor. I have a book I can read until he comes."

"You do that, honey. I'm going to get ready for bed. Though I suppose I should sit up with you two."

Cori laid a hand on Evie's arm. "I... I promised Clay we could take a ride in his buggy. Do you mind? I'll mind myself. I promise."

"Now, you know I don't like it when you girls talk me into shenanigans." Evie knit her brows. "Lainey and Zane would toss me out if I let you go out at night without a chaperone."

"Please, Evie. You can trust me."

"Yes." Evie studied her, "Yes, I can at that." She shook her finger. "But what about young Mr. Dalton?"

"You know we won't do anything to jeopardize ourselves." Cori kissed her cheek. "Remember our secret?"

"Yes, you're getting married." Evie rolled her eyes and smiled. "When are you going to announce it?"

"After Gran and Gramp get settled in. I'm sure we'll talk about it tonight." She gave Evie a quick squeeze and whispered, "On our buggy ride."

"Oh... go on, then. I suppose you will. Just make sure that boy minds his manners. I can't wait until your folks get back. You girls are too much for me in my old age."

Cori laughed. Evie was only in her forties, the same age as her parents. Although her hair was a little grayer than Mama's, and she carried some extra pounds *of pure love*, as she called them, Evie was still pretty spry.

Her chuckle followed Cori out of the kitchen. Cori wandered into the parlor to wait, lighting the gas and a candle as well. She curled up with her book and read mindlessly for twenty minutes before her patience wore one shift too thin.

An hour later, she snapped the book shut, its contents unremembered. She paced across the room, pausing to flick the curtain back for yet another look out at the dark street. With a heavy breath, she gave up waiting and climbed the steps to her room. The hour had gotten too late for any respectful girl to go out on a ride, even with her betrothed. Cori pulled the pins from her hair and yanked a brush through it. Static jumped from the clinging red waves. She braided it with deft fingers.

I can't believe he stood me up. He'd better have a good explanation for this. Tomorrow, my family will be home. He ruined what could have been our perfect evening alone together.

She flung the hairbrush onto the dresser and stared into the mirror. Her face looked like white stone; her eyes, like twin blue flames. "You'd better have a *very* good explanation, Clayton Dalton."

*****

Jesi's body, liquid and warm, melted into the bed. Her hair, a fiery mass in the candlelight, lay tangled all around her. Her eyelids drooped. She wanted nothing better than to curl against Clay and sleep until morning, but she didn't dare. Someone might discover she hadn't gone to Clara's.

Jesi didn't care. She loved Clay more than her sister ever could, and everything she'd done would soon be worth it.

"It's time to go," he whispered, tracing a hand across her shoulder.

"I know. I don't want to leave you now."

"Someone might look for you."

She wanted to ask whom he meant, whether he had any idea who she was. She sat up abruptly.

"What's the matter?"

She shook her head.

He pulled her back against him. "Are you sorry?"

Tears threatened. She'd hoped that somehow he'd known. That somehow he'd realized she was Jesilyn, not Cori, and that he wanted it that way.

"Cori, once we're married this will all be put right."

Her heart burned. She turned and looked at him. "Don't say that."

"But it will."

"Yes, just stop saying..." She shook her head and leaned against him. She couldn't say it -- *Stop calling me Cori* -- she just couldn't say it.

"Come on. I'll take you home."

She sat up and tugged on her corset. "Light the lamp, will you? I can't see well enough to buckle my stays."

The mattress lifted as he rose and turned on the gas. A moment later, the room glowed more brightly.

"How long will your friend be away?"

Clay snickered. "A few days longer, I should say. Why do you ask?"

She turned to him and smiled.

"You are a vixen." He slipped his shirt sleeves over his arms and froze. He gazed at her again, and his expression changed, only subtly.

She licked her lips. "Um... do you need any help?"

"No. I think I have it." He fumbled with the buttons on his shirt.

She stepped nearer. "I can help you with those buttons if you want."

"It's all right."

She stood in front of him and slowly hooked his buttons into their proper holes, working her way up his shirt front until she gazed into his eyes.

He studied her oddly, and she was sure, then, that he knew.

Something had triggered his subconscious. Maybe he had finally recognized her face, her features, the shade of her eyes. Dare she say it now?

"I love you, Clay."

He blushed and chuckled as if embarrassed by her admission. She didn't move away, but instead stood close, forcing him to acknowledge her words. "I -- I love you, too, Co--" He kissed her on the cheek, just a quick peck, nothing like before.

She frowned. He *did* know. He wouldn't call her Cori.

Well, then.

"I promised Ma I'd take some flowers by the church for Sunday's service. I can meet you there after I drop them off."

"We'll see."

So, that's how it was going to be. He must know, but he wasn't going to admit it. *We'll see, indeed.*

He turned away and reached for the lamp.

She put her hand on his arm. "Wait."

His face turned her way slowly. "What is it?"

"You know, don't you?"

"What do you mean?" A muscle in his jaw twitched. His eyelids flickered, but his gaze didn't rest on hers. "I'd better get you home." He turned away again.

Boldness filled her, straightening her spine. "Say my name."

He stilled, his shoulder to her, and glanced at his feet. "Cori."

"Don't you mean a different name?"

"Darling, then." He glanced at her sharply. His lips stretched in a taut smile, and he reached for her hand. She let him hold it, but she didn't move her feet as he tugged her toward the door.

"You know, Clay. I know that you do. I felt it from the beginning. Ever since we sat in the buggy by the lake. You know my name. Say it."

"Cori, if you're playing tricks, it isn't very nice."

"Jesilyn. Say it. You know it's me."

"Cori--"

"Jesi. Oh, Clay." She crushed herself against him. His arms came up to hers and pushed her back, but she fought against him and pushed close.

"You're Cori."

"No. No, I'm not. It's me, Jesilyn, and you know it. You've known all along, and you've wanted me just as badly as I've wanted you. Nothing is truer than that."

"Jesi, stop it."

"I told you." She backed away and stared at him. "You *did* know."

He ran one hand through his hair, planted the other on his hip, and paced in a small circle. "Why did you deceive me?"

"That's just it. I didn't deceive you. You wondered the moment I met you at the buggy. You wanted it to be me, and not Cori."

He shook his head.

"I love you, Clay. You love me, too. I'm sure of it."

"You don't know anything."

"I do. Clay, I'm yours now. You've made it so. You have to acknowledge it, accept it. You want it."

He flicked off the gas, and in one step clutched her arm and propelled her out the door. The candle in his other hand cast jerky shadows on the wall as he trotted her down the stairs.

He pushed her out the door and turned to lock it, then hurried her to the buggy. "Get in."

She waited for his help.

After lifting her arm to steady her, he dashed around and leapt up beside her. Cracking the reins, Clay kept his gaze straight ahead as the buggy jolted forward. He snapped a quirt over the horse's back, and Jesi clutched the seat as they bounced and careened along.

"I don't know why you're angry. You got what you wanted, and I don't think you're one lick unhappy about whom you got it from."

"Stop it."

"You've wanted me since the beginning. You've been sorry for months that you chose to court Cori instead of me. Well, it's not too late. I won't let it be, because *I'm* the one for you."

He didn't say anything. He turned the corner, and moonlight flashed across his face, silhouetting the stony set of his jaw. Silence fell thick like Lake Superior fog between them for the rest of the ride. But she couldn't let it be. When he yanked on the reins, stopping them abruptly at the end of the walk in front of her home, she took the opportunity to reach up and run her fingers across the hair at the back of his neck.

Clay shrugged her hand away, but she didn't relent. She leaned closer to nuzzle his neck.

He stilled.

"Clay..."

He turned suddenly and grasped her to him. He kissed her, pushing her back against the seat of the buggy, nearly swallowing her. She came up breathless, gasping.

He pushed her arm away. "Go inside."

She nodded and stumbled down out of the buggy.

Clay did not assist her.

Chapter Three

Seated on a northbound train facing her aging parents, Lainey Beaumont thought about the days ahead when she would be home again with Zane and the girls, and now her parents, once they were settled in. Her father slept, his head resting on her mother's shoulder as she gazed out the window at the passing scenery of tamarack and marsh grass, worrying a fingernail between her teeth.

"I'm sorry, Ma. We'll be home soon, so he can rest better."

Her mother, Colette Kade, smiled at her. "I know. I'm so thankful you have room for us."

"Zane is glad you're coming, too."

Colette dropped a kiss on her husband's forehead. "He'll do better just being near you."

"I know Gray's sorry he couldn't be around more to help you out."

"Gray and Eldon are too busy with the business to have to worry about us. Now with Kenton having that new wife and a baby on the way, he's got his hands full, too. I'm glad they'll be able to live in the house, but no new wife wants the added task of taking care of her in-laws."

"You don't need taking care of, Ma."

"You know what I mean."

Lainey nodded. Ever since her father, Manason, had taken ill, her mother had aged. She was only sixty-six, and her hair still held a good deal of honey brown threaded through the gray, but today she looked her years. Weariness and creases of worry for Lainey's pa had thickened the skin around her eyes.

"We'll make sure he forgets he's sick. The girls will see to that."

Her ma smiled again, revealing the beauty she'd once been. "I can't wait to see them. I haven't been with any of you in over a year, but surely they can't have changed too much since then."

"They're eighteen now. You'd be surprised how every year brings a new nuance."

"Eighteen." Colette sighed. "I remember when you were eighteen. That year changed your life."

Lainey propped her elbow on the armrest and put a finger on the crow's feet pulling at her eyes as reminiscences gathered like dust in the corners of her memory. "It did, at that."

"Within two years, you'd married Zane."

"He was always the only one for me."

"Well, he's certainly done well for you, and given you those two beautiful girls, besides."

"Yes." Lainey chuckled. "He still calls them *his roses*. They were only eight when I first planted the rose garden. He's called them that ever since."

"It's appropriate."

Lainey stretched her back. "You know, Corianne can't wait for you to meet Clayton."

"We can't wait to meet him. You said he comes from a good family."

"Yes. His father is a banker. Clay works with him during the summers, but will return to Madison before long to complete his studies and graduate from the state university next spring."

"That's good. They'll have a good start."

"An education will pave the way for them."

"What about Jesilyn? Has anyone spoken for her yet?"

Lainey laughed. "Jesilyn receives no shortage of attention, but I'm afraid she's a bit too much like her mother. She hasn't settled on anyone yet."

"At eighteen, it's time for her to think about that."

Lainey gasped. "Ma, think of what you're saying."

"You would've been married by then if things hadn't happened differently."

"I don't know." Lainey's voice turned wistful. "I think I was destined to wait for Zane."

"Yes, I think you were, at that." Colette smiled and glanced out the window again. The terrain had changed. They now rolled through balsam and poplar, broken occasionally by an oak ridge. "Will I be able to tell them apart? Last time was hard."

"They don't often dress alike or wear their hair the same anymore. And if you look carefully, you can tell Jesilyn's eyes are a lighter shade of blue than Cori's. More like Zane's than mine."

"That's right. I remember. Anything else?"

Lainey frowned. "You'll be able to discern their attitudes."

"Oh-oh. That doesn't sound good."

"It's not bad." She shrugged. "But you'll soon note that Cori is more patient than Jesi, and less prone to temper."

"So Jesi is more like you in that respect?" her mother teased, and they both laughed.

Her pa lifted his head. "Wh-what's going on?" He blinked and tried to get his bearings.

"We're almost home, Pa, at Superior."

"That's good. My joints are complaining."

"You're a tough old buzzard, Pa. I'm sure they can't be complaining too hard." Lainey flicked a glance at her mother and kept the laughing tone in her voice. It was hard, knowing how sick he was. She didn't know what she'd do -- in fact, she didn't know what her *ma* would do if and when they lost her pa. She didn't like to think about it, but she was afraid they'd have to sooner or later. *Please God, let it be much, much later...*

*****

Zane Beaumont stood on the platform of the Hurley depot and recalled a saying as he waited for his train to take him back home to Superior. *The four hottest places on a Saturday night are Cumberland, Hayward, Hurley, and hell. The four toughest places on earth.*

His gaze traveled up Silver Street, a route that alone boasted more than fifty saloons along its plank sidewalks, each one bawdier than the next as they lined their way toward the infamous lower block.

The town had boomed over the last eight years, as soon as rails had connected it to the port at Ashland. Even now, despite recent hard times and the financial panic sweeping the country, the future of Wisconsin's Lake Superior rim looked bright to Zane. Hard to believe that only twenty years ago, none of these towns had existed. Logging, mining, railroads, and shipping had brought development to the country, and he'd ridden track right along with the surge.

After marrying Lainey, Zane had gotten a job with the Wisconsin Central building a line north through the wilderness, lakes, and highlands from Stevens Point in central Wisconsin, and south from the newly developed bay city of Ashland with its population of five, across the Penokee Range so settlers could flood in. And flood in they had, growing these towns quicker than a hillside of young poplar sprouting in a cutover. That work eventually led to his position with the Duluth, Atlantic, and South Shore, and that had brought him to settle his young family in the bursting port of Superior on the western tip of the lake by the same name. He hadn't run out of work since. Still, the new panic stirred upheaval.

Friday ushered in the end of another work week, and if that wasn't enough cause for raucousness in the small mining and logging towns of Wisconsin's northeast corner, then the men losing jobs and worrying about their futures added to it. Mines and factories kept shutting down or cutting jobs. Demands for lumber had slowed in the hard economy, despite the needs of the settlements cropping up out on the plains. Men found debauchery an easy way to manage their worries against the backdrop of such tough times.

Zane checked his pocket watch. His train wouldn't arrive for another half hour, and he'd already eaten at one of the local diners. He might as well sit down to wait. A few other passengers had accumulated at the station, and he got comfortable on a slatted bench.

Travel had gotten so much easier than it used to be, with more trains heading east, west, and south every day. He wondered if Lainey and her folks had made it back to Superior yet. Too bad about Manason.

He'd always acted like a real father to Zane, as much as he'd been to Lainey. Zane would hate to lose him. Maybe when he got back, they could all--

A sudden commotion up the street caught his attention and scattered his thoughts to the wind. Two men tumbled out of the nearest saloon and rolled into the street. Too early yet for a brawl, but maybe they'd been in the saloon since breakfast. A third man leading his horse up the street tried to get out of the way when the two tumbled in front of him, spooking his horse. It reared up, its nostrils flaring. He tried to hold the animal, but one of the brawlers fell against the man's legs and knocked him sideways. The horse trotted off as the man righted himself and stepped between the two swarthy giants fighting in the street.

Zane leaned forward, his interest deepening along with that of the other onlookers on the platform. He shouldn't enjoy watching the brawl, but he couldn't help recalling some of the days he'd spent with his brother Kelly when they were young bucks like those fellows, stirring up trouble. More folks stepped out onto the boardwalk on both sides of Silver Street, taking in the scene, but no one intruded.

He leaned back again, chagrined to recall how unhappy he'd been during those youthful days. Who was to say these fellows were having fun? They looked ready to kill each other, if they didn't each get themselves killed first.

Then faster than a blink, a fist flew out, and the other fellow who'd been trying to intervene went flying into the dirt. Zane jumped to his feet as one of the scuffling men picked up the interloper and belted him once in the gut, then again right in the face. The fellow stumbled backward and sprawled flat.

A gasp went up over the crowd on the platform, and Zane bounded off the steps and into the street. The two brawlers, staggering as much from drink as from their mutual beatings, lurched off in opposite directions, while the third man lay in the dirt and dung on the street. He appeared conscious, though. He pulled his leg up, rolled to one side, and suppressed an audible groan.

Zane knelt beside him. "You alive, then?"

The fellow drew up his arm with a jerk, covering his blood-and-mud smeared cheek.

"I'm not gonna hit you. Here, give me your hand."

He blinked up at Zane once, then twice, and extended his hand. Zane yanked him to his feet, ignoring his sharp gasp.

"Gonna make it?"

The fellow nodded.

"You got yourself into bit of a mess there. I was over at the station. Thought I'd come and make sure you didn't get run down lying out here."

"Thanks." The fellow bent to pick up his hat and brushed the dirt off it before placing it carefully over his lank brown hair. "Did you happen to see where my horse went?"

Zane nodded behind him, where the brown mare stood half a block away, drinking out of a trough.

"You're not too full of drink yourself to hold the saddle, are you?"

The fellow's face split into a wry grin, and he chuckled. "Well, that's a good one. Did I look drunk when I was trying to break up those two men?"

"No, just making sure you're not going to topple off as soon as you're on your way."

"Names Winter -- Paul Winter." He extended his hand and Zane shook it, surprised by the strength of the man's grip. He was of average height, but not a big man. His face was narrow; his build, wiry. "It might surprise you to know I'm a chaplain."

"A chaplain?" Zane couldn't keep the surprise out of his voice, or the grin off his face. "Well, now. You did get yourself in a mix-up then, didn't you?"

"Trust me, it wasn't my intention. I was just heading out of town."

He walked toward the horse, and Zane wandered along beside him. The gawking crowd dispersed back into the stores and saloons. Folks on the station platform lost interest as well.

"You a circuit rider?"

"On occasion. I'm not a pastor. I don't have a church. My sister and I live out on the road to Spring Camp Falls a few miles west, and I do what I can for the men in the camps out there, especially in these tough times. I'm sorry, what did you say your name is?"

"I didn't, but since you asked, it's Beaumont. Zane's my first name. I'm a railroad man from Superior."

Paul caught Zane's gaze. "You a Christian, Mr. Beaumont?"

"That I am, son, and I mean that." Zane gave him a smile. "It's a great thing you're doing out here. My own brother had similar ambitions some years back."

"Oh?"

Zane nodded. "He died at Peshtigo. He loved the Lord, though."

"I'm sorry."

"Time heals." Zane shrugged. "He had a big influence on me and my wife. You never know what your work will do, or how your life will touch someone else's. Remember that when you're out there trying to reach them rowdies."

"I will. Thanks again."

A train whistled in the distance, rumbling in its approach. "I'd better get back to the station. It's been a pleasure meeting you. Maybe I'll look you up again sometime, just to make sure you've been staying out of street fights."

Paul laughed as he climbed up into the saddle. "That might not be a bad idea."

He tipped his hat at Zane and turned his horse down a side street. Zane watched him a moment longer. He seemed like a real likeable young man. Maybe *too* young for the work he'd cut out for himself.

*****

Paul prodded his horse along the trail next to the rail spur boring into the woods away from the main line. Rail lines had changed the way everything worked for the logging companies. They were able to thrust deeper into the woods than ever before, counting on railcars to haul their pine out to main lines, lakes, and rivers. For that reason alone, Paul wondered how many years it would be before the trees were stripped clean, and the whole of Wisconsin was turned to stumpage and plow. With the financial panic currently upon them, he figured it would hold out for a few years longer anyhow.

Solid dark settled down by the time he made it back to his and Marie's cabin near the west branch of the Montreal River. His shoulders slumped even further, and he sighed inwardly. Would any of the men he'd spoken to today find their way into a church on Sunday? And if they did, would they take to heart even a single bit of the Word? Lord knew they didn't seem to hang onto much of what he preached.

Plenty of times some fellow would ask for Paul's help, come to him worried and suddenly prayerful about his wife being alone with a new baby, or letting him pray over an injury. They showed up for preaching on Sundays when there wasn't anything more interesting to distract them. But Paul often wondered if he really had any impact at all on their lives. Certainly, some of them had no real relationship with God whatsoever. Theirs was just a cultural faith, not a heart reliance. Not once had anyone come to him seeking to really grow in faith, or to be truly introduced to Christ for the first time. Not once.

Four years. He'd be twenty-seven before winter.

Paul sighed. His life wasn't the way he'd imagined it would be when God had first stirred a fire inside him to come up to this wilderness country. As a missionary chaplain, trying to give guidance while traveling around the camps, he'd seen more moral depredation than he'd ever cared to see. He longed to witness growth and change, but his ministry was apparently destined to be hard fought and seldom won. Not the vision he'd had for it at all.

A handful of men stayed behind at the camp each weekend, not usually more than a half dozen. Most of them would sleep in on Sunday. If he were blessed, three, maybe four would make their way to hear him preach in the cook shack, more out of having something to do than having any real desire to hear from God's Word.

He jerked his saddle free and set it in the corner of the stable while he turned to grain and brush down Sarah, his mare. Once he got her bedded in, he headed across the camp to his cabin near a tiny tributary creek that trickled into the Montreal. A single lamp burned in the window. Marie had probably waited up for him, worrying herself about all manner of trouble that might befall him along his journey, just like she always did. Well, she wouldn't expect to hear he'd been part of a drunken hullabaloo. He probably should have cleaned up before coming home. The dried blood on his face might scare her.

When he cracked open the door, he realized his vision out of his left eye had gotten pretty fuzzy. He patted at it with his fingertips and cringed at the pain that darted over his cheekbone. His eye had swollen almost closed. Terrific. Maybe she wouldn't notice.

"Paul Winter! What in the world have you done to yourself?"

Well, her not noticing had been too much to hope for.

Marie jumped to her feet and hurried over to get a closer look. "What happened? A branch slap you or something?"

He'd judged his sister wrong. She didn't sound overly worried. More put out, like a scolding mother. He smirked. "Or something."

"Well, sit down there at the table." She frowned as she pumped out a bowl full of water and grabbed a clean cloth. "I'll fix you up."

"I think you like this," he said while she dabbed at the blood and swelling around his eye and along his jaw.

She smiled, long creases dimpling her cheeks and softening her brown eyes. "Maybe a little."

Smiling hurt, but he couldn't help it. "I thought you'd be worried."

"I was." She slapped the rag playfully against his arm. "But you're alive and only slightly damaged. You ready to tell me what really happened?"

"I had the misfortune of getting in the way of a fight -- and while I was minding my own business, I might add."

"Since when do you ever mind your own business?" She plopped the rag into the bowl and planted her hands on her hips. "What was the fight about?"

"No idea. Couple of men just stumbled out into the street in front of me. Scared Sarah half to death and let me have it."

"I see. Probably knew you were a preacher and thought it was their chance to get even."

He shrugged. "Could be, but I doubt it."

"So there you were, getting a good licking in the middle of the street. Anyone else around who could've stepped in to stop them?"

"Oh, plenty." He looked into a hand mirror she offered him and scowled, turning his face to the right and left as he assessed the damage. He laid down the mirror. "One fellow came out after to see if I was alive. That was all. A railroad man waiting for his train. Said he was a Christian."

"Well, at least it's nice to know there's one good Samaritan somewhere in this godforsaken country."

She seemed to catch herself, regretting the remark as soon as she'd said it. But she was right. And Paul inwardly agreed. This place did seem to be godforsaken. Despite the churches on the streets in Hurley, despite the handful of men like him trying to make a difference, despite wives and daughters hoping to mold their corner of the world into something civilized and God fearing, nothing ever seemed to propel their community in that direction. Instead, Hurley seemed to be running toward the devil with arms wide open.

"I shouldn't have said that." She opened the door and tossed out the dirty water, then went to the icebox.

"What's the difference if you say it or just think it? It's not like I haven't thought the same."

"I didn't come along with you to discourage you." She pulled out a hunk of left-over venison roast, cut off a slice of meat along with some bread, and laid it out for him.

"I'm not discouraged, at least not by that."

"But you are discouraged?"

Paul ignored the food and peered at her through his swollen eye. "When's the last time we had a single soul really want to know God?"

"You're planting seeds, Paul." Marie patted his hand and sighed. "God will give the increase in His time."

He nodded. He knew it, but it was hard to keep pressing on, believing it. "You're right. You know, maybe I'm just dog tired. I think tomorrow I'll rest up. Go hunt some squirrels. Maybe something good'll happen on Sunday."

"We'll pray for it. But Paul--" She gripped his hand, and strength flowed out of her for him. "If God only brought you up here for one single person, and it was going to take a lifetime for that person to cross your path, then you are in the center of His will. You have to believe that, and trust it to be true."

He nodded. He'd said the same thing to himself a hundred times. Every time the ugly head of dismay rose up inside him, he said it again.

He'd given up a lot to come up here. He'd been offered the pastorate of a thriving church in Appleton. He could've married Imogene Gillette and started a family. When she'd fumed he couldn't possibly expect her to go with him to such a remote place when he had every opportunity to make a successful life for them in a decent, civilized city, he'd turned their relationship over to God, and God had pressed him to leave her behind. Paul had felt certain of God's leading and blessing. So why, then, if God had asked Paul to give it all away, would He not give back even a little? Was one small soul wanting to be saved just asking too much?

Chapter Four

Jesi's fork clinked against her plate as she plowed through her breakfast. Why was she in such a hurry? Cori propped both elbows beside her plate, framed her toast with both sets of fingers, and delicately munched another bite. Her twin picked up her milk glass and swilled down its contents before clunking the empty glass onto the table.

Jesi's eyes flashed up. "What?"

"Nothing." Cori was surprised her sister had even noticed her, she'd been so absorbed in finishing her food. "Why are you in such a hurry?"

"Who said I am?"

Cori paused chewing and raised her brow.

"Mrs. Taylor is picking me up to take flowers to the church for service on Sunday. I promised."

"Oh." Cori ate the last bit of crust and brushed her fingers on her napkin. "You remember the garden party at Mayor Pattison's begins at one o'clock, right?"

Jesi stilled for a moment and stared at her. Of course she'd forgotten. Cori couldn't help wondering what was on Jesi's mind these days. Every time she turned around, distracted Jesi forgot something else. And if she wasn't forgetful, then she was aloof, absorbed in a world of her own thoughts. Then suddenly, like now, she'd realize other people existed, and her eyes would momentarily lose their faraway look.

Cori sighed. "Did you really forget?"

"No, I didn't. I just had to remember for a moment, that's all. I've got this chore for Mama on my mind. I don't want her to take Gran and Gramp to church on Sunday and see that I forgot to take care of the flower arrangements."

Not so long ago, Cori and Jesi had made a habit of sharing their innermost thoughts and desires with one another. Lately, however, that hadn't been the case. Cori sipped her milk. No. Now that she thought about it, *she* had always done most of the sharing. Jesi could be very unforthcoming about her own secrets. Was that what was going on now? Maybe Jesi had secret things going on in her life.

Perhaps it was Cori's fault Jesi had grown distant. As Cori and Clay's courtship had grown stronger, she'd become more concerned about spending time with him than with Jesi -- though her parents still called Jesi Cori's *other self,* and vice versa.

Maybe she should try to restore some of that openness with Jesi. Maybe she should tell her sister about what had happened last night.

Obviously in a hurry, Jesi pushed back her chair. She reached for a knife to cut the tough, thorny stems of the roses while Cori dabbed her lips with her napkin and jumped up to follow.

"I'll help you get the flowers."

"All right. Thanks." Jesi sounded kind of surprised.

"Did Evie tell you about my buggy ride with Clay last night?"

Jesi's steps faltered. Her movements slowed. "No."

"That's because there wasn't one."

"Oh?" Jesi glanced her way. "Why not?"

She sounded curious, and Cori suddenly wished Jesi had been there last night to help get her through her anger, or to rage along beside her. "Mr. Clayton Dalton stood me up."

"Really?" Jesi glanced at her again as they went outside and wandered along the winding footpath between the roses and other late summer flowers. "Did he say why?"

"No. I have no idea."

Jesi stopped to select some flowers, and Cori put her hands on her hips.

"I haven't even spoken to him. Two days ago, he couldn't wait to see me -- *alone*." Her voice thickened, then popped back up. "Then given the chance last night, he didn't even show up. Can you believe that man? I have to admit I went to bed pretty angry toward him last night. I can't wait to hear his explanation."

"Well..." Jesi stood holding three blushing pink blooms. She handed them to Cori and then went back to cutting. "I'm sure he had a good reason for not coming."

"I hope so. I suppose any number of things could have kept him away."

"Yes, certainly." Jesi bent away from her. "Maybe he was involved... with his studies."

"Possibly." Cori tapped the bouquet against her chin. The bouquet drooped. "At least I know he couldn't have been off seeing another girl."

Jesi's back stiffened. "You're sure?"

"Yes." Cori ignored the far away tone in her sister's voice. Jesi always teased. "I'm sure -- of that, at least. I just hope nothing else is wrong."

"Well, I guess you'll find out soon enough if it is." Jesi turned to her and lifted the bouquet from her fingers just as Mrs. Taylor and her daughter pulled up in their buggy. "Thank you for your help."

"You're welcome. I'll see you when you get back."

Jesi barely nodded as she hurried away down the walk.

*****

Corianne twirled in front of the mirror and twisted her neck to gaze back at the reflection of her skirt flowing down her backside. How stunning she looked.

The new dress was worth every over-priced cent she'd spent after saving her allowance from Papa for weeks in order to afford it. Her parents were very generous with her clothing allowance, but this was something special. She'd had to save for it over time, preferring not to spend her pennies on the regular hair ribbons, blouses, stockings, and camisoles as she might have. The lacy white garden dress looked absolutely fetching. Her ringlets blazed to an even brighter copper red, and her eyes danced like bright blue flames against all that white. Clayton Dalton had better take care, or some other fellow might sit up and take notice.

She giggled. She fully intended to marry into the Dalton name and money, but there was no reason why she shouldn't keep him mindful of just how absolutely smitten he was with his bride-to-be, especially after last night's disappearing act.

As soon as Mama returned with Grandma and Grandpa Kade, and Pa got home from the railroad, they'd announce the date they'd set for next June. Ten whole months away. How would she ever stand the wait?

She set the mirror on her dressing table and paced across the room. Clay should've arrived half an hour ago. What could be keeping him this time? She flicked back the curtain and eyed the street. No sign of him yet. *Hurry up, Clay.*

She imagined herself tucking her arm through his and letting him stroll her around Mama's rose garden in her white dress, while she twirled her parasol and listened to him make his apologies for last night. She'd already decided to forgive him. He'd probably be apologetic and look as handsome as ever in a dove gray suit and tie. They'd hold hands, and she'd let him kiss her. Then they'd be off to the garden party at Mayor Pattison's mansion.

She whirled off down the hall, poking her head first into Jesi's room before going downstairs.

"Evie, isn't Jesi back yet?" she called, assuming their housekeeper was the one scuttling about in the other bedrooms. "I thought she was only going to be gone for an hour."

"I haven't seen her yet," Evie called back. "She's probably gotten side-tracked with the Taylor ladies."

Cori rolled her eyes and went down to the front parlor to watch out the window for Clay's buggy. Jesi was supposed to ride with them to the garden party. They had plenty of time, but if she didn't hurry and get home, she wouldn't have much time to change her dress.

Plopping down on the settee, Cori thumbed through a Sears catalog without really looking at anything. *Why does everyone have to be late today, of all days?*

She glanced at the clock on the granite fireplace mantel. Eleven-fifty. The party started at one. She stood up and looked out at the intersection cornering their house. Her heart jumped when a carriage appeared in the distance, steering around the ruts in the road.

"Well, it's about time." She patted her hair and brushed imaginary wrinkles from her dress. She wouldn't go to the door just yet. No need for Clay to find her too anxious. She glanced toward the window again. It framed the buggy just so as it pulled up to the walk. She frowned. Was that Jesi with Clay?

Her gaze lingered. What was Jesi doing riding home with him?

She forgot her resolve to wait for Clay to come to the door and swung it wide as they dismounted from the buggy. He lent a hand to her sister.

Cori marched down the porch steps. "I've been wondering about you. Jesi, do you realize how late it is? The party starts in less than an hour. Where's Mrs. Taylor?"

"Clay happened to be driving by the church as we were about to leave." Jesi brushed her gloved hands over her russet gown and only flicked Cori a glance as she strode up the walk. "He graciously offered to save Mrs. Taylor the trip since we were heading to the same place."

"Oh, I see." Her sister had spoken so sharply, Cori wondered if she had offended Jesi in some way. "Well, I hope you had a pleasant ride."

Jesi didn't answer her, but instead brushed past and mounted the steps.

Cori turned her attention to Clay, remembering her new dress and awaiting his reaction. He barely looked at her.

Jesi paused at the door. "I suppose you two have a lot to talk about, so I'll take my time dressing." She raked her gaze over Cori's dress. "You look nice."

"Thank you," Cori murmured, as Jesi turned and stepped through the door. Cori looked back at Clay.

He cleared his throat. "Yes. Yes, Cori, you look lovely, as usual. Is that a new dress?"

"Yes." She went to him and laid her palm on his arm. "Is everything all right? What took you so long? I've been waiting."

"Oh, it was nothing. I was just delayed a bit in town, that's all. Then I bumped into your sister and Mrs. Taylor and stopped to chat for a while."

For the strangest moment, an unwelcome sensation stole over Cori, but it quickly disappeared. She couldn't have named it, or even described it. It just... unsettled her. She took a breath. "I'm glad it was nothing."

She linked her arm through his, and they wandered onto the path between the roses. She realized she'd forgotten her parasol, so the affect she'd hoped to achieve remained incomplete. Clay was dressed in a suit, just as she'd known he'd be, but his tie was crooked, and his collar was wrinkled. That wasn't like him, to not be impeccable about his appearance. A scuttling worked its way through her. Something was wrong, but she couldn't say what.

She reached down and plucked a light pink rose. She held it to her nose then handed it to him. "Pink means admiration and joy. I admire you, Clay, and you make me happy."

"Do I?"

She frowned. That didn't sound like a rhetorical question at all. "I suppose Jesi told you I was upset last night."

His face was expressionless. "Last night?"

"Oh. She didn't tell you."

"Oh, last night." He turned her to him. "I'm sorry about the buggy ride. I was held up with my studies. There's to be an exam--"

"It's all right, Clay." She held up her hand. "I'm not angry. I knew you must have a good reason for not picking me up. I did so look forward to being with you, but I understand your obligation to your studies. We'll have other buggy rides."

"Yes, I suppose we will." He turned his face away.

She touched his chin and urged him to turn his face back toward her. His handsome profile was troubled. His faint blonde mustache twitched with uncertainty.

"Clay--"

"Cori--" They both spoke at once.

"Let's sit down," he suggested, and they settled together on an iron bench beside the path. Clay twirled the pink rose in his fingers as he gazed at the garden.

"Is school all right?" she asked, still feeling as if something were wrong.

He nodded. Then he opened his mouth to speak and closed it again.

"I don't want to pry, Clay, darling, but is something else wrong?"

"No." He sighed and finally looked at her. "Nothing is wrong. At least, nothing that can't be righted easily enough."

He took her hand, and she sighed. The warmth of his fingers wrapping around hers eased the unsteadiness of her mind. Cori knew that sometimes she was a flighty girl. She placed too much care, she realized, on surface things. Yet when it came to the things and people that really mattered, she remained steadfast.

She studied his blue eyes, so like her own. They were bright, but momentarily fathomless. "I'm glad if it's true. I just hope you know you can tell me if you have some kind of trouble. I don't want you to think I have no wits about me, or that I would fall apart at the first bad news you had to share."

He lifted his hand and grazed the back of his fingers across her cheek. "I know you wouldn't. In fact, I'm counting on that."

Chapter Five

Jesi twisted the buttons on her party dress. She couldn't wait to get it off. Fancy tea parties and prim gatherings were nothing but an annoyance, especially when she had to watch her sister parade around on Clay's arm. Why didn't he just tell Cori the truth?

The three of them had driven to the party in near silence. Cori kept trying to draw Jesi and Clay into conversation, but her attempts had been ineffective. Jesi shook her head. *How could I possibly feel like chatting while I was stuck in the carriage with Cori squeezed between Clay and me?*

For the thousandth time, the morning's events seared like hot steam through every crevice of her mind. Clay had sought out Jesi, just as she had known he would. He'd come to the church and found her. They'd stolen away together and had been late getting home.

Jesi smirked. If only her proper sister knew the truth about the man she aimed for, that he loved *Jesi,* and not Cori. Jesi had won him, and that settled it. Well, he had better tell Cori soon. Jesi couldn't keep up the pretense for long. If Clay found confessing his feelings to be so difficult, then maybe he needed some help. After all, she'd had to prod him to recognize his attraction to her. Maybe she should prod him to come forth with his love for her, too.

She hooked the last button on the neck of her everyday dress just as a knock rattled the door. Good. She would face Cori right now.

Prepared for battle, she slung open the door. Evie stood in the hallway.

"Your mama and her parents are home. She and your grandma want to get your grandfather settled in, so you'd best go downstairs and say hello. They can use your help."

"Oh." Jesi had almost forgotten. Cori would have to wait.

Down in the drawing room, their mother plumped pillows around their grandpa on the settee. "We'll get you all settled in upstairs right after you have something to eat," Lainey said. "Ma can get some rest then, too."

Jesi's grandmother looked her way, then clasped her hands to her cheeks."Oh, my, Jesi. Look at you. Or are you Cori?"

"I'm Jesi, Gran."

"I thought so." Grandma Colette opened her arms to embrace Jesi. "You're even more beautiful than I remember."

All of the women in their family were tall, and even growing older, Jesi's grandma still had an innate strength and erectness about her that defied her years. She beamed at Jesi, and Jesi reveled in her embrace.

"I was beginning to wonder when you all were going to get here."

"It's going to be so good to be here with you children." Gran looped her arm through Jesi's and gazed about their group. "Grandpa and I will enjoy soaking it in."

Jesi kissed her grandma's soft cheek. "We're glad you came."

"Now, where is your sister?"

Indeed, where was Cori? She was usually the first to make their guests welcome. She'd been so excited about their grandparents moving in with them, her absence struck Jesi as odd.

"She knew to expect us," Lainey said. "She must not have heard us arrive."

"I haven't seen much of her since we got back from the Pattison's party," Jesi said. "I'll see if she's in her room."

"Not until I get my hug." The deep voice stopped her, and she turned. Her grandfather sat nestled in the corner of the settee with a blanket tucked around his legs. His chocolate brown eyes twinkled out from his rugged face, his graying hair brushed back in smooth waves. He grinned over his thick, neatly combed beard.

"Oh, Gramp, I'm sorry. I wouldn't think of running off without getting my bear hug." Jesi lunged into his arms just like she had when she was a little girl. She'd forgotten just how good her grandpa's engulfing hugs felt, even though this one didn't seem as tight as usual. Was that just because she was older, or had Gramp gotten weaker? A pang struck her at the thought as he released her.

She straightened and smiled down at him. "I'll go find Cori. She's been waiting for a hug from you, too."

Jesi trotted up the staircase and rapped on Cori's door. When she got no answer, she tried the knob. The door was locked. She jiggled the doorknob back and forth.

"Cori? Gran and Gramp are here. They're waiting to see you."

"Tell them..." Her sister's voice sounded tight, choked, as she let the words trail away. "Tell them I'll be down in a bit."

"Cori?" Jesi leaned her head closer to the door and waited. A moment later, the lock turned, and the door opened. Cori walked away and slumped onto the bed. Her face was red, as if she'd just wiped away tears.

Jesi's heart tripped. "What's the matter?"

Cori shrugged.

"Well? You've been crying. That's obvious. What happened? Did -- did you and Clay have a fight?"

"Not exactly" Cori flashed her a look, her blue eyes as watery as Lake Superior in the sunshine. Then she frowned and picked at a thread in her hands. "Not at all. But something is wrong. I know it is. Did you see the way he acted at the party today? Quite a bit different than the last time we were together, wouldn't you say?"

Jesi chose her words carefully, her heart racing. "What do you mean?"

"Remember the other night? You saw how he behaved toward me. If I'd have given the slightest cue, he would have taken me in his arms right then, swept me up, and driven me off to who-knows-where. But today he acted just -- I don't know. Cold and indifferent."

"Maybe he had something important on his mind."

"Humph. He seemed talkative enough with other people. Why, even with you--"

"Even with me, what?"

Cori cast her a quick, sideways glance. Her lips trembled. "Nothing."

"No. Even with me, what?"

"I saw him laughing with you by the cake."

"You didn't think he was just being friendly?"

"I don't know."

"Cori?" Jesi stepped close and sat beside her sister, then licked her lips and took a quick breath. "Are you jealous?"

"Jealous? Of whom?"

Jesi didn't answer. She waited for Cori to look at her, to read her eyes and think her thoughts. Well, not *think them,* exactly. She wanted her sister to see her point, like they used to always be able to do as girls.

"Of you?" She harrumphed again. "Why would I be jealous of *you?"*

Jesi scowled. "Well, we do look *exactly* alike. Why mightn't he be attracted?"

"You think Clay is attracted to you? That's absurd."

"Is it?

"Clay is in love with me."

"So he says. But are you sure he's playing straight with you?"

"I can't believe you're suggesting this. You think Clay's behavior today was the result of some stray attraction to you, just because he laughed with you at the cake table?" Cori stood, paced to her bureau, and absent-mindedly arranged the hair pins and ribbons on its top.

Jesi stood so she could see Cori's face in the mirror. "What if I told you I think it's the truth? What if I told you I've sensed Clay's attraction?"

"You haven't."

"Actually, I have."

Cori's knuckles whitened on the frippery in her fingers. She glanced up into the mirror and down again. "It's nothing."

"Is it? I rode from the church with him today. He was more than agreeable during our ride."

That wasn't entirely true. In fact, Clay's guilt had nearly driven him into stony silence. Yet when she'd suggested they meet again tomorrow, he hadn't declined.

Cori spun around. "If you're trying to worry me, it isn't working.

Clay is in love with *me.* It's only natural he might enjoy your company. After all, as you pointed out, we do look alike. But he chose me. He won't change his mind. And besides, as far as you're concerned, there are plenty of other fish in the sea, isn't that right? You don't need to spend any of your charm on Clayton."

"I'm just warning you. If you can't trust him, maybe you should give him up while there's still time."

"I do trust Clay."

Jesi rose to leave the room, but as she reached for the door, Cori stopped her.

"I'm going to ask him about this. I'll try not to embarrass you, of course. But you wait and see. Clay's heart is well in the palm of my hand, and it's going to stay there."

Jesi pulled open the door. "You do that, Cori. I'm more than curious to know how it comes out."

*****

Jesi woke the next morning to someone tugging on her toes through her blankets. She pulled her feet up, but the teasing continued as the covers slowly slid away. She grasped their upper edge and yanked back, but was instantly caught in a tug of war. She groaned and kept her eyes shut, denying the daylight access behind her eyelids.

"Wakey, wakey. It's time for eggs and bacey."

"Daddy," she moaned. "It's too early."

"Come on, Rosebud, roll out of bed. Your mama's got some errands for you to run down to the mercantile."

Her eyes fluttered against the light. She'd forgotten. Last night, Mama and Evie had made her a list. It was the perfect excuse she needed to get out and meet Clay.

"There she is." Her pa grinned as she blinked at him.

Jesi flung back the covers and dove into her father's arms.

"Glad to see you made it home," she said, laughing at his look of surprise. "You woke me up. Now you have to put up with me."

Zane chuckled and grabbed her in a hug. "I guess so. Apparently, you're well rested. Well, hurry and get dressed and get downstairs." He swatted her backside as she turned away.

"Hey. What was that for?"

"That's for what you thought you got by with." He chuckled again as he let himself out.

If you only knew, Daddy.

She grinned. If he only *did* know, she'd be getting married today. That is, if he didn't kill Clay Dalton first.

Half an hour later, after giving more care to her appearance than she usually gave for a trip to the mercantile, she drove away in the buggy in the direction of downtown. She'd asked for a little extra time, using the excuse of wanting to look at some catalogs for a winter cape. Instead, she headed for an obscure diner near the university where Clay usually ate lunch. If anyone who knew them saw them there together, they would just suppose her to be Cori.

She found a place at a corner table covered in a cheery blue gingham cloth and sat down to wait. Before long, he strolled in through the door with some companions. When he saw her, he lost his grin and made excuses to his friends.

"Why are you here?" His tone was even, but his look remained guarded as he yanked out the chair next to her. He certainly had come to recognize her quickly in just a couple of days.

She caressed him with a smile. Hopefully it was provocative enough to calm him down. "We promised to meet, remember?"

"I never promised."

"You didn't disagree."

He rubbed his clean-shaven chin and raised his hand at the waitress. "Water, please." She scurried away with a nod and Clay turned to look at Jesi again. "Look, Jesi... I didn't mean for this to happen."

"Yes, you did."

"Not the way you think."

"What other ways are there?" She forced a laugh. "You meant to woo me first?"

"No." He glanced around, looking embarrassed for sounding emphatic.

A chill raced down Jesi's spine, but she remained calm. "All this guilty talk and behavior, Clay, is going to eat you up. As soon as we marry, it'll all be made right… just like you said the other night."

"No." His head shot forward. "*We* are not getting married."

"Of course we are." Her jaw dropped.

The waitress set a glass of water on the table for each of them and told them about the special lunch menu. Jesi didn't hear her for the sound of the blood rushing through her head, drowning her brain.

"I'll have whatever they're ordering," Clay said, dipping his head toward his companions across the room. "The lady isn't staying."

When the waitress walked away, Clay chugged at his water like a man thirsting to death.

"Clay?"

His glass clattered against the wood beneath the tablecloth as he set it down. He looked hard at her. "You might as well understand -- I'm still marrying Cori."

"What do you mean?" Jesi gasped. She gripped his arm. "You can't possibly."

"I can. I will. And you won't stand in our way."

"You'd like to think I won't, but I'm already in the way. In your heart, you know it. I'll always be in the way because it's *me* you really want."

"Want." He smirked. "That's exactly right."

She pushed at his arm, leaned back, and tucked her hands beneath her. She blinked against the burning in her eyes and looked out the window.

"What, Jesi? Tears, really?"

"I love you." The tears leaked out.

He pulled a handkerchief from his breast pocket and held it out to her. She snatched it from his hand and dabbed her eyes.

Anger rose to burn in her chest, smothering the pain. "Why can't you just admit you feel the same way? What is it about Cori that makes you want to marry her? She doesn't love you."

"We'll get along without it."

"But why? Why condemn yourself to that? You can't be marrying her for her looks. They're the same as mine. And if it's because of some old fashioned idea of propriety, I'm older by nearly ten minutes. I will inherit just the same as her. I'm willing to love you completely."

He harrumphed.

"Cori teases you. She pretends to offer you something that she will never fully give. Is that it? You like being teased? You think it means she'll deliver?"

Clay shook his head, then lowered it into his tented fingers.

Not waiting for him to speak, Jesi went on. "She'll always hold you at arm's length, even once you're married."

His head shot up. His jaw hardened. "I doubt that. But even if it were true, maybe that's why I trust her."

"Clay…" Jesi's heart nearly stopped. "If you're saying that you don't trust me, I -- well, I can't believe it."

He didn't say anything.

Her anger welled away, and she slumped her shoulders. "I've given myself to you completely." Her voice rose, and he glanced around. "You've taken every part of me, and I would never give it to someone else. I've loved you for a very long time. Just you. You owe me, Clay. You owe me."

She scooted her chair back and rose, nearly taking the blue gingham tablecloth with her. Her water glass tumbled over, soaking the cloth and running into a puddle on the floor.

Red splotches shot up Clay's neck and flushed over his face. With a fleeting glance at the people staring at them, he stood and reached for her. "Jesi, wait..."

"You think you're going to marry Cori?" She stepped back. "Well, you'd better get rid of that idea because I'm not so sure Cori still plans to marry you."

"What are you talking about?" Clay hurried behind her as she stormed toward the door.

She ignored the smirks on the faces of his friends and the others in the diner. Yanking open the door, she marched out to her buggy, but he stayed at her heels. She had one foot on the step when his fingers dug into her arm and he twirled her to face him.

Blonde hair spilled over his forehead. Fury settled between his brows and flared his nostrils. "Are you threatening me? Don't do it. Don't even try. If you intend to come between your sister and me, you'll be sorry."

"Come between you? I've already come between you. I don't have to say anything at all to Cori. She knows something is wrong between the two of you. She suspects it. In fact, she even thinks you might have compromised your feelings for her."

His jaw slackened and his face went white, but he didn't loosen his grip.

"Let go, Clay."

He leaned into her, clenching tighter until she slapped him. Her fingers left prints across his cheek, even though it hadn't been such a hard blow. But it stunned him enough that he released her arm. She turned and climbed into the buggy, and this time he let her go.

She picked up the reins and snapped them over the horse's back. The buggy lurched away.

Fear spiraled like a corkscrew through her heart. How could he say those things? He couldn't possibly mean them. They made no sense, no sense at all.

He couldn't marry Cori. He couldn't.

Jesi might not know Clay Dalton well, but what if he really did mean it? What if his will was stronger than her own? What if she'd given her virtue to him for nothing? How could she live, seeing him married to her sister, while the intimacy of their past hung over them like a monstrous shadow? How could she stand it?

She couldn't. That was it. She just couldn't. Jesi should go away rather than watch him marry Cori. Better to never watch him fall truly in love with her sister, to give her his children. Anything would be better than that.

She pushed her sleeve across her face. A veil of tears blinded her as she rushed her buggy down the street. One of the wheels struck a hole, jarring her. A sob ripped from her throat.

Anything would be better. *Anything.*

Chapter Six

Cori and Clay stood in her family's parlor. She faced him and twisted her hands. Emotions she hadn't realized ran so deep bubbled to the surface, choking her.

"Do you have feelings for my sister?" Cori blurted, even though that hadn't been her intention.

"What?" Shock passed over Clay, reddening his neck. He looked like a school boy, caught in a lie. Was he shocked, or merely embarrassed? She feared the latter.

"You heard me." The words rushed out of her like a madness. "Do you have feelings for my sister? Are you attracted to her? Does she appeal to you?"

All during the Sunday sermon, while the minister droned on, Cori had worried the fabric of her dress, plucking at it while her thoughts tormented her. She couldn't repeat back a single syllable of the message. She kept glancing at Clay next to her on her right, but whenever he looked her way, she averted her gaze. Then she looked to the left, past her parents, to Jesi seated between her pa and her grandma. Jesi stared straight ahead, her body still as stone, her profile the picture of grave attention.

Cori bit the inside of her cheek. Jesi hardly ever paid attention in church, but that didn't mean she wasn't good at faking it. Who knew what was going on in her sister's mind? She followed the line of Jesi's gaze to the reverend. Or was she focused on the vase of flowers sitting on the floor below the podium? Jesi had brought them to the church yesterday and then rode home with Clay.

Clay's hand stole gently over Cori's, but she could hardly sit still long enough to let it linger. So many questions burned through her, one foremost of all. Was he attracted to Jesi?

When the service finally ended, she let out a breath that did nothing to unravel the knot in her stomach. Finally the church doors opened, and they had escaped into the sunshine.

Clay's hand on her elbow had guided her out the door.

Now they were back home. Ma and Gran were in the kitchen helping Evie with the Sunday meal. Pa was smoking on the back porch while Gramp soaked up some sun and read the paper. She didn't know or care where Jesi was, but she and Clay had the parlor to themselves.

"Just answer the question, Clay."

He stood before the fireplace with both hands planted on his hips. "The way you look at me makes me feel like it doesn't matter what I say. Don't I get just a moment to be stunned by your question?"

"You shouldn't need a moment if your answer is no. But if that's not your answer..."

"No." His defiant blond shank of hair dropped over his eyes. He pushed it back and took a stride forward, rubbing her shoulders with his thumbs. "Why would you think such things? Why such accusation? Have you been listening to some kind of crazy gossip?"

"Gossip?" Cori frowned. The knots tightened inside her. "There's been no talk that I know of. But there's something wrong, and you won't tell me what it is. Yet you have no problem talking to Jesi."

"What do you mean, I don't have problems talking to Jesi?" Clayton's shoulders relaxed and he let out an unnatural chuckle."Is this because I had a little bit of conversation with your sister at the party the other day? I certainly haven't talked to Jesi about anything serious. If I had a real problem I would tell you. You know," he said, as one corner of his mouth curved up, "she *is* going to be my sister-in-law. I have to at least be friendly. Trust me, darling. Nothing is wrong."

Cori's heart raced. She wanted to believe him. She wanted to believe his adamant response was real, but was it? He seemed almost too convincing. She bit her lip. Jesi had said she *felt* Clay's attraction. Would a woman's own intuition lie? Or had Jesi said it only because she wished it? Who should Cori believe?

She covered her face in her hands.

Clay gripped her forearms. His voice dropped on octave. "Cori, you shouldn't always listen to your sister."

"What makes you think I'm listening to Jesi?" Her eyes, glassy with tears, shot up to look at him.

He shook his head. "Nothing. I just suspect it."

"And even if I did, what would she say?"

"Who knows? You know how she is, and how she likes to fool me."

"I don't know what you're talking about." Cori pulled her arms free. What did he mean that Jesi liked to fool him? Her heart did another somersault. She thought she might be sick.

He blushed, giving away the fact that he'd slipped and told her something private.

"Jesi fools you? How?"

"By pretending to be you." He rubbed the back of his neck and shrugged. "When she lets me in the door, she pretends to be you sometimes. Then if she fools me, she laughs."

Cori's eyes dried as she puzzled over his admission. "How does she pretend?"

"Just by saying she's you."

"Does she flirt with you?"

"No," he said, but his shrug told her the truth.

*****

Jesi leaned against the parlor doorway and observed the interchange between Cori and Clay. She grew anxious at Clay's stumbling responses to her sister's questions. Her heart hoped, even while she witnessed Cori's heart crumbling into ruins.

"When else?"

"When else, what?"

"When has she fooled you?"

"I don't know." He paced toward the window and looked out at the tree lined street. "Just... on occasion."

"How badly does she fool you? Has she held your hand?" Cori blanched. "Have you kissed her, thinking she was me?"

Clay spun and froze. His gaze landed on Jesi standing in the doorway.

She stepped into the room with her arms folded across her middle. "So is this your first lover's quarrel?"

Cori gasped just enough to cover Clay's curse. Her eyes teared up again, and Jesi's conscience smarted for her, but not enough to subdue the pain she'd feel over giving Clay up if she still had any chance at all of making him love her.

She straightened and stepped closer, her gaze searching his with unspoken longing.

Cori wept. "I just want somebody to tell me the truth."

Clay turned, leaned his elbows against the mantel, and tented his hands against his forehead.

"What truth, Cori?" Jesi asked. "You want to know if Clay kissed me?"

"Yes, and anything else. You said he's interested in you."

"That's a lie," he said, his back still turned.

Cori whimpered. "Is that the truth? Or do the two of you care for each other? I want to know if you're hiding your feelings because of me."

"I'll tell you." Jesi pushed her shoulders back.

Clay's spine stiffened.

Cori's eyes shone unusually bright, and Jesi recognized the hope growing behind them. Alas, she would soon shatter it like glass.

"Clay and I *have* grown closer. We didn't mean for it to happen. At least, Clay didn't. I've believed for a long time I could develop an attachment to him. Even before he courted you, Cori. And now, it seems, he returns my feelings. That's why I tried to warn you--"

Clay spun toward her like a lion, his face contorted, his lips twisting. "Don't listen to her, Cori. She's nothing like you. She's deceitful and envious and plotting. She's nothing but a common--"

His lips clamped shut on the word, but Jesi knew what it was. Faintness stole over her, swallowing her up. Would he still deny his feelings, even now that every door was open for him to reveal them?

Yet Cori was the one who staggered and dropped onto the settee, her head in her hands.

Jesi reached out, searching for Clay's arm, for something to hold onto, but he went to Cori instead. Jesi stumbled back against the door frame.

He patted Cori's hand and pulled her into his embrace.

Jesi's hand stole to her throat and pushed at her collar. She needed air. "Clay, how can you say such things? You came to *me.* You sought *me* out. You made it clear you loved *me.*"

"Did he really seek you out?" Cori asked, her voice a mere whisper. Her eyes shot open, and she darted a look between them.

Clay scowled at Jesi, but she ignored it. If he really meant to cast her off, then Cori would know the truth. "He did, Cori. More than that. He sought me out, more than once. I only fooled him the first time we kissed. But then he knew, and he still wanted me."

"Stop," Clay growled.

"We met secretly. He wanted me, Cori. He wanted me and loved me just as much as I wanted and loved him."

"I said 'stop'!"

"We were together, Cori... completely."

Cori cried out and bit the back of her hand as she leapt off the settee. Clay tried to stop her, but she broke free and fled. She pushed Jesi aside and ran down the hall. Clay moved to follow her, calling her name.

Jesi put a hand on his chest. Tears climbed into her eyes. Her voice wavered. "She'll never want you now."

He stopped and looked at her. His shoulders wilted, and she knew she had defeated him.

Her throat constricted. "I warned you."

"Then we all lost," he said with a nod. He walked past her. A moment later, the front door slammed.

*****

Jesi knocked on Cori's bedroom door, but her sister didn't answer. Everyone knew something had gone wrong, that Cori had fallen out with Clay, but no one knew why except for Jesi. No one bothered to notice the agony in *her* eyes.

"Cori?"

Cori had been mad at Jesi before, and had never been one to give in easily whenever she held a grudge. This time Jesi suspected her sister might hold her silence for weeks.

She turned to go. No use trying to talk to Cori now, or to try and make her see that her breakup with Clay had been destined to happen. He would never be Cori's, even if Jesi hadn't come along. Only now, he'd never be *hers,* either.

"Wait."

She hadn't even heard Cori's door open. She turned and followed her sister into her room.

Cori folded her arms like a shield in front of her and glared. "Well?"

"I didn't come to apologize."

"What did you come to do, then?" Cori gaped at her. "Gloat about seducing Clay?"

"I just want you to understand--"

"Understand? Understand you threw yourself at my fiancé and shamed me?"

"No."

"That you defiled yourself out of jealousy and spite?"

"I didn't--"

"That you want me to forgive you for such a despicable, immoral act? Well, I won't."

"Cori..." Jesi let her words trail away, and they stared at one another, mirror images with their fists clenched by their sides.

"What?" Cori spat. "Go ahead. Explain."

"I'm not asking for your forgiveness. I only want to tell you why I did it."

"You have a good reason, I suppose, for ruining yourself."

Jesi ignored the barb. "I realized I cared for Clay more than you do."

Cori gasped, but Jesi continued.

"I loved him more and more each day. I couldn't bear to have him think he loved you, when each time we spoke or looked at one another I knew it wasn't true. He loves *me.*"

"*Loves* you? He spit you out like sour milk. How can you still think he loves you?"

"I..." Jesi looked down at her feet. She frowned. Why did she still think so? Was she really so deluded she couldn't distinguish Clay's lust from his love?

Cori laughed in derision. "Are you so full of yourself you can't see the truth? You tricked the man I was going to marry, and he used you like a tramp. Nothing more. He hates you. And I hate you, too. I... I couldn't care less if I ever saw either of you again. Get out."

Jesi lifted her lashes slowly, only to see Cori's back. Suddenly she felt dirty. Filthy, in fact. Like the slash of a knife, the name that had hung on the edge of Clay's lips felt rightly stamped on her.

"Fine. I'll go."

Cori squared her shoulders in silence. They would share no forgiveness or reconciliation. And Jesi would still not have Clay.

Sooner or later, her family would learn the truth. Cori wouldn't be able to hide her resentment, and without Clay deciding to marry Jesi to set things right, they'd all see her the same as Cori did now: as a shameful, immoral girl who had allowed Clay to ruin her.

She clamped a hand over her mouth and fled Cori's presence. If only she could flee her own.

She remembered how she felt just yesterday, when she and Clay had quarreled at the restaurant. She had believed then anything would be better than watching Clay give his love to her sister. Now, she believed that would be a thousand times better than having him hate her. Cori was right. He *did* hate her. He'd used her and thrown her aside like garbage. The affection he had given her had turned sour. Gall was all he felt for her now.

Jesi thought she might throw up. She went into her room and locked the door. A moment later, she heaved. The room spun, and she fell across her bed.

Hours later, after the house had fallen quiet, she peeked into her grandparents' room. The elderly couple whispered in the lamplight.

"Gran?"

"Come in, honey." Her grandmother Colette lifted her head. "Is your sister with you?"

"No, it's just me. Jesi," she said, in case they weren't sure. "I didn't think you'd both still be awake."

"We're old, but we're still pretty spry." Her grandmother scooted closer to her grandpa, leaving space for Jesi to settle on the edge of the bed on her side. "Grandpa is telling stories about Lake Superior."

"I'd like to hear them."

Gramp reached over and patted her hand. "Oh, I've got enough stories to tell you to keep your ears warm all winter."

"That's good. Winter's even longer up here than down in Chippewa Falls, according to Ma. I just came to say goodnight."

Gran opened her arms, and Jesi fell into her caress. She lingered as long as she dared. If she stayed in her grandma's embrace too long, she might sense something was wrong. They all knew Cori had broken up with Clay. Jesi didn't have much time.

She hugged Grandpa Nase, too, and kissed his rough cheek. "Feel good tomorrow, Gramp, okay?"

"I don't think I'll have much choice around here."

She smiled and stood up. "I'll talk to you later."

"All right, honey. See you in the morning."

She didn't answer, but let her gaze linger on them just a moment longer. "I love you both," she said, straining to keep her voice strong.

"Love you, too."

"Mm-hm. G'night."

"Night."

Jesi backed out the door and closed it without a sound. She squeezed her eyelids shut and pushed back her tears. Telling them goodbye was even harder than she had thought it would be.

She wished she could do the same with her ma and pa, but she hadn't gone to their room to say goodnight in years. They'd want to talk about Cori and end up being suspicious, and she decided it best they fall asleep as quickly as possible.

Jesi went back to her room and picked up her case, an old carpetbag her father had used years ago and had given her to keep her doll clothes in. Now it had a new purpose. She didn't feel right taking any of the good luggage with her, or anything else that belonged to her family.

If Jesi was going to run away and start her life over, she needed to do it completely on her own, and that was it.

She drew on her coat and made sure she had her reticule. It held every scrap of money she had -- not much, but hopefully enough to last until she found a job. The train ticket alone would cost her dearly.

Jesi slipped out of the house a half hour later. No sense waiting around once her parents fell asleep. She could doze at the station until time for her train to leave. Walking to the station would take a while. She'd be exhausted once she reached it, but maybe that was a blessing. She would be able to sleep during the long train ride into her unknown future.

Chapter Seven

Seated at the table in the middle of his cabin's main room, Paul Winter stared at the letter in his hands. As candlelight flickered over it, he silently re-read his words, checking for mistakes, making sure the tone of the missive sounded professional enough. Finally, satisfied, he set it down and signed his name at the bottom.

Behind him, lamplight bathed the open corner kitchen. Marie's wooden spoon struck the sides of her heavy bowl with a *whap* as she mixed biscuits for the next morning.

"What's that you're working on?" she asked. "A sermon?"

"No, no. Just a letter."

"To whom?"

"Just some folks down in Oshkosh."

"Oshkosh? Who do you know in Oshkosh?"

"No one you've heard of." Paul folded the letter and shrugged.

Marie plopped the wooden spoon in her mixing bowl and stared at him. "You're up to something."

"Why do you say that?" Paul turned to look at her. Then he pushed back from the table and rose. "Can't a man know some people his big, nosey sister doesn't know?"

She grinned and commenced to beating the batter. As it stiffened, she set the spoon aside and dumped the lump of dough onto a floured bread board. She pressed her knuckles into it. "Go ahead, act aghast. You and I both know I'm right. You're up to something."

"Go ahead and believe that if you want." Paul stuffed the letter into his back pocket and reached for an apple in the dish at the table's center. He snuffed out the tallow candle that had heavy dollops of wax pooled around its base.

"Play nonchalant. It's all right with me. It must not be too important, or you wouldn't be crushing it all up in your britches pocket."

Before he could think twice, he wrinkled his forehead, snatched the letter back out, and smoothed it on the table. He'd stuck it into his pocket as a reaction to Marie's sudden curiosity without really thinking. It was pretty messed up.

Marie laughed and pointed a floury finger at him. "That was a pretty fast draw."

Paul scowled. What was he doing, anyway? He re-lit the candle and looked again at the wrinkles and creases of his carefully constructed letter. With a sigh, he held the contentious missive over the flame. When it flared too close to his finger, he dropped it onto the puncheon floor and stomped it to ash.

"What did you do that for?" Marie stared at him, and her bantering tone fell away. "I'm sorry for teasing you."

"It's all right. I don't think I was supposed to send it, anyway." He pursed his lips and pushed a hand through his hair.

Marie rested her hands in the dough. "Paul, are you okay?"

Was he okay? He grunted mildly and went for the broom. Truth was he hadn't been okay in a while. Not since that day in town when all the doubts and questions started assailing him double-time. He hadn't been able to stop dwelling on what he'd given up four years ago in order to answer God's call to come north. The more he mulled it over, the more he second-guessed it. Maybe he should move on. Or maybe he shouldn't. He didn't know what to do.

He opened the door and tossed the ashes from the dustpan off the front step. Setting the tools aside, he crossed his arms and faced Marie.

"It was a letter about a church position."

"A church position? In Oshkosh?"

He nodded. "I thought about applying, but maybe now isn't the right time."

"You aren't sure if you should? You wrote the whole letter and then changed your mind?"

"Isn't it obvious? I'm not sure about a single, solitary thing." He shrugged. "I'm not sure if I should stay here, not sure if I should go. I'm not sure I've made a right decision since day one."

"Paul," she brushed her hands together and, in two strides, stood eye to eye with him. She touched his shoulder. "If you're not sure, then what about me?"

"What do you mean?"

"I mean, I'm sure. I knew without a moment's hesitation that God called me to go with you when you came up here. I feel like my ministry, slight as it is -- baking bread for the cookee, having a smile for the lumberjacks when they're tired, studying the Bible with Charlie's daughters, and especially nursing hurts -- is exactly what God wants of me. He hasn't called me to quit."

"So you think God sent me up here to take care of you so *you* can minister? I'm not so sure if that doesn't make it even worse."

"We've had this conversation before." She frowned. "In a way, yes. He *does* want you to take care of me. Only, He didn't send you up here just for that. He also wants you to plant seed."

She turned and went back to her dough board.

Yes, they had discussed this before. Paul sensed her frustration, while failure heckled him. It plagued him like a Bible leprosy, and he couldn't shake it. Was he so weak-minded that the devil could just keep taunting him this way and win so easily?

"I don't want to be indecisive, sis. It's not that. I guess I do believe God called me up here, but that was four years ago, and now I'm starting to wonder if He wants me to stay."

"Write the letter again, then."

"What?"

"You heard me. Write the letter again. Maybe if you're discontented, or you just aren't feeling God is keeping you here, you should write to that church in Oshkosh and see what He does. If He wants you down there, He may set me on a different course, too. After all, it's not like you've *had* to take care of me."

He offered her a weak smile as he remembered the suitors who'd tried to whisk Marie off into the north woods. "You'd never have married Bob Kelick or Jude Selzner whether or not I was here to take care of you."

"Don't be too sure." She cut out the biscuits.

Paul hadn't expected her to say what she had about testing God's will by sending the letter. But maybe she was right. Maybe he wouldn't know what to do until he stepped out in faith and did *something*. What had his dad always said? *You can't move a parked buggy.* Maybe if he unlocked the hubs of his own rusty faith, God would move him forward. If not, then maybe He'd show Paul this was the place for him to stay after all.

He strolled over and reached for a piece of dough. "Are you sure? You sound pretty happy here. What if God does call me on? You think you'll be ready for that kind of change?"

"What do you think?" She gave a mocking gasp. "That an old maid like me is too set to change course and try something new? It's not as if I'm enamored of Hurley." She rolled her eyes. "I might up and surprise you good one of these days. But right now, I'm content. God knows He's in charge of changing that when need be."

"An old maid? Don't kid yourself." Paul grinned. He'd seen the appreciative looks that still came her way. Marie was only thirty-two. She didn't have to remain unmarried if she didn't want to. He put his hands on his hips and nodded. "All right then. I'll write it again."

Paul dipped his pen into the ink well and squared his shoulders. Knowing he wasn't keeping anything from Marie and that she had given him her blessing made him feel better. He wished he'd talked about the idea with her in the first place. Sometimes, she was still the big sister.

"I'll ride in and post this in the morning."

"Maybe you can pick me up some things while you're in town."

"Want to come along?"

"Not this time. I've got Bible study with the girls in the afternoon, and I promised a pie to the Schmidt brothers after they fixed the broken pump handle last week."

"Yes, that was nice of them. Just leave me a list, then. I'll leave early."

"See if you can keep from running into trouble while you're there this time," she added with a teasing note in her voice, her brown eyes sparkling.

He laughed. "Oh, I'll side-step that, I promise you."

*****

Seven whole days had passed since Jesi stepped off the train at the Hurley depot and planted her feet in Wisconsin's northeast corner. Now, standing in front of a mercantile squashed between two of Silver Street's saloons, she stepped out of the way of passersby and set her bag on the wooden walk. Sweat stuck her sleeves to her underarms and dampened the back of her neck. Dust clung to the hem of her brown dress.

She shaded her eyes against the late August sun and glanced up the road. Worry ran like rivers up her veins. If she didn't find a job soon, she didn't know what she'd do. She had already applied for work at every inn and café, looking for a job cleaning, cooking, waitressing, doing laundry, clerking, or performing secretarial work, even though she wasn't in the least bit qualified to be a secretary. She didn't know what else to look for, at least nothing else she was capable of doing. She'd entered every reputable establishment she could find, and knocked on a lot of private doors besides. None of them, even the big, beautiful Bardon Hotel, needed so much as a dishwasher or someone to change the sheets. Apparently times were harder than she had first realized. With so many men out of work, giving a job to a single woman didn't seem reasonable, when the men needed to provide for their families.

Jesi was almost out of money. She hadn't expected it to disappear so fast, or for her hunt for work to be so hard. She could no longer stay at the modest but pleasant hotel where she'd been registered, even though it had begun to feel like home. She liked the pretty white curtains fluttering against the window, and the single tick mattress covered with a homemade calico quilt. The fare was simple but good, and she was responsible to no one. But she'd have to find lesser accommodations now, and her choices at the moment looked less than inviting.

Most of the rooms she could afford were upstairs above saloons, and heaven only knew what else went on in them.

She pulled in a deep breath. Where she lived didn't matter. *When it comes down to it, I'm no perfect flower any longer, so I've got no right to judge. If I'm going to stay here and make it on my own, then I'll just have to get used to that fact.*

She'd do whatever it took to keep from slinking back home in disgrace to face the judgment of her family and friends -- and Cori's wrath.

No, better for her to stay here, whatever the accommodations.

She glanced across the street at another *Rooms* sign swinging above the door of a saloon.

"Maisey's Place," she murmured, reading the name of the establishment. "Well, Maisey, your name sounds welcoming, at least."

Jesi hefted the worn carpet bag and stepped toward the street. The door of the mercantile opened about the same time and someone slammed into her, sending her lurching forward off the walk. She stumbled, and as the dirt raced up to meet her, a hand grasped her arm.

Gasping, she turned around and pulled free, her face a foot from that of her rescuer. "You almost killed me."

"I'm so sorry. I came out the door without looking where I was going. Here, let me help you with your bag."

Jesi frowned and clutched her bag more tightly. Her breath came out in a ragged rhythm, and her heart pattered. "No. It's all right. I have it."

"Please. I insist." The man smiled and took off his hat. "I'd hate to have it on my conscience that I almost killed you and didn't do anything to make amends."

He smiled, squinting a little into the western sun. He looked sincere, but she caught the humorous tone of his words. A breeze moved the lank brown hair across his brow.

She gave him a cursory, distrustful once-over. "I didn't mean to over-react. You didn't almost kill me, but you did scare me. I might have twisted my ankle or something."

"You might have. That's why I insist you let me carry your bag to... wherever you're going."

Jesi flitted a glance at Maisey's Place. Unnatural heat crawled up her neck, making her glad for her high fitting collar. "No, really. I don't have far to go."

"Then may I buy you a cup of coffee by way of an apology?"

She frowned. Her heavy bag tugged on her arm, and she was tired of this man. "Look, mister, all you did was bump into me. I'm all right."

He gazed at her a moment longer. Then his glance stole to the saloon across the street. She flushed.

"Are you in need of a room?"

"It's none of your business." She turned and walked away. What kind of man made such rude inquiries of a woman he'd never met? Only *one* kind. Why should she feel embarrassed? Who was he, anyway? Just some stranger who'd nearly ploughed her into the ground.

"Look, I'm really just sorry." His voice carried into the street after her.

She ignored him and picked up her pace, not bothering to look back. She widened her stride, her purpose bent on Maisey's. When she'd successfully crossed the street without being hit by a streetcar or a buggy, she pushed open the door to the dim establishment. With only a brief glance behind her, certain he wouldn't be able to see her inside the shadowed enclosure, she noted the man had disappeared.

*****

The redhead marched across the street, her head bent with determination. Paul shrugged and walked a dozen yards to the rail where he'd hitched his horse Sarah. The girl pushed open the door and the darkness of Maisey's Place swallowed her.

"Save her from her anger and pain, Lord," he muttered as he loaded Marie's goods into his saddle bags. He'd seen that look in other girls' faces around town. The haunted appearance of those whose lives had turned astray and who depended on the living they made in barely disguised brothels like Maisey's. He wished she would have taken up his offer of coffee. Maybe he could have spoken with her about the Lord and offered her some hope for the future.

Such encounters never seemed to work out that way.

Paul climbed onto Sarah's back and headed up the street. This was his first time back in town since the day he'd gotten hung up in the street fight. He laughed.

"God, you sure do have a sense of humor." Seems he couldn't come into town without colliding with trouble -- literally. Marie would enjoy a good laugh about this one, too.

While he ate lunch at his favorite cafe, Paul thought of the girl again. If only he could do something to let her know he wasn't like the men she usually met in that place. He'd simply wanted to offer her his apologies and let her know people cared about... well, cared about girls like her. Some of them did, anyway. He and Marie did.

She had looked tired and a little thin. Paul supposed those kinds of girls had seen more than their fair share of suffering and struggle, and they also probably dealt with the inner burdens of self-contempt and guilt, even if they didn't want to admit it.

I pray you'll reach this one, Lord.

The waitress brought him apple pie for dessert. It sure did look good. Then he remembered Marie was baking an apple pie for the Schmidt brothers. She'd bake two, for sure, so he'd find apple pie waiting for him at home, too.

"Ma'am?"

The waitress turned around.

"Would you mind wrapping this up for me?" He patted his stomach above his narrow waist. "I just remembered my sister has pie waiting at home, and I don't want to offend her by not having room for any when I get there. I don't want this to go to waste, though. A girl across the street, a redhead, 'bout twenty-years-old, would probably like it. Maybe I can send it over to her. She looked pretty hungry."

"Always trying to help some soul, aren't you?" The middle-aged waitress smiled. "Still preaching to them boys up in the woods?"

"I try."

She nodded. "I'll be right back."

"Might I borrow your pencil and a slip of paper off your pad while I wait?"

"Sure." She handed him the implements and picked up the pie. "I'll be back in a jiffy."

He wrote: *Dear Miss. Again, I'd like to offer my apologies for knocking into you today. Here's something I hope will make up for my clumsiness. Perhaps next time I bump into you, it will not be quite so literal, and we can have that cup of coffee I mentioned.*

He thought about signing it *pastor,* but decided that sounded pretentious. He wanted to say he was praying for her, but she'd likely think it smug. In the end, he just signed his name, *Paul Winter,* and vowed to keep praying for her. Maybe someday, someone else would come along and plant a greater seed.

Chapter Eight

At home in Superior, Cori lay on her back and stared up at the afternoon shadows playing on the white ceiling above her bed, willing the past weeks to disappear along with the hurt. She wondered whose betrayal pained her more. Jesi's or Clay's?

If only Cori could erase the memories all together. Life wasn't fair. She had always done the right thing, and then Jesi's choices had ruined her future. It just wasn't fair. She'd kept to propriety. She'd guarded her and Clay's courtship. But her sister -- her own flesh and blood -- had destroyed what should have been a perfect, beautiful thing. Clay should have been guarding their relationship, as well. Cori had trusted him, and he'd spoiled it in the most complete way possible. What kind of real man did such a thing?

I should be planning my wedding and having an engagement party. She and Clay should be talking about their future and the family they'd raise, where they'd live, and what they'd do in the years ahead. Now Cori's future stretched empty and bleak, holding absolutely nothing.

Tears welled up in her eyes, spilled out, and trickled into her ears. She pumped her fist against the quilt. For one moment, her heart raged at Clay; then the next, it fumed at Jesi. She'd never thought she could really hate someone, but right now her feelings for her sister couldn't be called love.

"I don't care if she ever comes back." She ground out the words through gritted teeth.

She sat up and wiped her eyes on her blanket. Mama and Papa were worried sick. Not knowing the full truth, only that Cori and Jesi had gotten into a fight over Clay, they couldn't figure out why Jesi had run off like she had. Gran and Gramp weren't doing too well over it, either. Didn't Jesi care what something like this would do to them? Was she so selfish that she didn't care about hurting people? Gramp had gone downhill with lightning speed after she ran away. The last few days had drained what little bit of strength he had left right out of him.

If he dies...

Cori bit her lip. If Gramp died, Jesi would be at fault.

She stormed out of her room. Where was Mama? Papa had gotten on a train to try and find her prodigal sister. He didn't even know where to head. His first thought was to go to Duluth, then to St. Paul. From there, he would complete the triangle back to Eau Clair and come north again. He hoped to find some trace of her along the way. She'd certainly not left them a trail here at home. If she had taken a train, as everyone believed she had, she must have used a false name. They had found no record of a ticket sold to Jesilyn Beaumont.

Jesi was smart. Of course she was. She would know better than to use her real name. She'd been smart enough to keep her affair with Clay secret and had devised ways to be with him. Certainly, running away would be a circus for her.

Again, the affair sent swirls of unwanted thoughts through Cori's head. What a desperate act. For Clay to have fallen for Jesi's tricks so easily only deepened the burn inside Cori.

Rage warmed her again. What kind of man was he, anyway? What kind of man planning to be a husband would do such a wicked thing? Cori couldn't help but believe Jesi's claims that Clay hadn't been fooled. He really had realized he'd dallied with Jesi, not Cori. He'd realized it, and he'd gone back to her.

Cori charged through the house. "Mama?"

"In here." Her mother's voice sounded tired, and she looked it when Cori found her in the kitchen dicing potatoes and carrots for a stew.

She reined in her temper and calmed her voice. "Where are Gran and Evie?"

"Evie's hanging out some wash." Her mama's voice shook. "Grandma's sitting with Gramp"

"I'm sorry, Mama. You must be afraid."

"I am." Lainey nodded. "Gramp isn't doing any better. A doctor's coming over tomorrow to give him another examination. And I'm worried about Jesi, too, of course, but she's traveled before and knows how to take care of herself. I only hope she took enough money and writes to at least let us know where she is."

"She's made me so mad." Cori slapped her hand on the work table between them. "You shouldn't have to worry about her. It's her fault Gramp is worse. It's her fault for *everything.*"

"She didn't mean to care for Clay, I'm sure." Lainey dashed away a tear with the back of her hand and continued dicing. "She didn't mean to come between you. Maybe going away was the only way she could think of for the two of you to work things out."

"Work things out with Clay? *Never*. Mama, if you only knew."

Her mother looked at her with widened eyes. Cori had kept Jesi's shame secret only because it embarrassed her and heightened the wound the lovers had given her. She had never divulged all the things that had spilled out of Jesi that day. She'd only said that her sister had tried to steal Clay, and that he hadn't been innocent in the matter. As far as her parents understood the situation, Cori and Clay had only suffered a little rivalry and jealousy that would pass eventually.

"What do you mean?"

"I'm sorry." Cori swallowed and turned away. "It's nothing."

"Are you sure?"

The paring knife clattered as her mother set it down and walked around the table, her skirt swishing. She came to stand beside Cori, who threw herself into her mother's arms. Cori shuddered as the hateful tears came back.

"It'll be all right." Her mother's hands gently brushed her back.

She shook her head and gulped. "I don't think *all right* is a possibility."

She lifted her head and gazed steadily at her mother. A different look had come into Mama's eyes, a new fear.

"What is it?" she whispered. "What don't I know?"

"Mama, she--" Cori wanted to tell. She *needed* to tell. She'd railed in her room for three weeks and could no longer keep the horror of it inside, yet she didn't want to hurt Mama. She sighed, and tears welled in her eyes again. Oh, how she wished they wouldn't. "Mama, Jesi and Clay, they..."

Her mother's hand tightened on Cori's shoulders.

"They *had* each other."

Her mother gripped Cori and stared at her until she finally winced. Then Mama dropped her hands, covered her mouth, and turned around. Now Cori needed to comfort her.

"I didn't want to tell you, but I couldn't stand it anymore. Jesi and Clay, they snuck away. They met places. And he still pretended to love me, to want to marry *me.* Oh, what if I had? What if I'd married him and then found out? What if they'd continued to be together?" A sob clawed back up her throat. "What then, Mama? What then?"

Mama turned back, her eyes wide with shock, and hugged her again.

"I'm so sorry, my darling girl. I'm so sorry Clay did this to you."

"Jesi did it!" Cori shouted. Her fury at her sister rushed to the forefront again. For just a split second, she believed Clay to be a victim of her sister's plotting. The blaze of anger roaring through her came pouring out. "She schemed, and she planned. She fooled him! Tricked him into thinking she was me! He thought she *was* me, and then he knew she wasn't... and he didn't stop! He stayed in the trap. He and Jesi kept--"

She cried again. And all the while she cried, she hated Jesi, and she wondered when the tears would ever stop. Finally, after raging on for several more minutes, she went limp with exhaustion. Both women wiped tears away and startled when Colette came in.

Cori tried to smile.

"Don't worry about stopping your tears on my account," Gran said. She sighed and dropped onto a chair.

Cori swallowed. "Is Gramp okay?"

"He's asleep, but he moans. I think the sickness is working overtime. My strong, handsome Nase isn't going to get any better. I know that now."

Lainey put a hand over her mother's, and Cori experienced an even deeper pain at witnessing theirs. How could they survive so much hurt and sorrow?

Gran lifted her gaze to Mama. "I think we should send a letter to your brothers. Nase may not have many weeks left."

Cori gasped and curled her hand into a fist against the work table. She needed to be strong for them now, even more than for herself. Whatever Clay had done to ruin their future, whatever Jesi had done to steal it, didn't compare to the loss these dearest of women would feel when Gramp passed on.

For a moment, Cori almost prayed. She longed to beg God for more time for her grandfather. But she didn't. She *couldn't.* Her bitterness toward Jesi stood in the way. She recognized it, an impenetrable wall standing between her and God, a wall she couldn't climb over until she wanted to badly enough. And she didn't want to, because that would mean asking for forgiveness. Cori couldn't ask for forgiveness, because she wasn't ready to give it; wasn't ready to let go of the hatred and anger. Clutching them close filled her with satisfaction.

She could never forgive her sister.

*****

Jesi curled tighter into the covers and pressed her hands over her ears. No matter how hard she tried, she couldn't drown out the cacophony rising up from the barroom down below, or the grating, high-pitched laughter of the women earning their living in Maisey's. If her stomach didn't hurt so bad, maybe she could fall asleep and block it out.

Two weeks had passed since her first night of lodging at Maisey's. Meanwhile, a decent job continued to elude her, even though she had searched everywhere. She also tried to adapt to her surroundings. She had been going out in the mornings to look for a job, though now, more often than not, after giving up, she just stayed in. She'd run out of ideas. She never left her room after suppertime. She'd figured out pretty quickly what type of business Maisey ran, and she didn't want to be mistaken for one of *Maisey's girls.*

The women weren't really so bad. A couple of them had seemed almost nice when she'd met them in the hall on her way from the bath. Yet they could be ornery, too. Once she'd stayed in the tub too long, and the one named Betty almost blew the door down with her string of curses. Jesi made sure to take her baths earlier in the morning after that episode, and she steered clear of Betty, who'd been pointing barbs at her ever since.

Jesi could do for a hot soak now. She shuddered. Her one blanket wasn't enough tonight with the cold seeping in. September was like that sometimes, warm during the day, then temperatures dropping down at night. The window rattled with each tiny wind gust. The winter would be cold if she was forced to stay here.

Jesi cringed at the thought. *Forced to stay here... what a laugh.* She would be lucky if Miss Maisey let her stay another night. She was a week behind in her rent, and she had no hope of getting any money. No matter how many doors she knocked on, no job seemed forthcoming.

What was I thinking? Why did I come here? I could have gone down to Chippewa Falls or Eau Claire -- anyplace might have held the better hope of finding a job.

But she knew what had brought her to Hurley. The town lay in the last direction her family would think of looking for her. At most, they might go to Ashland, realizing she wouldn't have had the money to travel far. But she'd gone just out of reach, just far enough and into a lesser desired place to throw them off her trail, in case they managed to pick it up at all. By train, she was only a few hours from home. Just the right few hours to keep her out of their reach.

Jesi turned over. Piano music blared from downstairs. Her mattress felt even lumpier than ever, if that were possible. No pretty white curtains decorated the one smudged window in her room. Only a heavy piece of dusty red drapery hung there. Even in the darkness, she could smell the dust. Despair wormed its way into her. She had to find a job somewhere, no matter what.

Her stomach pinched again, and she forced her eyes to stay closed. If she could block out the sounds and forget how hungry she was, she might fall asleep. That was the only escape she could hope for.

She must have gotten her wish. The next time she lifted her eyelids, a ghostly light filtered the room. Morning of another day. Now those hours of distance from home felt like thousands of miles. Jesi didn't know when she'd finally fallen asleep.

The new day only made her desperation more acute, however, and when Miss Maisey knocked on her door the second she got out of bed, she drove the point home.

Jesi recognized the woman's sharp-knuckled rap and cringed. *It's too early for her to be up. This can't be good.* Maisey's didn't house any early birds.

When Jesi didn't get to the door fast enough, Maisey thrust the key into the lock and let herself inside. Jesi gasped and clutched her dress to her chest. She hadn't had a chance to pull it on over her shift.

"Well? You're a week late. Are you going to be able to pay?"

"I... I don't have it right now. Maybe later today--"

"Look, Miss Barton," the middle-aged woman said, using the name Jesi had given her. She stared hard, though not unsympathetically, at Jesi from beneath disheveled, unnaturally blonde hair. Her pink robe was cinched beneath her ample bosom over layers of diaphanous drapery. "I don't like to be hard on anyone in these times, but I can't have you taking up space if you can't pay your rent. I have to make my own living, and I've got to think of my employees."

"I know. I don't expect you to do that. It's just that I--"

"I know. You haven't got a job, and you can't find a job. When's the last time you've eaten? You haven't bought a meal here in at least two days."

Jesi flinched as Maisey's eyes raked up the length of her. "I had a sandwich."

"When? Tuesday? Wednesday? You're starving yourself. I can see that. Why don't you come downstairs. I'll have Mary fix you something. Then you'll have to be on your way."

"Please." Jesi reached out to Maisey, stopping her just as she turned to go.

"What?"

"I don't have any place to go." She retracted her hand and the woman's eyes narrowed, studying her.

"What are you asking? I already said you can't stay here. That is..." She paused and gave Jesi a more serious perusal. "Not unless you want to work."

Jesi clenched her dress. *Yes.* She wanted to work. She closed her eyes for a moment, her head spinning. "Oh, yes."

"You'd better understand me clearly. I'm not asking you to do the cleaning. Hilda does that. Walter serves the bar, and Mary cooks. It's another kind of work I have available."

Jesi's breathing nearly stopped. She couldn't speak, couldn't swallow. She stared back at Maisey.

"Well, I see you're not interested. Too bad. My clients would like you." She turned to go.

"Wait." Jesi found her voice. Her lips trembled, but she managed the words. "I can do that. I-I need the job." Her legs shook, and she plopped down onto the bed.

Maisey took another look at her and came to stand over her. She took Jesi by the chin and lifted her face, shifting her head from side to side.

"Yes. All right, then. I'll send you up some breakfast. Don't worry. Meals are free, along with lodging. You can start tonight. After breakfast, take a nice long bath. I'll tell Betty not to pester you. Then take another nap if you want. Dinner is at four. Be in the bar ready to work by six."

Jesi nodded. "Thank you."

Maisey walked out but paused before pulling the door closed. "What's your first name?"

"Jane. My name is Jane."

"Welcome to Maisey's, Jane."

Chapter Nine

The oil lamp on Jesi's nightstand washed the room in shadows. Standing before the long cracked mirror in the corner beside it, she couldn't help noticing how pale the skin of her arms and neck looked, exposed in her filmy, midnight blue dress. The dress Maisey had given her hung looser than she would have liked, but she'd dropped weight during the past several weeks. Did how it fit really matter? She understood what sort of message it was meant to convey.

As soon as the thought came to her, she pushed it aside. She wouldn't think at all. She'd just go downstairs, serve some drinks, talk to the customers, and make friends.

A shudder ran up her torso and out to her fingertips. She told herself it only happened because she was cold.

She rubbed her arms and took one last look in the mirror. Maisey had said to leave her hair down. The long waves glowed like copper coins in her reflection. Only, her eyes didn't seem so bright.

Turning away, she strode to the door. She laid her hand on the brass knob and took a deep breath, then flung it open. The gas-lit hall and the rumble of voices from down below pulled her into the world. She had a job. She would ignore the fact that it had been born out of desperation. The work would keep her fed and provide her with a roof over her head. Maybe something else would turn up soon, and within a few days or a couple of weeks, she would be able to put it behind her and close the door on this memory.

Gaslight filled the barroom, making it brighter than her dingy room upstairs. She took another deep breath as she reached the landing, her insides scrambling. Only four or five patrons sat at the bar. The night was early yet. That was Maisey's intention, no doubt, to ease her into the job. As she strolled into the room, heads turned to notice her before the men returned their attention to their drinks. Betty flicked a glance in her direction before lifting her nose and sauntering away to lean against the other end of the bar. Jesi turned toward the piano and ignored Betty's abrasive laugh as the woman joked with patrons.

A thin man with his shirt sleeves rolled up over his boney elbows warmed up at the piano. His hair was greasy, but combed, and stubble marked his chin with hints of glittering white. He glanced up at her for a moment with red-rimmed eyes.

"You new?"

"Y--" Jesi nodded and cleared her throat, then finally found her voice. "Yes."

He nodded and started a slow run up the keys with knobby fingers. "Name's Gravy."

"Gravy?"

He nodded.

She wanted to ask about the moniker, but why bother? "I'm Jane. Jane Barton."

He acted as if he hadn't heard her as he started in on a slow, relaxing song. The music warmed and soothed her. For the first time all day, tranquility washed over her. When he looked up at her again, she smiled. He changed the tempo to a livelier tune. Her shoulders swayed.

"You dance?"

Jesi thought of the few formal dances she'd been to. She didn't think that was what Gravy had in mind. "A little."

"Good. I like it when people dance. Maybe later you can find yourself a partner and dance while I play."

She smiled again.

Find a partner? She looked around the room again and tried to imagine a man like Clay coming in through the doors to dance with her. That wouldn't be so bad.

From the corner of her eye, she noticed Maisey watching her from the far recesses of the room near the curtained doorway leading to the storage room behind the bar. Jesi lifted her shoulders and smiled. Maisey flipped a nod toward the patrons, and Jesi got the message. She forced her feet forward toward the bar.

She'd only gone a few feet when three men burst through the front door of the saloon. The one in front was a big man, well over six feet tall, with shoulders that filled the doorway for the brief moment he was in it. Thick waves of black hair shrouded his head, and a full beard covered his chin. His eyes were big and dark and lively.

"Where is everyone?" he bellowed. "Maisey, why hasn't this party started?"

Betty hurried over to give the man a friendly welcome, lacing her arm in his, and Maisey greeted him, too, shaking his hand and kissing his cheek. Walter the bartender set up another round of drinks, and Gravy began a new tune.

"Hey there, Johnny Ray. Where've you been?"

Jesi slid up to the end of the bar and listened. So his name was John. He was as big as a bear, and looked almost as frightful except he had a big smile, and folks seemed to like him.

"Here and there. Mostly there. Mine's running slow, so I'm in town for a while."

"You get let off?"

He cussed. "They wouldn't lay me off."

The other fellows at the bar laughed.

Suddenly his gaze lifted and met Jesi's. He stared down the length of the bar.

"Well, then, now we won't be so bored," another fellow said with a guffaw. "With big John in town, we'll have some fun."

Big John laughed and took a long swallow from his beer mug. Then his eyes came back to her again, and he watched her like a bear.

"What's your name?" he asked, his voice hushing the others in the bar as they all turned to look at her.

She straightened and flipped her hair over her shoulder. Being intimidated by this beast wouldn't do. "I'm Jane."

"Jane, huh? But not Plain Jane." His look took in all of her. One side of his mouth lifted in a grin, and he slugged back the rest of his beer. Big John pushed his glass toward the bartender. "Why don't you come over here and stand next to me, Jane?"

She could feel Maisey, not to mention everyone else at the bar, watching her. Betty scowled. The two or three other girls who worked at Maisey's had appeared without her noticing their entrance, and the barroom had gotten crowded.

Jesi's hands hung at her sides, and she became very aware of the loose dress fluttering around her legs and hips as she walked slowly toward Big John. When she stopped in front of him, he grazed the length of her with his black stare.

"Is that all the closer you're gonna come?" His voice, low and rumbling, both dared and commanded her at once. She took another step closer. Big John moved over, exposing a thin space between him and his friend at the bar, and his expression challenged her. "Here's room for you."

She squeezed into the space, the heat of his big body pressing into her.

"Now, that's better." He slid his arm down her back. "Walt, where's my beer?"

For the better part of an hour, Jesi stood next to Big John, eventually finding breathing space when the other fellow moved away. But John didn't let her leave his side. He kept putting his arm around her, and now and then his hand moved where she had to will herself with all her mind to allow it. She agreed to drink a glass of beer with him. She'd never done so before, and afterward she felt woozy and light-headed.

The fog in her mind helped her ignore Big John's hands. His voice had gotten louder, and he filled the bar with laughter. His course jokes drew a raucous response from the others gathered around him. As the night wore on, more patrons and music filled the room. Jesi wished she could be Gravy. He must be tired, but at least everyone left him alone.

This is what it would probably be like, night after night. The noise, the drinking, men like Big Johnny Ray.

Another man squeezed in beside her and pressed her tight to Big

John. She recognized him as one of the men who'd arrived with him.

"Hey, Johnny, guess what?"

"What's that, Lou? You need another drink?"

"Absolutely. But that's not all. Gravy says this gal can dance."

Big John draped an arm across her shoulders, weighing her down as much with his breath as with the weight of his body against her, crushing her between the two of them.

"Is that right?" he slurred. "Well, I feel like dancin'."

He pulled Jesi away from the bar and over to the piano, where Gravy barked out a spirited melody on the keys. Pulling her to him, Big John held her in a swaying dance, his rhythm well off-kilter. She swayed with him, trapped by his giant arms and bear-like paws roving over her.

She willed herself to ignore the rasp of his breath in her ear and his intense hold on her. *Soon.* Soon he would get tired, or go back to drinking, or maybe even pass out.

"Come on." He suddenly lurched away, captured her hand, and pulled her up the stairs.

Jesi's heart raced. Her earlier wooziness fled, and a new weakness flushed over her. The blare from the bar muted as the rush of blood in her ears magnified.

"Which room?"

They stood in the gaslight of the upper hall where five doors led into four bedrooms and one bath. Jesi tilted her head. Her voice shook. "That one."

He pushed open the door, pulled her inside, and kicked it shut behind him.

*****

"They're here." Lainey paced away from the window and smiled down at Cori. Her mother's brothers, Gray, Eldon, and Kenton, hadn't come up to Superior for a visit in years. Now, they were all here at once.

Cori closed her book and sighed. "I suppose you're excited to see them. I wish they weren't coming for such a gloomy reason."

"Yes, honey, I know." Her mother's momentary elation snuffed out. "But your daddy and I learned years ago to hang onto joy wherever we can find it, because Lord knows, enough times it's hard to find. Try and wear a smile today, all right?"

She patted Cori on the back as a knock sounded at the front door.

"I've got it," Evie said, hanging her apron on a hook in the hall and scooting to the door.

Lainey grabbed Cori's hand and pulled her aside as their relations filled the doorway.

"Lainey."

"Hi, Kent." She tumbled forward into her youngest brother's

embrace. Behind Kent stood his wife Gracie holding their baby. "I can't believe you made it."

"I don't want to miss being with Pa. We figured we could endure the trip, and so could little Bonnie."

Cori's mother smiled at the infant, who stretched in her sleep.

"Hey, don't forget us," Gray said. He and Eldon grasped Lainey in their arms, and everyone moved inside.

Gray caught Cori watching them. "Which one is this?"

Cori stepped forward. "It's me, Corianne, Uncle Gray."

She took a deep breath, summoning joy, but found nothing but bitterness. How were they going to explain Jesi's absence to her uncles without hurting and embarrassing Mama more?

"How grown up and beautiful you've gotten. Makes me feel as old as last year's dirt."

She smiled at his saying and tried not to dwell on the unpleasant explanations to come. A knock on the open door brought up her gaze.

"Oh, we forgot to tell you we brought company," Eldon said.

A man with mostly salt-and-pepper hair that curled at his collar stood in the doorway. His dark eyes held amusement, and his face lifted in a crooked smile to match theirs.

Lainey hurried to hug him. "Uncle Joe! You came along?"

"I'm here, like it or not. I had to see Nase again, and I couldn't stand to think of your mother going through this without offering her my support."

Solemnness washed over all of them as they stopped to ponder the gravity of the situation. Cori's grandfather, Manason Kade, was dying, and no one wanted to let him go, especially not her grandmother, Colette.

"Ma's with him now. She'll be down in a little bit," Lainey said.

Joe Gilbert nodded. He stepped out of the way as another figure stepped through the door.

"Lainey, you remember Jamie," Joe said. "I don't think you got to see him while you were down in Chippewa Falls."

Joe's son James -- Jamie -- nodded at them and smiled. His smile, dimples, and black curls, so like his father's, made their relationship clear. He'd clearly gotten his dark complexion from his Indian mother. Cori couldn't remember exactly, but she thought the woman had died when Jamie was a baby.

"I'm glad to meet you again," he said. "I think I was only about twelve the last time."

"Yes, it has been a long time." Lainey shook his hand. "How old are you now, Jamie?"

"I'm twenty-two."

She pressed her cheek to his and took in the whole family with her smile. "It's very good to see you again. We're so glad you could come. I feel better just knowing all of you are here."

Cori breathed a sigh. Mama glanced at her again, as if she could read the apprehension tingling in her limbs, and Cori wondered if Mama had recognized her hesitation. Or was she just sad that Jesi had abandoned them when they needed her most?

Mama would probably forgive Jesi, but Cori never would, not seeing over and over the pain her sister had inflicted upon everyone.

"Oh, my heavens, look at all of you in one room."

Cori looked up. Gran stood in the corridor. Tall and lovely, though clearly weary with care, she made her way into the parlor between them and hugged them all.

When she reached Joe and Jamie Gilbert, she stopped. Warmth spread over her face, and she looked fifteen years younger.

"Joe." Gran clasped Joe's shoulders. Her eyes shone with moisture.

Joe hugged her. "Lettie, girl. I'm so sorry."

She sniffed and drew back. Joe handed her a hankie.

"I'll be all right." She dabbed her eyes and nose. "And I bet the sight of everyone together will have Nase all right, too."

"You're absolutely right, Ma," Lainey said "Come on everyone. We have soup and coffee. Cori, why don't you run and help Evie get a tray for the parlor?"

Cori's eyes held the floor as she scooted between her uncles and her mother's other relations. She glanced up only briefly at Jamie Gilbert, who stepped back to let her pass.

She hadn't seen any of her cousins or other distant relations in a long time. She tried to piece them all together in their correct places. But no matter how she did it, she couldn't figure out where Jamie fit.

That didn't really matter, however. They would all be well acquainted before long. And together, all of them -- except Jesi -- would comfort one another while her grandfather died.

Chapter Ten

In the dim bedroom above Maisey's bar, Jesi struggled against Big John, fighting as if trying to heave herself free from a brick enclosure. "No. No!"

Why had she ever thought she could do this? Did she really think she could close her eyes and it would be no different than being with Clay? Tears choked her, and she clawed her fingers into the enormous brute, trying harder to squirm free of his grip.

Guided by only a pale slice of moonlight coming in through the crack between the dirty red curtains, he pushed her toward the bed and wrapped his arms around her waist.

"Come on, now," he said, kissing her neck and scratching her with his rough beard, "don't be like that. I like a little fight in a gal, but that ain't what I'm payin' for tonight."

"Please," she gasped, sucking in air as he held her tight and tugged at the shoulder of her flimsy dress. "I--"

"Take it off."

Blood roared through her head like a train engine as panic took full hold. She pushed at him again, fighting in earnest now. Tears leaked out of the corners of her eyes, and she knotted her fists against his chest. She tried to draw up her legs, to turn, to somehow escape.

"What is this?" he growled, his dark eyes glittering and fierce with anger.

Jesi closed her eyes and thrashed as hard as she could, more fear than she'd ever known oozing from her pores. A guttural scream climbed to her lips as he pinched her arms in his grip, effectively manacling her. A blow across the head silenced her and sent her reeling against the mangy pillow. Then suddenly he was off her, and she could breathe. The metallic taste of blood coated the back of her throat, and more blood ran out of her nose. A flare of light startled her, and she winced as she opened her eyes and saw he'd lit the lamp.

This was her moment to escape. She scrambled to her feet and rushed for the door. He turned to look at her just as she moved and like a viper, swept out his arm and reeled her against him again. She kicked and bit and swung her elbows until he pulled her head back by her hair, wrapping it in his meaty fist.

"Look at you," he snarled. "Clean up."

He shoved her head forward, releasing her to stumble against the rickety dresser, where a bowl and half full pitcher of water waited beside her hairbrush and washcloth.

Jesi steadied herself and stared, dazed, into the bowl. He would have her. She understood that now. She had no way to fight Big John's strength. She should just resign herself to the fact. This is what she had become. Tears pooled in her eyes, and she couldn't see well as she reached for the washcloth. Blood dripped from her nose and splatted against the inside of the white porcelain bowl.

"Stop your crying. I didn't come here for that, either. "

She sniffed and reached for the water pitcher. Hands shaking, she tipped it to dribble water onto the cloth. She could hardly hold it steady. Try as she might to hold it still, the pitcher wobbled back and forth, and her tears continued. She gripped the handle tighter. The vessel felt weighted in her hands.

Heavy.

She blinked. With the pitcher in her right hand and the cloth in her left, she wiped the tears from her vision and smeared the blood away.

"Don't stand there all night, red. I need some attention over here."

"I-I'm... coming." She stepped backwards and found her voice. "I'll give you some... attention."

Then she turned. And with her arm outstretched and the pitcher extended away from her, she swung it toward Big John, belting the container across his head. It broke into pieces, and water sprayed the room. Big John stumbled back onto the bed, his knees buckling and his arm coming up to his face.

With strength and speed she'd thought had fled, Jesi wrenched open the door and fled into the hall. She bolted down the steps and across the barroom, shoving her way past patrons who stared at her and moved out of her path.

Before she reached the door of the saloon, Big John's bellow echoed down the stairs. With a startled cry, Jesi punched open the door and tumbled into the street, tripping over her gown and falling. Dirt clenched in her fists, she pushed herself up and ran. She hiked up the dress, moving as fast as she could, diving around the nearest corner into the blackness between the buildings. Making for an even darker shadow, she dove behind a stack of empty crates pushed up against a brick wall. Burying her head in her arms to stifle the sound, she sobbed.

I haven't gotten far enough. He's going to find me.

His voice and other voices, too, barked into the night. A mayhem of angry snarls and deep throated chuckles, even a woman's caustic tones. Jesi curled tighter into her hiding place, peeking to glance farther up the side street. They would know -- Big John would know -- she hadn't gone far. How could she have?

She bit back a scream when feet shuffled by off the boardwalk at the corner. She couldn't hear them in the soft dirt of the road. Her heart thumped in her throat, and she fought the urge to bolt and run helter-skelter up the street. The only thing preventing her was the sure knowledge that she wouldn't be fast enough if they pursued her. Her dress would entangle her and her tired, quivering legs would give out. They would catch her. And if they did, they'd take her back to Maisey's, to that room. And *he* would be there.

Afraid to move, she wiped her face on her skirt with a shaky hand. Blood still trickled onto her lip. Nausea crept up her insides, and her head wanted to fall forward. She didn't dare pass out. Not now.

Another pair of feet padded along the boardwalk. Her pursuer, if he *was* a pursuer, paused, and then moved on.

Jesi leaned her head against the bricks and drew in a shallow breath. She clutched her waist. Cold night air seeped into her bones, and she shuddered. Rising slightly, she peered up the road. Lights from the other buildings, saloons mostly, dappled the darkness, helping her to adjust her vision accordingly. Other night sounds met her ears. Laughter from far away. Singing. A horse's whinny, and the plodding of more feet. Normal sounds. She slumped back down and closed her eyes. Normal night sounds she didn't want to hear.

Maybe she could sleep. Maybe she could escape the horror by drifting away. In the morning, she would decide what to do.

A mottled gray mist outlined the street corner several hours later. Jesi hugged herself. She ached from head to foot, and she was damp, cold, and tired. She hadn't slept much. Her escape from reality had been brief and harrowed by nightmares as real as day. Big John figured prominently in all of them. She couldn't stay here any longer.

Her dress stuck to her skin as the mist turned into actual rain droplets. As the light of day crawled out like a leery mouse from its hole, the blood smears stood out on her dress, along with the dirt and grime the fabric had collected from her night spent on the street behind the crates. Her hair was matted in knots, and her hands were filthy. She could only imagine what her face looked like. If she didn't move now, someone would see her like this.

Her body rebelled against movement, and at the same time thirsted for it. Pain shot up both legs as she uncurled them, and her circulation returned. She pushed herself up among the crates and held on to them, making sure her light-headedness passed before she ventured out. She brushed dirt and debris from her shabby gown and clutched its open throat closed at the neck.

Looking first one way and then another, Jesi moved up the road. The first two people she saw were a grocer and a teamster unloading parts of a beef carcass off a wagon in an alley across Silver Street. They were far enough away and paid her no mind. She hiked herself up onto the boardwalk and scooted faster, heading away from Maisey's. She would have to go back there eventually, but she didn't want to go too soon, worried Big John had spent the night.

Passing another side street, she saw a horse trough and headed for it. No windows nearby faced the street and Jesi thought she could at least clean herself up without notice.

Splashing water on her face and rubbing the dirt off her hands and the sweat off her neck felt good. She shook out her skirt. Wasn't much else she could do for it. She finger-combed her hair, mostly just rearranging its snarls. By the time she finished, the day had dawned completely. The raindrops had stopped falling for the time being, but the sky didn't look as if they would stay away for long.

Hunger pinched her stomach, and that pang competed with her need for a real bed to lie in. She thought that maybe in another hour, she could go back to Maisey's. If she went in through the back door, perhaps she could stay with Mary in the kitchen until it was safe enough for her to return to her room. Then she would try to explain to Maisey about last night. Maybe the woman would find something else for her to do, and also keep her clear of Big John.

Best for her to keep out of sight for the time being. Rain pattered down again, so Jesi hunted for an eave to stand under. She shivered. Goose bumps covered her arms, and she rubbed her hands over them. Gazing out into the gathering storm as the rain picked up its intensity, she let out a cheerless grunt. Life had certainly not gotten any brighter or more hopeful since she'd fled the shame she faced at home. If anything, her shame had increased.

When the rain finally subsided once again, she couldn't stand waiting any longer and decided to go back to the saloon. Facing Maisey wouldn't be the easiest thing she'd ever done, but after last night, it wouldn't be the hardest, either. Maybe she should've just swallowed back her bile and submitted to Big John. Then she would at least be warm and dry, and she might even still be asleep.

She dodged soggy horse droppings and puddles in the wagon ruts, while street mud oozed around her shoes and collected along the hem of her dress.

Maisey's stood dark and silent, a testament to a late night. Jesi didn't want to linger out in front of the building, just in case. With a deep breath, she gripped the sides of her skirt and walked through the alley to the back. The rear door stood propped open to relieve some of the heat building up in the kitchen from the cook stove, and inside Mary clattered dishes and pans as she fixed breakfast.

Jesi smelled sausage sizzling, and the delicious aroma propelled her to the door faster. Not wanting to startle the woman, she knocked on the door frame. Mary's head jerked up, wisps of her dull brown hair falling from her forehead into her eyes. For the first time, as she stood there in her greasy apron, her eyes staring wide, Jesi noticed the white scar running from beneath Mary's ear to the corner of her left eye. The skin at the corner of her eye was pinched, making her eyes look disproportionate in size. Her lips clamped shut then opened again.

"What are you doing there, standing in the rain and scaring me like that?" She waved her inside. "Look at you. Where you been? Wipe your feet before you go tracking slop across the floor."

Jesi obeyed, hoping not to have to explain anything on an empty stomach.

"The sausage smells good," she said weakly.

Mary grunted and eyed her suspiciously, but must have sensed she wasn't going to get a direct answer right away. She grabbed an empty plate and tossed two sausage patties onto it. Scraping a spoonful of scrambled eggs beside them, she plunked the plate onto the table in front of Jesi. "Might as well eat as drool. How come you're up so early? Didn't expect to see anybody but Gravy coming around this time of day."

Jesi thought of Gravy while shoveling in her breakfast. He'd seemed like a nice man. Then again, he was the one who'd told the tale about her knowing how to dance. She frowned and reached for the coffee cup that followed along after her plate.

Mary folded her arms and watched her. "Hungry today."

She nodded.

"Big first night for you."

Jesi lowered her cup slowly. Mary's stare pierced her.

A loud voice broke her stare. "Mary, I need a complete list--"

Jesi set down the cup and rose as the door between the kitchen and the dining room swung open, and Maisey came to a stop in the middle of the passage. Jesi lowered her hands to her sides and dropped into a short curtsy as Maisey glazed her with a sharp, pinched look.

"So, you're back." Her sharp tone needled Jesi. She let the door swing shut and folded her arms across her bosom so that, together, she and Mary created quite a fortress. "What for?"

Jesi tried to think of an appropriate response. "I need a-a place to stay."

"Well it's not going to be at my place. Mary, get the bag by the stairs." With a frown, Maisey flicked her head in the direction of the outer room and glared hard at Jesi. "I got no place for girls who don't want to work." She cut Jesi off as soon as she opened her mouth to speak. "*And* I've got no place for someone who mistreats my best customers."

Maisey came around the table and leaned into Jesi's face. "Johnny Ray is well-liked around here. He's good to us and very good to the girls. If you hadn't acted like a little fool, you'd know that."

Jesi blinked in the face of Maisey's anger.

"Well," Maisey said, leaning back and planting her fist on the table. "I don't have time for fools."

Jesi jumped when the woman rapped on the wood. She folded her hands together.

"Please, Maisey. You must understand. I didn't mean to cause trouble. I was just afraid."

"Afraid of Johnny Ray? You must be out of your mind. Why, Big

John would've treated you like a queen if you'd have played your hand with some brains."

Jesi thought of the sharp blow across the head that had fazed her last night. Her hand stole to her cheek where the flesh was still tender.

"So, you're blaming that on my customer. If a girl is smart, she doesn't get herself in a position to get hit. She does what's wanted of her, and everything turns out fine."

Was that true? Jesi batted her eyes to drive away the threat of tears.

Mary strode back into the kitchen and plunked down a half closed carpet bag. Jesi recognized her belongings.

"Please, Maisey." Her voice sounded pleading, desperate. "You can tell Johnny Ray I'm sorry. I'll try and do better."

"You'll try? You bet you'll try." Maisey hoisted up the bag and walked to the back door. "But it won't be here." She flung the bag out the door. It fell open, and Jesi's clothes spilled into the mud. "Now, get out."

Maisey leered at Jesi with her fake blond curls falling around her shoulders like dirty yellow rags. Jesi backed up, glanced at her few belongings being beaten by the rain, and gulped.

"Hurry up, before I send *you* out the same way." Maisey's slovenly pink gown gaped as she pointed out the door.

Jesi sniffed and slid past her, half expecting Maisey to strike her. Maisey stepped out and pushed the prop from the door, slamming it shut in her wake.

Rain pelted Jesi's skin and beat on her clothes heaped in the alley. She quickly bent to collect them, shoving them along with some dirt and debris into the worn bag. Bunching it closed, she hefted it and trudged back down the alley to Silver Street. She had nowhere to go, nowhere to stay. Nothing to look forward to, even the saving of her own life.

Chapter Eleven

Sunshine finally broke through the clouds. Jesi left the shelter of the eave she'd huddled under while the rain drummed puddles around her feet. She'd come to a decision while standing there for the past hour. In the lulls between downpours, she'd considered the string of saloons and bawdy houses lining the street and pondered marching into the cleanest looking one first and picking up where she left off at Maisey's -- if they'd have her. At least three times she'd stepped out into the soppy street and braced herself for the task of what she had to do, what she simply *must* do. She intended to simply steel herself against the gall of it when the time came. This time she'd squelch her fear and revulsion. She wouldn't think about what was taking place when she was with someone like Big Johnny Ray. For all she knew, she *would* be with Big Johnny Ray.

Each time the rain started to fall again, though, and she'd hesitate. Driven back into her meager shelter, she'd change her mind, only to change it again a few moments later. Finally, fed up with her indecision and apprehension, another idea squirreled into her brain.

She would leave Hurley.

Ironwood, Michigan lay just across the river. She'd gone there days ago and found no work, but perhaps instead of heading in that direction she'd find work further south. If not... well, then she'd do what she must. She decided to set out toward Montreal and Mellen. Mellen was a good distance away, and to get there she'd have to cross over the Penokee Range. Maybe she could find work at a logging camp. She could do laundry or help the cookee.

Hope spurred in her chest. While part of her doubted the opportunity to find such work, she buried the thought. She simply had to keep hoping.

Her pores opened up, soaking in the heat of the sun's rays. At least she wasn't hungry yet. Mary's sausage and eggs were still stuck to her insides. Jesi had no idea where her next meal would come from, so she figured she'd best make as much track as she could while she still had her strength.

She ducked her head and hurried out of town, not looking up at the saloons or storefronts as she passed. She set out behind the depot along the southwesterly railroad grade, putting some stride into her steps. Before long, however, the carpetbag grew heavy and she had to set it down and rest.

The sun rode ever higher in the sky. Trees and brush smelling of autumn leaves and rain-dampened earth crowded up against the railroad line. She took a heady whiff. She should really take advantage of the sun to dry her clothes. By nightfall, the air would be chilly. If she didn't find a place to stay by then, she'd be forced to spend another night out in the open, a grim prospect indeed. But if she could exchange this awful dress for one of her regular dresses and a shawl, it wouldn't be nearly as bad. If only she had packed a coat. She really hadn't thought she would need one so soon.

Opening the bag, she pulled out her muddy apparel. She couldn't do much except shake out the debris and spread the garments on the tracks to dry. She could see a good distance in each direction and would have no problem scooping them up if a train came along.

Once she'd finished spreading the garments in the sun, Jesi took inventory. She had two dresses with shifts, two pairs of stockings, and the appropriate undergarments. A hat. One glove... She must have lost the other one back at Maisey's. Her only shoes were on her feet. Thankfully, she hadn't had to run away without them last night. Lord Bless whoever had packed her belongings for her. She could be missing much more than a glove.

She checked herself. Who was *she* to ask God to bless anyone? He didn't even know she was alive, and to her, He wasn't, either.

Jesi curled up in the thick grass growing along the embankment, closed her eyes, and let the sun soak into her. When had she last rested, really? Even now, her dire situation didn't allow her to completely put her troubles out of her mind. At least she could close her eyes for a little while, while she was warm and not hungry, and enjoy that.

She woke with a start. A noise called her from her sleep. Jerking upright, groggy and confused, she looked around and struggled to gather her bearings. Grass clung to her arms and the bawdy saloon dress. A train's rumble cleared things up for her. She crawled on her hands and knees up the slight slope to the gravel railroad grade. Jumping up, she swept her dry clothes into her arms. The train rumbled closer down the tracks. She shoved the things back into her carpet bag and scurried off the grade.

Edging up to the woods, Jesi locked her gaze on the train as it lumbered by. A man stood behind the engine. A few workers rode on a flatbed car. One passenger car looked mostly empty. If anyone had seen her standing there beside the thick forest, they gave no notice. A minute later, the train was gone.

Jesi climbed back onto the railway line. Gripping her bag tighter, she set out in the opposite direction of the train. With uneven steps, she hiked from tie to tie, heading toward what looked to be a long, long journey.

*****

Paul rested his gun on his shoulder and stepped high over the gnarled brush blocking his path. The cutover provided good bird cover, especially where poplar seedlings had grown over the area. He'd no more than set his foot back down when a pair of grouse flushed from the grass, their wings beating the air in a fury. He spun the gun into position and fired, knocking down one of the birds. The other tilted and curved away into the trees.

"There we go," he said, smiling, as he stepped over another fallen tree in search of his quarry. He picked up the dead grouse and ran his hand over its smooth, brown feathers and barred tail. "Nice sized bird."

He stuffed his prize into his oversized coat pocket and reloaded his gun. On days like today, peace washed over him. Maybe from the sense of having made a decision and knowing whatever happened next was up to God. Perhaps in another week or so he'd hear back from the church in Oshkosh. He would like to start over someplace with a ready-made congregation.

Of course, moving would mean a lot of adjustments. Folks there would have to get used to him, just the same as he'd have to get used to them. Was this how he would have felt if he'd done as Imogene had wanted? If he'd never come north, would he be settled in as a regular pastor, holding Sunday services and Wednesday Bible studies, visiting from house to house, encouraging his flock? Would he baptize people? Would the ladies aid bring him a hearty meal now and then? Would he teach Sunday school? Maybe he wouldn't have missed out on so much if he had listened to Imogene and trusted her instincts.

What was she doing now? She was probably married to some preacher in Appleton or Green Bay. She probably even had a baby or two by now. Imogene would make a good mother, and she'd make some pastor an excellent wife.

Paul kicked at another pile of brush, hoping to scare up a rabbit. Nothing emerged, so he kept walking. Hunting felt good.

Would he have time for such frivolities as hunting down in Oshkosh? Probably not right away. He'd need to put in extra time at the church, establishing himself, studying, making a right and proper impression. In a city, his church might actually grow. He hoped it would at least grow strong spiritually, if not in numbers.

But if numbers didn't matter, then why shouldn't he just stay where he was?

Paul made a small turn and carefully eyed the area around him. Northern Wisconsin was quite a country. Forests and rivers, hills and lakes, rugged wilderness stretching as far as forever. Somewhere up north, Lake Superior became the only stopping point.

In all those woods -- men lived. Families pressed on, bent on carving civilization out of the boondocks. Beauty filled this rough country; beauty unsurpassed by anything he'd seen in his youth. Far from being a wasteland, Wisconsin's north woods filled him with wonder.

How could he ever leave it?

Paul frowned, watching his feet now more than the swales and sloughs he skirted. He hoped God would show him *what next* pretty soon. He didn't know how much longer he could put up with his own wavering uncertainties.

*****

Jesi pushed an arm across her forehead. Even though the sun now hung lower in the western sky, drawing long, deep shadows over the narrow railroad tracks, she was warm. Sweat stuck under her arms. Fatigue pulled at her shoulders. Finally, she plunked the heavy bag onto the tracks and sat on one of the steel rails. Hard and narrow, it didn't offer much for seating.

"I'll never make it." She lowered her head onto her arms. Her stomach growled, and a sob erupted from her chest. More sobs came and she cried hard, her body shaking as she slid off the steel onto the tar-covered ties in the gravel bed.

Finally, she rubbed her eyes with the heels of her hands. Night would come fast. She had maybe two hours of walking left before dark, but it would seem like much less in the middle of the thick woods. Mosquitoes burrowed under her hair line and hummed around her face. She waved a hand at them, but they kept coming back, biting her knuckles, buzzing in her ears.

"Oh, please... please," she cried, sniffling. She had to keep moving. She stood again, but this time she could hardly lift the carpet bag. Frustrated, she yanked it open and pulled out her shawl and bonnet. Hands trembling, she tied the bonnet on and slung the shawl over her shoulders. Warm as she was, the garments would protect her from the biting insects, and besides, dew would soon fall. She pulled a pair of undergarments out of the bag, knotted them into one spare dress, and hooked the garments over her shoulder. Then she kicked the bag off the track and plunged on, tripping over ties she meant to step on.

For another hour, she stumbled on and cried. Her nose dripped. Her clothes and hair and body felt filthy. Surely the bugs would eat her alive. How would she ever be able to stop and sleep? Not a single human sound met her ears. Now and then birds twittered or screeched, or she startled a deer grazing along the side of the railroad. Once, a coyote slunk across her path. But not once did she see or hear another human being.

Finally stars popped out. First singly, and then in groups, they cast glitter across the deep blue twilight. Looking up at them, Jesi was too tired to think about their beauty or wonder at their creation. They were just there. She blinked and stared down the dark track.

The toe of Jesi's shoe caught the edge of a railroad tie as her gaze fell away from the heavens, and she lurched forward. She fell hard, hitting her knee on the rough surface. A cry burst out of her. She pushed herself up, but stumbled again. This time, she hit her hip on the rail and fell just beyond it. Her hands skidded across the gravel and into the grass as she rolled twice, stopping on the slope.

What was she thinking? She would never make it to the next town -- not as weary and worn as she was. Even if she did, the people there would take one look at her and close their doors. She would have no job, no shelter, no hope. She, Jesilyn Beaumont, had reached the end.

Her ragged gasps fell away, and she grew quiet. Calm spread over her as she closed her eyes. She ignored the raging cloud of mosquitoes lighting on her, and the ticks crawling through her clothes. Her breathing grew shallow and darkness fell even deeper behind her eyes as she drifted away, knowing her sleep would not be natural.

*****

Paul's feet crunched along the gravel between the railroad ties. He'd stayed out later than planned. Marie would wonder what had become of him. He didn't think she'd worry, though. His hunting trips sometimes turned into chances to get away in prayer with God. He'd eaten his supper on a rock next to a stream and had cleaned the birds there, too. He'd managed to bag three grouse and one woodcock. Not bad. Then he'd taken time to talk with God, once again pouring out his frustration and indecision, once more asking God to show him what to do.

Their talk had taken awhile, but God had reassured him, yet again, that He would make Paul's path straight. He'd just have to wait to find out how.

At least getting home in the dark wouldn't be a problem. He had this fine railroad line to follow as far as the tote road. From there, he would have just a short hike to the base camp and his cabin. He narrowed his eyes when something a few yards ahead caught his attention. A lump lay next to the track. At first he thought it might be an animal, but when he got closer, he saw it appeared to be just something someone had lost.

"What on earth?" He bent to have a look. A dress. Paul turned the garment over in his hands. Didn't seem to be anything wrong with it a good washing couldn't fix. "Hmm. Won't Marie be surprised when I bring her a new dress?"

He grinned and was about to move on when he noticed more things lying a few feet off the track. He went through the grass, barely able to make out the shapes in the darkness, but soon found other women's items and an empty carpet bag. None of it was worth much. The clasp on the bag was broken, but he stuffed the items inside anyway and took it along with him.

"Must've fallen off a train," he said to himself.

Carrying the bag in one hand and his gun in the other, Paul picked up his pace, the featherless birds still stuffed inside his coat pocket. He trotted on down the track, working up a sweat and wondering what Marie had on the back of the stove for dinner. Biscuits, hopefully. And maybe some of those tomatoes Horace had given her.

He panted after a while. Thankfully, the tote road lay just ahead, or he wouldn't feel like carrying all this stuff. The road was nearly in view when Paul stopped short and stared into the darkness at yet another object lying off the track. His heart rammed into his throat. This lump was large, and not just a pile of clothing. He walked closer.

"Good Lord." He dropped the bag and laid the gun across it. He shrugged out of his coat, stooped down, and grasped the shoulder of the woman who lay crumpled in the grass. "Ma'am?"

He shook her.

Nothing.

"God, no." He turned her over. Copper-colored hair blanketed her face. He pushed it back and gasped. "Pie Girl."

He'd thought of her as *pie girl* ever since the day he'd sent her the pie from the restaurant. He never really realized how often he'd thought of her since then, but the incident of meeting her had crept into his memory at odd times, and he'd prayed God would save her. Now it seemed his prayers hadn't been answered.

"Miss?" Paul smoothed her hair away from her face with gentle hands, then bent over to put an ear to her lips. A faint breath brushed his earlobe. *Thank God. She isn't dead.*

"Miss? I'm going to pick you up. You'll be fine. Don't be afraid, now." Paul spoke softly as he wedged his arms beneath her shoulders and legs and lifted her off the ground. He planted his foot against the embankment, trying to maintain his balance as he rose, holding her in his arms like Marie would hold one of her baby dolls when they were kids.

He tucked her close so her head rested on his chest, and her arms hung loose. She was thin, but tall. As fast as he could, Paul carried her toward the tote road and home.

"Don't you leave me, Pie Girl. I'm going to get you someplace safe."

Twenty minutes later, Paul kicked the cabin door and Marie yanked it open.

"Good grief! What--" Marie's eyes popped wide as Paul pushed past her into the cabin and crossed into his bedroom with the girl. He deposited her onto his bed as gently as he could.

"Fetch some water, please," he said, as he caught his breath.

Marie hurried to the kitchen and returned a minute later with a glass of cold water, a clean cloth, and a pitcher of warm water to pour into the wash bowl. She set down the items and poured the warm water into the bowl. Rinsing the cloth and wringing it well, she handed it to Paul, who sat on the bed next to his patient.

He'd been unable to tear his eyes off the woman. His heart hadn't slowed down, even without the weight of her in his arms. She looked so ill and so vulnerable. Shadows circled her closed eyes, and her skin was unnaturally pale except for the welts on her face and hands where mosquitoes and gnats had feasted. Her hair and clothing were dirty, but she didn't seem to have lice or anything. Mud streaked her cheeks and throat, openly exposed by her shabby, gauzy dress. She'd lost a shoe, and Paul made a mental note to look for it later when he went back for his gun and other things.

Marie leaned over him. "Poor thing. She looks next to death."

"I may have gotten to her just in time. If she'd lain out there all night, no telling what would have happened to her." He dabbed the rag at her cheeks a bit, pausing at the sight of her heart beating in the hollow of her throat. He turned and stood, handing the rag back to Marie. "You're better at this than I am."

Marie took his place on the bed and began her ministrations, cleaning the girl's face, neck, and hands. Slowly a frown formed on the young woman's brow. She turned her head to the side and moaned.

Marie shushed her. "Don't be afraid. You're safe. Just lie still."

The girl complied, and suddenly her brow smoothed as she seemed to fall into a more peaceful sleep.

Paul leaned over Marie's shoulder. How had Pie Girl ended up out in the woods, and where was she going? Had she missed a train somewhere along the way and decided to walk to meet another? That seemed unlikely, but nothing else made sense. The last Paul had known, she'd been intent on staying at Maisey's Saloon.

He scanned the length of her body. Her dress didn't hide much. He tried not to let his gaze linger too long, but he could tell she was just as half-starved looking as he had suspected when he'd carried her home. He moved to the end of the bed and removed her single shoe. Taking an extra folded blanket from where it hung over the footrest, Paul covered her, gently tucking the edge of the blanket under her chin.

The girl frowned again, and her tongue slipped out over her dry lips.

Marie held out her hand. "Hand me the water, Paul."

He did so.

"Help me lift her head."

Paul moved around to the head of the bed and slipped his arms beneath the girl's neck again, gently raising her shoulders. She gave a weepy moan.

"Here you go, take a sip," Marie coaxed.

The girl tilted forward. Small dribbles of water ran into her mouth and down her chin. Paul used his free hand to cup beneath it.

"A little more."

She took a little better sip this time and pushed her head back. Paul laid it against his pillow. He couldn't help but stroke the tangled red hair back off her forehead.

"We'll let her sleep now," Marie said.

"You think she'll be all right?"

"I think what she needs is rest in a warm bed. Tomorrow I'll get her to eat. Come on."

Marie rose and led the way out of the bedroom. Paul glanced back at the girl before he closed the door. She seemed to be sleeping peacefully.

"Are you going to tell me how you found her?"

"I came upon her next to the tracks." Paul went to the cook stove and lifted the lid, then picked up two sticks of wood and worked them into place inside the stove. "She looked like she'd dropped right there. I found a bag with some clothes scattered around it another hundred yards back. Hers, I suppose."

Marie came up beside him and folded her arms. "She's obviously from one of those dens of iniquity in Hurley."

"I suppose it's a fair guess." He glanced at Marie. "I've met her once before."

Her eyes widened, and she unfolded her arms. "How's that?"

"I bumped into her coming out of the mercantile. Nearly sent her sprawling into the street."

"You're sure it was the same girl?"

"She didn't look like she does now, of course."

"The dirt, you mean."

"The dirt… and the dress."

Marie arched a brow. "So she wasn't wearing the clothes of a bawdy house girl before, or were they simply cleaner?"

"She was dressed like any girl. In an ordinary day dress." He thought of the clothes scattered beside the tracks, and it dawned on him that the dress he'd first picked up was the one Pie Girl had been wearing when they'd met in the street.

"She was looking for a place to stay, if I recall."

"So you spoke to her?"

"Only briefly. I apologized for plowing into her and offered to buy her a cup of coffee. She wasn't interested."

"I see."

"She seemed determined to go to Maisey's. That's one of the taverns near the mercantile. I had a piece of pie sent over to her later."

"You went out of your way."

"She looked hungry. She's a lost soul. I knew it then, and isn't it obvious now?"

"Of course it is. I think you did right. I'm surprised you didn't mention it."

"I had other things on my mind."

"I suppose so. Well, regardless, we'll get her fixed up. Maybe we can talk her out of going back to that place." Marie glanced over at the bedroom door. "Do you know her name?"

Paul shook his head.

"I suppose we'll find out tomorrow."

Paul sighed. "Well, I'd better head out and get my gun and those birds. She'll want those clothes too, so she has something else to wear when she wakes up."

"Be careful."

"I will. I don't know what else I can run into."

Chapter Twelve

Cori was grateful for the distraction her relatives offered. While Gramp rested quietly upstairs, the house hummed with activity down below. Her aunt Gracie seemed relieved by Cori's attention to tiny baby Bonnie. Bouncing the infant on her lap, walking her about to gaze at shiny objects in the house, and singing to her while rocking in the chair, all helped to lure Cori's thoughts from the sorrow of Clay's infidelity.

Her uncle Eldon wouldn't let her get through a day without at least one game of checkers, and Mama kept her busy helping her and Evie in the kitchen. As much as it pained her to realize why they'd all come, she was glad for the activity.

Now she carried a tray of dirty cups and saucers from the dining room into the kitchen. She set them on the work table, brushed her hands together, and turned to go back for more, but wheeled directly into Jamie Gilbert, who came through the doorway with a stack of plates in each hand.

"Oh! I'm sorry. I didn't know you were behind me. Here, let me take those from you."

"It's all right. I've got them." He smiled and stepped past her to deposit the dishes next to the tray she'd left on the table.

Gran, seated close by, laid a dish towel on a stack of silver and reached for Jamie's hand. She patted it. "Thank you, Jamie. It's nice to see what a helpful young man Joe's raised. You're so like him."

Cori lingered in the doorway, curious about Jamie and Joe, and about her grandmother's youth.

Jamie grinned, and Cori noticed, not for the first time, the resemblance of his smile to her uncle Joe's. *No, he's not my uncle.*

"Thank you, Mrs. Kade," Jamie said. "Da will be glad to know you think so, though he might doubt it's true sometimes."

"I keep thinking you and I are cousins," Cori said, frowning. "But Joe's not really my uncle..."

The women in the kitchen chuckled. Gran squeezed Jamie's hand. "This young man might have been your brother, but no, he's not even your cousin." Her eyes twinkled. "Though I wouldn't have minded calling him mine, right along with Gray and Eldon and Kenton. He certainly feels like one of my own."

Mama grinned. "So are you going to tell us the story about that? I've only heard it second hand before. I had to depend on Gray's version."

Gran *tsked*. "You children. All of you are adults now, and you're still trying to figure out us old folk."

Cori stepped forward and pulled out a chair next to her

grandmother. Evie paused to listen, and Mama folded her arms across her apron as she leaned against the dry sink. Jamie, too, pulled out a chair and sat.

Gran eyed each of them. "Joe courted me, but I only had eyes for your Gramp. Course, he didn't know it, and we hadn't seen each other in years." Her eyes looked into the past as she spoke. "Then I married Lainey's father, Harris. I was Mrs. Eastman then."

She glanced at Jamie, then looked away again. "He was a hard man. He knew what he wanted, and nothing could stop him."

"What about Gramp?" Cori asked softly.

"As I said, I didn't think I'd ever see him again, so I agreed to marry Harris."

"And Da?"

Grandma patted Jamie's hand again. "Your da and I had an argument, and he went away to the camps. I didn't expect things to happen with Harris the way they did. I didn't love him, and your da knew it. But he never knew about Manason. Joe was very angry and hurt when he came back."

"And then he married my mother," Jamie said.

Gran nodded and gazed around at them all, a wan smile on her lips. "He loved that Indian girl, and she loved him. I was glad for them."

Mama stepped forward and put a hand on her mother's shoulder. "That isn't the end of the story, is it? Wasn't there a late-coming proposal from Joe?"

Colette's shoulders jumped as she giggled like a school girl. "That Joe. He asked me to marry him after Harris had his heart attack. He found out I was expecting you, Lainey, and he didn't want me to face that business alone. He was willing to sacrifice his own happiness for my security."

"That's my da," Jamie said, dimples riveting his profile.

"He was my best friend in those days."

"That's so romantic," Cori said, enthralled by the story. "You lost your true love, or so you'd thought. Your best friend tried to spare you a frightening and uncertain future, and probably loved you too. And then you finally married Gramp."

She blushed as she realized what she'd said about Jamie's pa loving her grandma.

"Joe and I cared a great deal about each other. We still do." Gran made the remark with finality, as if daring anyone to challenge it or to misconstrue it. "Now, this young man..." She wrapped her fingers around Jamie's wrist, slid her hand into his, and gave it another squeeze. "He takes after his father, but has the good fortune of having gained some of his mother's gentler side. I think he's likely to be less of a scalawag than young Joe."

The ladies laughed, and so did Jamie. Cori used the moment to study him. He was almost devastatingly handsome, with his coppery skin and thick black curls. His chocolate brown eyes and dimples would likely magnetize many a young woman. She wondered why he wasn't married.

"Why don't you tell us about yourself, Jamie?" she asked. "We're practically related, after all, and I don't really know anything about you."

"Not much to tell." He smiled. "I work with Da and your uncles."

"I thought you went to school," Lainey said.

He folded his arms across his chest and leaned back in his chair. "I would like to go to school, if there was such a thing as a school for forestry conservation."

"Why is that?" Cori asked. "You already work in the forest, don't you?"

He swiveled his gaze her way again. Intelligence lurked behind his handsome façade. "There's more to working in the forest than cutting down trees and making them into lumber." His voice was soft, challenging. "Surely you've heard concerns about deforestation."

"Yes, of course. But it's hard to believe. We've so many woods here."

"Here, right in northern Wisconsin, yes. But in the southern regions, and in places like Michigan and farther west, the trees are playing out. What we have are millions of acres of cutover land, stumpage, and brush."

"But aren't the farmers turning it to plow? That's always useful."

"In much of the country, yes." He nodded, one of his thumbs rubbing his elbow thoughtfully. "Farmers are indeed turning forest land to crop land. But that does nothing to replenish the supply of timber."

"I see. And that's what interests you -- replenishing the timber?"

"Yes." He smiled again. "That's what I'm hoping to understand better -- ways to do that, and other things as well."

Cori's interest piqued. "What other things?"

"Well, places like Wisconsin need a more effective fire control program, for one." He glanced at Cori's mother. "You would certainly agree to that, wouldn't you, Mrs. Beaumont?"

Cori's mother had barely survived the great Peshtigo fire of '73. Cori's uncle had died in the conflagration, along with thousands of others. Millions of acres had burned, including the entire town of Peshtigo, Wisconsin.

"I would indeed, Jamie. I hope many heads like yours come together and devise a better plan for alleviating such terrible disasters as the one Zane, Kelly, and I went through."

"I hope so, too." He looked again at Cori. "Right now, no school teaches that kind of thing. So in the meantime, I'm studying conservation on my own, anyway I can. I use what I learn at the Kade Forest Works."

"That's admirable." Cori didn't think she'd ever met a young person so self-motivated to learn, especially to learn something so obviously useful for the future. Clay had gone to school because he could, and because it was expected of him. For Jamie, his desire for understanding alone was enough to drive him. "I'm sure you're a great asset to my grandfather and uncles."

"You'd have to ask them, I guess."

He rose, pushing in his empty chair, and Cori stood, too. "I'd like to know how you study such things, without going to school. Maybe later you can explain it to me."

"I'd like that."

Just then the front door opened, and Cori peered past Jamie into the hall, where her father stood. He took off his hat.

"Hello, everyone."

They greeted Zane. He looked directly at Cori. "I'd like a word with you, if you aren't busy."

"Sure, Pa. Excuse me." She glanced at Jamie before following her father to his study.

She turned to face him as he closed the door. He sighed and ran a hand through his strawberry blonde hair. "Are you holding up okay?"

"As well as everyone else. Gramp is sleeping a lot today."

"I meant about the other business, with Clay."

She shrugged and clasped her hands. "I don't really want to talk about that, Papa."

"Well, it's important. You're going to have to talk about it."

"Why? As far as I'm concerned, Clay's not a part of my life anymore."

Zane took her by the shoulders and squeezed them gently. "Are you sure about that?"

"After what he did?" she nearly shouted. Then she quieted and gathered her self-control. "After what he and *Jesi* did?"

The bile that churned inside her hadn't lessened. She thought it might rise up.

"Corianne, I need you to be sure. Clay's in town. I talked to him today."

"You did?" Her gaze leapt up, and her breathing quickened. "Why? What did you say?" She scowled. "I hope you told him he was a no good skunk."

"Well... close. I told him I'd lost a good deal of respect for him, and only self respect and my friendship with his father kept me from kicking him like a piece of trash in the street."

"I wish you would have."

"He wants to talk to you." Papa stroked her cheek and drew up her chin so he could look into her eyes. His gaze grew soft. "He asked me for another chance and wants to know if you'll give him one, too."

Cori pulled away and strode over to her father's desk, where she fingered a paper weight modeled after a train engine. Her heart heaved.

Part of her wanted to give Clay a second chance and put things back the way they had been, but the other part, the part she knew and understood best, realized she couldn't. She could never look at him again without seeing him with her sister. She could never look at either of them again, any other way.

"I think I hate him, Papa." Her throat burned. She dashed a hand at the maddening moisture rising in her eyes. She spun to face her pa. "Yes, I know I do."

"Hate's a strong word, Cori. Too strong." Papa frowned. He looked sad.

Did he know she meant her words toward Jesi, too? She wouldn't take them back though. She hung her head.

Papa sighed. "He's outside. Shall I send him away?"

Cori nodded. Clay wasn't worth her time or her trouble. Maybe she should tell him so. Maybe he should hear it straight from her lips. "Papa, wait."

Zane had turned toward the door, but he stopped and swung back.

"Tell him I'll see him. I have some things I need to say."

He nodded, his features drawn, resigned, and closed the door quietly on his way out.

Cori fidgeted. She paced to the desk and then the window, flicking back the curtain's edge to see if she could spot Clay coming up the walk. He must have parked further down the block. She toyed with her fingers and walked around the room again before sitting in the chair beside her father's bookcase. She straightened her dress and cleared her throat, nestling her hands in her lap just as a brief knock sounded on the oaken door.

"Come in."

Clay stepped into the room. He looked as handsome as ever with his lank blond hair just brushing the edge of his collar, and his ascot fixed perfectly in place. He nodded and turned his hat in his hand. "Cori."

"Clay. What do you want?"

"It's been hard to concentrate on my studies." He flushed. "I just... wanted to talk to you."

"I can't imagine what for."

He took a step toward her and she frowned, effectively halting him. "I hoped to have a word with you, to see you again... and tell you how sorry I am."

She closed her eyes and forced back her pain as the bile threatened to rise again.

"I beg for your forgiveness."

"My *forgiveness*?" Her eyes sprang open, and she jumped to her feet. "Are you mad? You had an affair with my *sister*."

Clay's redness deepened as it climbed up his neck and ears. "I can't even forgive myself."

"You shouldn't. You should carry your stink with you. What's it been anyway, a few weeks? And you think I can forget what you did so fast? You dare to ask my forgiveness as though it were the easiest thing." She crossed her arms, clutching them around her middle as she spun and paced to the window. She stared outside.

"I only want you to know how sorry I am. I don't expect anything more than that."

A knock rattled the door again, and Cori imagined it was probably her pa.

"Come in," she demanded.

Jamie stepped into the room, smiling. "I thought I'd show you a book I brought along. It might help you to see what I was talking about earlier."

Suddenly, he noticed Clay. He halted.

Cori thought their tension must be evident. She could feel it oozing out of her pores. And there stood Clay, looking like a weasel begging for a meal at the hen house.

"I'm sorry. I didn't know you had a guest. I'll come back later."

She straightened and lowered her arms to her sides. "No, Jamie, wait. Don't leave."

Jamie turned toward them again, his dark gaze flitting between them. He put out his hand toward Clay. "I'm James. James Gilbert."

Clay gave a slight cough into his fist before stretching out his hand to Jamie. His discomfiture was obvious. "Oh, sorry. Clay Dalton."

"Yes, Jamie, do stay. Clay is leaving. And your introduction was unnecessary. He won't be returning."

Clay stared at her, his mouth opening and closing again like a fish gasping for air. She felt triumphant at his expression, at the shock and the degradation he must feel -- that she wanted him to feel. Jamie moved aside, his chin tucked down as he turned the book over absently in his hands.

Clay stepped forward. "Cori, don't be rash. I beg you to think about this."

"I've been thinking for days, Clay." Her answer came out in a rush. "And I'm tired of thinking. I wish you'd go away. Find Jesi if you want to. Find her and spend the rest of your life with her, but leave me alone."

Clay looked at her a moment longer, then glanced at Jamie.

"Excuse me," he said. He planted his hat on his head and shouldered past Jamie. He turned back to Cori one last time as he flung open the door. "Find Jesi, you say. Both of you can go to the devil. That's what I say!"

He slammed the door and it shuddered, matching the shudder that ran down Cori's back.

Chapter Thirteen

Jesi lay in a log bedstead in an unfamiliar room, taking inventory of her surroundings. Obviously she was in someone's cabin. How had she gotten here? Foggy pictures drifted in and out of her brain. She vaguely recalled someone carrying her and speaking softly, gently even.

Now, a pair of hushed voices reached her from the outer room.

Her heart pitched as the door opened and a strange woman entered carrying a tray. She beamed at Jesi. "It's good to see you looking rested."

A man stood just inside the doorway while the woman settled the tray holding a bowl of steaming soup next to Jesi. She scooted back into her pillows. "I can come out to the kitchen to eat. There's nothing wrong with me. I don't feel right, you treating me like a queen."

"Never mind that today. You can come out for breakfast," the woman said. "Right now, we just want you rested and feeling strong."

She figured there was no point in arguing, and truth be told, she enjoyed their attention. She'd forgotten what it was like to be cared for over the last grueling month and more.

"Thank you," she muttered as she picked up the spoon.

"At least you're well enough to talk," the woman added. "My name is Marie Winter. This is my brother, Paul."

Jesi glanced only briefly at the man, then looked back at Marie. She was tall and raw-boned, about the same size as Jesi, but not as rounded. Jesi figured she was nestled into the other woman's bedclothes. The pink nightgown was soft and smelled good, like the woman smelled when she leaned over the bed. She was young, too, sort of. Maybe in her late twenties or possibly even thirty -- a spinster, apparently. She did look a little like her brother. Jesi checked him out again with another glance. They both had straight brown hair. Marie's was in a bun, with a few loose strands falling across her cheeks. The man's was lank and a little too long, occasionally dropping over his light brown eyes.

"I'm glad to know you. Thank you for helping me and feeding me." She glanced down at the sleeves of her gown. "And lending me something clean to rest up in."

"Paul found you. But don't worry; he found your bag, too. Your clothes are all washed and dried. You'll be able to have something of your own to wear tomorrow."

"Thank you." She didn't think she'd be able to stop saying those words.

Paul stepped forward into the room. "I don't suppose you remember me?"

Jesi halted with the spoon midway to her mouth. She squinted, thinking. He did look familiar in a way that reached beyond her shadowy memories of rescue. A pulse of fear jumped in her chest. Could he have been at the bar that night? No... It didn't seem possible.

"I'm sorry, I don't recall..."

He stepped over to the bed so the full light of the oil lamp shone on his features. "I bumped into you in the street once, quite literally, I'm sorry to say. I almost knocked you down."

Of course. She remembered now. She forced a small smile. "Yes, now I remember. You were very apologetic, as I recall."

"I did feel badly about it."

Jesi remembered it all; how he'd asked where she stayed, how he seemed disturbed by her going to Maisey's. She still didn't see how it was any of his business. How was she to know what he was after? Now here she sat, inside his house. She flushed and looked down at her soup, quickly taking another bite.

"I sent you some pie."

"Yes," she murmured. He had sent pie that fateful day. It probably wouldn't have been delivered to her, but she happened to be paying for her room when it arrived, and the person who'd delivered it made it loud and clear that it was for the young woman with the red hair. Everyone in the establishment at the time had looked her way. She could do nothing but accept the gift. In the end, she had been grateful for the delicacy.

"I never did get your name that day."

Was it the soup, or did fear cause heat to rush over her? She scrambled for a name. It wouldn't do to tell her who she really was and have them send her home to her family. She grasped for the name she'd gone by at Maisey's.

"My name is Jane," she said, glancing up at them through her lashes before sipping her soup.

"Well, that's good to know. It's much better than *Pie Girl,* the name I've been calling you."

"Pie Girl?" She looked at him, and he flushed.

"Yeah... but now you're Jane. Do you have a last name, Jane, if you don't mind my asking?"

"I'm Jane Barton."

Marie patted her leg. "Well, you eat up and get some more sleep. You don't have to be in any hurry to go anywhere. We've got room for you as long as you'd like to stay, isn't that right, Paul?"

He nodded. "You bet."

Jesi's heart slowed. She wouldn't be forced out in the morning. She wouldn't have to move on down the line just yet. Sweet blessedness. She'd be safe for a while. She glanced covertly between the two of them smiling over her. As long as Mr. Winter kept his distance, she'd be safe as safe could be. Nothing had ever sounded so good.

*****

Paul crossed an ankle over his knee in the straight-backed chair before the fireplace and glanced at Marie while she mended yet another sock. She always had a lot of thoughts and opinions spinning around in her head. She was probably just waiting for his invitation to spill them. Jane slept quietly in his room. Still, he felt the need to whisper.

"What do you think?"

"She's afraid. You're going to have to tread very carefully, if I don't miss my guess. Something happened to her back in Hurley."

"Doesn't something always happen to those girls?"

"*Those* girls? What girls, Paul? Those poor, lost souls who find themselves in a heap of trouble with no place to turn?"

"You know I'm compassionate." He shifted. "I just wonder sometimes."

"That's because a lot of them are hard. They have to be. Especially if the years wear on them. But Jane's not hard, not yet. I can see it in her eyes."

"You might be right."

"'Course I am." She smiled, her eyes twinkling, her fingers never missing a stitch with the needle. "That's why you have to be careful. In fact, you'd better start thinking about moving some of your things out to the woodshed."

"You think she'll stay that long?"

"I'm hoping so."

"I've prayed for her ever since the day I ran into her." Paul stared into the orange blaze. "But I never expected that God would turn around and use you or me to answer that prayer."

Marie paused and stared, too. "It's a miracle."

"*Miracle* is a strong word. Maybe this is just the sort of thing God does every day."

"You might be right."

"Sure I am," Paul said, laughter in his whisper. "After all, I'm a preacher. In this case, I'd better be right."

The next morning, he came in from graining Sarah, his horse, to find Jane helping Marie set plates on the table. He nodded at her before hanging his hat and coat on the hook by the door.

"Did you wash?" Marie asked as she turned sausage in a pan on the cook stove.

"Psht."He gave a mock frown and turned his hands backward and forward in a show of cleanliness. He caught Jane's eyes and smiled at her. "Nice to see you up. How're you feeling?"

"Quite well, thanks." She smiled back meekly, and he couldn't help being seized by her loveliness. Marie was right. She wasn't hardened.

He rubbed his hands together, then pulled out a chair at the table.

"Mm-mm. Nothing like the smell of pork sausage. I need to eat up. Lots to do today."

"I'll start the bread right after breakfast. Anything you need help with?"

"No. I'm just going to move a few of my things."

Jane poured coffee into each of their cups while Marie slid a plate stacked with flapjacks onto the table. He noticed the way Jane's brows flicked in curiosity.

"You'll be able to stay in the back bedroom as long as you like. I'm fixing myself a nice spot in the workroom behind the woodshed."

She paused with the coffee pot and frowned. "I don't want to put you out."

"Oh, it's no problem. I've an extra bedroll out there, and a chest to keep a few things in. I'll be okay for awhile. I'm a country boy. I don't mind roughing it a little."

"Really, Jane," Marie said, "he's not kidding. He'll enjoy the privacy."

"If you're sure..."

"We are," they answered together, and laughed.

Jane's shoulders relaxed, and she smiled. Paul thought she looked like an angel with her penny-red hair shining all around her.

*****

Paul set down his empty cup. "I'm off to get my sleeping quarters set up. I have a lot of studying to do this afternoon."

Jesi wanted to ask what he studied, but she thought it best to keep quiet. He was a congenial fellow, but it wouldn't do to seem too interested. Men got the wrong idea when a girl seemed interested -- especially a girl like her.

"I need to start on the evening's bread for Cookee. Maybe you won't mind giving me a hand, Jane."

"Not at all," Jesi said shyly. Fingers of relief stretched through her. Having a task to do would be good, what with the way she had taken advantage of their hospitality and all, and them not knowing a thing about her except that she'd come from Hurley. She glanced sideways at Paul as he moved in and out of the bedroom she'd slept in, gathering up a few books and blankets and a lantern. He whistled a hymn she recognized but couldn't name. He knew where she'd come from. He'd seen her making her determined way to Maisey's. But maybe he didn't know she'd taken a job there. A little flame of hope leapt inside her.

"I bake two double batches -- that's eight loaves a day -- and run them over to the cook shack. Poor Cookee has enough to do trying to keep all the lumberjacks fed. My baking bread gives him a little bit of a break, and I have the time."

"I see." But she didn't, not really. If they lived on the skirts of a lumberjack camp, why hadn't Paul headed off into the woods this morning? Why did he live here with his sister, and why would he spend his afternoon studying? Was he a teacher?

She approached Marie. "Are there children in the camp?"

Marie paused from washing the breakfast dishes. "Just Charlie Hanke's girls."

"Oh." She was more confused than ever. "Do they go to school?"

"Charlie's a widower, but he gets them books, and he's done an admirable job of teaching them to read and cipher. They're nice young ladies. I'll introduce you to them when we take the bread over." Marie went back to sloshing plates and cups in and out of the dishwater while Jesi dried them with a towel. Suddenly Marie stopped again. "You aren't a teacher, are you?"

"Oh, no." Jesi blushed. "I was only wondering."

"I see." Marie's hands moved slowly as she circled her dishcloth round and round a kettle. "Jane, do you mind me asking about how you ended up beside the railroad tracks? I take it you're not from Hurley, or you'd be going back home. Paul mentioned to me that you were looking for a place to stay when he bumped into you."

Shame flooded through Jesi, and she turned away to set a plate on the shelf so she wouldn't have to look at Marie. "I couldn't afford the train ticket to Mellen, so I decided to walk."

"You were going to walk all the way to Mellen?"

Jesi turned toward her again and ducked her chin. "Yes. I know it was a foolish idea."

"Well, maybe not if you were stronger and more prepared."

"I know. For some reason, I didn't expect it to be so difficult."

"Mellen is nearly forty miles away."

"Oh. I didn't know it was so far."

"And you'd have to march over the Penokees."

Jesi nodded, feeling more foolish and embarrassed with each of Marie's statements. What had she been thinking? *Escape. I was thinking only about escape. I'd do it again, too.*

She hoped to re-direct the conversation as she put the last fork away. "Was Mr. Winter out working with the woods crew when he found me? It must've appeared as though I'd fallen off a train."

"No, he was out hunting, actually. He was on his way home, taking the tracks since it was near dark, when he found you. God must've been watching over you to bring him across you like that."

Jesi's eyebrows lifted, but she had no idea how to respond. Telling Marie God had no interest in whether she lived or died would seem callous, as would explaining that Jesi didn't care whether He did or not.

"You must be wondering about us, too," Marie said, surprising Jesi.

"I don't want to pry. The two of you have been so good to me."

"It's all right. Paul and I moved up here a few years ago as missionaries. He's a chaplain here at the camp."

Paul was a preacher? Well, that explained a lot about him.

"He speaks to the men on Sundays -- those who stick around to listen." Marie's chagrin was evident, and Jesi knew why. She knew exactly where most of the men ended up on the weekends.

But did that mean she might run into some of Maisey's patrons out here in the camp? "Do you go to his services?"

"Certainly. I wouldn't get to hear much preaching otherwise. There've been a few times we've made a group outing into town for a Sunday meeting, but not too often."

"I see." Jesi had no doubt she would have to attend services with them, too, if she stayed. She wasn't fond of the idea, yet she hoped she wouldn't have to leave. Not soon, anyway. "I guess I'll get to hear him preach, then."

"I hope so." Marie smiled, warming her. "You know, Jane, we mean it when we say you don't have to be in any hurry to leave. But if you were heading to Mellen to stay with someone, we can certainly make sure you don't have to walk there."

Marie set a mixing bowl and flour on the work table, then went about gathering her other bread-making supplies by rote. Trying to decide what to say, Jesi watched her. Lies circled all around her. Maybe it would be best if she were honest in some part.

"No. I don't know anyone in Mellen. I was going there to try to find a job."

Marie's head bobbed up. She set down her measuring cup and a jar of honey and touched Jesi's arm. "Then you should stay. We have plenty, and I would love the companionship." She laughed. "Lord knows there's enough to do with all this baking to keep two of us busy."

Tears threatened to well up in Jesi's eyes, whether for Marie's kindness, or her own relief, she couldn't tell. "I don't know what to say to such a gracious offer."

"Say you will."

"I would be so very relieved to have a place to stay and work to do. I can be a hard worker, though I admit, my talents aren't great." A trickle escaped the corner of her eye, and she tried to cover her emotion with a laugh. "I'm a terrible seamstress."

"This will be wonderful." Marie took her by the shoulders and gazed at her, then drew her into a hug. "I can't wait to tell Paul."

"Are you sure Mr. Winter won't mind, truly?"

"Paul will be very happy you've decided to stay, I can assure you."

Jesi wondered why it would matter to him.

"He's been feeling out of sorts lately, and trying to figure out if he's doing any good up here. Right now, it does him good to have you here as a reminder that God is still using him."

Jesi stuffed her hands into her dress pockets. "Well, I guess I can't argue with the fact that I'd probably be dead by now if he hadn't found me, though it doesn't necessarily do much for his role as a preacher, except maybe give him one more body in the audience on Sunday morning."

She smiled at Marie, and Marie laughed.

"We might give him the idea he has a full congregation before we know it. Come now, I'll show you how I do this."

"If you have an extra bowl, I can do the other batch alongside you."

"Good idea." Marie's skirts twirled as she spun about to retrieve her spare bowl.

Half an hour later, both batches of bread were rising under a clean cloth on the warming shelf above the cook stove. Jesi had gone outside to bring in more wood for the oven while Marie cleaned up their mess. Then the two of them went out to the root cellar to get some apples for a pie.

"One of the men brought back two bushels for me a couple of weeks ago. Such a treasure."

"I love pie," Jesi said. "Mr. Winter wasn't far off when he called me *Pie Girl.*" She chuckled softly. In fact, she rather liked the moniker.

When they came back inside, they found Paul seated at a small desk in the corner of the main room. He looked up from his studies and removed a pair of spectacles. "Hello. I was wondering where you two had gone."

Jesi went into the corner kitchen to empty her apron full of apples.

Marie hung her shawl on a peg. "I showed Jane the root cellar. We're going to make pie for dessert, and we might make an extra one for breakfast."

"Good food for study. She isn't working you too hard, is she, Jane?"

Jesi turned back to the pair and grinned. "Not at all. I'm enjoying it quite a bit, actually."

"Jane mixes bread as if she's been doing it for years. I have a feeling she has a natural talent."

Jesi didn't know what to think of that compliment. She'd always enjoyed baking, but she'd never really considered it to be a talent before. "I like to keep busy."

"Well, you'll be busy around here, and don't you doubt it," Paul said. "Marie has more than enough work to do to keep you occupied. Even if it's mostly self-imposed work."

"It's ministry, Paul."

"Yes, that's true."

Jesi brushed her hands against her apron. "Ministry?"

"I don't *have* to bake the bread for the cookee, or bring pies and treats to the men."

"Or mend their clothes and nurse them when they're sick," Paul added. "She does it just because she has a big heart."

"You take care of them when they're sick?"

"I try. Someone has to."

Jesi wondered about Marie's many talents. What would drive her to care so much about all those men... about someone like *her?*

Paul turned back to his studies, and Jesi's lips twisted.

"Did you always want to be a missionary?" she asked Marie as the other woman got out the bread pans to grease.

Marie pulled the bowls of risen bread dough down off the warming shelf and punched them down. "Not particularly. But I wanted to be a nurse, and coming up here offered me the chance to put my desire to good use."

"That's remarkable." Jesi rested her hands on the back of a chair. "Why didn't you just become a nurse?"

"I got some training. Then God called Paul to come up here." Marie split the dough from one bowl in quarters and handed two of the dough balls to Jesi. "Our parents had both passed on, so I came along to make use of what training I had."

"I see."

Together they rolled out dough and patted it into smooth loaves, filling all eight pans.

"I would like to get more training again someday. But for now, I'll wait until God shows me it's time."

Jesi nodded, content to let Marie talk, unsure how anyone could ever expect to know from day to day what God wanted of them or how He led them. Her own parents lived like that, but she'd never been able to grasp the notion that God was personal.

"Well, for what it's worth, I think you'd make a wonderful nurse," she said to Marie as she watched her cover the loaves to rise again. "I hope you can get the training you want someday."

Chapter Fourteen

"Paul, I have a list of things I need from town," Marie announced. "When can you take me to get them?"

Jesilyn looked up from the vegetables she was slicing on the cutting board. She enjoyed working alongside Marie. The past couple of weeks had given her a routine.

Paul dropped an armful of firewood into the wood box by the stove. "We can go today if you want. I just finished helping Adam wrestle the wheel on the spare wagon. All I have to do is wash up. Plus, that'll give me a chance stop by and invite the Kirschners to next Sunday's meeting."

"Good. I'll get ready right away." She pulled the knot loose on the back of her apron.

"I can finish the stew," Jesi said.

"We can finish cutting up vegetables tonight and cook the stew tomorrow. I think today we'll get Paul to take us to his favorite restaurant."

"Oh... I don't have to go."

Marie stilled and looked at her. "Why, of course you do. You'll go stir crazy if we keep you here all the time, won't she, Paul?" Marie turned to her brother, who shrugged.

"I suppose she might." A question appeared in his eyes, and Jesi wondered if he might be uncomfortable about her riding with them into town. Maybe he knew, as she guessed, that people would ask questions. Maybe she'd put him into a predicament.

"No, really. I don't want to impose on you anymore than I've already done. I don't expect you to take me to restaurants or anything."

"Nonsense." Paul's face relaxed in a warm smile. "It'll do me good to be seen with two such lovely ladies."

Marie whacked him with her apron and giggled, but heat climbed into Jesi's cheeks. She glanced at him and found him looking at her again, the question returning to his eyes.

"I... I'll get ready then." She wiped her hands on a dish cloth and took off her apron.

A few minutes later, she had freshened up and sat on the wagon with Marie between her and Paul. She was surprised she hadn't gotten any farther from town. Driving there took them less than an hour, but she could have sworn she had been a half day's ride away. Why, she couldn't have been more than seven or eight miles out.

The sight of Hurley's clapboard buildings with their bright signs, its dusty street with the horse drawn trolley rolling up the track, and the drinking establishments lining the roadways brought a lump rising into her throat and pressing against her chest. She tried to keep her eyes down on her lap, and then realized she had clenched her hands into fists.

Marie reached over and laid a hand on them. Her gaze flew to Marie's, and Marie curved her mouth in a knowing, yet reassuring, smile. While it did ease Jesi in one way, it also shamed her. She wanted to tell Marie she'd never done what Maisey had asked of her, but why would Marie believe her? After all, pretending she was innocent would be a lie. Clay, with her consent, had made certain she wasn't.

She wished she could erase the past. She wished she'd met Marie and Paul under different circumstances and could be their friend. But if she had met them long ago, would she be their friend? Or would she still be running after things she couldn't have -- things she'd *never* have?

Paul pulled the wagon over at the mercantile, the same store he'd emerged from, nearly running her down, the day they'd met. It stood directly across from Maisey's.

Marie took Paul's hand and descended from the wagon. "I'm going to be a while. Do you need some things, too, Paul?"

"No, not here. I'm going to go talk with the parson over at the Congregational Church. I'll come back for you in a bit." He held out his hand to Jesi. "Marie will look after you."

He seemed so sure. Suddenly, she wished he'd stay. Yet she couldn't do anything about it. She took a breath, climbed down, and tried to focus on Marie's chatter.

Together they went into the store. Jesi hadn't been inside this particular one since she'd come here looking for work. The clerk didn't recognize her, nor did she recognize him. After realizing no familiar people were about, she relaxed a little and looked around. She helped Marie select some fabric and a few dry goods. Before she knew it, Paul came back. She couldn't help the sigh that escaped her when the bell over the door jangled and he stepped through.

"Are you ladies done shopping yet? I'm getting hungry."

"Paul," Marie laid her hand on his arm, "would you mind taking Jesi over to the diner and ordering for us? I have some personal business to see to before I join you."

The mysterious tone of her voice sent alarm bells off in Jesi. Marie's face was a mask, though. So her business couldn't be anything too serious. Still, Paul frowned, too.

"Are you sure?"

She nodded. "I'll tell you about it later, when the time is right."

"Hmm." He raised his eyebrows with a teasing smile. "I don't know if I like that my big sister is keeping secrets from me."

She grinned back. "Oh, go on with you."

No, it must not be too serious at all.

Paul winked, then turned to Jesi. "We'll walk, if that's okay with you. My favorite eatery is just a couple of blocks down. It's the one that makes that terrific pie you've already sampled."

"Ah." Jesi smiled and followed him out of the store. Walking and talking with Paul, even without Marie's presence, felt good. She didn't know when she'd gotten more comfortable around him. A mere two weeks had passed since they'd taken her in.

He held open the door of the restaurant, and she stepped inside. A cheery room greeted them, a picture of light. Papered walls and blue-checked tablecloths brightened the place. A mixture of the tasty odors of beef, pie, and coffee wafted through the room on a warm draft coming from the kitchen. Paul pulled out a chair at a table along the wall and sat across from her.

"I can already see why you like this place."

"I come in for Lulu's pie."

"I'm beginning to see you have a penchant for pie."

"That I do. In fact, come summer, I'll take you and Marie blueberry picking. There's nothing better than a blueberry pie."

Did he hear what he'd just said? About next June? Why, it was only the end of September. How long did he expect her to stay? *It's just conversation. It doesn't mean anything.*

"I have to agree with that. I do love a good blueberry pie."

"I had a feeling you would."

His smile seemed so genuine and kind, she enjoyed the chatter. But she doubted he'd be quite so relaxed with her if her past ever rose to the surface in their conversations. She didn't know which he'd despise most, Jesi the almost-prostitute, or Jesi the liar who'd done the worst possible thing to sabotage her sister's engagement -- in the name of love? Chances were he'd reject them both.

The waitress took their order, and they sat back to enjoy their coffee.

"What do you suppose Marie is up to?" she asked, trying to stir up conversation.

"Knowing my sister..." He laughed. "I have no idea. She comes up with notions sometimes, and doesn't let me in on them until she has the whole plan worked out in her head. That way there's no room for argument."

"Sounds like my mama," she said, blanching as the words left her mouth. *Why did I say that? I nearly gave myself away.*

He looked long into her face.

"My mama used to always steer my pa that way," she added in a rush. Jesi raised her coffee cup and let it hover there in front of her lips. She blew on it even though the liquid was plenty cool.

A pause stretched between them before Paul finally spoke. "Well, Marie will know how to handle a husband when she finally decides she wants one. That's for sure."

He grinned, and Jesi was grateful he didn't pursue her with questions about her family. "I'm surprised she hasn't married. Marie is a very handsome woman and would make some man a wonderful wife."

"She's comely enough, and smart enough, and would probably like to raise a bunch of kids. But I suspect she thinks she has too much to do taking care of me and tending to this bunch of woodsmen up here."

Jesi lowered the cup. "You mean she's sacrificed her dreams to be a missionary?"

"Not sacrificed them. Just put them on hold. She's a fine one for reminding me we don't understand eternity. Our weeks, our months, our years, are just a breath to God."

"What do you mean?"

"Marie says people who are in a big hurry have forgotten how to trust, and that's all God wants from any of us is a little trust -- faith and trust to let Him control things. Instead of running our lives like we're frantic to get to the next thing, we need to rest easy and let God unfold our destinies."

"Our destinies? You're talking above me. I can't get past next week, much less imagine some grand destiny for my life."

"Next week is all you do have to worry about. Then after that, the next one. Eventually, if we keep trusting and asking Him to guide us, it becomes the whole kit and caboodle. Our talents, our dreams, our jobs, and the families He's given us are for His glory. Even our drives and desires. We're supposed to let Him do the worrying, while we just do our best to find out where He's leading us from one day to the next."

"That seems too easy, and at the same time, too hard."

Paul laughed, and Jesi liked the sound of it. She hadn't known a preacher like him who was so prone to laughter, or so young. She chuckled along with him, and studied him as their laughter faded. Paul Winter was a unique individual. His sister didn't have the market cornered on that.

"Well, I admit it isn't always easy. I'm a shoe-in example of a person who has difficulty with that."

"But you're a preacher. How can that be?"

Paul's eyes steadied and his jovial tone mellowed. "Well, Jane, I guess because, first and foremost, I'm a man."

*****

Paul leaned back and looked at Jane. The swish of skirts between the tables told him Marie had arrived, but he couldn't pull his gaze away from Pie Girl's startled, silvery-blue eyes. She had pulled up her mane of red hair and tucked it into a snood, but a fair amount of it threatened to escape the netting. Freckles dotted her nose, and her red, perfect lips formed a little *oh* of surprise. Staring at her, pulled into those depthless eyes, he couldn't have said anything with more truth. He'd never felt more like a man than at this moment.

And that was dangerous.

He cleared his throat, reminding himself others were in the room, thankful she released him from the power of her gaze and turned to look at Marie.

Marie pulled out a chair and sat between the two of them. "Did you order for me?"

As if in response to Marie's question, the waitress arrived with three plates of beef and potatoes.

Paul leaned back as the waitress set their food before them. "Were you able to complete your mysterious mission?"

"As much as possible for now. Mmm... Doesn't this look delicious?"

Paul winked at Jane. "See how she evades us?"

She blushed and picked up her fork. His heart thudded.

What had come over him? He could hardly keep his thoughts on the conversation or the meal. He'd sat across from her and shared a meal a dozen times. Yet never had he so engaged her in conversation. *God, how can I minister to her when I can't keep my flesh out of it?*

He attempted humor. He smirked at Marie. "Ol' Jude isn't courting you again, is he?"

She snapped her napkin over her lap. "Go ahead and tease. I shall not tell you a thing."

He laughed along with both women. Marie must have something up her sleeve that was worth waiting to hear about, but it would be fruitless to try and pry it out of her.

Marie talked with Jane about their shopping and Paul just listened while he enjoyed his beef and potatoes. Jane had been so easy with him today, almost as easy as she was with Marie. He thought of how she'd looked when he'd found her. Today she glowed with health -- health and beauty.

He steered his gaze to the food on his plate. Best keep it there... as much as possible.

By midday, they were ready to head out of town. Marie and Jane strolled ahead of him the short distance to the wagon. Marie chattered, but Jane had quieted once they stepped outdoors. Her eyes darted up and down the street, even while she seemed attentive to Marie. Again Paul remembered what her life had been here. He glanced at the stretch of buildings housing Maisey's Place. Of what her life had been *there*. Her working there didn't seem possible, but facts were facts.

He lent Marie his hand while she climbed into the buggy, then turned to Jane. She grasped his fingers and pulled herself up. Suddenly her head lifted and her gaze travelled to Maisey's. She dropped her glove and stepped back to the ground.

"Let me."

"No, no. I have it." She bent to retrieve it, then lingered, tucked between the wagon and Paul, fussing with the dusty glove.

Her hand shook. Something -- *someone* -- had startled her. Paul's eyes darted up in search of the cause. A thin man leaned against the building outside Maisey's door, puffing nonchalantly on a pipe as he took in the slight comings and goings on the street. He looked their way.

Paul's spine straightened as he caught the man's gaze. He spoke softly. "Ready?"

"I--" Jane couldn't hide her troubled expression.

"I'll help you." He smiled at her. Did she understand he meant more than simply lifting her into the wagon? She had nothing to fear while she was with him and his sister.

Jane hesitated, then nodded. She slipped the glove onto her hand and allowed Paul to steady her elbow while she climbed into the wagon. She didn't turn her head or lift her gaze toward Maisey's again.

*****

Leaves, crispy and brown, blew across the walk in front of the Beaumont's Superior home. A stiff breeze gusted off the lake and shook the bushes. Cori sat on the bench beside the walk and drew her coat tighter around her shoulders.

For most of her eighteen years, she'd reveled in the fall of the year. Now, the season seemed as lifeless as her heart.

Pools of rose petals had fallen, leaving behind only shriveled, reddish-brown rose hips. Some flower heads remained, but they drooped, faded and dry on their stems. She reached down and broke off one. A thorn stabbed her finger.

"Ouch!" With a frown, she sucked at the injury.

"Doing battle with the remnants of summer?"

She jumped at the sound of the voice behind her. "Oh, Jamie. You startled me."

"Sorry." He came and stood near her, glancing at the bench.

"Would you like to join me?"

"If you don't mind my company."

She scooted over and he sat down, tucking his hands into his coat pockets.

He scanned the garden. "Your family likes roses."

"My mother, mostly."

"But not you?"

"Oh, I like them. They're flowers, after all. What girl in her right mind doesn't like flowers?"

He chuckled, a deep sound that vibrated out of him. "I know a lot about trees, but not much about flowers. I've never seen so many rose bushes. I didn't know they'd do so well in this climate."

"They take special care. We have to cover them well to protect them over winter. I should probably be doing that. Usually Jesi helps." She looked away. She didn't even like saying Jesi's name and wished she hadn't.

"I understand your sister has left home."

She shrugged. "Left home is a polite way to say it. She ran away in shame."

"Ah."

Cori thought he might ask more about it, and she would have gladly given him an earful about her wayward sister, but he said nothing more. She took a deep breath. What good would it do anyway? Jamie certainly hadn't come out here to listen to her complain. He'd already endured her emotional discharge against Clay.

"I'm sorry you had to hear all of that between me and Clay in Pa's study the other day."

He shrugged and glanced at her with a warm smile. "I figured it didn't hurt your case to have backup available."

"Backup?"

"You know, someone to be there in case the fellow got out of line. And who knows, maybe I roused his jealousy just a bit."

"Jealousy?" She blinked. "I... I don't know what you mean."

He shrugged, his pockets lifting with his hands stuffed inside. "Maybe he thought I was someone important to you."

"I see." A slow smile stretched across her face as she understood. "He might have thought I was moving on."

"It's possible."

"He probably thinks you're my cousin."

"But I'm not."

His smile fell away, leaving his face smooth and serious, his eyes deep and thoughtful, and they pulled Cori in. Sitting next to him, she suddenly realized how tall he was, and how broad his shoulders were. No, he was definitely *not* her cousin, and they were sitting quite close.

Her heart fluttered, and she came to her feet. "Would you like to know about the roses?"

"You're a horticulturist?"

"No. I don't mean about how they grow. I'll explain the meanings of their colors."

"Oh, yes. I do understand that sending posies with deep and sometimes nefarious meanings is all the rage these days."

"Yes, something like that." His dimples returned, and she blushed. She held up the rose in her hands. It had been yellow, but its edges had faded to a brittle, washed out hue. "A yellow rose is a symbol of joy and friendship." With a little hesitation, she held it out to him. "It might be a rose I'd give to you."

He stood and accepted the rose, grasping the stem just above her fingers so their hands touched. A tingle passed through Cori. She took a quick breath and looked away.

"There's a pink one," she said quickly as she pointed. "It can stand for grace and elegance, or be a simple symbol of appreciation or even admiration."

She flicked him a glance and moved on down the path. He ambled along behind her, his nearness doing something to her she hadn't expected.

"What about that one? It looks nearly orange, or is it just a deeper yellow?"

She looked where he pointed, though she knew the bush he had found. "No, you're right. It's one of my mother's favorites. Papa brought it home for her on their anniversary a couple of years ago." She dared not look at him. "It means passion and excitement. It's a symbol of fervent romance."

"Ah." His deep chuckle reached into her again. "I can see why it made the perfect anniversary gift."

She cleared her throat. "Yes."

"I thought the red rose stood for romance."

"Oh, it does. It's the most common, popular rose, of course. It's best given to say 'I love you."

"It looks like your mother planted lots of red ones."

"Yes. There are different types, sizes, and so on."

"That one must have been a very delicious red."

"Yes." She faltered at his description of the deep, dark flower, still open, but beginning to lose its petals. "You might think of it differently, however, if I told you it's called a *black* rose because its shade of red is so dark."

He frowned. "Oh... it symbolizes death, then, I take it? Somberness and gloom?"

She couldn't help giggling. "Yes, and revenge."

"So beautiful, yet so sinister."

"Yes. Not unlike some people." She thought of Jesilyn. So beautiful, yet so wicked. She turned to face him. "There are others." She forced a laugh and spoke in a prim voice. "But that's your lesson for today, class. I'll give you a test next week."

"Yes, ma'am."

She swung away to walk up the path, but stumbled on the edge of a paving stone. Jamie's hand shot out, and he grasped her arm. She pulled in a startled breath.

"You'd better take my arm. Apparently rose gardens can be dangerous places for ladies to walk alone."

"Perhaps." She looped her arm in his and smiled at him as thoughts of Clay slipped far, far away.

Chapter Fifteen

Paul's breath rushed out in misty trails as he stomped debris off his boots on the doorstep. The noisy effort was as much to let the women know he was coming in as to keep Marie's floor clean of barn fodder. As he opened the door, warm air rushed out to meet him, and his stomach growled in response to the aroma of grease and eggs frying on the stove.

"Morning, ladies." He shucked out of his heavy coat and hung it on a peg, at the same time noting Jane's pleasant smile.

"Good morning," both women chimed.

"It must be pretty crisp out there," Marie said. "I can feel the cold air rolling in with you."

"I reckon the real cold will be here any day." He yanked off his boots and wandered over to the kitchen area in his stocking feet. "Toast smells good. Coffee, too."

"Come in and have your breakfast."

October had sped by, and November was already upon them. He'd hardly noticed it. They'd fallen into an easy routine together, Jane fitting in with him and Marie as though she'd always been there. She seemed like a younger sister. Almost. Daily she grew more at ease with them -- with him.

He rubbed his palms together and whistled when she plunked a plateful of steaming hash browns and eggs in front of him. "Fresh eggs? I thought Rosie's chickens were molting and starting their winter strike."

"Oh, they are." Marie added a cup of cold water to the coffee pot to settle the grounds. "So I let Cookee pay me in eggs this week."

"You're charging Cookee for baking now?"

"Now and then he feels better when he can send something my way. I don't ever ask for anything or expect it."

"I'll be sure and thank him." Paul pinched some salt out of a bowl on the table and sprinkled it over his food.

Marie set two more platefuls on the table and poured coffee while Jane turned the toast on the stove. Paul glanced at her discreetly as she forked the golden brown pieces onto a plate and settled it in the center of the table. He gathered a slice and slathered butter on it as Jane pulled out a chair and sat down to her breakfast.

Marie yanked out a chair and joined them, blowing a wisp of hair off her brow. "I have some news to share with the two of you after breakfast."

Paul grinned. "Another offer of matrimony from Mr. Kelick?" He winked at Jane.

Marie returned his smirk. "I can assure you that such is not the case."

"What do you think, Jane?" Paul continued to tease. "Has someone been courting Marie when I've had my back turned?"

"I don't think so," she said with a giggle, the sound warming Paul up even more. "It must be a different kind of news."

"Art Miller's horse must've foaled, then."

Marie gestured with her fork. "You're wasting your time."

"Any guesses, Jane?"

"I think Marie will tell us when she's ready."

"Hmm. So you're not going to help me, then." He looked back at Marie, who had grown thoughtful. "I hope it's nothing too serious."

"Paul," Marie's voice did sound solemn. "How are you doing out in the lean-to? It must be getting cold."

He shrugged. Truth be told, he wasn't sure what he was going to do about the days ahead. He couldn't very well stay out in the lean-to behind the woodshed all winter. Any day now, they'd get snow, and if the next month flew by like the last one, they'd be in a deep freeze before long. "I get by all right."

"I think you should move back inside."

His mouth moved in slow motion as he chewed. He swallowed his hash browns and cast a quick glance at Jane."How do you figure?"

"Well, I can't very well have you freezing out there, now can I?" She sipped her coffee. "I don't think your moving back in would be inappropriate. Anyone would understand."

"Would they?" Paul pushed back in his chair and leveled a gaze at his sister.

"Of course. Everyone in the camp knows Jane came to us in despair, and that she's been nothing but a blessing to us since she's come."

Jane's cheeks turned pink, and with the back of her hand she brushed some stray, coppery tendrils off her brow. "I do feel badly about keeping you out of your own room for so long."

"She can share my room," Marie said. "We're quite comfortable with one another, and I have more than enough space."

Paul considered their offer. "I just don't want there to be any gossip."

"I don't see any reason why there would be. Do you?"

A month ago, he wouldn't have. He'd only been thinking of Jane's discomfort. But somewhere between that time and now, his feelings had gotten into a tangle. He was attracted to Jane. What if someone else noticed? He was surprised Marie hadn't already, not that he'd done anything to follow up on it. But what if some unconscious gesture revealed his feelings? What if someone caught him looking at her? He'd caught himself often enough. He never meant to stare at her or study her, but it just happened sometimes, like when he was supposed to be studying his sermon notes and she was helping Marie with the meals, or when she read by the firelight in the evening.

He liked helping her by carrying the washtub or hauling water and firewood. He liked talking about books with her. She was well-read, and that surprised him. He liked the way she smelled. A time or two, she'd been near enough for him to notice the flowery scent of her skin. He shook himself inwardly to bring his thoughts back to where they ought to be.

"I just don't want there to be any trouble for Jane."

"I'm sure my reputation can't get any worse," she said, sounding suddenly sour.

Paul caught Marie's glance. "People forget after a while," she said.

"No they don't. I saw some of the men in camp at Maisey's."

Paul's hackles rose, and he clenched his knee beneath the table.

Her eyes flew up to his. "Oh, not that way."

His nerves settled some, but not completely. He had become distracted enough by Jane's pleasant nature to forget for a while where she'd come from. But she didn't seem ready to forget, and now she'd reminded him.

Marie slid her plate aside and folded her hands on the table. "Do you want to tell us about Maisey's, Jane? It might help."

"Well..." Jane studied Marie, only flicking her gaze briefly at Paul. He sensed her embarrassment. "I only went there for a room, but I ran out of money and couldn't find a job." Her voice climbed. "I was desperate."

"Of course you were."

"I had no place left to turn."

Paul shifted uncomfortably.

Then suddenly she looked at him. "I never was with any of those men. I ran away. That's why I was out on the tracks heading to Mellen or whatever place I could find. There was this big man, dark, a big talker--"

"Johnny Ray?"

"Yes, that's him." She nodded, her face looking frightened still. "I clobbered him and ran, but he came after me."

Paul's heart thumped. She'd *clobbered* him?

"I was so afraid of what he'd do if he caught me. I hid all night. Then I went back the next day. I was hungry, and I started to think I was a fool." Her face blushed fire red. "I thought I was a fool for leaving. I knew I wouldn't make it on my own."

"But you said you ran away," Paul cut in.

"I did." Her lids drooped over her blue eyes. "I just couldn't stay away. I was hungry and cold. I went back, but Maisey threw me out. That's when I left town, and... you know the rest."

"You were desperate, just like you said." Marie reached for Jane's hand across the table, her words soft.

"Jane," Paul said, frowning, "I don't think less of you for the situation you found yourself in. Neither of us do. We've both been forgiven for our share of foolish mistakes, and God doesn't place a measuring stick on sin saying this one is worse than that one. He died for all of them, just the same. But I'm wondering, what happened before Hurley? What brought you here?"

She looked away and stood. She took her plate to the sink and slid it into the wash tub, keeping her back to them. "I'm not really ready to talk about that yet."

Paul and Marie exchanged glances. What could be worse than her experience at Maisey's? What in her past kept her from speaking about it? Had she been on her own for long? Was she running from someone else?

A charge exploded up Paul's spine. *Is she married?*

"We don't have to talk about it if you don't want to," Marie said, cutting off Paul's thoughts. "We can talk about other things, like my news."

Jane's shoulder's straightened and she turned toward them, but Paul noticed the glassy sheen in her eyes.

"We're having a community Thanksgiving social in town later this month. I told Mrs. Larson I'd help her and some of the other women with planning and decorations. Jane, I thought that maybe you'd like to help with the food. You're a good cook."

She nodded and offered a weak smile. "Yes. Sure."

"I told her I'd ride into town tomorrow to talk with her about it. Would you like to go?"

Jane shook her head. "Maybe you can just tell me what I'll need to do. I don't feel much like visiting right now."

Paul sighed. "You don't have to feel embarrassed to be seen in public. I hope you know that."

She nodded, but didn't look directly at him as she cleaned up the kitchen. "I know."

*****

The next day, Jesi tried to keep herself busy when Marie rode into town with Charlie Hanke's two girls, Rosie and Charlotte, to meet with Mrs. Larson and the rest of the planning committee. She wasn't ready to go back to town again so soon. She was sure Gravy, Maisey's piano player, had recognized her on her last trip when he'd stood staring at them from across the street. He'd been a nice enough man, but that meant nothing. What if he whispered to Johnny Ray that he'd seen her? What if the men in camp who knew where she'd come from mentioned where he could find her?

Fear spread wings inside her. Paul had assured her she was safe with him and Marie, but what if he was wrong? Johnny Ray was a powerful man, used to getting his way. *Please let him have forgotten me by now.* The words in her head were almost a prayer.

Paul planned to spend part of the day moving his things back into his room just as soon as she moved hers into Marie's.

Jesi had never been at home alone with him before, but she felt comfortable, and as safe as she could hope to feel. In a strange way, she felt better for having told them about her experience at Maisey's. Now they knew she wasn't really one of *those* girls. Her heart tripped at the deception. She was still a fallen woman, a mere tart who'd given herself away in the hope of buying love.

And what of Clay and Corianne? Had they mended things between them? Perhaps, but she doubted it. She'd done irreparable damage and was sure Cori would never forgive either of them. As for Clay, what if he realized his mistake and came looking for her someday? What if he found her, walking down the streets of Hurley, and wanted her back?

Clarity washed over her thoughts. She'd go back to him. She'd fall into his arms as helplessly as ever. She should be ashamed to admit it, even to herself, and in a way, she was. But that didn't make it any less true. As much as she hated him, she was afraid she'd fall prey to his charms again if given the chance.

"Jane, do you mind helping me carry a few books?"

She flushed, wondering if her wayward thoughts were written all over her face. Paul smiled, and she had to look away. "I'd be happy to. Lead on."

She followed him out the door to the lean-to behind the woodshed. Cold wind pressed her sleeves against her arms.

"Here we go." They stepped into the small room where he'd been sleeping. It certainly wasn't much. His stack of books had grown over the weeks, yet the two of them could manage carrying them all in one trip.

Paul placed a small pile in her arms. His dimples creased again, and his brown eyes were warm. "Not too heavy, are they?"

"No. I can manage."

"Good." He bent to pick up a taller pile, his shirt straining across his shoulders. Jesi would never have taken him for a preacher.

"You've read all these just since you've been staying out here?"

"No, not entirely. They're mostly study books I use for reference."

She followed him into the house to his room. It looked different already. She'd only ever known it from the day she'd awakened in it and found her few things nearby. Already it seemed changed by Paul's presence, his books, and his blanket spread across the bed.

"Let's set these here," he said, plopping them onto the mattress.

She dropped her load beside his. "I'm glad you're not staying out there anymore. I'm freezing. I can't imagine you sleeping in such quarters." She rubbed her arms.

"Let's warm up by the fire."

Paul added logs to the fireplace while Jesi made them some tea. "Do you think we'll have snow pretty soon?"

"I suspect so. I'd like to bring down some venison before long."

"What's it like to hunt?"

Paul shrugged. "It's a challenge. A conquest. Of course we do it for the meat, too, but I can't deny I find pleasure in it."

"I'd like to try."

He grinned at her. Whenever he smiled, and that happened quite often, Jesi realized what a handsome man Paul Winter was. He looked nothing like Clay. He wasn't dapper, or distinguished -- or proud. He was rugged, but still young. His eyes always sparkled as if he were ready to pop open with ideas. Yet he readily admitted he didn't quite understand the world yet.

Clay thought he knew everything. That thought alone made her wonder why she would ever want to go back to him. Some things, she supposed, couldn't be understood or explained.

After their tea, Jesi planned to make dinner. But Paul told her she needed to take a break. He suggested they eat sandwiches and enjoy their dinner hour with some reading aloud while they waited for Marie to return.

Jesi eagerly agreed. While preparing their light meal, Paul told her how Marie's feisty pranks as a child often got them both into trouble. Then, while they ate, he told her how Marie had been the first to commit her life to Christ, and then had persuaded Paul to do the same.

"She's been such a big influence on you."

"Older siblings are often that way."

He looked at her with that deep, studying way of his, and Jesi wondered if he was trying to figure out whether or not she had siblings, and whether or not she was older or younger than they might be. She chewed her food slowly. *I'll not yield to your curiosity, Paul. Not yet.*

Instead, she changed the subject. "What do you suppose I'll be expected to bring to the social? Nothing too difficult, I hope."

The creaking of a wagon alerted them that someone was outside. "Sounds like Marie is home. I suppose she'll tell you the answer to that."

Paul had barely risen from his chair when his sister came through the door, her skirts swishing as she spun to close it. She swept off her bonnet and gloves and unbuttoned her long coat. "Looks like we'll have a storm. I'm glad I made it home before it arrives."

She rubbed her hands together and came to stand by the fire next to Jesi and Paul.

Paul picked up a poker, stooped down, and shifted the logs. The fire blazed higher. "How was your meeting?"

"Am I to cook a mountain of food?" Jesi asked.

"My meeting was... eventful." She lifted her shoulders in a slight shrug and gazed at Paul in a way Jesi recognized as filled with an undercurrent of meaning. She and Cori had shared those kinds of signals.

Paul sat. His forehead furrowed. "Well? What happened? Don't keep us in suspense."

Wondering as well, Jesi waited. She didn't know enough about the locals to care about any gossip, not that Marie was one to bear tales.

"Today I had a very interesting visit with an acquaintance of mine from Ashland. She works as a nurse in the Ashland hospital." Marie's gaze swung back and forth between them. She sucked in her breath, and expelled it again in a gasp. "She wants me to come there, to work in the hospital."

Paul stared at her.

"We've written back and forth a couple of times."

"So that's what you've been up to."

Marie nodded. "I have an idea, Paul. I'd like to talk to you about it later, if you don't mind."

Jesi's safety net dropped away. A job for Marie in the Ashland hospital? Where would that leave her?

Chapter Sixteen

Cori pulled the drapes across the window, shutting out the wet snow pelting the pane. She bent to kiss her grandfather's cheek before sitting at the little table next to his bed.

"Just because I get a kiss doesn't mean I'll let you beat me."

She set the chess board between them. "You're on, Gramp. Are you sure you're up to this?"

"I'm feeling a lot better than I did. I just needed to stop worrying. You know," he said, his look drifting far away, "your sister used to be able to beat me."

"Don't worry." Cori frowned. "Jesi will be fine. She always is."

"So you keep saying." He harrumphed. "Don't you wonder what she's doing, or where she is?"

"No." She picked up a rook.

He reached for her arm, and she paused with the chess piece in her fingers. "You're too young and pretty to grow old fast by hanging on to your anger."

"Humph." She pulled away and set up the last pieces. "I get to go first."

"Go ahead." He chuckled and shrugged. "Use your advantage."

Cori moved her first pawn.

"You and Joe's boy are getting on pretty well, aren't you?"

She darted a look at him. "How did you know that?"

"So I'm right."

"Oh, you're good." She squinted at him. "You only guessed."

"Those Gilberts have a way about them."

"What do you mean?"

"Joe tried to snatch up your grandma ahead of me."

"So I've heard." Cori smiled. "You aren't worried about him hanging around here now, are you, Gramp?"

"No." He snickered. "Joe's a good friend. If I have to go, I know he won't let anything happen to your grandma."

Cori's heart wilted. "Don't say things like that, okay?"

"Just facing facts."

"Facts, facts. Nothing's a fact until it happens."

Gramp's hand hovered over the chess board, and a moment later, Cori's pawn disappeared. She crossed her arms and studied her next move.

"So what can I tell you about James?"

"James who?"

He chuckled again. "Jamie Gilbert."

"Oh. Jamie." She peeked up at him. "What an old match-maker you are, Gramp. I thought that was the sort of thing only women were supposed to get up to."

"Nothing much else for me to do."

"Hmm. Well, all right then. Has Jamie ever courted anyone?"

"Your knight's in trouble."

Her shoulders jerked. Oh, the game. She made a quick move to save her knight.

"No, not so far as I know. He's a hard worker. Hasn't taken time for the girls, I guess."

"But they must take time for him, I bet."

Gramp laughed out loud. "There never was a Gilbert who couldn't get the ladies' attention."

Cori captured a pawn and settled back in her chair with a smug smile. "Take that."

"All right." Gramp leaned forward, slid his knight around her bishop, and captured her rook.

She frowned. "You cheated."

"Did not. Your move."

"Jamie is leaving soon, so I don't suppose it matters. The woods call."

"Absence makes the heart grow fonder."

"Just a saying," she said, making another move.

"I was separated from your grandmother by miles and years. And through it all, something grew we couldn't lessen, much less stop."

"You two are sweet."

"We might have gone our separate ways, and we even tried to for a while."

She forgot about the chess game and rested her chin in her fist. "Did you ever court anyone else besides Gran?"

"I had a girl named Margie once. But I didn't really court her."

"My, that doesn't sound good."

"It was a mess, to tell you the truth."

"Like me and Clayton."

"Those things happen." He adjusted his shoulders against his pillows. "You just learn from them and move on. It's best to do it without adding bitterness."

"That's a tall order, you know."

"Have you prayed about it?"

Cori sighed. "Not really."

"Do your old grandpa a favor and do that. Okay?"

"First I'm going to pray that I beat you."

"Well, don't count on Him answering that one."

He smiled and reached for another piece just as a knock at the door called their attention. Lainey strode into the room and sat on the other side of Cori's grandfather.

"You look good today, Pa."

"This daughter of yours is keeping me on my toes."

"That's good. Are you hungry?"

He smiled wanly. He was rarely hungry these days. "I could try a little something if you want me to."

"Cori, will you go see what Evie has?"

Cori nodded and stood, sliding the table back so they could finish their game later. She grinned at the old man in the bed. "No cheating and moving pieces while I'm gone,"

His eyes twinkled, and he waggled his brows.

Cori laughed and left the room. She met Jamie in the hall coming out of his room.

"Hello." His smile warmed her, and she thought about what Gramp had said. *There never was a Gilbert who couldn't get the ladies' attention.* Jamie had certainly gotten hers.

"Hi."

They turned to go downstairs together. "How's your granddad?"

"Doing pretty well. He's beating me badly at chess right now."

"Interesting. I played a game against him once. Never tried again."

"I plan to beat him one of these days."

"That's good." He followed her into the kitchen. "Hearing you say so is a sign of hope."

Cori was indeed hopeful. The doctor seeing Gramp had diagnosed a tumor he thought might be operable. Her parents and grandparents had discussed what to do about it. Thinking about the doctor cutting open her old grandfather and removing the tumor frightened her. He could die, or the tumor could grow back. The disease that had caused it might have spread. But they'd all decided it was worth the risk. To leave the tumor there would destroy any chance he might have.

Evie wasn't in the kitchen, so Cori looked for something palatable her grandfather could eat.

"I'm glad I found you. I wanted to have a chance to talk with you again before Da and I leave. We'll take the train on Friday."

"Oh..." Cori frowned. Jamie had kept her mind off the sorrows surrounding her during the past weeks. Her friendship with him had happened quickly, and she realized suddenly that she would miss him. She'd hoped he'd be there while Gramp went through surgery. If he went away, she'd feel alone again. She feared what her thoughts would turn to once the time came.

"I'm wondering..." His voice faltered, causing her to turn from the breadbox and look at him. "Corianne, I know you've just been through that -- that courtship -- and it has you feeling a little mixed up and hurt." He lifted his gaze into hers, and her heart pattered. "I'd like to write to you, if you don't mind."

"That would be fine." She swallowed. "I'd like that."

"I'd also like to come back and see you again, maybe over Christmas."

"You would?"

"My da will want to know how your grandparents are doing."

"Oh, of course."

"And I would like the chance to see you again."

"You would?"

He chuckled softly. "You seem surprised."

Cori's heart twisted as a terrible thought encroached on her. Would Jamie's interest in her be confused if Jesi were home? Cori stretched her fingers against her sides and wet her lips. "I guess I'm a little untrusting."

"I hope I won't do anything to earn that." He frowned. "I haven't already, have I?"

"No." She came around the work table and stood next to him. "I didn't mean it like that. It's all because of Jesi and Clay."

She looked away. He touched her arm, and she turned to him again. His eyes were soft and gentle, and dark like coffee.

"I'm still so angry."

"But not at me, I hope."

"I'm grateful for you. I'm glad we met. It's reminded me that everyone isn't like Clay. And that I'm not like Jesi."

"I hope you and your sister don't remain at odds."

"What about my staying at odds with Clay?" She stood only a foot away from Jamie, and couldn't help teasing him. Somehow, saying Clay's name didn't mean anything.

"I hope the space between you stays just the way it is." His expression grew more serious, and Cori could tell he wanted to kiss her. She wanted to kiss him, too.

She backed away and took a breath. "We'll go skating when you come back. I love to skate. Do you?"

He nodded, his dimples returning. "I'll look forward to doing that with you. I can hardly wait until Christmas now."

*****

Marie stood in Paul's bedroom with her hands on her hips, waiting for him to argue his case. Thank the Lord Jane was nowhere near to hear.

She had gone to deliver the new batch of bread to Cookee. Paul didn't mind her going alone when all the men were off working in the woods and gone from the camp. A few knew where Jane had come from and occasionally made suggestive remarks to her and let their stares sweep over her unabashed. Paul put his foot down on it, but still, he didn't like her wandering through the camp alone if he could help it. Right now, only the office manager and Cookee were about the place.

She'd be safe around them.

Paul admitted to himself that at first he'd worried about her safety alone. But somehow, his concerns had managed to become a sort of jealousy that crept over him whenever another man noticed her. He had no such business feeling that way. Not even given the outrageous scheme Marie had concocted to protect their reputations.

Marie's fingers tapped her hips impatiently. "Well? Isn't it a perfect solution?"

"I can't marry her." He dropped to his knees and dug through a trunk beneath the window.

"Why not? If you marry Jane, she'll be protected, your reputation will remain untarnished, and I'll be free to move to Ashland."

"You've always been free to move to Ashland or anywhere else you've had a mind to go. There are other ways to solve the problem of Jane being here."

"Oh? What are they?"

He glanced up. "Maybe you should both move to Ashland."

"Paul." She gasped and crossed her arms, "I'll be studying and learning a new job. I could end up becoming a full-fledged nurse one day, but that'll take work and school. So you know how impossible that idea is."

"It sounds a lot more possible than this -- this *notion* of yours. Do you even know how crazy it sounds? I can't imagine what Jane would think." He stopped rustling through the trunk. Resting his hands on its edge, he stared at her as panic seized him. "You didn't already mention it to her, did you?"

"Of course not. Paul--" Marie scowled and pinched her eyelids shut. She took two strides toward him and squatted beside the trunk. "Think about it for a minute before you get all excited. You and Jane get along perfectly. She's a wonderful cook and a good housekeeper, she enjoys baking the bread for Cookee, and she has never once complained about your preaching." Marie smiled, then laughed when he caught on to her joke.

"Oh, ha ha."

"She'd make a good minister's wife."

"She would? Haven't you forgotten something?"

"Love?"

"No." His neck warmed. "I'm talking about her faith. *Be not unequally yoked together,* the scripture says."

Marie stood and bit her fingernail. "Yes, that's true. But I think she's open. She may just need a little nudge."

Paul dropped the lid to the chest and stood, brushing past her. "This is foolishness."

"You like her, Paul."

"Of course I do. She's a sweet girl. She's had some misfortune."

"Sweet?"

He looked up and was met by Marie's precocious grin. "You know what I mean."

"You like her."

Paul strode into the main room and looked for something to do. He stirred the fire and added more wood, prolonging the activity. Marie shadowed him.

"You like her a lot. I've seen you looking at her."

"Marie..." So she *had* noticed. Paul had feared that. No use arguing now. "Yes, I'm very aware of her, and I am attracted to her. But too many things stand in the way. The main one, I've already mentioned. Then again, she hasn't shown the slightest interest in me. She'd probably run off scared out of her wits if you even brought up this idea."

"Maybe not."

He scowled and stared into the fire.

"She needs us. It's obvious she has no place to go, no one to turn to. I think she'd consider the idea."

"Marie, you're not talking about me *protecting* her. You're talking about me *marrying* her. That's something else entirely."

"Paul, surely you've heard of marriages of convenience."

"I've never planned to be part of one." His thoughts swept to Imogene Gillette, the girl he'd nearly married. The girl he had *loved.*

"Of course not." Marie's voice softened. She moved next to him and looped her arm through his. "But what if it's God's will? What if this is the soul you've been praying for? What if a marriage of convenience could become a perfect union of love and a lifetime of commitment?"

"What if it can't?" The *lifetime* part worried him the most.

To that, Marie fell silent.

The door swung open, and they looked up from the fire. Jane hurried in out of the wind as light snow flurried down. She swept off her bonnet. Her bun tumbled askew, and her face was flushed with cold. Her beauty made Paul blush when he realized, once again, he was transfixed... and now Marie knew.

She strode over to take the empty basket from Jane."How did it go?"

"Perfectly, as usual." She unbuttoned the heavy coat she'd borrowed from Marie. "Cookee said to tell you he has some venison hind quarter in the smoker and that you should come get some later, Paul." She smiled at him, and her eyes shone.

What if Marie is right? He swallowed, trying to imagine the possibility, while at the same time his instincts warred inside him. *What if it is* the *answer... God's answer?*

"Uh," he stepped forward, snapping himself out of his melee of thought. "Did he say what time?"

"No." She gave him a confused frown, then another smile and a shrug. "I suppose anytime will be fine."

He licked his lips, and Marie cast him a swift glance.

She clasped her hands. "I'm going to be busy for the next half hour or so. I have some correspondence to do, and then I'll plan what to take with me to Ashland. So I'll be in our room if you need me." She glanced at Jane and then darted her gaze to Paul, shooting arrows of meaning along with it.

"All right," Jane said. "I'm going to sit by the fire for a while and warm up. Maybe I'll tackle some of the mending." The chagrin was clear in her voice. Paul knew she didn't favor the task.

"I'll keep you company," he offered, "as long as you let me throw in my wool socks." He smiled, and she returned it. His heartbeat sped up. Marie had given him this chance to feel out the situation with Jane, and she would pray for him as well, asking God to show him whether or not this idea of marrying the young woman was what he should really do or even consider. "I'll pour us some tea, first. I think the pot's still hot."

Paul got the tea while Jane collected her basket of mending. During those minutes, he gave his own fervent thoughts to God. *Show me what You want me to do. I want what's best for Jane, Father. And I can't deny I dare not trust my own feelings. I wholly depend upon You.*

She sat in a straight-back chair facing the fireplace where he handed her a cup. Then he pulled up another chair and sat beside her. For a moment, they stared at the fire and sipped their tea, or rather, she did. He barely touched his.

"Is something bothering you, Paul?" she asked at last.

He straightened and tried a little laugh. "You're very intuitive, did you know that?"

She shrugged. "It's not hard to figure out, unless you're just tired. You cut up a lot of wood this morning."

"Nah, I'm not tired." He stretched his shoulders and then turned toward her to discover her watching him closely. "It's this thing with Marie moving to Ashland."

Jane frowned. "You don't think she should?"

"Oh, of course she should. She's always wanted to take up nursing. She's not getting any younger. She can get some training there -- not necessarily the schooling she wants -- but she'll learn a lot while she helps take care of patients."

"The men here depend on her whenever they're sick or hurt."

"Yes, and they'll miss her." He sipped his tepid tea. "But you've been helping her a lot. You've learned some of her ways, I'll bet."

"No." Jane shook her head and glanced down at her cup. "I only try to make them feel less afraid."

"There's healing in that," he said, his voice falling to nearly a whisper.

Hope filled the gaze she lifted to his, and he prayed she'd found some sort of worth. His heart quailed as he realized how very little Jane thought of herself. She really was intuitive. She had a way about her others found pleasing and comforting, and she had an easy-going, pleasant nature. What had seemed at first to be shyness fell away as she'd gotten to know him and Marie. He didn't think she was really very shy at all. She'd just stumbled into dire circumstances and lost her trust along the way

He cleared his voice and spoke levelly again. "Jane, are you afraid of what'll happen when Marie leaves?"

"Naturally." She laughed, but without humor. "I can't very well stay here living with the preacher, now, can I?"

She'd nailed it without beating around the bush on that one. "No, I guess you can't. But..." He paused until she looked at him again. "I do think God has a plan for you, and I know you shouldn't worry about it. Do you trust that?"

"Trust God, you mean? I used to."

Her answer was more than he'd hoped for. He leaned forward and rested his forearms on his knees. "You used to?"

"You and I have talked about that before, at the eatery. Remember? And you don't think I can listen to your preaching Sunday after Sunday without knowing in my heart I owed Him that much, do you?" She grinned.

"Is it really that bad?"

She giggled, then suddenly reached over and touched his arm, giving him a squeeze through his flannel shirt that jolted him.

"No, it's not bad. You're a good preacher, actually. Better than my old pastor."

Her hand fell away, and his whirring thoughts slowed. "So you used to go to church?"

"Yes." She finished her tea and set the cup aside. She bent to pick up a darning needle and a sock. She concentrated on the work in her lap.

Paul leaned back. "Are you a believer? I've wanted to ask, but I didn't want to pry."

"I believe in Christ. But I'm not a faithful Christian, if that's what you mean. You asked me if I trust God's plan, yet I don't think He has one. I used to believe it, but somewhere along the way He let go of me. Or maybe I ran away from Him. I don't know."

She was hurting, even more deeply than he'd imagined if she thought God had released her. *My sheep hear my voice, and I know them, and they follow me. I give them eternal life, and they will never perish, and no one will snatch them out of my hand.* The passage from John's gospel leapt through Paul's brain.

"You're still in God's hand. It's just that His hands are so large you can't always feel them grasped around you. He'll never let you go."

"Hmm... Maybe not. But that doesn't keep me from leaving of my own accord."

He quoted the end of the passage. "'My Father, who has given them to me, is greater than all, and no one is able to snatch them out of my Father's hand.' *No one* even includes us."

"So you're trying to tell me I'm still in His hand, even though I ran off and made a mess of my life, even though I willingly offered to work for Maisey." She raised her voice. "Even though I left a trail of ruin in my wake."

Her eyes lit with a fire he'd never seen before, and then they suddenly watered. She sniffed and fisted the clean sock over them. Paul had all he could do not to gather her in his arms and comfort her. The best he could do was to reach out with more words. "I believe God brought you to us. Whatever happened before, no matter how terrible, He took it and turned it to good by leading you here."

She lowered the sock and stared at him. Was that hope brimming in her eyes?

"That's what I believe."

"You do?" Her voice wavered, and she shook her head. "How can you, Paul? You have no idea what I've done."

"No. I don't. But God does, and he loves you anyway."

"Marie is still going away." Jane's shoulders quivered with a sigh. "So where does that leave me?"

Paul's heart pounded. *I'm going to step out on this one, Lord. If I'm wrong, then dear God, show me. Please show me.*

"I have an idea." He chuckled and tried to draw space to breathe. "Actually, Marie thought of it." He shouldn't have said that. She might hate him for not sounding genuine. "It's an idea worth considering." His neck grew hot.

She watched him expectantly. He didn't know how to get the words out. "I'm a little worried about what you'll say. I don't want to give you the wrong idea."

"The wrong idea?"

She looked perplexed, and if Paul had a back leg, he'd have kicked himself with it.

"Jane..." He almost reached for her hand, then constrained himself and grasped his hands together in his lap instead. "Jane, what if I asked you to marry me?"

The fire crackled. She stopped breathing and stared at him.

Yes, she was holding her breath. Finally, she let it escaped with a whoosh. "*If* you were to ask me? Is that what you're doing?"

He couldn't tell if she sounded more shocked, put out, or simply perplexed. Now he did take her hand. She let him, but it lay limp in his.

"I'm just trying to help you. If I marry you, no one will think poorly of you staying."

"Such charity."

"Not necessarily."

Her eyes widened. "I don't love you."

"No... No, of course you don't." He had been unprepared for the sting of her words. "I'm not expecting that."

"I see." She frowned and pulled her hand away. Her eyes glinted suspiciously. "What is it you do expect?"

He stood, stepped closer to the fire, and then turned to face her. "I don't expect anything. I don't even expect you to accept my proposal. I know it sounds crazy. It even sounded crazy to me when Marie suggested it."

"Why even suggest it, then?" Her mouth gaped. She let out a harsh laugh. "You're right. It's crazy."

She jumped to her feet, the forgotten mending tumbling off her skirt to the floor. She almost spun away, but Paul caught her arm, forcing her to stop and look at him.

"It sounds crazy... but it also sounds like an answer. Look, Jane…" He held his grip on her arm. "I don't know where else you can go. And I... well, I like having you here. We get along all right. You seem content with the things you have to do. I think we could get along fine."

"I don't... love you," she said again, whispering the words.

He let go of her arm.

She walked a few feet away, as if to go into the kitchen and leave the conversation alone, but then she stopped and looked back. "You really wouldn't expect anything from me? I mean, any... marital obligations?"

Her face looked pink even in the dim cabin. Paul's pulsed quickened. He knew what she meant, all right. "No. Nothing like that. We'll just be a help to each other. I'll look out for you, and you'll help me in my ministry."

She nodded and turned away. Paul's pulse kept up its frantic throbbing. Was she considering it?

Chapter Seventeen

Daylight would soon creep in, but for now the cabin stood in heavy darkness. Jesilyn stared into the void, her heart and mind restless. Beside her, Marie slept on in utter stillness. Jesi couldn't even detect her breathing. She turned her back on her bedmate and tugged Marie's pretty patchwork quilt closer under her chin.

Her tattered carpetbag lay tucked under the bed, just beneath her. She pondered sliding out of the covers, retrieving it, and slipping away into the pre-dawn light with whatever belongings she dared gather. Her instincts cried for flight. And yet--

And yet, this time she had no money. This time, she had no way to buy a railroad ticket. This time, she had no plan to punctuate her thoughts with ideas of independence.

Where would she go? Back to Maisey's or one of the other brothels in Hurley? How would that be different than marrying Paul? Either way, she'd belong to someone to whom she had never intended to belong. At least in binding herself to Paul, she would belong only to him, not to uncounted others besides. She shuddered despite the quilt, and not from cold. Big Johnny Ray's face loomed out of the darkness in front of her, chilling her to the bone more thoroughly than the night air ever could.

If only Paul were Clay. And yet, Paul was a decidedly better man than Clay. He was honest and steady and a good provider. He was nice looking, too. And he was safe.

Safety was what she needed most.

A gray haze filtered in through the room's one small window. A thud echoed from the other side of the bedroom wall. Paul must be up. Logs thumped onto the hearth, and she imagined him stirring the coals into a blaze.

Marie groaned softly and stretched her legs.

Jesilyn nested deeper into her pillow. When had she come to feel so comfortable here? Why should she think of leaving? She pictured Paul out there now, his lank brown hair askew from sleep, a day's growth of beard prickling his cheeks, his broad shoulders heaving with an armload of firewood. A smile tugging at the corners of his eyes, brightening them.

What if she said yes? What if she stayed here and lived with Paul?

Just the two of them... alone here all the time. For another moment, she remembered Clay and their intense intimacy. Would Paul really respect a boundary between himself and Jesi, one not even her imagination could cross?

Marie slung back the covers and dragged her legs over the side of the bed.

"You're letting in the cold," Jesi murmured.

"You're awake."

"Yes. I don't want to be."

She sensed Marie's sleepy smile. "Time for breakfast and chores, I suppose."

Jesi didn't answer. The mattress shifted as Marie rose and dressed in the shadowy darkness. Marie seemed like a sister, a feeling Jesi had nearly forgotten. When had Cori last stirred any sensation of sibling affection? Not since Jesi had met Clay. If Jesi married Paul, then Marie would indeed be her sister.

But she couldn't marry Paul. She simply couldn't.

Marie slipped out of the room, but Jesi lingered in bed. Restlessness wound through her, but she didn't want to face him yet. Marie must have sensed her heightened emotional state, because she didn't return to rouse Jesi. Before long, she smelled their breakfast cooking. The door closed as Paul went out to do his chores. A while later, it opened again.

By then, Jesi had made up her mind.

She got up and dressed. No use lingering. What would be, would be. She brushed her hair and knotted it at the back of her head, not taking the time to do it carefully. Pouring some icy water from the pitcher on the nightstand into the wash bowl on the dresser, she splashed her face and shivered through to her core. She patted her skin dry and put the towel aside. An oval mirror above the dresser reflected her chagrin.

She spoke to her reflection. "I have no other choice."

Entering the brightly lit main room, warm air rushed to meet her along with the scent of biscuits and gravy. Life sparked in her veins. Marie cast her a smile that said more than *good morning*. A question lay behind it. Paul sat at the table with his Bible lying open in front of him. He glanced up at her, too, his look almost sheepish.

"Paul." He looked up again when she stopped in front of him. His brown eyes steadied, and his shoulders relaxed. Jesi's fingertips teased the edge of the table. "Did you really mean it, when you said you'd marry me?"

He pushed back his chair and rose slowly. His gaze didn't leave hers. "Yes, I did. I prayed about it for a long time last night, and I still do."

She looked to Marie who watched them, riveted, with a wooden spoon in her hand. "Marie, do you really think this is a wise idea?"

Marie looked as if she had much to say, but after opening her mouth, she merely nodded.

"I don't lo--"

"I know," Paul broke in, holding up his hand to stop her. "You've already told me. I'm offering you protection and shelter. My name, too, if you'll have it. I'm not asking for anything in return."

"But you're a good man. You deserve a wife who'll love you."

"What's to say *you* won't love him someday?" Marie said, still holding the spoon.

Paul stepped around the table and closed the space between them. "Forget about all that, Jane. Just forget about it. Just relax and let me take care of you. That's all I want."

A strange light shone in his eyes, one Jesilyn had never seen before. Was that truly all he asked of her -- just camaraderie?

"Then if that's good enough for you, I guess... I mean... if you can be content with someone like me, even for a little while--"

He took her hand and squeezed it. "Not for just a little while."

His fingers were warm and rough, almost reassuring. He might believe what he said now, but what if they never grew affectionate toward one another? He'd change his mind then. After all, he'd said nothing about loving her, either.

She tried a little smile, one meant to bolster her own confidence as much as Paul's. "Then I'll marry you so Marie can be off to Ashland."

Marie gasped, and Paul chuckled in what sounded like nervous relief. Jesilyn didn't know if they were truly happy about her choice, or merely relieved she hadn't left them wondering. Yet Paul seemed sure. She couldn't imagine why.

His words came back to her. *I'm offering you my name, too.* Deep shame, like a river current, pulled her down and washed over her. She plucked a plate from the shelf and dished up her breakfast, all to avoid looking at them as they talked about the upcoming nuptials. *He doesn't even know my name. He thinks he knows a little something about me because of what I've told him. But he doesn't even know who I really am.*

Maybe she wouldn't have to tell him. Maybe she'd just keep up the charade. What would it matter if he married Jesilyn Beaumont or Jane Barton?

"Janie Winter. I like that," Marie said as she set the coffee pot on the table. "It has a real nice ring to it. The men in camp will get used to you being the preacher's wife quickly enough."

Marie's comment skewered Jesi's thoughts. She glanced up at Paul, who smiled awkwardly and sat back down to his Bible. What was she thinking? How could she dare become the wife of this fine man who loved God when he wouldn't even know whom he'd married? Would they even be legally wed if she kept up the lie?

Part of her didn't want it to matter. If they weren't legally wed, she could leave again when things turned sour. Nothing would hold her to him. Yet her conscience argued that Paul and Marie only meant her good. As much as Jesi feared what might happen as an outcome of her decision, she dreaded hurting them more. She was forced into yet another choice. Either tell them the truth, or go back home.

I can't go back.

Yet what if they sent her back once they knew?

They think I'm Jane Barton now, and they haven't tried to discover my roots, so I doubt they'll try to discover where Jesi Beaumont is from, either.

She sat down in front of her meal, but laid her fork beside her plate without touching it. "Before you get too accustomed to the sound of my name with yours, Paul, I need to say something."

They both looked at her expectantly.

"Go ahead, Jane. I'm listening." Paul's expression lay open, accepting. Telling him the truth would be even harder than she'd thought.

"I'm not sure what you'll think. Maybe you'll change your mind." She stroked the fork beside her plate. "This is so difficult."

"Jane," He reached over and laid his hand on hers. "Just go ahead and say it. I understand your doubts about this arrangement. You don't have to hide anything."

"Well, it's like this." She squinted at him, wishing she could understand what made him so long-suffering. "I haven't told you some things about myself. You might get mad."

"You're not going to tell me you're married, are you?" Paul laughed, but it didn't help. She couldn't join in his attempt at levity.

"No."

He fell silent and grew serious. Did he feel her pulse hammering in her hand?

"My real name isn't Jane."

Marie stepped toward her and stopped.

Jesilyn's gaze swung her way. "It's not Jane Barton."

Paul's hand slowly slipped away from hers, and coolness took its place. She closed her palm and withdrew it to her lap.

"Mind if I ask what your name is?"

"You know I didn't want to lie, but I was afraid when I first came here."

"We know, Jane..." The false name died away on Marie's lips, and the woman slid her gaze to the floor.

"Then when you let me stay, I was afraid to bring it up and tell you the truth. After a while, I thought I really was her."

"Her?" Paul said. "Is there another Jane Barton?"

She'd no idea what he could be imagining, but she had to stop it now. "No. It's me. I'm Jane, and yet I'm not. I just made her up because I didn't want anyone to know who I was, in case someone came looking for me."

Paul's frown deepened, and his expression glinted with mistrust. "Are you in some other trouble besides the trouble you got into at Maisey's?"

"No... not trouble, really. I just left home and didn't want anyone to find me."

Marie sighed. Paul leaned back in his chair looking somewhat relieved. "That's it? You ran away from home?"

Jesi nodded. "I can't go back. Please don't send me back."

"I'm not going to send you back." Paul shushed her. "But I have to know more. I can't keep you here, knowing someone might be worried about you, or that you could be in danger, without the truth. I'll wait until you're ready."

Marie sat back down at the table. She reached for Jesi's hand, and Jesi clung to her. "I left because of my sister. We quarreled."

Paul's expression was unreadable.

Jesi squirmed. "Well... not quarreled, really. My sister, see... she was about to announce her engagement, and I was jealous. I-I'd fallen in love with her fiancé." She tightened her grip on Marie's hand. "I tried to steal him from her."

Jesi squeezed her eyelids together and tears oozed out, trickling over her cheeks. She had to tell them, had to get it out. But she couldn't bear them looking at her. She covered her face with her free hand.

"He let me think he loved me, too, but he didn't. He cast me aside." Her voice took on a harsh edge. "But it was too late. I'd done things... to keep him. Things that made me think I could work at a place like Maisey's."

Their silence screamed at her.

"I was desperate." She flashed a look at them, then dropped her gaze again. "I didn't want to work there, but I thought I could do those things again. It wasn't the same. I'd loved Clay."

Jesi hadn't meant to say his name, but it came out, and with it a sob tore from her chest. Marie came close and wrapped her arm around Jesi.

"Love makes people do strange things. Sometimes the same thing happens when we mistake something else for love."

She cried in Marie's arms, sobbing and sniffling, torn between remembered pain, the agony of confessing, and the hint in Marie's words that perhaps Jesi's feelings toward Clay hadn't been love. Finally the torment ebbed away. She straightened and ran a finger under her eyes. Paul hadn't moved. He hadn't said a word. He sat there with his arms crossed, worrying his lower lip between his teeth.

She forced herself to look him in the eye, her throat still tight. "You can change your mind. It's all right."

He would do it. She could at least make it easier for him.

The chair screeched when he pushed it back and stood. He came around and offered her his hand. "Come with me."

She glanced at Marie, put her hand in his, and rose. Together they walked to the door, and Paul opened it wide. A wintry gust pushed at her skirt and blasted through her body. Paul seemed hardly to notice it.

"Look over there." He pointed across the logging camp a hundred yards away. "What do you think all this is?"

"A lumber camp?" Her teeth chattered, as much from cold as from the dancing of her nerves.

"Yes. It's a lumber camp. It's also a mission field, full of men who sin every day, just like you and I do."

"Don't compare yourself to them, or to me, Paul." She tugged her hand free and stepped back. "You don't even know what sin is."

"You mean lust? Is that the kind of sin you're talking about? Or do you only consider the physical act to be sin enough to set you apart from God?" The wind sucked all the warmth out of the cabin. Paul ignored it while it whipped around him.

"It's one thing to think about it, and another to do it."

"Is it? Who told you that? God says whoever looks at a woman to lust after her has already committed adultery with her in his heart."

"You're only telling me that so I won't feel so dirty. But it'll always be there -- the shame and the dirt. You say God will take it away, but I don't believe it. I feel it. I know what I did. I know my sister will never forgive me. The rest of my family won't forget. They'll be ashamed each and every time they look at me."

"You don't give them very much credit." He stepped inside, drew her in after him, and closed the door. The flames in the fireplace danced. Marie lifted the lid off the kitchen stove and added more wood.

"As dirty as I feel, I really did love Clay." She squared her shoulders, but her anger dissolved. "I don't regret wanting him at all. Just don't make me go back. Okay?"

"I already said I wouldn't do that."

"But now you'd rather not claim me either. I don't blame you."

"Is that what you think? I don't even know who I supposedly don't want to *claim*. You still haven't told us your real name."

"It's Jesi." She raised her chin. "Short for Jesilyn. Jesilyn Beaumont."

Paul nodded his head and considered her new identity. She sensed his thoughts churning like cream, trying to come together. He walked over to her, and while they'd sat next to each other on any number of other occasions, Jesi didn't recall ever standing so close to him before. At least, not with him looking down at her like he was. She was tall, but she still had to glance up into his eyes. She found them dark and unreadable.

"Jesilyn Beaumont," Paul asked, pausing and working his jaw, "will you be my wife?"

She stared at him in surprise. His jaw worked some more, and she wondered what he could be thinking. She felt like Red Riding Hood, about to be eaten by the big bad wolf. *My, what big eyes you have.* Then suddenly, his eyes grew tender.

She knew he really didn't want to marry her. He didn't want to spend his life with a used woman. She'd just heaped sin upon sin, and now he'd be trapped with her.

Unfortunately, I've got no other choice.

She lifted her chin. "If you think Jesi Winter has a tolerable ring to it, then yes. I'll marry you."

Chapter Eighteen

Cori poked the needle through the fabric of her embroidery and flicked a glance at her mother. Lainey ran her hand across the package lying in her lap. Her face looked drawn, as though she might choke on a sob any moment. Cori frowned. "Mama?"

"It's nothing." Mama laid the package under the Christmas tree next to another one the same shape and size. "I'll be all right."

Her papa stepped into the room and halted, giving out a slow whistle. "Look at that tree. But it isn't near as pretty as my ladies."

They both smiled up at him, but Mama held his gaze. Tears welled in her eyes. Papa's smile wilted. He held out his hands and pulled her to her feet. The rigid tension left her body as she fell into the comfort of his embrace.

He kissed her forehead and smoothed loose strands of dark hair away from her face. His eyes, from where Cori sat, looked serious, smoky. Jesilyn's eyes appeared like that sometimes, too. Cori looked away.

"If we only knew where she was, that she was all right," Mama whispered.

Cori tried to concentrate on her stitches as they moved in and out on either side of the wooden hoop.

"Shh..." Papa kissed away her mother's tears. "She's not out of God's sight."

"Yes. You're right." Mama sucked in a breath. "I just... I just miss her." She pulled away and dashed a finger across her cheek.

Cori stared at them. Where *had* Jesi gone? Didn't she realize how worried their parents would be? Cori had no worries about Jesi's ability to land on her feet. Still, would it kill her to at least send a telegram or a letter to let them know that's what she'd done?

Part of Cori -- just a small part -- almost wished Jesi would return, just to ease her mama's suffering. Yet the bigger part of her hoped she'd stay away longer still. Cori wasn't ready to forgive her. Not now, maybe not ever.

"Either He'll lead us to her, or she'll come back," Papa said matter-of-factly. "She just isn't ready to be found yet, that's all. God's working on her. He has to be."

Cori let her handwork lay limp in her lap. "Pa's right, Mama. Jesi's smart. She'll take care of herself."

"I know she's smart, and strong." Mama looked directly at Pa. "But we both know God sometimes allows us to stumble and face difficulty so we might recognize Him waiting for us with open arms. Didn't we learn that lesson ourselves, Zane?"

Papa pursed his lips and nodded. Then he braced mama's arms and gave her a loving smile. "I'm leaving for Michigan next week, right after Christmas. I have to meet a man in Escanaba about laying some new line out there once these hard times let up. Who knows? Maybe someone will have word of her. I've got to believe she must be homesick missing Christmas."

"Thank you for trying so hard."

A log tumbled in the fireplace, sending cinders dancing up the chimney. The parlor was cozy despite the snow blanketing the deep December night and the cold etching its crystal patterns on the window panes. Was Jesilyn enjoying a cozy Christmas season? Did she have a hearth to sit by and someone to share it with?

Cori's heart winced. She didn't want Jesi to be hurt or in trouble. But she also didn't want her to enjoy herself. Maybe she was indeed a little homesick.

"I think Papa's right. Jesi loves Christmas." Cori snorted. "Jesi loves getting presents, anyway. I wouldn't be at all surprised if she came strolling in on Christmas morning, acting as if she'd never left."

Mama's lips lifted in a wan smile. "Well, if she does, I'd be glad. And I bet she'll be sorry for everything that happened."

"For your sake, Mama, I'll be glad too." Cori looked up from the fire to Mama. "But I won't get my hopes up about Jesi ever being sorry. It's just not in her."

She gathered her embroidery and rose from the settee.

"Not off to bed this early, are you?" Papa asked.

"No. I think I'll write a letter."

He gave her a wry grin. "To the young Mr. Gilbert?"

"Perhaps. And don't you start teas--"

A knock on the door interrupted them.

"I'll get it." Papa turned away.

Lainey stood next to Cori. "I wonder who that could be. It's snowing out, and it's getting late."

They waited as voices entered the hall. Papa's sounded cheerful and surprised. She couldn't tell about the other voice. A few moments later, Papa returned with Jamie Gilbert, who looked flushed with cold.

Mama clasped her hands together. "Why, Jamie. What a surprise."

"Hello, Mrs. Beaumont. I hope you'll forgive me for coming here unannounced."

"We don't mind at all. I think Cori was just going up to write to you."

"Mama..."

"Well, weren't you?"

Cori ignored her. "Hello, Jamie."

"Cori." He reached to take her hand, and warmth climbed into her heart. She admired Jamie. He was a dedicated, hard-working man. He certainly was handsome, and he didn't seem at all like the sort to dally with a girl's affections. One thing she didn't need was someone who would do that. Not after Clay.

Mama gestured to the settee. "Why don't you have a seat while Zane puts away your coat, and I'll get us all something hot to drink."

"That would be wonderful. The train came in without any trouble, but getting across town with the snow coming down wasn't easy."

Jamie sat on the opposite end of the settee from Cori, and Papa engaged him in a discussion. A little while later, Mama returned with a tray of spiced cider.

"So hopefully Wisconsin can establish an effective fire control program sometime soon. With all these cutover areas, well... you know what can happen."

"Don't I ever." Papa took a cup from the tray and winked at Cori's mother. The Peshtigo Fire never seemed far from her parents' memories even though the event had happened a couple of years before Cori was born. They'd told her about the devastation. She figured there would always be images in their memories as fresh to them as though it had only just taken place.

"Tell me," Papa said. "Do you think we need to start a re-forestation program here, too? Some folks say no. They think the pine will never run out."

Jamie palmed the cup of cider and held it between his broad hands. "I think you and I know better, don't we?"

"So you're a true conservationist, then."

"I'd like to study forestry, if there was a school in the state."

"Someday, maybe you'll get the chance. But if you did, what then?"

"A lot will be going on. There's talk of building nurseries for starting seedlings, for one."

Papa grinned. "So while your pa and your uncles cut down trees, you'll be working on replanting them."

"Something like that." Jamie sipped his cider. Lowering the cup, he smiled. "But I'm a logger, too. I know how much we need those trees. I aim to make it possible for my children to continue the tradition, if I can."

Children. Cori's cheeks warmed, and she glanced down at her hands when Mama caught her eyes. Was she falling in love with Jamie Gilbert? She didn't recall blushing so easily with Clay.

Mama must have noticed. "Children, you say? So you do intend to settle down with a family then, someday -- between all your studying and working, I mean."

Now Jamie blushed. "Yes, ma'am. I hope I'll be so blessed."

Cori's heartbeat kicked up a notch.

Zane whistled. "You've got more figured out about the future than I did at your age, I'll tell you that."

"It's good to have a plan." Cori scooted forward. "You always say so, Papa."

"Sure is. But right now, I plan on getting some wood for the fire so I can sleep snug tonight." He set down his cup and rose. Shaking Jamie's hand again, he said, "Glad you came, Jamie. Christmas will be brighter with a young man in the house to keep Cori on her toes."

She rolled her eyes but couldn't hide her smile. "Papa."

He wrapped his arm around Mama. "Come on, sweetheart. You can clean up your tea things while I stoke the fire. Then we'll go upstairs and get warm."

"Zane." Mama might have thought she was past blushing, but the flush on her pretty face told on her. Jamie Gilbert laughed.

The three days leading up to Christmas flew by. Cori couldn't help wishing they'd drag on forever, since Jamie could only stay with them until New Year's. But at least they'd get to spend both holidays together. They could sit by the fire and play cards. She could listen to him tell her about his ambitions for hours. They could take walks in the snow. Or, like today, they could skate on the lake ice where snow had been cleared off the edge of the bay.

He grasped both her hands in his and twirled her in a circle, their skates cutting sharp edges into the ice. She giggled, threw her head back, and nearly lost her footing.

"Oh!"

"Don't worry, I've got you." He pulled her close in a gesture more intimate than seemed necessary to keep her from tumbling to the ice. His lips brushed dangerously close to her ear. "I thought you said you could skate."

"I can. But you keep making me laugh."

"Good skaters keep their feet under all conditions. Bad ice. Cold wind. Even while having hysterics."

Leaning against his sturdy shoulder, she smiled up at him, then pulled free. She took off down the ice. "Race you!"

She had a head start, but in seconds his skates scraped up beside her and he flew past. He turned so that he skated backwards, then reached out to grasp her as she caught up. Together, they turned into another arc on the ice. Slowly they skated to the end of the rink.

Her chest rose and fell from the exertion."I'm all out of breath."

"Me, too. Maybe it's time for hot chocolate."

A short while later, they sipped chocolate in a café, warming their hands on their mugs.

Jamie gazed out the window at the young university across the street. It was small, but promising. "So that's it."

"The university? Yes, that's it."

He glanced at her, his eyes as dark and inviting as the cocoa in their drinks.

"What? Why are you looking at me like that?"

"Because I like to."

She took a long sip from her mug, closed her eyes behind the steam, and absorbed the sweet aroma.

"Do you ever think of going there?"

"To school?" She set down her mug. "Why would I?"

"Didn't you think about it when you were with that fellow?"

"With... oh, you mean Clayton." She shook her head. "It never occurred to me to go to school. I thought that once I married Clay, I'd just be..." She shrugged. "You know... his wife."

"Seems like a great way to start over."

She gazed over at the school again and wondered for the first time what went on inside its brick-walled classrooms. When she looked back at Jamie, she caught him studying her.

"You're still staring. But now you have something else going on. I can see it churning around up there in that head of yours." *That dark, handsome head.*

"Your mother tells me that you like to teach children."

"In Sunday school? Yes, I guess that's true. I like telling them stories and helping them learn. I like to do fun, creative things with them."

"Maybe God wants you to do more than that."

She straightened her shoulders. "What do you mean?"

"Maybe you should become a teacher."

Cori leaned forward. She didn't answer right at first. Jamie's suggestion both startled and thrilled her at once. *A teacher.*

"I-I don't think I could."

"Why not? Don't they have a new teacher's training program there?"

"I just..."

"A friend of mine who teaches in Eau Claire tells me there are only two normal schools in the state." He nodded at the university across the street. "Here you have one of them being founded in your back yard."

Suddenly Jamie leaned forward, too, and cupped his big hands over hers around her mug. "You're smart, Cori. You want something more than waiting under your parents' wings for a husband to come along."

His touch sent a bolt charging through her, but in the next instant it dissolved. Had she started to think of him beyond what she should? Was he about to squelch those thoughts?

She frowned. "You barely know me. What makes you think I can handle normal school, or that I'd even want to? And what's so bad about wanting to marry?"

She flushed. That hadn't come out sounding like she'd hoped.

He squeezed her hands. "There's nothing bad about it." His dimples winked at her. "But I think you want something else besides."

He let go of her hands and leaned back. Cori tucked her fists into her lap. A million thoughts scurried through her head. She'd successfully put her failed engagement to Clay behind her. Now Jamie had her attention, so why deny his pull on her heart? He was thrilling, smart, handsome, and he seemed more concerned about her as a person than Clay had ever been. He wanted things for her, not just for himself. Now, his suggestion pricked her with yearning. Maybe she did want those things, too.

"I haven't the first idea about getting into normal school."

"It can't be that hard to figure out. Maybe we can look into it before I leave."

"Really? You'd do that?"

"Cori," he said, his gaze tender, "I'd like to help you with anything you need."

Cori believed he meant it.

On Christmas Eve, Jamie attended church with Cori, her family, and Evie. Later, at home, they caroled for Gramp, and Jamie and Papa helped Gramp manage the stairs to join them in opening their gifts. Then they all enjoyed a hearty meal of roast pork, some tarts and puddings, and more spiced cider.

For Cori, Christmas was as festive as she could remember, especially since Jamie shared it with her. But she wished her grandfather was well, and she knew her parents longed for their missing child, and that made it difficult for Cori to push thoughts of Jesilyn out of her mind.

Blown glass ornaments had lately become the rage, and Cori received one from her parents. Another one similar to it remained unopened in a package bearing Jesilyn's name.

"I have something for you," Cori said, turning her gaze from Jesi's gift and pulling another package out from under the tree. She handed it to Jamie.

He unwrapped a soft, knitted scarf.

"You made it, didn't you? Thank you." He wrapped it around his neck and grinned. The twinkling in his eyes made Cori giddy. "I needed a new one."

"I'm glad you like it."

"I didn't exactly get you a present."

"Oh, that's all right. I didn't expect anything." She flushed. She caught Mama and Papa's grins out of the corner of her eye and wished she'd waited to give him the gift privately. But that wouldn't have exactly been appropriate.

"I thought before I bought you a gift, I should do something else."

Her head came up. She was unsure what he meant. He smiled at her and then looked at the others in the room. "Mr. and Mrs. Beaumont, I can't tell you when I've had such a wonderful Christmas. I always have a great time with my da and my sister's family, of course, but I think you realize this has been special.

"You must know your family has come to mean a lot to me." His brown eyes flashed, then riveted back on Cori. "And how much your daughter has come to mean to me."

Cori sucked in her breath. Her heart hammered in her ears.

"I would like your permission to court her, if you're willing to give it."

Lightness lifted Cori, and her breath escaped. In an almost dream-like panorama, she took in the reactions of the others in the room. Gran squeezed her hands together in her lap and let a soft smile play on her lips. Was she reminded of her youth? Gramp was tired, but his tender expression included a smile that reached to his eyes. He looked over at Gran. Papa scratched his chin, but both he and Mama soon broke into a laugh.

Evie jumped from her chair by the fireplace and clapped her hands. "I hope you're going to say yes."

Jamie grinned as the chuckling continued. He reached for her hand and enveloped it.

Papa folded his arms across his chest. "I've been wondering when you'd ask."

"Taking after his father, no doubt." Gramp's eyes glinted. "A bit slow."

"Nase." Gran gasped. She leaned over and wrapped her arm around his shoulder.

"What about you, honey?" Mama asked.

Cori looked from Mama to Jamie, and then flushed, biting her lip in her smile.

"That's it, then," Papa said. He shook Jamie's hand. "I hope this is just the first Christmas of many we'll have you with us."

"I hope so, too, Mr. Beaumont."

Chapter Nineteen

Jesilyn clasped her mittened hands in her lap beneath her heavy wool coat, trapping them from their longing to fidget. Her lips didn't require the same discipline. She doubted she could have uttered more than a squeak, even if she had tried. Bundled in the sleigh between Marie and Paul, she wondered what would be longer and more unendurable: the trip to Hurley to marry Paul, or the return trip home as his wife. Both journeys seemed to stretch on, and at the same time, ended much too quickly. Soon they'd be back at the cabin, and she would begin her life as Mrs. Paul Winter. She shuddered.

"Cold?" Marie leaned into her, as though she would somehow share a little more of her body's warmth.

"Not really."

"We'll be home soon. I hope there are coals left in the fire."

"I'll have it toasty as quickly as I can," Paul said. He snapped the reins over Sarah's back and hurried her down the trail.

They rounded a final bend on the tote road and emerged in view of the logging camp. Stumps marred the clearing carved out of thick pine, balsam, birch, and a few gnarly oaks. Low-roofed shanties spewed smoke out of their chimneys. One was a bunkhouse, and another acted as the manager's headquarters. Another housed a small company storehouse. The biggest was the cookhouse, where the men gathered for their meals. The sleigh lurched over ruts and bumps as they passed the small camp. Another sixty yards past its fringe stood Paul's lone cabin.

Home.

So... permanent.

Marie pushed herself out of the sleigh as soon as Paul pulled Sarah to a halt. He jumped out, too, but turned to offer Jesi a hand.

She pulled her fingers free as soon as she gained her feet. "I'll go inside and start supper."

"Jesi."

The firm way he said her name halted her.

"Relax."

She frowned, even after his lips lifted in a small smile. Then slowly, she nodded and turned to go inside.

Relax? How could she relax? She'd just gotten married. Not to Clay, but to a man whom, though he'd proven to be her friend and had a truly good heart, she didn't even love. She hurried to the kitchen stove, lifted the lid, and stirred the ashes, relieved that a few embers still glowed with life. She added several sticks of wood and hurried to pump some water. Once she set the kettle on the stove, she finally took off her coat. Paul busied himself stoking the fireplace and going back outside for more wood. Marie went into her room and emerged again in her old dress and apron.

"You'd better slip an apron on if you're going to stay in that lovely dress."

Jesi glanced down. She loved the new dress Marie had sewn for her wedding. Instead of a typical wedding gown, it was more an elegant tea dress she would be able to wear on many Sundays to come. Marie had chosen deep forest green material and sewn in Watteau pleats that hung down loosely from the back of Jesi's belted waist. Marie had trimmed the yoke with just enough lace to ornament it, and added leg 'o mutton sleeves that made the garment even more stylish. Jesi had never lacked for nice things, but she didn't know when she'd last appreciated such a simple act as Marie's so much.

"I'll put one on."

Marie pulled left-over meat pie from the icebox. "I have to admit, I'm really going to miss being here with the two of you. I've not been away from Paul, that's true. But I'm especially going to miss being here now that I have a new sister."

New sister. Such an addition didn't seem real. *This marriage isn't real. It's on a piece of paper, but I'm Paul's wife in name only.*

"I'll be back to visit often enough, and you'll have to come see me when I'm settled."

"I'll look forward to that a great deal," Jesi said.

They ate their evening meal, and then Jesi continued her normal evening routine. Paul didn't treat her any differently than he had before they were married. Maybe what he'd said was true. Maybe he wouldn't expect anything from her, and they could carry on as though nothing had changed between them.

Finally bedtime arrived. Jesi rose from her chair by the fire and stepped away. She halted. Paul lifted his head from his book.

"Everything all right?

"I'm to still sleep in my room?"

The silence that followed wasn't lengthy, but it balanced on a tenuous thread between them for far too long to suit Jesi. Paul set aside his book and stood. He held out his hand. She stared at it. So this was it, then.

She put her hand in his. His palm was warm and slightly rough, and in a confusing way that sent a reassuring rush up her spine.

He tugged on her hand, and she followed him. He walked her to her bedroom door.

"If I had courted you properly, I'd have at least walked you home." He squeezed her fingers. "Goodnight."

"Goodnight." His smile put her at ease. Once he released her hand, she slipped into her bedroom and closed the door, then undressed in the dark and crawled into the bed.

*****

Paul woke up praying, but his thoughts jumbled in every direction. *So much to understand, God, starting with whether I was wrong in what I thought You wanted me to do. I have to be honest, Father. I don't regret it. Jesi's my wife, and I'm glad of it. I think I've been waiting for the one You have for me for a long time. I just never expected she'd come along like this. But Lord God, what about her? I don't think she's looking at our marriage the way I am.*

His mind spun. The whole impact of having married Jesi washed over him like the pre-dawn light filtering slowly into his room. He had a wife.

Suddenly, out of the recoils of his memory, Imogene Gillette's face crept in. Beautiful Imogene. A little bit spoiled, but she did love the Lord. If only she'd loved Paul as much. They'd be serving God together now.

He flipped back the covers and got out of bed. Retrieving a small wooden box from the bottom drawer of his dresser, he sat back down and lifted the lid. A daguerreotype of his parents, some cuff links, a medal he'd won in school, and a few other mementos filled the box. Along with three letters. He pulled them out and opened them, spreading them on the bed and re-reading them, beginning with the first one:

> *Dear Paul,*
> *I've thought about it a great deal it, and I've prayed about it, too. I just don't think I could live so far away from bigger towns and people...*

The second one read:

> *Dear Paul,*
> *Part of me will always love you, but what you are asking is simply too much. I have family here, and friends. I think its best we let it go. I've gotten good advice from my friends. It's made me think much about the reality of things...*

And the last one:

> *Dear Paul,*
> *Please stop writing to me. I must tell you outright that I have no intention of ever moving so far. I've asked God to help me get over you, and I think He has. You remember George Weinhert...*

Paul was a married man now, and in all likelihood, Imogene was married, too. He should let the letters go. Conviction burned him. He set them aside for the fire.

The house lay quiet, but the smell of bacon frying seeped into his room. Marie would leave them tomorrow. She must be up already, full of nervous energy.

Today was Sunday, the day he'd reintroduce Jesi to the men in the camp who'd come for service. Many of them still looked at her with questions in their eyes. Figuring he knew the nature of some of those questions, he'd like to blacken those eyes. But he'd settle with making it clear that he was now her protector. Her husband.

Paul dressed hurriedly. *Husband. I like the sound of that.*

He'd have to endure a bit of back-slapping, no doubt. And they would embarrass Jesi, probably. My, she was pretty when she blushed. All that coppery hair framed her pink cheeks like a halo.

Paul smiled as he slipped his suspenders up over his shoulders. Whistling softly, he left the room with the letters for the fire in his hand.

"Mmm. Smells good. You're up before the chickens today."

Jesi turned from standing near the table and graced him with a smile.

"Oh. I thought you were Marie." He tucked Imogene's letters into his back pocket.

"She's still sleeping. I think she had a hard time falling asleep last night. Thinking about her move, I bet."

"You're probably right."

"Paul." Jesi stilled her busyness. She chewed her lip. "Do you think the men will wonder... I mean, do you think they'll find it strange, or... or anything... about your marrying me? I don't want you to suffer embarrassment on my behalf.

"I don't see how that would be possible." He looked at her, but her eyes refused to steady on his. "I didn't have to marry you, Jesi. Nor you, I. We chose this course, and I'm not sorry for an instant -- no matter what any of the men may think or say. I hope you believe me when I tell you that."

"But your ministry--"

"*Our* ministry."

She lifted her chin.

Paul grinned then shrugged. "You're my wife, Jesi Winter. I intend to take care of you, to protect you, and to include you in everything I do." He stepped closer, grateful she didn't back away. He reached up and caressed her shoulder tenderly. "To stand by you no matter what."

Marie stepped out of her bedroom, and Paul dropped his hand. Marie squared her shoulders and smiled. "Good morning."

*****

"Are you sure you have everything?" Paul asked.

Marie glanced at the carpetbag at her feet on the train platform and shrugged. "Well, if I don't, it's too late to worry about it now. My train boards in five minutes."

"We'll make a trip over in early spring, so if you think of anything important, send a letter and we'll bring it then.

Marie tilted her head and grinned. "*We*. I love the sound of that."

Paul rolled his eyes, but wallowed in the good feeling inside. "I'm not too certain Jesi thinks in terms of *we* just yet."

"Could've fooled me from the way you two looked at each other yesterday morning."

"That's wishful thinking on your part."

"I don't have to wish. I'm praying."

The train whistle blew, and the conductor called out for passengers to board. Paul grew serious. He hugged Marie. "Thank you for your prayers, sis. I covet every one of them."

"And I, yours." She loosened herself from his embrace and hoisted the bag, handing it off to a porter. "I'd better get on. Give Jesi one last hug for me."

"If she'll let me."

Marie smiled and squeezed his arm. Hitching up her long skirt, she boarded the train, and Paul watched her pass by the windows until she found her seat. He waved when she blew him a kiss. Minutes later, the train chugged away from the depot.

Paul sighed and turned to leave. How different things would be now, without Marie to encourage and cajole him. Would Jesilyn ever feel at ease enough with him to do those sorts of things?

She had decided not to come along to the station. She'd said it would be good for Paul and Marie to say their goodbyes together. And since it was so cold outside, Paul had thought it a good idea that she stay at home. But in truth, he wondered if she just wanted to avoid the long, quiet ride home with him alone. Sometimes she seemed to need to be by herself.

He was about to climb into the wagon he'd borrowed from Charlie Hanke to haul Marie's luggage when a hand grasped his shoulder. He turned, surprised to see a man with familiar gray-blue eyes. Familiar, but Paul's memory of the man was vague.

"Hello. Remember me?"

In a burst, the memory came back to him. He gave the man a brisk handshake. "Sure I do. You're the fellow who was good enough to make sure I didn't get run over in the street that day last summer."

"Yes, sir. Zane Beaumont."

Paul's heart lurched. He'd forgotten the man's name, and now the reminder slammed into his gut like a fist. And the man's eyes... he knew those eyes. They belonged to Jesilyn. Paul's mouth worked, and he blinked, trying to garner his thoughts.

"Good to meet you again, Mr. Beaumont. My name's Paul Winter, in case you forgot."

"I remember. So we meet again." The man chuckled. "It's good to see you're all in one piece and staying out of trouble."

"Yes, well... all in one piece, at least." Paul dipped his head. "What brings you back to Hurley?"

"I'm actually on my way to Escanaba. Rail business."

"Oh, yes. How is that these days? Miners here are barely keeping afloat. Logs are moving out slowly, too."

"Everybody's suffering. We're doing our best to keep as many men working as we can. How about you? Aren't tough times good for the preaching business?"

"You would think so, wouldn't you?" Paul shook his head at Zane's tongue-in-cheek question. "But seems they're better for the tavern business."

"People sometimes don't realize when they've hit bottom. By nature, they fight and cling and hang on, hoping they haven't really arrived there yet, or that they can do something, anything, really, to avoid turning to God for help."

Paul thought of Jesilyn. Is that what had happened to her? In leaving her distant home and this relative, who seemed like a decent fellow, had she refused God's help?

Zane Beaumont must be her father. The resemblance was remarkable. The more Paul studied him, the more the man reminded Paul of Jesi. Not just because of his eyes; it was his hair, too, although Mr. Beaumont's had faded. Paul recognized the lift of her smile, the set of her jaw. Her nose must be her mother's, and those full lips...

He shook himself. "Uh... so you're waiting for the next train?"

"Yes, that's right. I've got another hour or so if it runs on time."

Paul laughed. Funny, to hear a railroad man joking about the train schedule. "I'm in no hurry. Can I buy you a cup of coffee and some pie while you wait?"

"I sure wouldn't mind taking you up on that. What kind of man can pass up pie?"

Like father, like daughter.

"You sure I won't keep you from anything?" Zane asked.

Paul shook his head. Jesi probably wouldn't miss him if he stayed in town an extra hour. "No, I don't have anything pressing."

Ten minutes later, they stood inside Lulu's café, shrugging out of their heavy wool coats. A waitress brought them two pieces of cherry pie once they sat down.

Zane shook his napkin to open it. "Now, that looks good."

"Well, I can tell you from experience that it tastes as good as it looks. Dig in."

"So... tell me more about yourself. Do you have a place here in town?"

"No. I can't remember what I told you that day. I'm a chaplain out at one of the camps."

"Yes, yes. Now I remember."

"I have my own cabin. Sometimes I trail ride up to some of the further camps and preach there, too. This winter, though, I've stayed pretty close to home." Paul sipped on his coffee and scooped up another big bite of pie.

"Must be a lonely job sometimes."

He shrugged. "Oh, it's not too bad. I came up here a few years back from down around Sheboygan. I don't regret it. My sister came along, too."

"Oh, well, that's nice."

"She's why I'm in town today. I just put her on the train bound for Ashland. She's going there to work in the hospital."

"Ah, so you won't be seeing her so often."

"Right." *But I'm not alone. I have your daughter with me.* Part of him wanted to tell as much to this man. Surely he must be anxious to know the whereabouts of his child. But the stronger part of Paul would never betray Jesi that way. Still, what should he do?

"Sounds like you and your sister must be close."

"We haven't been apart much, that's for sure. She's a great encourager, but of course, she has to follow her own dreams, too."

Zane set down his fork and slowly, methodically wiped his fingers on a checked napkin. "Yes, dreams are important, as long as you don't get lost in them."

"Sir?"

"Call me Zane."

"I'm sorry, Zane, I don't follow."

"Dreams are gifts from God, wouldn't you agree?"

"Absolutely. I'm always telling... I always say God gives us desires as a way to lead us into His greater plan for our lives. That's part of the reason why I'm here in Hurley."

"Yes. But don't you think sometimes we get our dreams out of focus, and they can swallow us up?"

Paul thought about what Jesi's pa had said. He didn't think he'd understand if he didn't know about the man's situation with his daughter. Is that what Jesilyn's dreams had done, her dream to steal away her sister's betrothed? Could that even be called a dream? Or was Zane speaking of himself?

"I think I might know what you mean."

"At any rate, it's good about you and your sister. Seems God has set you both on a course worth following."

"Indeed He has." Paul dropped his eyes to his cup and lifted it to his lips. "And quite a course it's turning out to be."

"My brother and I were close like that. My wife and her brothers, too. My two girls, on the other hand... they used to be close, but then they had a rift. Now I wonder if things will ever be the way they once were."

Paul set his cup down and sat forward. Sounded as if Jesi had a big family.

"It was bad, the rift between your girls? Maybe they'll outgrow it."

"My girls are -- well -- they're grown. They're twins, see."

Paul pushed back his plate and rested his elbows on the table. He clasped his hands to keep from shaking. *Jesi is a twin?* Dear God. And she had tried to trick her sister's betrothed... Paul could see it in his mind's eye. She'd tried to steal her sister's future husband, and how much easier would such a task be for an identical twin?

"Twins?"

"Yes. Beautiful girls, my two roses." Zane smiled. "Forgive me for sounding like a father. My wife tends roses, and I've always called them that."

"I can understand."

"They're twins, but different on the inside. They had a falling out, and now one of them has run off."

"Run away?"

Zane nodded. "My Jesilyn. She... uh, I don't even know how to tell it. She came between her sister Corianne and Cori's fiancé. They used to think so much alike as youngsters, and share so many things. Seems that in this case, they both fell for the same fella."

Paul nodded. He could clearly imagine it, though it sent a sharp pang through him to think of Jesi caring so much for another man.

Zane shook his head. "Sad thing is, not only have I looked all over God's green earth to tfind her without success, Cori hasn't forgiven her. I'm afraid she intends to hang on to her bitterness, and I'm sorely afraid of what's become of my Jesi. I don't think she'll come home on her own." Zane gave a humorless chuckle. "Jesi and I, well... we're alike."

"How's that, if I may ask?"

"We're both stubborn."

Paul leaned back as Zane cut the remnant of his pie crust in two. He thought over the deluge of information while Zane cleaned his plate, wondering how he could offer comfort without telling on Jesi.

"Zane, you might think of me as a young preacher who's too zealous for his own good, but I'm going to assure you right now that God is taking care of your girl. He's keeping her safe and protected. One day she'll find her way home to you again. I trust that. Will you?"

"Seems I tell Lainey that all the time. Lainey's my wife. But it isn't always easy to believe that myself. I do believe I have the compassion of a young preacher, though, who'll not let go of praying for me and my girls. Am I right?"

"On that, you have my word." Paul reached across the table and grasped Zane's hand in a handshake he hoped conveyed every bit of promise he could make to a man he hoped to call *father* someday.

"Zane, if you don't mind, I'd like to write to you sometime, just to see how things are going with you and your family."

"That's thoughtful of you. And if you ever see a gal with long red hair and light blue eyes who's on the tall side, try and talk to her for me, and tell her she can come home. We'll gladly send money. Tell her her mama misses her. Oh, and that her grandpa's still with us."

"All right. You can be sure I'll do that -- should I see her." He would tell her all those things, the moment he got home. He felt hot, angry that he should be put in such a position to withhold the truth from her father. At the same time, however, he felt relief. Relief that God had not only seen fit to have him meet Zane Beaumont again today, but had also orchestrated Paul and Jesi's meeting, as well. If he'd had any doubts before about God's will in his marrying Jesi, meeting Zane had washed every last one of them away. The peace that thought brought rushed over him like a wave. Then one sudden thought broke the wave as it crashed on the shore of his heart.

He looked again at Zane. "I have one question. What about the fellow in the middle of all this? Did he and your other daughter work things out?"

"No." Zane frowned. "Matter of fact, she sent him off. Except for once, when he came back looking for a second chance, we haven't seen him. I sometimes worry he's gone off in search of Jesi himself. We don't really know how much he cared about her. I didn't think he cared too greatly, because his mind was still set on marrying Cori. But the fact that he did turn to Jesi, and had been seeing her, keeping it secret, makes me wonder if he wasn't pretty confused about his feelings.

"Except for the bitterness Cori seems to want to hang onto, she's turned her life in another direction. You mentioned dreams before." Zane laughed quietly. "Well, seems her dream now is to become a teacher. Lainey and I are proud of her for looking for something more." He shrugged. "And it doesn't hurt that a friend of the family, a young fella named James, also wants her to follow that dream. He's asked to court her, and she's agreed."

"Well, that's good news."

"Indeed it is. I try to stay focused on those kinds of things. But again, Paul, thank you for your prayers -- and for keeping a close eye out for Jesi. Her grandpa and her uncles are all loggers. I wouldn't be a bit surprised if she thought about looking for work in a town like Hurley, or even as a cook's helper in a camp somewhere. It'd be trouble for a girl, but Jesilyn wouldn't be the type to let that stop her."

"No, doesn't sound like she would."

Paul set money on the table for the pie, and they rose to leave.

"Thanks again for the pie and conversation. I'll walk back to the depot. I've got a few minutes to spare, and I need to stretch my legs before I get back on another train."

They headed out the door and shook hands one last time. As Zane Beaumont walked away, Paul thought again about all that had happened to the Beaumont family and wondered just what he'd say to his young wife when he got home.

Chapter Twenty

Jesi swept the floor where ashes had blown out from the fireplace. She was running out of things to do. She'd baked bread, gotten supper simmering on the stove, cleaned up the cabin, and stoked both fires. She'd read a little, and now the sun dipped close to disappearing. In another twenty minutes it would be dark. Night came on so suddenly in the winter months.

She thought about napping until Paul returned, but restless energy bound her. She wondered what it would be like to sit with him at the supper table tonight without Marie's presence. And while reading in the evening, or buttoning up the cabin at night. Would he walk her to her room like he had the past two nights?

Her gaze flicked toward his open bedroom door. She hadn't been inside the room since the day he'd moved back in from the woodshed. She could at least sweep the floor clean for him.

"It's not as though I'm trespassing," she said to herself, her voice breaking the silence.

She walked inside purposely, averting her eyes from his things as she swept. But soon her gaze fell on several small things: the pocket watch on his dresser he'd forgotten to take with him today, a pair of wool socks hanging over the footboard of his bed, the blankets askew since he hadn't had time to make up his bed this morning. His oil lamp needed refilling. She should see to that, too, and fill the others in the cabin as well.

After sweeping, she set the broom aside and looked again at the bed. She would just make it up for him, so it would be comfortable for him to crawl into tonight after the long, cold trek to Hurley.

No, that was too personal. She turned away, but then thought better of it. What did it matter? She strode over to make the bed. Lifting the blankets and shaking them over the mattress, she inhaled his scent. He always smelled like wood shavings and soap -- except for the times he'd worked hard outdoors. Then he smelled like wood shavings and sweat. Even then, it wasn't a bad smell. He was a man, and a man should smell like a man sometimes, after all.

She shook her head and hurried in her task. What in the world was she doing, thinking about the way Paul smelled?

She tucked the blankets around the foot of the bed and smoothed the top. Turning to go, she noticed that a wrinkled paper that had lain on the dresser beside his watch had drifted to the floor, probably from when she'd created a draft tossing the blankets onto the bed. She picked it up and hurried to replace it, but made the error of glancing at it first.

Dear Paul...

Feminine script.

Unable to help herself, she read the letter signed, *Ever Fondly, Imogene.*

She moved closer to the fading light falling through the window and read the other two letters folded with it. Paul had been spurned.

Clearly he'd asked *Imogene* to marry him, and she had said yes. Then he'd asked her to come to Hurley, and she had refused. What kind of foolish girl had she been, to turn him away?

Her heart caught. *The same kind of foolish girl I am, not to embrace a wonderful man like Paul. I should be glad Imogene left him. I should be glad I belong to him now. Still...*

She placed the letters back on the dresser and left the room to check on dinner, wondering about Paul and how he must have loved Imogene. He certainly must have given her his heart, because he'd saved her letters all this time, no doubt hoping she'd eventually change her mind. Why else would he keep such hurtful things in his possession? He'd taken them out to read them again. Was he still pining for Imogene? Did he need to remind himself she'd rejected him, just so he wouldn't regret marrying Jesi? She frowned. That was likely.

Would she keep such letters from Clay, knowing that each time she read his words an arrow would pierce her heart again?

Yet each time she had the slightest thought about their furious relationship, it hurt and angered her. Most times it even repulsed her, though now and again she longed for the sweet moments she chose to remember -- moments she'd mostly imagined, it seemed, since he'd kept on pretending to himself that she was Cori.

Jesilyn stirred the stew on the stove, so lost in reflections about her own past and the one she'd discovered of Paul's that she didn't hear the wagon come into the yard. Suddenly the door latch lifted, and Paul came in.

Jesi jumped and dropped the spoon onto the stovetop, where the drippings hissed.

"Sorry. Didn't mean to startle you," he said.

She dipped a rag into a tub of water and hurried to wipe off the mess, careful not to touch her fingers on the hot cast iron surface of the stove. "It's all right. I was daydreaming and didn't hear you drive up. Did you already unhitch Sarah and take her over to the barn?"

"I did." Paul shed his coat and came into the corner kitchen. "My, you really must've been lost in thought."

Her cheeks warmed, and she wasn't sure if it was because she was embarrassed by being so fuddle-headed, even though it didn't really bother her all that much, or because Paul stood so near her in the small kitchen. His shoulder brushed hers as he leaned over the stove to take a whiff of the stew.

"So glad I'm not going to go hungry with Marie gone." His eyes sparkled as he grinned at her, and she warmed even more.

She moved away and grabbed their plates. "It's all ready. You must be starved. I'll serve you some if you want to sit down."

"Actually, I'm hungry, but not starved. I stopped at Lulu's and had a piece of pie with an acquaintance today."

"Oh? Someone I've met?"

"I'd say so."

She glanced at him then ladled his stew. "Are you going to tell me who it was?"

"I'm thinking about it."

That made her nervous, but no, he couldn't be talking about any of the people she'd met in Hurley. He wouldn't have pie with any of Maisey's customers.

"Was it that man from the social? Mr. Babcock?" She had met a few people at the social they'd attended between the holidays. Not many of them stood out in her mind as Paul's friends. She'd been glad when the whole event was over. She'd helped Marie with her end of the preparations, and had attended dutifully. But being around Hurley's townsfolk always made her nervous. She wondered if she would ever stop feeling that way. How many of them had she begged for a job? How many had she passed in the street, dressed in Maisey's bawdy dress? How many had she seen going into one of the many bars and brothels on Silver Street? How many sterling citizens of Hurley were secretly responsible for lending credence to the town's coarse reputation for debauchery?

Perhaps she was harsh in her judgment. Good, decent people lived in the town, too. Paul and Marie had both assured her of that, and Charlie Hanke and his girls proved him right. Still, her past experiences clouded her outlook. Perhaps months or even years from now, she'd be free enough of her own black memories to enjoy a holiday social.

"No. Not Babcock. I did hear he's been laid off, though. I'll have to pay him a call and see how he's making do."

Paul took the plate of stew, but rather than sitting in his usual chair, he leaned against the work table. She faced him and folded her arms.

"Well, I guess I have no idea. Who was it?"

"A railroad man I met last fall right around the same time I met you."

"Oh." Jesi frowned. She didn't remember meeting any railroad men who knew Paul.

He forked a piece of meat. "Yes. He's from clear over in Superior."

Jesi's heart dropped into her toes. Surely he couldn't mean... no, that wasn't possible. He'd never met her father. Had to be someone else.

"I can't imagine who it might be. Are you sure I know him?"

"He talked about you."

"Did he?" *Please God, don't let it be one of Maisey's customers.*

"He's worried about you."

Jesi folded her arms and braced herself. She pinched her upper arms, telling herself that Paul couldn't be getting at what she feared he was getting at. Not a customer of Maisey's, but...

"I had pie with your father, Jesi." Paul said it and slowly set his plate on the work table.

He looked ready to step forward and catch her if she fainted. She almost felt as if he might need to grab her. She dropped her arms to her sides and turned away. "So you told him."

"No, I didn't."

"I see." He hadn't? She took a breath and wondered where this would lead. But she couldn't look at him. "How... how did you meet?"

"I met him in town last fall at the end of a rather bad day. Today he was at the depot, waiting for a train. Marie's train had left, and I was about to go, too. But he was there, and he recognized me. Our first meeting had been so brief, and truth be told, I was a bit of a mess. I didn't remember his name -- or at least it never came to mind when I learned yours. Beaumont. Zane Beaumont."

"Yes." Air rushed out of her lungs. "That's him."

"He sure does love you, Jesi."

She nodded. There was no use denying it, and why should she? "I know."

"Why would you run away when you know your parents love you no matter what?"

She shrugged.

"Jesi?"

"I don't know."

His hand fell on her shoulder, and he turned her to face him. "What do you mean, you don't know?"

"I just had to." His touch disconcerted her. Her eyes burned. "I-I told you what happened. I couldn't stay. Don't you understand? I fell in love with a man I couldn't have. Do you think I could stay there and endure my sister's hatred, not to mention Clay Dalton's scorn? And when they married and started a family, you think I could bear that? You *must* know something of that yourself, Paul." She clamped a hand over her mouth, then pushed her tears back into her hair.

He stared at her, a dumbstruck expression on his face, then quickly shook it off. "Jesilyn, I'm sorry for what happened to you. I'm even sorrier such a thing *could* happen. But your parents love you, and they're worried about you. You should at least write them and tell them where you are and that you're okay."

"But they'll want me to come home."

He stepped closer, and just like in his room, she smelled soap and wood shavings and all the other nuances that livened him to her.

"Jesi, you may never love me, and we may never come together, but I am not going to ever forget for one single moment that you are my wife. No one is going to take you home. *This* is your home for as long as I'm alive and living here."

She opened her teary eyes wide and stared at him. He'd said it so matter-of-factly, with no hesitation or side-stepping around the obvious. They were married, but they hadn't come together, and she didn't love him. *But he didn't say he doesn't love me...*

Was it possible Paul cared about her that way? What was that kind of love like, anyway? Did she even know?

"I've never known anyone like you, except for my father, of course." She thought of Paul's letters. "Aren't you afraid you'll get tired of this arrangement? Don't you worry about falling in love -- I mean *really* falling in love with some other girl -- and realizing you made a big mistake in marrying me?"

His look was so intent it would have unsettled her if she didn't trust him so. *I trust Paul.* The discovery stunned her by its depth.

"No. I'm not afraid of any such thing." He held her gaze, and she didn't flinch when he reached out and took her hand. "Come sit down. Eat your stew. Then I want you to tell me all about your family."

"All right."

Allowing herself a new freedom that came with trusting him, she took her plate to the table.

*****

Something strange had happened in the last few minutes. The protection Paul felt for Jesi surged and roared through him. His mind told him to hold back, but then collided with all those feelings in his heart. His arms ached to hold her, to love her.

I'm in love with her. I love my wife.

What would she think if she knew? She'd likely run back to Superior. Rather than worry about being forced home, she'd turn tail and head there herself if she realized he'd deceived both of them by wanting more.

He thought of his own words from moments ago. *You may never love me.* Oh, they stung. She might never, especially since she obviously still felt something for Clay Dalton. *I'd like to meet him in the street and...*

He chewed the piece of meat in his stew with greater vigor.

"Are you angry with me?"

His head jerked up.

"You aren't mad, are you?"

"'Course not. Not at you, anyway."

"But you're mad?"

He shook his head. "No. It's nothing. Tell me more about your father."

"He's worked for the railroad my whole life. He and my mother came to Superior right before Cori and I were born. He learned railroading in the army."

"I can see a lot of you in your father. You have his eyes."

She settled her gaze on him, and he liked the way those eyes shone. He was glad she didn't avert them now.

"My mother's eyes are deep blue. Corianne's look like hers. It's really about the only way to tell us apart, though some folks don't notice it for a while."

"I'll have to keep that in mind when you're both in the same room."

Jesi snorted. "You're hoping for a lot. I don't expect my sister and I will be in the same room for a long time to come. Maybe never."

"Is your father the one you both get your stubbornness from?"

Her chin jerked up and her eyebrows lifted. "You think I'm stubborn?"

He grinned at her. "I've only known you a few months, but I think the record has been established."

"You're assuming Cori's stubborn."

"You said your eyes are the only way to tell you apart. You must have similar personalities."

Jesi shrugged. "That depends. Some of my family might say Cori is the compliant one, the one with less temper. But that's only how she is on the outside. See, I don't believe in being one person on the outside and someone else on the inside."

"You don't?"

She flushed. Pink infused her neck and cheeks, and Paul might have felt bad for pointing out the flaw in what she'd just said, but he couldn't feel bad about how pretty she looked when she was embarrassed.

"I guess you've got me there. But I wear my opinions pretty much out in the open."

"Oh? Give me an example."

"All right. I think you don't have more men coming to church on Sunday because you're too nice. You talk to them about their spiritual lives, but you're so nice about it, they don't feel bad stepping on your toes and ignoring you."

He prickled, but listened.

"It would be nice to hear you tell them they'd better start paying attention to their eternal souls. It would be nice to hear you hassle them just a little bit. Don't let them get by with treating you like a no-backbone preacher boy."

Paul scowled. "I guess you do have an opinion, don't you?"

"Yes." She blushed again. "I warned you."

"Makes me sorry for your poor mother."

"Mama? Why, she's of a pretty sound mind herself. She practically ran away from home when she was my age, too."

"Practically?"

"Well, she had my grandma and grandpa's blessing, but she almost got herself killed in the Peshtigo Fire."

He studied her. She was animated now, first resting the heels of her hands against the edge of the table, then moving those pretty hands about.

"She met my pa and my uncle Kelly, who got killed. She did all sorts of things all because she got her mind set on them."

"So you really get that stubborn streak from her."

She folded her arms and jerked up her chin. "Maybe. Just don't go getting all kinds of ideas about how sweet it's going to be to have me and my sister and my ma all in the same room again."

"Well, in God's time we'll worry about that. After you have time to write to them and to pray about it -- a lot."

"What makes you think I'll do either?"

Paul stood up and rested his fists on the table. He bore her a look. "Because I said so."

"You say so, and you think I'm going to listen?"

"Yes, I said so." He might have thought she was really being argumentative, but a gleam in her eye egged him on to tease her. "I'm your husband, so you have to do what I say."

"Really?" Jesi squeezed her napkin into a ball and threw it at his chest. "Well, that's what I say to that."

She stood and faced him, their half-eaten stew on the small space of table between them.

"I don't think I can let that go."

"Oh? And what do you intend to do about it?"

Paul straightened and walked slowly around the table. Jesi backed away. As he rounded the corner toward her, she turned and squealed. He ran after her. She was quick, dodging him in the small cabin, running around the table again and rushing to the door. Before he could grab her, she lifted the latch and leapt out into the snow. She hiked up her dress and headed down the path, but he gained on her, catching her at last as she plummeted into the deeper snow.

He grabbed her waist, pulled her to him, and tickled her. She screamed and giggled, writhing for freedom.

"There now. What do you think of that?" He kept tickling her until she collapsed against him in defeat. Suddenly they stood still and silent in the cold, the fog of their panting breaths wrapping around them in the waning daylight.

Her head fell back, and she stared at him with those crystal eyes of hers. Her smile relaxed. He didn't want to let her go, but slowly he loosened his hold, and she backed out of his grasp.

She hugged herself. "Brrr."

"We'd better go back inside before you catch cold."

She nodded and turned away, trudging through the snow and back onto the path. Paul followed, his gaze on the slender curve of her waist, still holding her in his thoughts.

Chapter Twenty-One

Under Jesi's watchful eye, widower Charlie Hanke's two girls, Rosie and Charlotte, combined the shortening and flour for pie crusts into each of their bowls.

"Mix it with your fork until it turns into a nice, crumbly texture," Jesi said. "Then we'll add the other ingredients."

Rosie was only twelve, almost three years younger than Charlotte, who'd turn fifteen in April. She'd be turning heads soon, too. She was a sweet, lovely girl. Jesi thought it was too bad she had to spend her days out here in the backwoods, without any schooling or social life that benefited other girls her age.

Her father seemed to regret it, too. But he couldn't haul the girls into Hurley for school and still work his job. These days, a job was a valuable thing. He might not find another.

Jesi decided she could at least take the girls under her wing and help them learn a few womanly skills -- such as she had to share. While she still found her seamstress skills lacking, she really did have a natural penchant for cooking. And the girls were already pretty good with a needle anyway, so that didn't worry her.

Her attention to them wasn't totally for their benefit, however. She enjoyed their company. She'd come to realize how terribly she missed womanly companionship. With Marie gone, she only heard Paul's or Cookee's or some other fellow's voice during the dark winter days. Who'd have thought how dreadfully she'd miss the camaraderie of women? In Superior, she'd only thought of Clay's company.

"Don't play with the dough too long. That will make your crust tough. Watch me."

Jesi turned her pie crust onto the table's wooden surface and kneaded the pliant dough. "See? It's a little sticky, but that's okay. Our crusts will be nice and flaky."

"Mine's too thick to squeeze," Rosie said.

"It's just that you're not strong enough. Here, I'll help you."

"How's mine?" Charlotte asked.

"Lovely. You can flour the table and grease your pan. Won't your papa be surprised when you bring him home a pumpkin pie?"

Rosie giggled and squealed. "He'll eat the whole thing."

Half an hour later, while the pies baked, Jesi sat by the fireplace with the girls and read to them out of one of Paul's books. She'd read *The Five Little Peppers* before, but had fun doing it aloud, sharing the tale with Rosie and Charlotte.

"It's so romantic. That silly Joel gets into so much mischief. But I'm glad that Polly and Jasper--"

Paul's bedroom door clicked open, and he leaned against the door frame. "What's going on in here? What's that smell?"

"We made pumpkin pies." Rosie leapt up from her chair. "Three of them. Two for our papa, and one for you."

Paul rubbed his hands together. "Sounds like my kind of dinner."

"It's dessert."

"Don't you ever eat pies for dinner at your house?" he teased.

"We have to eat our meat and vegetables first."

"Pumpkin is sort of a vegetable, isn't it?"

"Actually, it's a berry," Jesi said.

"Yes, Preacher," Charlotte said. "That's why it makes such good pie."

"I see." He sauntered over to them. "Well, it still sounds like a good supper to me."

"Mrs. Winter is making chicken and dumplings for your supper. She said so. That means your pie will have to wait. 'Sides, it'll be too hot to cut, won't it, Mrs. Winter?"

Jesi laughed. "Yes. And remember, we're friends. You can call me Jesi."

Charlotte blushed.

"How about when those pies are done, Jesi and I walk you home before it gets dark?"

Rosie moaned. "I wish we could stay."

Paul chuckled. "It's good to know that if I ever have to be gone for the night, I can count on you two girls to come keep Jesi company."

"That would be fun," Charlotte said, and Jesi nodded in agreement.

"Maybe we'll have to chase the preacher off sometime, just to do it," she said.

Rosie clapped.

"We'd better check our pies."

After the pies were done, Paul carried them while he and Jesi walked the girls back across the lumber camp to their cabin.

Jesi hugged them each goodbye at their door. "If you come back next Saturday, we'll make something else."

"Papa, can we?" Charlotte asked.

Charlie chuckled. "Long as you keep bringing home goodies for your pa."

About an hour of daylight remained. With winter waning, the sun stayed up a little bit later, just long enough to remind them the cold wouldn't last forever. A breeze blew, hinting at a coming thaw. Jesilyn and Paul started back down the trail toward home.

"Glad the weather's warming up," she said. "Can hardly believe March is upon us."

"I'll be glad for spring. Maybe things will look up for the mines and jobs. Some of the men will find work on farms."

"That will be good for them."

He cast her a glance. "Are you cold?"

"Not really. It's a nice evening."

"Would you care to go on a little horseback ride?"

She smiled at him. All the talk about her family and her past made smiling at Paul easy these days. The honesty felt good. She'd hardly remembered how this cleanness felt.

"Sounds nice."

"Come on." He reached for her hand and tucked it in the crook of his arm, as though touching her were natural. Didn't it feel so? Did Paul take notice of such things?

"I hope Sarah doesn't mind doing double duty."

"She'll love the attention, just like most females."

She gave him a little shove, but didn't let go of his arm, and he laughed. A nice sound.

At the camp barn, Paul saddled Sarah and climbed up. He reached for Jesi's hand and gave her the stirrup, then hoisted her up behind him. "Are you comfortable?"

She adjusted her weight and her long skirt so that it wrapped close to her legs, though she straddled the horse. She grasped his coat.

"Better hang on. The snow's still deep, and the ride could get bumpy."

She put her arms around him, feeling the shape of him through his wool coat -- his firm, narrow waist, and his muscles flexing in response to the horse's movements. She clenched her arms tight and squeezed the wool in her fists. "I'm hanging on."

"Okay."

They passed through camp, heading down the tote road at a slow walk. Lights burned in the cook house where a couple of men wandered in for their evening meal. Paul and Jesi waved, and the men waved back.

"Lookin' cozy, Preacher!" a lumberjack called.

Paul gave a laugh and waved him off. Jesi cleared her throat, and her body reacted by settling against Paul's back. One of his big gloved hands covered hers, holding her arms to his waist.

His voice sounded deep and comforting in the winter air. "I hope you don't mind their teasing."

"We've only been wed for a short time. They've a right to it."

"I'm glad it doesn't upset you."

"Why should it?"

He shrugged. "It shouldn't, I guess. But I thought it might."

"We're married. I guess only you and I know it's only for looks."

Paul didn't say anything to that. Anxiety crept through Jesi like cold cat's paws. She hadn't said anything that wasn't true. Their marriage *was* only for looks. They hadn't consummated it, and they most likely wouldn't. She'd made it clear to Paul from the very beginning that she didn't love him.

Still, his smile had the tendency to light up her day. Why just this morning, he'd come out of his bedroom in his long johns, apparently surprised to find her reading by the firelight. She'd laughed and shook her head, and he'd hurried back into his room to put on some pants. She'd kept giggling to herself for the next fifteen minutes, and Paul had actually looked embarrassed. Even so, seeing him first thing every day lightened her heart.

They had also enjoyed that game of chase that had ended in her yearning to kiss him. At first she'd told herself *no,* she didn't want that. Yet the truth had stared her down. She *had* wanted to kiss Paul.

She loved it when he read to her at night. She found his stories and even his sermon illustrations exhilarating. Lately, he'd talked to her about what he planned to preach, and sometimes she let him practice on her.

If he didn't do such a great job, she'd boo and hiss, and he'd threaten to throw her into a snow bank. Sometimes, though, his sermons stirred her blood. She found herself thrilled by Bible passages that had hitherto been meaningless to her.

She also cleaned his room more regularly. He must've noticed, because what she did to his bed and his clothing was obvious. Still, he never remarked on it.

The letters she'd found from the mysterious Imogene had disappeared. She wondered where he kept them. Imogene was a fool. If Jesi ever met her, she'd tell her so. Yet she hoped she'd never meet the woman. If she did, it would be because of Paul, and Jesi didn't ever want Imogene to come between them. The woman burning a page on Paul's memories was bad enough.

Jesi tightened her hold on Paul's waist, hardly noticing the beauty of the twilight falling on the balsams and the weight of the snow pulling down the branches. Jealousy gored her. How could that be?

She inhaled, smelling the woodsy wool of his coat. She tingled. He was in her arms. Dare she like it so much? Dare she want to be this close to him and have it be real? She focused her thoughts on his hand, still covering hers. Had she imagined it, or had his fingers stroked hers softly through their gloves?

Carefully, she laid her head against his back and closed her eyes. They rode on in silence while she wished their ride might never end.

When she opened her eyes again, stars twinkled down the corridor above her head, lighting their path home. Sarah seemed to know the way back to her barn. As they stopped outside the cabin door, Jesi finally pulled away from Paul's back. He held her hand as she slid to the ground. Then he dismounted and faced her.

The moon hung full above them, and for a crazy moment, Jesi thought of that full moon months ago that had found her hoping to trick

Clay. Tonight she stood before Paul with no mystery or secret between them. He already knew more about her than anyone did, at least in the heart sense of knowing. He knew about her blights.

His breath came out between them.

"Jesi..." His dark eyes bore into hers. "Am I imagining it, or is something--" He broke off and glanced away for a second, as if searching for words. "Or is something changing between us?"

She reached up and stroked Sarah. What had happened on their horseback ride, anyway? Had the moon caused it? Or maybe her own aching loneliness? Was she really just getting desperate, or was something stronger, more permanent growing inside her? Was she falling in love with Paul?

"You don't have to answer if you're not sure."

He reached for Sarah's reins, but Jesi put a hand on his arm and stopped him. She couldn't seem to keep from stepping closer. "I think so."

"You do?"

She shrugged at first, then nodded. Yes, she now had no doubt. Something had changed. She might not know how to explain it, but their relationship felt different. As though their bond had solidified, and neither of them could break free.

She looked up into his eyes, so fathomless, so dark. They pulled at her, and she leaned closer.

*****

Paul wondered about the change in Jesi, and it thrilled him to the core. What was going on behind those starlight eyes of hers? Were they beckoning or daring him? They definitely magnetized him and pulled him closer. Her full lips looked sweet, and he'd never had such a desire to taste a thing in his life. A breeze lifted the hair at her temple, and he raised a finger to move it away from her face. He leaned closer.

Then he feared she might regret it later. She should know for sure if his nearness was what she wanted. He didn't want her to hate him. So with every ounce of self-denial he'd built up in his twenty-seven years, he pulled back. His throat felt hoarse, his whole body tight.

"I'd better get Sarah bedded." Speaking choked him. He took the reins again and walked past Jesi. She followed him.

He looked at her. "You can go on in and get warm."

"I'd rather stay with you."

Such simple words, and yet they shot him to the stars. She must be chilled, but she stayed with him while he brushed down Sarah and filled her oat bag. They talked casually and comfortably about the men in camp, the Hanke girls, and Marie, wondering how she fared in Ashland.

By the time they left the barn and headed indoors, the hour was well past dinner time.

"What do you say we just eat pie tonight?" she asked with a smile.

"Sounds good to me."

He tried not to stare as she moved about, cutting their pie and serving him. Why shouldn't he? *She's my wife.* And she'd admitted something had happened between them.

Her gaze flicked to his, and she smiled. Her eyelashes dropped. Was she still flushed from the cold outside, or was she blushing?

Paul had told himself he would wait years for Jesi to love him, and even then it might never happen at all. Now here they were, married only a little more than two months, and out there in the twilight she'd seemed ready to give at least a part of herself to him in a kiss, even though he hadn't taken it. He'd held her arm around him on the horseback ride. They'd shared a level of closeness beyond their earlier friendship. Even that brief, self-conscious smile held the suggestion of a promise.

God, is my wife falling in love with me? I want her to come to me with certainty, Lord. I don't want her to feel obligated and then be sorry. Jesi still was haunted by her past and seemed to regret it terribly. Yet did she regret her choices, or just their outcome? He wasn't certain she'd ever taken all of her decisions and wounds to God.

Lord, as much as I want Jesi, I know You want her even more. I pray she comes home to both of us.

Chapter Twenty-Two

Corianne pinched the envelope between her fingers and stared at the lettering. Jesi's hand always flowed hard to the right and heavy, as though she couldn't get words down fast enough. The letter was postmarked from Hurley.

So that's where she'd gone.

With a sigh, Cori decided she should have figured as much. *Hayward, Hurley, Cumberland, and Hell.* Everyone knew the saying. *Any of them were a natural place for Jesi to land.*

Cori's jaw ached. She'd clenched it for ten solid minutes. She yearned to tear the letter open and read it, but at the same time didn't want to read one single word of Jesi's bragging or begging, whichever it might be. She longed more urgently to fling the hateful thing into the fireplace. Yet that would do less to assuage her bitterness than to hurt Mama and Papa even more.

Mama was upstairs now with Gran and Gramp. The doctor had removed Gramp's tumor, but his recuperation had been slow, painful, and filled with uncertainties. She should just take Jesi's letter to Mama and stop thinking about it, stop worrying Jesi might come home.

The letter was thick. More than a single page must be folded inside. Would Jesi have so much to say? *She must either be terribly desperate or things have gone well and she can't wait to tell us all about it. Maybe Clay found her.*

Stalling on the steps, Cori looked at the envelope again. What if he had? She hadn't seen Clay all winter. Not once since the day he'd stormed off from their house. She hadn't even bumped into him in any of their social circles, though he must have certainly returned home from his studies to visit his family from time to time. Could he have gone in search of Jesi, after all?

Cori went limp with anger and pain and dropped to the steps. She stared again at the letter. If that were the case, he had fully betrayed her. That must be it. He had finally done the last, most terrible thing he could. He'd accepted Jesi in Cori's place.

Fuming, Cori rose, stomped upstairs, and marched straight into her grandfather's bedroom. Her mother's and grandparents' eyes widened as she snapped the letter onto the bedside table before whipping around to leave. Then she stormed into her room and slammed the door, where she could finally let her sobs heave out.

An hour later, a tap rattled her door. Her rage had all seeped out, and she sat brushing her hair thinking about how different she and Jesi were. How Clay could have ever allowed himself to be deceived by her sister, she couldn't fathom. Then again, she could. Jesi's promiscuous charm had taken Clay in. He had followed her like a dumb sheep.

"Come in."

Grandma Colette peeked into her room. "Are you all right?"

Cori nodded.

Gran stepped into the room and closed the door. "So we know where to find your sister now, and I take it you aren't too happy about that."

"It's not that."

Her grandmother sauntered to her and took the hairbrush from her hand. She turned Cori's shoulders and gently stroked her curls. "Want to tell me about it?"

Cori shrugged, then caught a glimpse of Gran's knowing gaze in the mirror.

"Maybe you won't be so angry when you hear her letter."

"Maybe it'll only infuriate me more."

Gran's lips tweaked in a small smile. "It might."

"Is she coming home, then?"

"I don't know." Gran fluffed her hand through Cori's hair. "Your father opened the letter, but he hasn't read it to anyone accept your mama. He'd like you to come down and hear it, though."

Cori harrumphed. Another pang of defiance slid through her.

"Aren't you just a bit curious? I am."

"Well, it's obvious nothing's terribly wrong, or Mama would have let on to you, and you wouldn't be smiling and teasing me like this."

Grandma Colette bent and kissed her cheek. "When you're ready, then." She set the hair brush on the dresser and let herself out. The door barely made a sound when she closed it.

Cori frowned at her reflection. Her hair looked like a poufy red halo. "What do I care? Maybe Jesi and Clay are going far, far away, and they'll never come home."

She flung herself out of the chair and marched downstairs. Papa waited at the bottom.

"I thought I heard you leave your room."

"So what now? I know Jesi's all right."

"You haven't heard the whole of it."

"I don't really care."

"Enough of your pouting." Papa's brows furrowed. "Come into the parlor."

She folded her arms and followed him. His tone breached no argument. Very well, they could force her to talk about Jesi, to hear about her sister's forays of independence. They could make her accept the fact that she'd gotten Clay after all, but they couldn't make her forgive Jesi.

Mama patted the settee, and Cori plopped down beside her.

Papa sat in his favorite oversized chair and unfolded two pages from the envelope.

"A few months ago I met a man in Hurley, a camp preacher by the name of Paul Winter. Fine fellow. A bit young and inexperienced for a preacher, maybe, but that'll come in time. This first page is from him." He indicated the page with a brief lift of his hand. "I'll get right to the point. He met Jesi just shortly after our encounter. However, he didn't know her name then. Seems she was going by the name of Jane Barton. He doesn't say exactly how, but apparently he and his sister Marie crossed paths with Jesi as she was about at the end of her rope." His voice dropped. "He doesn't elaborate on that."

Lines deepened on Papa's forehead, and she wondered what he was thinking.

"God, it seems, used this young preacher in a mighty way to save her."

Cori snorted. "Save her? Jesi, coming to God?"

"No, that's not what I mean. But I believe Jesi knows the Lord, and she'll come back to him as soon as she finds the way."

"How can you say that, Papa, after what she did? You call that Christian?"

"Christians sin, Corianne. Christians get greedy, they tell lies, they cheat, and they even kill sometimes."

Her heart pounded. How could Papa believe that? Why, then, did they even pretend to know God?

"Jesi believed when she was just five-years-old, two years before you did, Cori," Mama said softly.

Gran wagged her head. "I made many a-foolish mistake in my Christian youth."

"Me, too, Ma." Mama smiled.

Cori twisted toward her. "You didn't play the whore with your sister's fiancé. You never did anything worse than play cards and run off places without a chaperone. You told me so yourself."

"I don't ever want to hear such a thing come out of your mouth again." Mama gripped her arm and squeezed it. "Do you hear me? I don't care how old and grown up you are. I don't care how full of resentment you are. I don't care how much of a martyr you feel. You just don't speak that way."

"She'll throw it in my face forever, Mama. Her and Clay both."

"What are you talking about?" Mama dropped her hand and wrinkled her brow in puzzlement.

Cori buried her face in her hands.

Papa cleared his throat. "Your ma's right, Cori. You best hold your tongue and listen.

As I was saying, Jesi's been rescued by this young preacher. I ran into him again, just a few weeks ago. Only then he hadn't put two and two together. We had a nice visit, shared some pie. That's when he figured things out. Jesi had come clean about her real name. She had to... in order to marry him."

Cori's head shot up. Her tears halted. Mama's hands lay clasped in her lap. Gran leaned forward, her hand reaching for her chin to tremble over her lips.

Papa took a deep breath. "He didn't tell me at the time. He didn't think he could break Jesi's trust that way. He went home and talked with her first. That's why we got the letter.

"This one from him," Pa said, waving the sheet in his hand, "explaining why he didn't tell me what had happened." He lifted the second page. "This one is hers."

A string of thoughts wove in and out of Cori's head like the tail of a kite she couldn't quite grasp. Bouncing up and down on its end was the main detail: *Jesi didn't go with Clay. He isn't in the picture at all.*

Mama reached for her hand. Cori looked at her. "I can't imagine how..."

"Frankly, honey, neither can we. There's a lot we don't understand. But we do know Jesilyn is safe, and this man seems to know a lot about her and is being very kind to her."

"I don't know how she does it."

Pa frowned. "Does what, Cori?"

"Always lands on her feet."

"God's looking out for her, same as He looks out for you," Gran said. "Same as He looked out for me when I got ahead of Him. Same as He looked out for your mama when she ran off. Same as He looked out for your Pa when life ran him over. Same as He looked out for Grandpa when--"

"I understand." Cori held up her hand in surrender. "Not really, but--"

"Jesi's sorry for making us worry." Papa lifted the other sheet of paper. "Says she knows it was the wrong thing to do. She admits that for awhile, she didn't know what she would do. Getting work was harder than she'd thought. She thought she'd found something, but it didn't work out, and pretty soon she ran out of money. She started walking to Mellen, but was overtaken by the journey and got sick. Mr. Winter found her unable to go on. He took her home to his sister, who nursed her back to health.

"She says they were willing to let her stay on, but then Mr. Winter's sister took a call to get nurse's training in Ashland." Papa fiddled with the papers, and Cori could tell by the way the next words came out that he didn't believe their authenticity anymore than she did.

"They got married before Marie left, and they're doing well. They'll come see us when the days are warm again."

"How did she get him to do that, do you suppose? To just marry her--" Cori snapped her fingers. "Like that? I can just about guess how."

Mama leaned back against the cushions and sighed. Even Gran scowled at her.

"It wouldn't have looked good for them to be living there alone. That's what Mr. Winter said."

Cori didn't relent. "Of course she'd put him in that predicament just to catch him. It's not likely she'd just get on a train and come home."

"Mr. Winter said she was afraid to come home and face up to what had happened between you," Mama said.

"In other words, she's not sorry. Just scared."

"We don't know. But Mr. Winter truly seems to care for her."

Cori stood and walked toward the parlor door. She paused and turned to face them one last time. "Well, then, let's hope he doesn't get his heart ripped out."

The next morning when Cori woke, water dripped off the eave past her window. Sun beat on her face. She flung back the covers and peered outside. Puddles formed pockets in the snow.

"Corianne!"

She flung her robe around her and poked her head out her door. "Did you call me, Evie?"

"Come take this tray up to your grandpa."

She belted her robe and slipped out in her bare feet to fetch Gramp's breakfast. Scrambled eggs, coffee, and a slice of toasted bread on the tray made her stomach growl. She pushed open the door to his room and found him propped against his pillows, waiting for her.

Gran had helped him comb his mane of hair and beard.

"You're looking very handsome this morning, Gramp."

"I have to keep impressing your grandmother. She never lets me rest." He snickered, winking at Colette.

"That's right," Gran said. "Else Joe Gilbert might come and steal me away."

"Humph. *Joe Gilbert.*" Gramp shook his head. "Those Gilbert men. Always flirting with my girls."

"Great Uncle Rob is a Gilbert man. You don't have anything against him, do you?"

"He stole my sister."

"I bet you didn't mind it at all."

"He didn't" Gran said. "He was as happy as a lark when Jean set her cap for Robbie."

"He was a sight better than that--" Gramp snapped his fingers in frustration. "What was his name, anyway?"

"Virgil Holcomb?"

"Whatever happened to him? He just seemed to sort of slither off the earth with the other snakes.

Gran chuckled.

Cori settled the tray in front of him and stepped back. "He sounds a lot like Clay."

"He was. A lot."

"Did you chase him off?"

Gramp picked up his toast with his thick, gnarled fingers. "Would've, but he ran off on his own before I had the chance."

Gran clucked her tongue. "Back then, you were too busy chasing Miss Margaret around to take time defending Jean."

Gramp feigned surprise. "Margaret who?"

Gran rolled her eyes and bent to kiss his cheek.

"Well, I wish you'd have been around sooner to chase Clay off."

Gran patted Cori's shoulder. "Seems you're truly rid of him, though. And that means..."

"What, Gran? Go ahead and say it."

"Means it's time to forgive your sister."

"Why should I? She hasn't asked for it. Besides, I still don't trust her. Her marriage isn't real. Anybody could tell that even without her ever saying so. She married that preacher to save her own hide. Who knows what she would've done otherwise? He sounds like a pretty gullible fellow, to take up with her."

"Those are harsh words and hard thoughts, young lady," Gramp said. "Careful, or they'll turn you hard clear through. You won't have any softness left in you to grow on. And it's my guess that James Gilbert wants a woman with a little softness in her."

Stung, Cori considered what he had just said. Was she really growing a callous heart? She might have never thought about it if Gramp hadn't mentioned Jamie. Would he find her thick-skinned and pitiless eventually?

"I-I didn't mean that about the preacher. He's probably a good man. Good men can be fooled." She frowned. Her explanation still didn't sound right.

"We're not going to stop praying for Jesi. Sounds like God might be doing something real important in her life." Gran's eyes twinkled. "And we're not going to stop praying for you either, just like we have been since you first came into the world, surprising us all."

Cori knew her parents hadn't expected twins. She'd come a few minutes after Jesi, astonishing everyone.

Her grandpa laughed. "I didn't think your pa would ever come down off that cloud."

Cori had no idea what it had been like for them, but she did have early memories. They always involved Jesi. The two of them had spent every waking minute together until they'd gotten older. Until they'd met Clay. Would Jesi act differently now that she was married? Would she be faithful to her new husband, or would Cori always have to live in distrust, wondering when Jesi's thoughts would stray toward one who didn't belong to her?

"Jamie's coming back in May. Last night, Papa mentioned that Jesi and the preacher will visit, too, once the days get warm. I can't honestly say I'm looking forward to that. I hope it's not when Jamie's here. It'll suit me if she never meets him, if you want to know the truth."

Gran sighed, and Gramp patted her hand.

Chapter Twenty-Three

Which is warmer? The sun on my shoulders, or the joy in my heart? Jesi smiled to herself as she strolled along the path where the melting snow allowed bursts of grass to shoot from the brown earth. She didn't know when she'd ever been so content.

Stepping carefully, she crossed a muddy rut, heading toward the pussy willow bushes growing along the ditch. She bent and twisted the willow, finally pulling a kitchen knife from her apron pocket to cut it free. In a matter of minutes, she had enough branches for a bouquet.

"First flowers of spring."

Though not truly flowers, they would look cheerful on the table in the center of the cabin.

The weeks had flown by. Her mind skipped over them like a spring brook running over pebbles. She and Paul had shared evening walks and deep talks by the fireside, simple meals and special desserts, doing chores together and reading books.

Paul frequently stared at her, clearly enjoying watching her as she went about the plainest tasks, not bothering to conceal his admiration. Yet it didn't offend her. He never made advances toward her beyond occasionally holding her hand as they walked along, or lingering over-long in a touch when he helped her into or out of the wagon.

They'd gone on no more horseback rides, and Jesi regretted that. Maybe someday soon, he'd take her again.

They even talked about their new life together. She recalled the conversation they'd had one night after he'd studied his Bible. She'd sat across from him at the table, making a list of things she hoped to try growing in the kitchen garden come spring. His voice, mellow and deep, interrupted her thoughts and sent them scattering to the corners of the cabin like dust.

"Jesi... I'm finding it harder not to feel for you... more deeply than I thought I would."

Warmth tingled all the way to her fingertips. He looked serious, and a little bothered by the fact.

She twisted the pen between her fingers. Ink spots dribbled onto her list. "Does that upset you?"

"Of course not. But I don't want it to upset you either. I just felt I ought to be frank. I won't break my word. I'll keep the promise I made you."

"Didn't we agree that something had happened between us? Something -- nice?

He pulled the spectacles off his face and set them aside to study her.

"Did you hear me, Jesi? My feelings are..."

"What?"

"I care. I care a great deal."

"But if that's true, wouldn't you... want me?"

His eyes flashed, looking like ebony beyond the glow of the oil lamp. "It's not that I don't." He pushed back his chair and rose. "It's only that I won't let myself."

He spun on his heel and left the cabin, leaving a draft in his wake that blew through her soul. What was he waiting for, anyway? Why did he have to keep his word? She'd have gladly kissed him if he'd so much as brushed close enough.

I really am too loose for my own good. She frowned. *But I am his wife, after all.*

For the hundredth time since that conversation, her thoughts lingered over the look of desire in his eyes and the realization that she'd liked it. Plucking her way back through the mud to the cabin, she went inside and stood the pussy willows in an empty jar. They would dry and last for a good many days. She plucked a green hair ribbon off her dresser and tied it around the jar to brighten it.

No matter what happened between her and Paul, she knew he had to be thinking about their talk, too. A smile lifted the edges of her mouth.

I'd better get changed.

He'd be back from his meeting with the camp boss any time now, and he'd promised her a special day. They were going to Hurley. She hadn't been there in over a month, and their supplies had gotten low. Paul planned a couple of brief visits along the way, and she hoped to get some material for sewing with Charlie's girls. She figured this would be their chance to show her their expertise, and the Lord knew she could use some, too.

After shopping, Paul would take her out to dinner. Her body buzzed with excitement as she thought about what a romantic day it might be, spent almost exclusively with him.

She whistled and hummed as she changed into an orange and yellow gingham day dress and coiffed her hair.

She turned about in front of the mirror on her dresser and admired the dress Paul had ordered for her. It was a simple piece of attire with slightly puffed sleeves that gave it just enough flair. The full, fluted skirt gathered into a flattering point at her waist, front and back. She gazed at her reflection. "I do look like a preacher's wife."

A good and proper way to look in Hurley. I won't be afraid to be seen in town anymore. Not when I'm with him.

"Jesi?"

Paul. She hadn't heard him come in. "I'm in here."

"Are you ready to go?"

She stepped into the main room. "Ready as can be."

Paul turned from hanging his coat on a peg and stopped. His smile reached right up to his eyes, and he whistled. "Look at you. Guess I'd better go get shined up if I don't want people wondering how I ever got you to marry me."

She flushed.

"I'll hurry."

She listened to him singing while he got ready in his room. When he came back out a short while later, he looked finer than a Sunday morning in June. He had on a clean white shirt and a pair of dark blue suspenders stretched up over his shoulders, though he certainly didn't need them for any functional purpose. Paul's waist was trim; his shoulders, broad. He wasn't big, but he certainly had an athletic build.

She blinked when she realized how she'd been pleasantly perusing him. "I-I guess we'd better get going."

His smile told her he'd noticed her appreciation. "The buggy's all ready."

"Buggy?"

He explained it on the way out. "I've got a surprise. I bought Matt Thompson's buggy. He owed the Schmidt brothers some money, so I thought I'd help him out."

"Can you afford it?"

"The back axel was broken, so it didn't cost me much. And the Schmidt brothers offered to help me fix it if I bought it so they could get their money from Matt. It all worked out, in a roundabout way."

The buggy was not only fixed, but shone with new care. It wasn't a fancy buggy like Pa's or Clay Dalton's. The seat wasn't covered with padding and leather. It was just simple wood, and some of the paint had worn away. But it was sturdy, and it would be better than riding all the way into town in Charlie's wagon.

Paul settled in next to her and laid his hand over hers, squeezing gently before taking the reins and giving them a slight snap over Sarah's backside.

"I saw you found some pussy willows."

"In another month or so, I'll be able to look for marsh marigolds. They don't live long, but they're so pretty. Brighter than butter."

"You must like flowers.

"I guess most girls love flowers."

"I'll have to remember that."

"My mama raises roses." Jesi smiled. "She started doing it back when my sister and I were little."

"Then it's not just that you're a girl. You had a love of flowers trained into you."

"That could be."

They talked for a long while about the roses in her mama's gardens and about the hours she and Cori had spent tending them over the years.

She told him about her Papa's nicknames for the two of them -- his roses, or his little rosebuds.

"You sound as if you wouldn't mind doing those things again with your sister."

Jesi flashed him a glance, but she didn't know what to say. She doubted that was worth hoping for. Cori would never forget what Jesi had done. Never.

Just outside of Hurley, Paul stopped to meet a man who'd been laid off from the woods crew the season before. He'd managed to find some repair work in town, but the work wasn't steady, and the pay was slim. His wife took in wash, and they were content, but if things didn't look up soon, they'd have to think about moving off. Paul prayed with him and told him not to hesitate if there was anything he and Jesi could do.

Jesi felt their frustration. She knew as well as anyone what it was like to fall on hard times -- even though hers had been of her own making.

She touched Paul's arm as they rode into town. "Paul, if there's anything I can do for them, to help you, you will tell me, won't you? I don't want what you said to them to be mere sentiment. I really do want to help."

"I will." His expression gentled. "I promise."

Sarah trotted down the street. The sights and sounds of downtown Hurley hadn't changed, other than the streets being muddier and the storefronts dingier from the lingering colorlessness of winter clinging to them. Ladies' hems collected cakey mud, and their pointed boots sunk into the ooze as they crossed the streets. Piano music eroded the quiet with tinny notes as they drove past one saloon and another, even though it was the middle of the day. In front of the stores, a few people clomped down the wooden sidewalk. On the corner of Cotton Street and Fifth Avenue, the prestigious Bardon Hotel still reigned as the most inviting establishment in town, though the new three-story brick courthouse could certainly compete. The trolley passed by them on its tracks, its bell ringing.

"I'll leave you at the store while I go over to the metal shop. I told Adam I'd pick up some parts he needs. I'll only be about twenty minutes. Will that give you time to look at things?"

"You're going to help me with the list, right?"

"You bet." He jumped down and came around to help her alight from the buggy. "Just take your time with your bolts of cloth and whatever other woman things you want to wish over."

She slapped his chest with her glove and chuckled.

He smiled. "I'll see you in just a bit."

"All right. Goodbye."

An uncomfortable tingle prickled over her as he got into the buggy and drove away. *He'll be back. He said he wouldn't be long.*

Why had this sudden panic crept over her? They had enjoyed a wonderful day so far. Paul had treated her like a lady, like a *wife*. Why would such fears even encroach on that?

It's this town. The memories...

"May I help you?"

She'd wandered inside and stood rooted by the door, almost unaware of her surroundings.

"Oh. I'm sorry. I was daydreaming." She straightened her shoulders. "May I look at some fabric?"

"Certainly. Right this way."

The woman pranced between displays until they reached a large corner section filled with bolts of cloth, laces, spools of thread, needles, patterns, and a hundred other things Jesi generally shunned. She took a deep breath and concentrated on the task, anyway. Charlie's girls were counting on her to bring back something they'd all like.

Her hands roved over the bolts, one after another.

This one -- no. This. She paused. *Uh-uh.* She fingered a piece of dark blue velveteen. *This is pretty.*

Someone stood behind her. She stepped closer to the display to allow them room to pass. But they didn't. She turned the bolt over and smoothed the material with her palm so the grain lay one way, then the other. She remained intent on ignoring the person behind her.

"Jesilyn?"

Spoken so low, she almost thought she'd imagined hearing her name. But the familiarity of the voice rose like a specter out of a dark gloom. She whirled around.

Her hand came up, reaching for a button at the top of her collar with which she had the habit of fiddling. Only... she wasn't wearing her everyday shirtwaist. She lowered her hand. Her fingers trembled.

Clay Dalton stared at her. She stared back.

"It *is* you," he said. He stepped closer until he stood only inches away looking at her as though he might swallow her whole. His gaze roved over her face and took in her hair twisted into a coif at her neck. It traveled down her neckline, over her dress, reading her through.

Jesi squirmed, blinking away her discomfort. "Clay. I -- what are you doing here?"

"Me?" He gasped. "What are *you* doing here?"

Heat raced through her limbs, up her neck, and she knew her face was red. "I live here."

"You live in *Hurley*?"

Jesi frowned.

Clay pinched his forehead. "Forgive my shock."

"And mine."

A slow smile lifted his lips, and he snickered. "I'm so surprised. You've been here all this time?"

She nodded, still not sure what to make of him. He spoke politely, if not with a bit of bemusement. She tried to smile. He grinned back. He flicked his head to the side so his shock of pale hair smoothed back off his face. His features had changed. Some of his leanness had gone, and he looked better for it. More mature, perhaps.

Suddenly she hated the way her heart pounded. "I'd better go. I'm meeting someone."

She'd no idea what to do. Paul was meeting her here. She was afraid of staying, though, of being with Clay. Afraid of her own heart.

He reached for her arm. "Jesi, wait. There are some things I'd like to say."

She stalled. *Go. Leave now. Don't listen to him.* But her feet held fast. "All right."

"Can we walk?"

She hadn't been in the store five minutes and had plenty of time before Paul would return. She nodded.

Clay's hand on her elbow guided her between the displays and out the building. His touch sent lightning blazing though her sleeve and up her arm. When he let go and they strolled along the sidewalk, she let out her breath.

"You look well."

She glanced at him. He seemed sincere. "Thank you."

"I mean, you really do. You look -- very lovely, in fact."

"You're kind to say so."

"Kind?" He said nothing more for a moment. Neither of them did. Finally, he said, "I can't believe I ran into you. I've wondered for months now how you were getting by, what you've been doing, if you're well. I've berated myself over a thousand times for what happened."

A lump crept into her throat. "Oh?"

She hadn't realized he held a hat. Now, as they made their way slowly along the boardwalk, he turned it around and around in his hands. "I was such an idiot."

"Yes. You were."

"I guess I deserved to hear that." He halted and stared at her for a second before moving on. "Though I'm pretty sure I've heard you say something like it before."

"Is Cori still angry with you?" Boldness lifted her shoulders, and she tried to keep her voice relaxed. "We... we don't talk, you see. She despises me."

"So that is why you left Superior." He shifted a glance at her. "Because of me."

"Because of Cori and you." She turned to face him. "It seemed like the best thing. My reputation was ruined."

"No." He shook his head slowly. "Cori hasn't forgiven me, either."

"But you wish she would."

"No. Not anymore."

She doubted him, but only for a moment. He sounded reconciled over it, over Cori or whatever state of mind he'd been in last summer.

"Jesi." He took her hand and stepped closer to make room for someone passing them on the boardwalk. He looked at her then in a way he never had before. For the first time, she realized, he looked at her with unguarded longing as herself, and not in denial or with pretense that she was someone else. "I'm staying at the Bardon for a couple of days. Will you consider having dinner with me there? Tonight?"

His fingers gentled hers, and nervous excitement crept up her spine.

"I don't expect anything," he hurried on to say. "I'd just like to get to know you again, as you."

He appeared so sincere, so trustworthy. She stood taller, an unconscious move that brought her closer to him. She smelled his shaving cream, and with it came a dizzying rush of emotions and memories.

Clay was beckoning her. *Her.* Not just an image of Cori, or with the idea he would be able to go back to her sister. Not believing he would gain anything beyond Jesi's heart. Could she do it?

Paul's face flashed before her. *Paul.* Her Paul.

But Paul was only protecting me when he married me. He doesn't love me. Does he? He has strong feelings for me, but what is that? It's not love, is it? Maybe...

Her heart twisted in confusion. *Was* Paul truly in love with her? Oh, if only he'd kissed her that day, or on a dozen others, and shown her the depth of his feelings. Then she'd know, wouldn't she? Or would that have meant anything at all?

Now here stood Clay, the one she'd waited for, longed for, given herself for, offering her a chance. Had that chance gone fleeting away? She fisted her free hand against her breast and searched Clay's face for something there that would tell her what to do. Even then, she saw Paul. Had her heart truly skipped off to find something better and more lasting in a camp preacher? Had she ever really loved Clay, or did she love Paul? *Paul... God, I don't know what to do.* And still, her feet shuffled and she let her hand linger in Clay's.

A loud, deep voice broke the spell. "Hey, mister. You're standing in front of the door."

Jesi jumped back, and Clay dropped her hand. "Pardon me."

The man's black eyes narrowed in a broad face marked by a day's grizzle. He was a giant in flannel and overalls. *Big Johnny Ray.*

Chapter Twenty-Four

Jesi's stomach flipped. She hadn't even realized they stood in front of Maisey's Bar. She gasped and ducked her head, but it was too late.

Johnny Ray leered at her. "Well... look who the dogs dragged back. I know you, red. You're the little gal who left me with the sore head and a whole lot of unfinished business."

He stepped close and jerked her chin up with his beefy fingers.

Clay laid a hand across Big John's forearm. "See here, mister."

The bear shook him off like a pesky black fly. "And now, here you are. Right back where we last met. We can pick up where we left off, but maybe we'll have a drink and a dance first."

Johnny Ray gripped her arm and twisted her toward the door.

"No!" She yanked free and fell against Clay, clutching him.

Clay backed up looking dumbfounded, with Jesi clinging to his coat front.

"Oh. I see. You're busy now." He threw Clay a look. "Better mind yourself, mister. Don't turn your head. She's a thieving, mean little thing."

She shook her head and glanced at Clay. He scowled and removed her hand from his coat. "Jesi?"

"Clay--"

"*Jesi*?" Another voice came from the street.

Jesi twisted her head. Paul hoofed it around a pair of mud holes as he crossed the road. She turned back to Clay. His face had changed. His jaw was now set, and his brow dipped. His face had taken on the tell-tale shade of red it always seemed to turn when he was angry.

"What've you become?" he asked, his voice tight.

"Clay, no."

Big John burst out laughing. "What'd you think she was, mister? I can tell you what." He jerked his head toward Maisey's dark interior. "So can anyone in this fine establishment."

She shook her head. Tears blurred her vision. Gravy's piano playing clinked discordant tones in the background.

"Jesi?" Paul's voice, even but heavy with worry she recognized, rang out as he leapt onto the boardwalk. She turned to him, but didn't dare meet his gaze. She wiped the back of her hand across her eyes.

Big John kept laughing. Clay just stared at her, his countenance growing harder by the second. His eyes took on the shade of thunderclouds over Lake Superior.

"Is this how you've been *living* in Hurley?" His look scathed her. "Yet you were ready to try and fool me again."

She had no breath, no courage to deny it. Her heart had momentarily soared to the peaks, and then crashed down in a hideous mess.

His face contorted. "You're still nothing but a common trollop."

Paul's fist shot out without warning, catching Clay square in the jaw. He reeled backward off the boardwalk into the mud.

"Who the blazes are you?" John thundered, reaching for Paul's shirt.

Jesi covered her mouth and bit her palm.

Paul shoved a fist in his gut, but the big man merely cringed and pushed Paul back. "What's your stake in all this?"

Paul found his footing. He glanced briefly at Clay, who'd gotten up and stood brushing mud off his suit.

"I'll tell you." Paul took a run at Big John, crashing into his shoulder so that the brute fell hard against the side of the building. "She's my wife."

"What?" Clay gawked and rubbed his jaw.

Jesi blinked, panic rising through her like bubbles up a straw.

Paul rubbed his knuckles, but John didn't just lie there. He jumped to his feet, moving faster than a big man should, fast as Jesi remembered -- and feared.

"Your wife, huh?" Johnny Ray's coal black stare burned a whole through Paul. He turned his head and spat, landing a wad inches from Clay's feet. "Well I'm going to get some satisfaction out of this somehow."

He pushed up his sleeve and swung hard, sending Paul stumbling.

Jesi screamed and rushed toward him, but Clay grabbed her arm and yanked her toward him. Paul righted himself and swung back, landing a solid cuff to the side of Johnny Ray's head.

Johnny shook it off and focused on Paul as he rushed again, connecting one more punch to Johnny's chin. Big John's face swiveled toward Paul, and he roared before drawing back and placing a blow that sent Paul spiraling to the boards beneath their feet.

Jesi jerked, but Clay tightened his grasp on her and glanced down at Paul. "Is he lying? Are you and he..."

Her chest rose and fell in fast breaths. She pinched her lips together, defiance rising up inside. She held out her hand bearing her wedding ring and gave a curt nod. Her words seethed out. "There. Now, do you still want to have dinner with me? Do you want to be seen with the town trollop?"

He rubbed the back of his hand across his mouth, smearing a trickle of blood that oozed out of his lip.

Big John grunted. "I got what I wanted, just about anyway." He raked his gaze over Jesi. "I guess you can have her now -- or *he* can." He sneered at Paul, who got up slowly.

"So you fooled somebody into marrying you," Clay said.

"She didn't fool anybody. If there's a fool to be found around here, I guess you must be Clay Dalton."

Clay straightened, his eyes widening. He dabbed again at his lip.

"You look surprised that I know your name. I've always thought I'd like to run into you in the street." Paul pushed his hair back, his expression as taut as ever. "Jesi told me all about you."

Clay picked up his hat and brushed if off. She recognized his visible attempt to play it calm. "I wonder -- if Jesilyn and I hadn't been stopped by that brute -- would you be feeling quite so chivalrous to discover that *your wife* had gone away with me? She was about to, you know."

Jesi's heart plummeted again. *No, Paul. Don't believe him.* She shook her head, but Paul's expression was inscrutable. He was waiting and allowed Clay to continue. *No, Paul. Please...*

Clay inclined his head with a slow grin. "We were just getting reacquainted. I'd invited her to my hotel for dinner. Why do you think she wasn't waiting for you back there?"

He dipped his head toward the mercantile.

She clenched her fists. "Stop it, Clay."

"I can imagine you don't want him to know. What would happen to your cozy little marriage? I take it he has some money."

Paul stepped toward him, and Clay moved back. He must've known he'd gone too far. Fear leapt back into his eyes.

"You're pretty confident for a man who was sent packing by the whole Beaumont family," Paul said, stepping closer.

Clay inched back. He smirked. "Sent me packing? Is that what *she* told you? I *left* Jesi and her spoiled sister."

"That's right. Because you had no choice."

"With that one, there's always a choice." Clay's glance slid suggestive accusation at Jesi.

Like a rock shot from a sling, Paul punched his snide face again. Then he hit him once more, doubling Clay over with a rocky fist to the gut. Blood spurted into the dirt from his panting nostrils.

Paul stood over him, hardly winded. "I'd tell my wife to go ahead and take a swing at you, too, but she's a lady."

Jesi stared at Clay, the bitter taste of gall climbing into her throat. Paul grasped her upper arm and gently steered her away from her accuser. Now she noticed a few people had stopped to watch the tussle. It wasn't a big crowd. Brawls weren't so unusual in Hurley. They shuffled off as she and Paul walked across the rutted street. Paul didn't let go of her, but shame stiffened her shoulders as he said not a word. His lips clamped tight. Inside, she trembled.

He helped her into their buggy, the shopping and the bolts of cloth forgotten. They would have no dinner, no day to spend together. The ride home would be interminable, she knew.

So this was Paul angry. She'd never seen him so before, not really. His face didn't register any real emotion, only the sense of shutters closing to his soul.

Her heart sorrowed. *Paul, I'm sorry. I'm so sorry.* If only she could speak the words.

She stared straight ahead, mindless of the sun beating down and birds swooping from branch to branch along the road home. As the buggy hit one rut, and another, she clung to the seat, afraid of brushing against him. Afraid of him hating her.

Why had she been so stupid? Why did she agree to walk with Clay, to listen to him? What had she really expected? To get some twisted sense of satisfaction? *Would I really have gone with him? Was he right in telling Paul I'd leave him?*

She gripped the bench beneath her. *No.*

If she had the courage, she'd tell Paul so now. But he wouldn't believe her. He'd only be angry and think she was making excuses. He'd listened to Clay's charges, and Johnny Ray had been there to add more lies to her scandal. Paul was sorry for marrying her now. He might be stoic, keeping his feelings stowed away in silence, but he regretted his hasty plan.

Tears filled her eyes. The world of the forest, the distant rush of the river beyond the trees, it all fell away. She was as trapped as she'd ever been. Trapped in her own pit of self-hatred and despair.

The moment the buggy reached the yard, she climbed down, not even waiting for Paul to engage the brake. She fled into the cabin, rushing through the dim main room to her bedroom. She pushed the door shut behind her and fell down against it, weeping.

*****

Paul took his time removing Sarah's harness and turning her back into her stall. Thankfully, no one was around the camp. Speaking to anyone right now would have been difficult. He closed the barn door and wandered toward the cabin, but went out to the woodshed instead. He removed his good coat and donned an old flannel shirt hanging on a peg above his axe. Never mind that he still had on his other white shirt, marred with specks of blood from Clay Dalton's nose. He picked up a log, steadied it, and yanked the ax into his grip. He swung a wide arc with it, splitting the chunk of wood in two with a loud *thunk.*

Then he picked up another.

Dear God.

He tried to pray, just as he'd been trying to do all the way back from Hurley. *Why? Why now?* The echo from the crack of the logs bounced back from the surrounding woods, his only answer. In ten minutes, he had a growing heap of wood on the ground. Pine chips flew from the bit of the ax. His shoulders heaved with exertion. Sweat ran down the side of his face, plastering his hair to his neck and forehead. He worked for answers.

Back there in Hurley, had Jesi really intended to just walk away, to exit his life as suddenly as she'd entered it? Was the Jesilyn he'd come to know truly as shallow and heartless as that? She'd told him about her past with Clay. She'd told him about her plan to deceive Cori and steal Clay from her. Paul could hardly believe it of Jesi when she'd spoken of it. Was she still that girl? To see her standing there on the street so brazenly clutching Clay had nearly taken his breath away. Right there in front of that *place*. Paul swung again, sticking the ax in a fat log. He wrenched it free and gritted his teeth. He swung again, but the log refused to crack. It was wet, still full of sap.

He stood there gripping the handle, puffing out his breath. He rubbed a hand over his sweaty brow. Yanking the ax free again, he grunted as he propelled it over his head, slamming it into the wood. The log cleaved in two.

Paul dropped the ax and leaned against the shed. Panting, he brushed his sleeve across his mouth. He braced his hands on his knees. *I didn't think anything could hurt this way, Father. If I could've imagined that man strutting into her life, even then I never would've dreamed she'd follow him. I thought... I thought she and I...*

"I can't let her go, and I can't make her love me," he murmured aloud.

He stepped out from behind the shed and looked at the cabin. What was she doing in there? Packing her bag?

No, he doubted that. But she was probably wishing she hadn't come back with him. She may have been crushed by Dalton's rejection, but she probably wished she didn't have to be with Paul, either.

He shed the old flannel shirt and hung it back on the peg. His good clothes had grown rank with sweat and dirt pretty quickly. He should stop by the outside pump and wash his face, but he didn't really care.

He pushed open the door and blinked, trying to focus in the dimness. All was still. Jesi's bedroom door was closed and not a sound came from inside. He sighed. What should he do? What *could* he do? He wished Marie were here. She'd talk to Jesi, find out what she wanted, sooth her -- all the things Paul, impotent in this situation, couldn't do. He stood in between Jesi and the man she truly wanted. Who could tell? Maybe she would've been able to explain the situation to Dalton about Johnny Ray if she'd had the chance. If Paul hadn't intruded to make her position worse, maybe those beautiful blue eyes of hers would have convinced Dalton to listen.

Paul went into his room and stripped out of his clothes. Glancing in the mirror, he noticed he had a black eye. Perfect. Twice now he'd been on the raw end of a public brawl in downtown Hurley. Some laughing stock of a preacher he was.

He poured water from the half full pitcher into the basin and washed the sweat off his face, neck, and arms. He wished he could so easily wash the grime from his thoughts.

As the afternoon waned, he tried to focus on the things he normally did. He opened his Bible to read, but the words drifted past his eyes, out of focus. He carried in more wood, swept the floor, shuffled to the kitchen to eat. Every so often he gazed at Jesi's door, but she didn't emerge. Finally he couldn't take it any longer.

He tapped on the door. "Jesi?"

No answer.

He tapped again. "You awake?"

Her voice was so soft, he could hardly hear it. "Yes."

"Are you hungry? I made a sandwich."

"No."

Paul turned to walk away, but he couldn't. He couldn't let it go. "Jesi?"

He reached for the knob, daring himself with one quick breath to let himself in. He cracked open the door. She lay in bed, her hair spread out around her on her pillow, her dress draped over her legs and hanging down the side of the bed.

She jerked when he drew close, realizing he'd come in. She pushed herself up on the bed and pulled her hair back around her neck, over her shoulder.

"I'm sorry for barging in, but..." Paul sat down next to her. He'd come in unbidden. Now he sat on her bed. He was crossing every line he'd promised to keep drawn. Propriety seemed to be crumbling like dust today. She didn't look at him. "What do you want?"

"What do *I* want?" His heart crashed. He didn't think there was any room left for it to fall. "I think the question is what do *you* want?"

Her gaze flashed up at him, and she blinked. She'd been crying. Her face was white; her eyes, red and puffy. He knew why. She'd lost Dalton again. Gall rose up inside. "Jesi, do you still want to go to him? If you do, then--"

She dropped her eyes and shook her head.

He wanted to reach out to her, to lift up her chin and make her look at him. "If he hadn't accused you of those things, would you have done what he said? Would you have gone with him?"

She stilled.

His voice dropped to a whisper. "Does he still have your heart?"

"No." She did look at him then, and she frowned.

Paul could only stare at her, trying somehow to read an explanation into her answer. What did he know of Jesi Beaumont really? What did she think and feel on the inside? Was she fooling him now?

Her lips worked to form words. "Paul, I--" Tears welled in her eyes and trickled down her cheeks. "I'm so full of shame. I don't love him." She rocked on the bed wringing her hands in her lap. "I hate myself."

"Jesi, no."

A sob slipped out. "I'm so full of disgust and humiliation. You must hate me."

"No, I don't." *Nothing could be further from the truth.* "I just don't want to stand in your way if--"

"Why not?" Her chin came up. "Why don't you want to stand in my way? You're ten times -- *no* -- you're a *hundred* times the man Clay is. You married me. Doesn't that give you every right to stand in my way?"

"In other circumstances, it might."

"What other circumstances?"

He sighed. She must know why. He didn't need to explain. *We're married only in name.*

She dropped back against the headboard. "I don't expect you to forgive me for what happened today."

He wanted to reach out and reassure her, but he didn't dare. Words failed him. His ability to know what to do failed him. "How can I not forgive you? You told me about your past. I accepted it."

"That's preacher talk." Bitterness leached into her tone. "But why shouldn't it be? What I've done will always be there like a dead thing in front of us. It'll keep us from *really* being man and wife forever."

Would it? Would her past always come between them? If he didn't figure out a way to hurdle it, it truly might.

Jesi stared hard at him for a moment, then sank down onto the bed and turned her back.

Paul's heart plummeted like a stone, aching in his chest. He pushed himself off the bed and quietly left the room.

Chapter Twenty-Five

Jesi pushed a shovel into the lumpy dirt and turned the soil, prodding up hairy roots and chopping them apart with the shovel's blade. She found it hard to believe Marie had grown a small garden in this same spot last year. The forest was so unyielding. If she kept at it, though, she might be able to plant it in a few weeks time and wind up with a productive patch -- if she didn't wear herself out first.

April had arrived with more sun than showers. Yet, it might as well have been winter still, for all the bleakness that filled Jesi's heart. She'd detested herself for months now, but since that day in Hurley, her self-loathing had reached epic proportions.

Paul had said he'd forgiven her, and he insisted God had, too. Only... when or how could she ever forgive herself?

She knew in the deepest regions of her soul that she'd wounded a place in Paul he'd been unable to defend. His pain had been evident that day, until he'd drawn the shutters over his feelings. Hadn't he admitted to caring for her a great deal? He might even love her, at least a little. But she'd squashed those feelings by paying mind to Clay, and then by soiling Paul's reputation in front of the whole wide world.

Clearly, any feelings for her he'd once entertained were gone, right along with the trust he'd grown in her. So for the past few weeks, they'd once again endured the awkwardness of living together though he clearly regretted marrying her. Repeatedly, she'd run a gamut of options through her tired mind. She couldn't run away. She was done running away forever. But *something* had to change. *Something* had to happen. Either they needed to agree to live as brother and sister until the awkwardness faded, or she needed to consider ways to live without interfering in his life. The third option, to live as husband and wife the way God intended -- well, that hardly seemed worth considering.

Somewhere off in the woods, the rhythmic whacking of an ax echoed. Moments later came a shout, and the crash and tear of branches breaking. The woods crew must not be not far off the trace. Most of the winter's logs had already gone downriver to the mills or been skidded out to the train tracks where they'd be loaded on the iron horse and taken even further away from the region.

"You look like you could use a hand."

Jesi startled, then straightened and leaned on the shovel. She hadn't expected anyone to walk up on her. Paul had gone to visit the family of a sick, elderly woman in Gile. A young lumberjack near her own age stood a few feet away. He wore overalls and tall boots. His red shirt sleeves were rolled up over his elbows, and his short-cropped yellow hair barely showed under his cap.

"I was passing on my way back to camp and saw you out here. Why don't you let me take that shovel and give you a rest?" He reached for the shovel and plucked it out of her hand before she could say yes or no. "You remember me, don't you? I'm Will Ackerson. I heard your mister preach at the camp a time or two when you were there."

She remembered. Her shoulders relaxed. "Yes, of course."

"My folks have a farm down near Upton. I make more money logging, but I admit to missing the farm chores. Don't tell my pa, though."

They chuckled together.

"This'll be good soil if you ever get rid of all the stump roots. Don't worry though. Everybody has to deal with it. The payoff is having all those nice, fresh vegetables right out your door."

Will planted his foot on the shovel and gave it a good, hard shove, then turned the dirt. He pushed and turned, pushed and turned. The way he chattered, it seemed he hardly used any effort at all. Jesi didn't say a word. She just listened.

"I think its jim-dandy that Mr. Winter went and got himself married. I wouldn't mind finding myself a gal, especially if she's a good looker like you."

Jesi smiled, warming up to Will's easy-going nature. "I'm sure you will, you being such a hard-worker and all."

"What do we have here?"

Jesi whirled; more startled to hear Paul's voice than she'd been when Will had surprised her.

Will rested his forearm on the shovel. "It's just me. I saw your missus out here tussling with this peaty dirt and thought she could use a hand."

"Tussling, was she?"

Will chortled. "That's right."

Jesi felt the need to explain. "He took right over. I didn't even ask him."

"I'm sure you didn't." Paul's brows rose and fell. "You must be tired out, Will. Can we get you a glass of water? I take it you'll be off to home soon."

"That's right. End of the week, and we'll be finished with this job. I'll hike on back to see the folks."

Jesi folded her arms. "You walk all the way?"

"Sure. Don't take long."

She thought about her own failed attempt to walk away from Hurley last fall. "Well, you better come get a drink after shoveling all that dirt. Thank you, by the way. I don't think I'd have gotten nearly so much done in so short an order."

Will pulled his cap off and dipped his head. "It was my pleasure."

Jesi led the way to the outdoor pump and with a few jerks of the handle handed him a cup of water. Paul followed. He seemed to have more on his mind than usual, but then, he was always quiet with her lately.

"Here you are."

"Thank you." Will gulped down the icy water and said goodbye.

Paul followed Jesi into the cabin. "He'll be tired tonight, after working in the woods *and* helping you turn the garden."

The tone in his voice pinched her nerves. "I didn't ask him to stop by, or to help me."

"You've already told me. But who could resist helping you?"

"What do you mean?"

"The woods aren't dripping pretty women."

"You mean like when you helped me?" Her hackles rose. "You couldn't resist, and now you wish you had?"

"No." His jaw loosened. "I don't mean that. I'm sorry."

Jesi turned away to pour water into the reservoir on the cook stove. His comment had cut her. It proved he was sorry, all right. Sorry for ever letting her into his life.

*****

Paul sighed and picked up the empty pail to refill. *No, Jesi, I meant you're beautiful and sweet and that any man would be a fool to turn his back on you. Why should a good-looking fellow like Will? I'm jealous. That's all...*

But of course, his words hadn't come across that way. They came across as suspicious. He'd tried to tell her he'd forgiven her, but until she believed it, she'd doubt him as much as she doubted herself.

"Paul." She spoke with her back turned. "I was wondering if you'd let me take the buggy into town. It won't be dark for a few hours yet, and I have a letter I'd like to send to my parents. It's been a while since I've written, and I don't want them to wonder."

"Can it wait until Monday? I have to go in then and get some feed. I need a little more time with my sermon."

"Aren't you preaching at one of the other camps tomorrow?"

Paul nodded. "That's why I need to get packed up this afternoon. So if you can wait until Monday--"

"I'd really rather not wait." She turned and looked at him, her face set. "You don't need to come along. I hate to take you from your work. But if you think it's all right for me to go in alone, I think I can handle it."

He knew she could drive a buggy. She'd tried it a time or two since their fateful trip to town that day. She'd said she'd been driving since she was twelve. Yet for her to go into Hurley alone after all that had happened there made him nervous.

He was glad she was conquering her fears. But she was still Jesilyn, and she turned heads. And Big John was there, and Hurley was a long drive alone, and--

"Paul? Is it all right?"

He frowned. "I suppose... if you really want to go."

"I'm not going to run off, if that's what you're thinking."

"I wasn't thinking that."

"Not that it probably wouldn't be better in the long run if I did."

"Jesi, don't say that. It's the last thing I want."

"Is it?" She wiped her hands on a towel and tossed it down.

In three brisk steps he took her by the arms, his touch gentle. "I'm just worried for your safety. I wish you'd believe that."

Did she believe him? Was the unspoken question in her eyes a sign of hope?

"Go ahead and take the buggy. It might be nice for you to have an afternoon away from here without me getting in your way. I'll go get it rigged."

"I'll have your lunch ready when you get back."

He gave her a smile. The trust had to start somewhere, didn't it?

Jesi left for town, and Paul spent the afternoon working on his sermon and packing his things for the trip up to the camps nearer Lake Superior. He'd light out before dawn and be back late the next night. Jesi would have the day to herself tomorrow, as well as today.

He paced the floor as the afternoon wore on. Dinnertime came. Where was she? Maybe she'd decided to take her meal in town. She might have even come home as far as Gile or Montreal and stopped by someone's house to eat. That was likely the case.

He took some deep breaths and fixed his own meal. After eating, he went back to studying. The sun sank lower in the sky. Spring had come and the days were getting longer, but the kiss of winter still lay on the evenings, and when the sun dropped, it dropped quickly.

Where could she be? What if she'd gotten hurt or was in trouble? *What if she had changed her mind about coming back?*

Paul stoked the kitchen stove to ward off the chill and pulled his coat from the peg on the wall. Time to saddle Sarah and hunt down Jesi.

He opened the door just as she pulled the buggy into the yard. He stayed in the doorway, watching Jesi climb down.

She caught sight of him. "Paul. You'll never believe what happened."

He walked out to unharness Sarah.

"The Bardon Hotel is on fire. The upper story, completely in flames. People were rushing everywhere. The fire department came right away, and the one from Ironwood came, too. That beautiful building... it's such a shame."

"How?"

"I don't know. Hopefully it won't be a complete loss." She followed him as he led Sarah across camp to the barn. "They seemed to be getting it under control by the time I left. I couldn't leave right away, of course. So much was happening. I wanted to find a way to help."

"Did you?"

"Not exactly."

"What do you mean?"

"I didn't help with the fire, but I ran into a woman I once knew. Her name is Betty. She worked at Maisey's."

Paul stared at her over Sarah's back as the horse munched oats out of a bag. Even in the shadows of the barn, her eyes sparkled.

"She was leaving Maisey's for good. I met her on her way to the station. We had a good talk, and I think -- I think I encouraged her."

Paul ducked under Sarah's head and stood near Jesi. Her excitement was as pungent as the fresh smelling hay. "Come on. Let's go inside, and you can tell me about it."

He followed her back into the cabin and helped her out of her coat. She took off her hat and gloves. Her cheeks were bright with cold, and he wished he'd built up the fire in the fireplace so she could sit by it.

"I thought Betty hated me. She was always curt with me, downright rude, even. When I met her on the street watching all the people rushing up and down, she stood there, just staring at the fire. At first I'd planned to walk past. You know how I worry about running into anyone..."

"Let's sit."

She pulled out a chair by the table, and Paul reached for the coffee pot. Thankfully, it had warmed since he'd stoked the stove. He poured her a cup, and she held it in both hands. Her voice fell into a whisper over the cup's rim. "She stopped me with one hard look. I didn't know what to say except *hello.*

"She remembered my name -- Jane, of course. I decided to tell her it isn't my name, and that I was glad to see her so I could tell her so. She seemed taken aback. I believe she thought she'd intimidate me."

"Why?"

"I don't know. She just always did. I think it helped her feel she was in control of her life."

"But she's not."

Jesi shook her head. "No, of course not."

Paul leaned back as she sipped her coffee. She understood. Then why didn't she let go completely? She'd turned so much of her life into fruit, but still held on so tightly to self-indictment.

"What happened then?"

"She changed. Tears sprang up in her eyes and she became a completely different Betty from the woman I'd known. She told me how she wanted to change, wanted to get away. She was going to take a train down to Green Bay, or maybe over to Duluth. She hadn't decided where. She just wanted to get away and start over.

"I offered her a ride over to the station. We had to go a roundabout way with all the commotion in the streets." Her voice softened again. "I told her what had happened to me and how I was sure God would make a way for her if she'd let Him."

Her lashes dropped, and Paul marveled. How precious she was to him, if only she knew.

She won't leave me. I can trust her heart. He knew it then, knew it like he had before, but he'd lost track of that trust for a while.

Suddenly she looked up and set her cup on the table. "I almost forgot."

She pushed back her chair and retrieved an envelope from her coat pocket. She handed it to him. "Your mail."

Her gaze flashed at his. He took a look at the envelope.

Imogene Weinhert.

He tapped the letter against his palm and glanced only briefly at Jesi. "Thank you for bringing it."

"Something important?"

The tone of her voice sounded more than casual. Paul shrugged. "People back in my home town. Friends of the family."

"I see." She lifted her shoulders and sighed. "This day has just worn me out. I think I'll go to bed early."

Paul stood. "I suppose you must be tired."

"Incredibly."

She'd been so enthused, so anxious to tell him about Betty. Now her voice had grown distant again. The letter hung from his fingertips. Did she know something about Imogene? That would be impossible, wouldn't it?

He didn't dare ask. That would open another can of worms. She reached for the door of her room. There must be something he could, or *should* say.

"Jesi?"

She paused. He wished she'd look at him, but she didn't.

"I'm glad you made it back all right."

"Goodnight, Paul."

Was she glad to be back? Now he wasn't sure. "Goodnight."

Chapter Twenty-Six

Jamie Gilbert smiled at Corianne as he strained against the oars of their rented pleasure boat, squinting one eye against the bright sun so it seemed he'd almost intentionally winked at her. She blushed and forced her gaze to wander over the bright expanse of water swirling around them. The St. Louis River, one of the big lake's largest tributaries, twisted it's broad, flat way along, separating the hills of Duluth from the sprawling Superior delta and pouring into the bay.

When she looked up at him again, his gaze was still on her, his shoulders moving in a smooth rhythm.

She answered his intense look with a coy smile. "Are we in a race?"

"Haven't I told you? I'm stealing you away."

Cori giggled. She shivered and hugged her wrap around her shoulders. Even though May was fully upon them, the brisk air coming off the water still held an icy touch. "You should have warned me, and I would have packed a bag."

His teeth gleamed. "I'd have your father and grandfather and even *my* father coming after me if I did such a thing."

"I suppose that's true."

"And besides, I don't want you to miss out on those classes you enrolled in for the fall."

"I still can't believe I'm going to be a teacher."

"You'll do wonderfully. You're a smart woman, Cori."

Cori warmed. She would turn nineteen in another month. No one had ever called her a woman even though she was fully grown. She'd grown up with young ladies who'd married at sixteen and were mothers already. Still, she and Jesi were always the Beaumont girls. Now Jesi was married, too. Had Clay Dalton thought of Jesi as a woman?

"You're blushing."

She touched her cheek. "Am I?"

"Because I said you're smart? Or because I'm admiring you in other ways?"

She tried to breathe, tried to calm the fluttering of her heart. "Both, I suppose. It's not fair that you can read my mind."

Jamie laughed. He rested his arms and the boat drifted slowly. "You'll be so busy by next Christmas you probably won't have time to write to me."

"I think I'll manage."

She'd prayed about attending normal school for four long months, and each time, before she'd even said amen, God had nudged her to follow up on Jamie's suggestion. He'd taken her to look into the program right after Christmas, and now it was all she could think about -- except for thinking about him, of course.

Jamie wants this for me almost as much as I want it for myself. What does that mean for the two of us?

She gathered him in with a warm glance. They'd grown close in their times spent together and had exchanged more than two dozen letters while they were apart. Schooling took time, and Jamie still had a long way to go in developing his own future. Would they ever marry and be together? *I want to marry this man, but does he want to marry me?*

He smiled at her again, and this time when her cheeks flushed, she didn't try to hide it. She raised a brow. "Are you getting hungry?"

"What did you bring us in that basket to eat?"

"Enough to feed the whole family, probably."

"Because Evie packed for your grandmother and my da to join us."

"Yes."

"It's too bad your grandfather couldn't convince her to come."

Cori wasn't sure. Sometimes she wondered about her grandfather. Some days, his recuperation went well and he acted as if he'd be around forever, and then on other days he behaved as though he was a goner. Today was one of the latter. Whenever he got like that, he made sure Gran had someone to lean on -- someone like Jamie's dad. He'd urged Gran to go boating with them, and Joe had been willing to bring her, but she refused to leave the house and enjoy the outing without Gramp. In a way, Cori was proud of her grandma. Proud of her for withstanding Gramp's ploys to push her toward the safety net of Joseph Gilbert. Gran was a smart old lady. She saw what Gramp was up to.

"I wish Gramp would get well. It's bad enough to think of losing him myself, but it about breaks my heart to think of what Gran must be going through."

"There's always hope, Cori, and there's always life. Your grandmother is a survivor. God will see her through *if* the time comes she has to go on without your grandfather."

"I sometimes forget you lost your own mother. Don't you wish you'd known her?"

"Of course. But Da tells me about her. You know she and your grandmother were friends."

Cori sighed. "Yes. Hard to imagine when your pa cared for them both. Imagine if he and Gran would've gotten married. Why, you'd be my -- my uncle." She laughed aloud.

"If I'd be at all, you mean."

"Oh, yes. That's true. Well, I'm glad things happened as they did, then."

His eyes twinkled with mischief. "Are you?"

"Jamie Gilbert, you are such a tease *and* a flirt."

"I don't flirt with anyone else."

Didn't he?

He penetrated her with a look she didn't know how to take.

"My mother was quite forgiving, or so it seems." He turned his eyes to the distant hills. "That's quite an attribute in a woman."

Her heart, soaring a second before, plunged off a cliff. Cori realized his thoughts, and her chest burned. *Jesilyn. Why does he spend so much energy wanting me to forgive her? Why doesn't he ever suggest* Jesi *should be the one begging for* my *forgiveness?*

Cori bowed her head and fiddled with the items in the basket. Her fingers fumbled over the sandwiches wrapped in brown paper.

Her prodigal sister had written twice since the letter confessing where she'd been. In telling them about her husband's work as a camp preacher, about the garden she hoped to plant, about the camp cookee and his daughters, she sounded not only well, but almost happy. So disheartening.

Cori handed Jamie a sandwich without looking up at him, and continued scrounging around for a napkin. Could Jesi ever truly be happy? To think she might have found contentment in some ruffian lumber camp was nearly impossible to believe. And though she talked of Paul in glowing terms, nothing in Jesi's letters convinced Cori her sister was in a honeymoon frame of mind.

"Cori?"

She glanced up. Jamie's face lay open, his eyes searching.

"What's wrong?"

"You always say things about Jesi." She raised her hand holding the sandwich and dropped it into her lap again with a shrug. "Oh -- I know what you're talking about even when you don't say her name. Your hints aren't lost on me. Why should I forgive her? She'll just act like she never did anything wrong. If you ask me, she should be the one begging *me* for forgiveness, rather than me just sitting here holding it out to her like she deserved a prize for her ill behavior."

She shifted beneath his intense gaze. Finally he answered, his voice soft and without incrimination. "It's important for her to want it, yes. But Cori, don't you think you'll be free of the bitterness eating you up inside if the forgiveness is there now, whether or not Jesi ever wants it?

"Eating me up? Why do you think that's happening? I'm... *bolstered* by what I feel because I know I'm right."

He shook his head and chortled like she was fooling herself.

She flushed. "Why do you laugh?"

"Let me ask you this, Cori. Do you think maybe God has an opinion about it? Have you talked to Him?"

"About forgiving Jesi?" Her voice pitched higher than she wanted it to, and her face heated.

He nodded. "I'm just saying if Jesus holds out forgiveness to every sinner willing to bow down and receive it, if it's there, waiting for them if and when they're ready, shouldn't we do the same thing?"

His words struck her like a slap across the face. Her face must be red with humiliation.

She gasped. "You think I'm sinning by not offering to forgive her?"

"To be quite honest, yes."

At one time she'd recognized her bitterness as sin standing between her and God, but she'd ignored it long enough to assuage her guilt. Clearly, God did not withhold His mercy, and she was to follow His example.

What if Jesi never wants forgiveness?

A voice answered her heart in whispers louder than the blood rushing through her head. *It's not for you to judge her, whether she does or doesn't. You just need to be ready to forgive.*

She fingered the wrapper on her sandwich, her mouth dry and choking. Embarrassment had stolen her appetite. Jamie had found her flawed.

"Don't be angry, Cori."

She couldn't help but look at him. Trying to avoid his brown eyes two feet in front of her was ridiculous. Yet he was all a blur. "I'm not angry."

"You're crying."

"No I'm not." She shook her head. In truth, she just wanted to get out of the boat. She wanted to get away from him. He was dissatisfied with her.

"Your da told me he expects she'll come home before long. He said your family got another letter from her."

"I suppose you're anxious to meet her." She regretted the accusation in her tone the moment the words were out.

"She's part of your family."

"A fact I'm constantly reminded of."

"Your twin. You'll always be part of one another."

"No. Jesi is *not* my twin." She flared at him. "We may look alike. We may sound and act alike, but we are very different on the inside. I wish people would understand that."

He reached for her hand. She tried to snap it away but he held fast, causing the boat to sway. He turned her hand over in his and caressed her palm. Lightning bolts raced up her arm. Her emotions rushed back and forth from fear and rejection, to love and longing.

His lips curved softly. "I think I know that."

He didn't let go, but with his other hand pulled a handkerchief from his pocket and dabbed at her cheek. She lifted her free hand and covered his.

"It's you I'm interested in, Cori. Not your sister."

He sounded so sincere, so loving. Humiliation filled her. She'd thought for a moment she was about to lose him.

She sniffled. "I-I feel so foolish."

"Don't feel that way." He dabbed her tears, then drew her face upward.

How had he leaned so close, until his face was just inches from hers? Cori blinked, her tears drying as she looked at him. She leaned nearer, her breath hardly coming, the world, the hills, the river swirling out of existence as their lips touched.

What if her grandmother had married Joe? What if her grandfather hadn't fallen ill so she and Jamie would meet? What if all those horrible things between her and Jesi and Clay hadn't happened?

I wouldn't be here, now.

She allowed the kiss to linger until Jamie leaned away, his eyes like coal. The sensation on her lips remained, soft and moist. The day suddenly felt warmer.

What if forgiving Jesi was possible, even out of the mire?

"Look over there."

She forced her gaze away. They'd drifted back downriver a good distance. An ore boat slid into the harbor.

"How solid steel so massive can carry tons of iron ore and float never ceases to amaze me."

"But you're the scientist."

"Not really. I'm just a woodsman, like my da."

"You're brilliant."

He turned to look at her again. She'd heard the gush of love in her voice with her own ears, but he might as well know how she thought of him.

He grinned. "What do you say we dock and have our lunch at the clubhouse?"

"Wherever you'd like to go. After all, you're the one stealing me away, remember?"

*****

Arriving back at the house late in the afternoon, they found Jamie's da in his overalls, toting a wheelbarrow of sod out of the yard. Cori's grandmother, Colette, knelt in the dirt.

Cori stood on the walk and grinned at the elderly pair. "You two are having an industrious afternoon."

"Yes." Gran swiped a wisp of hair out of her eyes and in doing so, streaked dirt across her cheek. "Your grandfather is sleeping, and I needed to do some thinking."

"Why is it that older people always seem to need to work in order to think?"

Joe harrumphed and dropped the wheelbarrow in its track. "Your day will come. We did our share of thinking once upon a time the way you two do -- long walks, fishing trips, lying on our backs, staring at the clouds." He pulled off his gloves. "I reckon we even thought about the same nonsense."

"Nonsense? Really?" Cori delivered her reprimand with a giggle.

Joe waved his hand. "I'm sure romance and nonsense is exactly what the two of you have on your minds."

She blushed in the face of Joe's mischievous grin.

Gran brushed the dirt off her hands and knees and came to stand in front of them. "Is Joe right?"

"Yes, Mrs. Kade. I'm sure you know Da well enough to read his mind and perceive when his judgment is sound. Romance and nonsense of the best kind is what we have on our minds today."

Gran cast Cori a smile as if to say, *he's very like his father.*

"So may I ask what you're thinking about that has you working so hard? Is Gramp feeling any better today?"

Colette patted her hand. "We got some news today while the two of you were out. The doctor came to see him. He believes your grandpa's chances are good. He still believes he removed the tumor before it spread anyplace else. But only time will tell for sure."

"We won't stop praying, Mrs. Kade."

"Thank you, Jamie. That means more than you can imagination."

Cori gave her a hug. "Is he asleep, or can we go up and see him?"

"He might be awake. You can peek in and see. He'll like that."

Jamie slipped his hand into hers and together, they walked up to the house. Life felt bright and welcoming. If Gramp could be healed, nearly everything would be in place.

Nearly everything.

Chapter Twenty-Seven

Jesi glanced at Paul out the corner of her eye while he sat at his desk, scratching away on a piece of paper. *Must be a doozey of a sermon. Lying, cheating, adultery... probably just a few of the sins he'd like to camp on.*

She opened the door and leaned against the frame, soaking in the dry breeze, wishing it could whisk away the agony that kept coming back. *Regret. That's all I have to look forward to.*

Paul paused, and the slump of his shoulders told her he was considering what to write next. He dipped his pen and continued.

She squinted into the bright sunlight and looked down over the garden where she'd planted some seed. Nothing had come up yet. If they didn't get some spring rain soon, she'd have to haul water from the pump to coax them to germinate. She felt just as dry inside, sapped of the moisture of life.

A sigh pressed past her lips. For a few hours on the day of the Bardon Hotel fire, she'd felt a surge of life. Talking to Betty about God had sparked a flame inside her own heart. But it had snuffed out when she'd handed Paul the letter from Imogene.

Regret.

Jesi turned aside. At her work table, she peeled back the skin of an onion. Her eyes burned. She sniffed.

"Jesi?"

She blinked. "What?"

"Stop whatever torture you're doing to yourself with that onion and go pack a bag. I've decided we're going to see Marie."

"We are?"

"Yes, and if we can make it on the five o'clock train, that'll be even better. I've made up my mind, and I don't want to wait until tomorrow."

Jesi stared at him for a minute, then loosened her apron. *Marie. Thank you, God.*

She wondered briefly what had caused Paul to make the decision. It was certainly spontaneous, or so it appeared. Really, his reasoning mattered little. They were going, and she would get away from the confinement of the camp and this tiny cabin where she was trapped with him, knowing how disappointed he was in her.

Packing didn't take her long. She didn't own many things. She decided to take nearly everything; the nightgown Marie had given her, the dress Paul had bought, as well as the one Marie had sewn for her wedding, and the one other day dress hanging on her hook. She'd leave behind the dirty work dress she had on.

Jesi changed and packed in less than half an hour. Paul tossed her bag into the boot at the back of the buggy and helped her up into the seat.

"What'll you do with the buggy when we get to town?"

"I'll leave it at the livery by the station."

She nodded, but Paul didn't seem willing to be drawn into conversation that might explain his sudden decision to visit Marie, so she decided to oblige his silence on the subject.

She bore the trip to town. She and Paul talked little the rest of the way and about nothing that mattered. On the train platform, she stood beside him, thinking about the circumstances of her last train ride.

I'm still on a reckless course.

Finally the whistle blew, and they boarded. They found their seats, and Jesi slid to the inside where she could look out the north-facing window where the woods stood just as thick as everyplace else.

"I suppose you'll be glad to have a woman to talk to again," Paul said. "You've been stuck with my conversation for so long now."

"I am."

Paul grinned.

Jesi flushed. "I didn't mean it to sound like there is anything wrong with your company. I'm always pleased when we talk."

She gazed out the window. No use looking to see if he had been pleased by the compliment. She knew better. Paul was always polite.

"I'm looking forward to seeing Marie, too. I guess I'm ever the younger brother, missing her influence."

She couldn't help the slight smile lifting one corner of her mouth.

"She may not get the wire we sent until we're almost upon her. It doesn't matter. We'll see her tomorrow. I'll get rooms for us at the hotel."

Jesi toyed with the string of her reticule. *Another awkward moment for Mr. and Mrs. Paul Winter.* That's what that would be.

Thankfully, with seemingly not much else to say, Paul dozed. Jesi relaxed. How peaceful he looked. She laid her head against the side of the train car and studied him. She hadn't been able to do that in a long while. Paul wasn't usually so close, or so still. And she had the benefit of him not being able to look back.

He'd forgotten to shave. A day's growth of dark beard stubbled his cheeks. His hair was a little too long, but she rather liked it. It came down almost to his collar and looked satiny. His straight bangs fell across his forehead and shadowed his eyelids with their dark lashes.

Such a handsome man.

A lump crawled up her throat, and she had to look away.

They got off the train in Ashland at just past supper time. Paul hailed a driver who took them to their hotel.

"Sorry, it's not the Chequamegon."

She didn't bother telling him she'd been to that elegant hotel before with her parents and sister. He'd only feel worse. They stayed at smaller lodgings that were just as comfortable though not as splendid as the magnificent white bay front establishment.

She wanted to ask if he could really afford two rooms, but she didn't want to point out the obvious awkwardness of their whole situation. The irregularities of their marriage stared at them from morning to dusk everyday as it was.

After registering them in the lobby, he walked up the stairs in front of her, carrying both of their bags. "I'll ask them to send up your meal. You're probably tired. I'll figure out our plans and come by to speak to you in the morning."

"All right."

She followed behind him as they walked down a corridor with several doors on either side. He stopped near the middle and pushed open a door. "Here you are. I'll be next door." He dipped his head toward his door. "Knock on the wall if you need me."

She stepped inside her room and nodded, waiting until he left and closing the door behind him. She sat on the edge of the bed and turned to look at the wallpaper in flowery stripes. Paul would only be a few feet away, on just the other side of a thin partition. Yet it felt like miles.

*****

The early morning came and went. Jesi had already paced for nearly an hour, wondering when Paul planned to come for her. Her gaze roved to the wall that separated them, and she thought about rapping on it, just to see if he was really still there or if he'd high-tailed it back to Hurley to leave her to her own devices.

But that would never be like Paul. She knew better.

She pulled the curtain back from the window and looked out into the street, anything to distract her. Wagons and buggies rolled by. The hotel was not on the lake, but near enough to see a glint of it in the sun. It reminded her of home. *Her* home.

She jumped when a knock pummeled the door. She spun from her gaze out the window to answer, but before she could, the door burst open and Marie hurried inside.

"Jesilyn. Oh, let me look at you." She grasped Jesi's arms and turned her toward the sunlight streaming in. "You look as beautiful as ever."

They embraced, and tears suddenly rushed into Jesi's eyes.

Her sister-in-law backed away and looked at her. "Oh... you're crying."

Jesi shook her head and blinked away the moisture.

"Don't be embarrassed. It makes me feel loved."

"I have missed you, Marie."

"I'm so excited that you've come. Paul said you're staying a whole week. Isn't it wonderful?"

"Really? I didn't know we'd stay so long."

Marie rolled her eyes. "You have to pry details out of him. Haven't you learned that yet?"

"I guess not."

She took Jesi's hand, pulled her to the bed, and sat next to her. "Tell me about things."

The pressure on Jesi's fingers and the steady, penetrating look on Marie's calm face told Jesi she wasn't asking for anything so simple as how Charlie Hanke and his girls were doing, or whether she was still baking bread, or if she'd managed to plant a garden, or if she were tiring of living on the outskirts of a lumber camp.

"They're all right."

"That's a lie, Jesi."

She shrugged and battled a return of her tears. In such cases, she'd always found it easier to be angry, to fix blame. But somehow she hadn't the heart to do so with Paul. She was the one who deserved all of *his* anger and blame... and his rejection.

"I thought by now I wouldn't find the two of you in separate rooms." Marie's voice was gentle. Understanding, yet probing.

Jesi cringed. "That cut to the point."

"Shouldn't it?"

She gave a tiny nod.

"When I left, the two of you seemed to share something -- some kind of spark. I saw it plain as day."

The hole inside Jesi's heart burned around the edges and grew wider. Oh, they had shared a spark, all right. Then the incident in town with Clay had snuffed it out -- at least, for Paul.

"I behaved foolishly, Marie. The spark you saw is gone."

"For you, or for Paul?"

She nearly said *both,* but caught herself. She blinked. "In truth? Paul can't love me. Not after what I did."

Marie frowned. "What on earth did you do?"

Jesi stumbled with the words at first, but after a few moments found talking so freeing she told Marie the whole sordid story. About how they'd been excited to spend the day together. How her heart had been filled with hope that they were about to embark on a new, *real* life together. Then Clay had stepped up to her in the store. How, like an idiot and a fool, she'd allowed him to take her outside, "just to talk", he'd said. How they'd run into big Johnny Ray, and lastly, about the brawl that put Paul in a compromising and embarrassing position.

"He believed Clay's lies that I was willing to leave with him."

"I can't imagine why he would. You told him the truth?"

"No." Jesi glanced at her. "I couldn't. Not then. But later I told him Clay didn't have my heart."

"And does Paul?" Marie leaned back and studied her.

Jesi closed her eyes, swallowed, and nodded. "Very much."

"Well, then."

Jesi blinked at her. "Well, then... what?"

"You love Paul." She sounded satisfied, even resolved.

"Paul doesn't love me, Marie. Not now. He might have felt something like that once. And I know he feels responsible for me. He made it clear when we married that he'd always be true to me, but love? I ruined any chance of that."

"Nonsense." She patted Jesi's leg. "He'll come around." She grinned, then giggled. "Paul can't seem to keep from running into trouble in that town. He ends up on the ground more often then he ends up in a pulpit."

Jesi's mouth fell open.

"He's my little brother. I can tease."

Jesi allowed herself a smile. She had been able to tease Paul for a brief time. Teasing him had been romantic. Was Marie right? Would those days come again?

"Marie, there's another thing."

Marie's smile faltered. "What else?"

"I've wanted to ask you about Imogene."

"Imogene Gillette?" Marie's brows shot up. "Whatever for?"

"Because Paul was in love with her, of course."

"You have nothing to be jealous about with her. He was infatuated. When she let him go, he was almost relieved of it in the end."

Jesi found that hard to believe. Imogene hadn't let him go. She'd rejected him. Jesi knew all too well what rejection felt like, especially the one-sided kind.

"I don't think she has, and I don't think he was ever relieved, either."

"How do you know about Imogene?" Marie frowned. "Did Paul tell you about her?"

"No. He has her old letters." She hurried on, "I didn't go snooping. They were just lying there open, on his dresser. I found them while I was dusting. A long time ago."

"You didn't talk to him about them?"

"No, I couldn't. At the time, it didn't matter. Now they've disappeared. I haven't seen them since."

"He must have thrown them away."

"He may have." Jesi shrugged. "But truly, they didn't bother me. At the time I felt only sorry for his loss." She clenched her hands together in her lap. "Then another letter arrived."

"What do you mean? When?"

"Just last week. He received another letter from her. He tucked it into his pocket. He didn't tell me what it said, and of course I couldn't ask. He doesn't know I know about her."

"I see." Marie stood and paced across the room. She crossed her arms and turned to Jesi. "I could try to get to the bottom of it, but I think it would be best if you asked him about the letter yourself. Trust me when I say this, Jesi, and... trust Paul. I don't think you have any need to be worried or jealous of Imogene."

"Truth be told, I hope to never be worried or jealous of anyone ever again."

Chapter Twenty-Eight

By midday, they'd seen the town, Ashland's new academy, the hospital, and the room Marie shared with another woman in the home of Hilda Berg, a widow who let rooms out to single ladies in her large, comfortable home. She offered them reduced rent in exchange for help with simple chores.

Marie seemed happy, incredibly so, and Paul was glad she'd followed her dream to come and train further through her job at the hospital. Clearly, she'd been able to discern God's leading.

If only he could say the same.

I need these days, Lord, and so does Jesi. Just refresh us both, I pray. Help us return to the work in Hurley with some clear direction for our future. I-I don't know what that future is, God.

Right now, Jesi helped Mrs. Berg and another boarder named Anna with their lunch dishes, while he and Marie sat in a pair of chairs out on the lawn. Marie leaned back, closed her eyes, and allowed the sun to soak warm rays into her face, not concerned that she might brown.

"Sure has been a beautiful spring."

"A bit too dry. Could be trouble if we don't get some rain."

"You're a pessimist, Paul, did anyone ever tell you that?"

"You have, often enough."

She smiled. His sister looked so pretty sitting there with her head tilted back and her eyes closed, such a gentle, teasing expression on her flawless face, he wondered when one of these northern men who'd noticed it would convince her to marry him.

"I'm just saying. Dry weather lasting too long could spell disaster. Been worried about sparks off the rail lines."

"You're right, I suppose. You and Jesi take care living back there in the woods, you hear me?"

"I hear you."

"Speaking of you and Jesi..." She winked one eye open at him. "Why haven't you made things right between the two of you?"

He straightened. His sister certainly had a bold way about her. "I'm not sure it's any of your business."

"Don't even say that, Paul." She sat up and leveled him with a stare. "You and Jesi will always be my business, like it or not. You've been married for months, living alone in that cabin together. I can't believe you haven't come together."

Paul flushed. "That's a bit indiscreet coming from a single, mission-minded lady."

"It's because I'm a mission-minded lady that I mind how you and your wife get along."

"We get along."

"You're like strangers." She pinched her lips in a straight line and tapped her fingers.

A quick glance told Paul she was stewing.

"Jesi told me what happened in Hurley."

"Good. I wondered if she would. I think she needed to talk about it."

"She would have been better off talking to you."

He shook his head. "I don't want to know any more about *Clay Dalton*."

"How can you expect your wife to open up and trust you if you won't let her?"

He gave her a sharp look, then laced his fingers together on his lap while he took a calming breath. "I've tried to help her open up to me. But after that business in front of Maisey's, everything got all stiff and uncomfortable between us."

"So do something about it."

Paul shrugged. He didn't know what to do.

"Have you wondered why things got all 'stiff and uncomfortable'?"

"Of course. I just figured she regretted her decision to stay, but that she'd reconciled herself to it."

"Is that what she said?"

Paul avoided answering, but Marie stared him down, waiting. "Well, no. She told me he doesn't have her heart." Saying it sounded foreign to his ears, but it sent a warm rush of blood through his body. *She'd really said those words.*

"Paul, have you been corresponding with Imogene?"

He jerked his head up, returning her stare. "What?"

"Jesi said you got a letter from her."

"I did, but she doesn't know about Imogene..." He suddenly recalled the measured look in Jesi's eyes the day she'd handed him the letter, and how her demeanor had changed. He'd noticed it then. It felt palpable, but he had no idea why. How could she have known?

He unfolded himself from the chair, walked across the lawn, and shoved his hands deep into his pockets. How in the world did Jesi know that the name on the letter meant anything to him? "Did you tell her about Imogene?"

Marie shook her head. "She told me she saw some letters once. She didn't mean to pry, but they were lying open on your dresser when she was cleaning."

Paul chewed his lip. So that was it. He pulled his hands from his pockets. *She must think...* He nearly moaned. The trouble between them always seemed to find a way to grow.

"What about this new letter, Paul?"

He waved her off with a brush of his hand. "It was nothing. Her father suggested she write to me about a pastorate opening up downstate. I have no intention of taking it. I wrote back and told her to tell him so. I'm staying where I am."

"Was he hoping something more would come of it... or was she?"

A small noise escaped his lips. "Hardly. She made point of the fact in the letter, and that was fine with me."

Marie stood up. "If it's that simple, then why are you pussyfooting around?"

"What do you mean?"

"You know exactly what I mean. You've watched a dozen lumberjacks go courting. Why, even Bob Kelick and Jude Selzner didn't waste the time you have, and they didn't have half so much chance." A flush rose into her cheeks. "If you love Jesi, why don't you court her -- and let her know it? You never did that before you were married, and now you have the chance. You *do* love her, don't you?"

Her imploring words plunged into his heart and pulled his feelings up like a bucket pulling water from a well. He pushed a hand through his hair and raised his gaze back at hers. Slowly, he nodded.

"Then love her like you mean it, Paul. Love her so fully she'll never doubt you. Ever."

*****

What day is it? Wednesday. Only Wednesday. Four more days to stay with Marie in Ashland. If only things could change before we have to go back. Can't they? Somehow?

Jesi thought of God's giant finger making swirls in her life, mixing it around, turning it into... what? Yet she'd prayed just now, really, hadn't she?

A soft rap on the door made her eyes pop open fully. Leaning into the pillow, she turned her head toward the sound. "Who is it?"

A voice, cheerful but muffled by the door called out, "Wake up, sleepy head. It's time for breakfast."

Paul?

She scrambled out of the blankets and jumped to the floor in her bare feet. "Um... okay." A wave of dizziness assailed her. "How soon should I be ready?"

"I'll be waiting next door. Just tap on the wall when you're dressed."

"All right."

Befuddlement had her turning in circles. She grasped for her things, mumbling along the way. "Where'd I leave my stockings? There they are."

She swiped them off the floor, laid them on the bed, and set out her dress and under-garments.

"I feel like a mess." She hurried to the wash basin and doused her face, then patted it dry with a fresh, white towel.

Her heart pounded, whether from the suddenness of rising, or from the bright tone in Paul's voice, she couldn't say. He sounded almost glad at the thought of having breakfast with her. Marie must be joining them. That was it. He was excited because of Marie.

She buttoned the long row of buttons running down the front of her dress, but had to do it again when she realized she'd gone crooked. She growled, but nimbly re-fit the buttons. Then, taming her wild hair with a brush as best she could, she wound it in a chignon at the base of her neck. Then she pulled on her shoes, looking around the room frantically for her button hook.

"Ah." Snatching it up, she set about buttoning them.

Don't leave without me.

Finally, she was dressed. She took one more look in the mirror and pinched her cheeks, then raised her hand to the wall. She hesitated, poised to knock, thinking how she'd almost done this very thing two nights ago. She gave three clipped taps and jumped back when Paul answered her knock with two more.

Moments later, he repeated his soft rap against her door. She smoothed her skirt and turned the knob.

His smile was as genuine as she'd ever seen it. "Good morning."

"Good morning."

"It's a beautiful day. Shall we?" He held out his arm. With an inward shrug, she looped hers through it. His shirt felt crisp, and he smelled of soap. The muscles of his upper arm filled her palm, sending a wave of pleasure through her.

She tried to match his cheer. "I think you needed a few days away from camp."

"I was turning into a bear, wasn't I? Yes, everyone needs a few days to refresh now and then."

Guiding her down the long staircase, through the lobby, and out the door, Paul paused on the walk. He looked left, then right. "Well, what do you say we go this way?"

He turned left and set a meandering pace.

"Where are we meeting Marie?"

"Marie had some things to attend to. I thought we'd just take a stroll."

A stroll? What's come over Paul?

She didn't know what had happened. He hadn't been so free and comfortable with her in weeks. Whatever the cause, she wasn't about to complain. Perhaps they could close some of the distance between them and at least be friends again.

"All right. Lead the way."

He smiled at her. Well, not *at her* exactly. More at the sunshine and the world around them. Still, she felt as if he'd smiled at her.

He fell quiet. She sneaked a peek at him. He had pursed his lips and drawn his eyebrows together in thought. Afraid his good mood might be nearing its end, she hurried to speak.

"It's been a joy to see Marie again. Thank you so much for bringing me."

"Bringing you? Did you think I'd leave you behind?"

"No, that's not what I meant. It's just that I'm glad we've come."

He chuckled. "I'm teasing. I knew what you meant."

Suddenly her stomach growled. She flinched.

"Was that you or me? Come on. There's a restaurant on the next block. I'll take you out for breakfast."

"Oh, but you didn't plan--"

"Who said I didn't?"

He did smile at her then, and Jesi's heart rolled over. He hadn't looked at her like that since... well, since before the day Clay and Big John caused the scene in Hurley. Warmth rushed up the length of her. "All right, big spender."

He laughed louder, and she dared join him.

During their breakfast of eggs and side pork, Paul continued to behave most pleasantly and attentively. Once he even reached across the small table and patted her hand while he talked. Almost as if he'd changed overnight. He *had* changed overnight. Could a few days away from home really cause such a transformation?

As they left the restaurant, she wondered what his next step would be. She didn't have to wait long to find out. He took her shopping, reminding her she'd never gotten the material for a dress he'd promised her, and saying he could use a new shirt as well.

"I've told you I'm not a very good seamstress."

"I'll like it just because you make it."

She stared back at him as he picked up the package wrapped in string and tucked it under his arm. He reached for her hand.

Now he was being more than generous. While her wonder grew, skepticism also reared its head. As he held her hand and guided her back down the street toward the hotel, questions gnawed at her heart. She pushed them away. Why should she be troubled when Paul was being so kind? But why, *why* was he being kind? Had Marie somehow reminded him he was a missionary, and that she, Jesi, was in need of his compassion?

The thought gagged her. *Compassion.* No, she deserved his judgment. All the harsh feelings that had sprung up between them since Clay's reappearance were deserved on her part. How she felt about Paul, how much she loved him, and how repentant she might be didn't matter. She could never be enough for him. She could never be as clean as he deserved his wife to be. Sooner or later, today's good will would reach an end and he would remember that, just like he had before.

The knot in her gut gave one final twist.

"You're holding my hand awfully tight. Am I walking too fast?"

A rush of air escaped her lungs. "I'm sorry. I didn't realize... no, you're not. I mean, I'm fine."

"I wasn't complaining. I like it." His pressure over her fingers increased, making up for the sudden release of her own.

This has to stop. I don't understand it at all.

"Paul--" Her voice caught.

He stopped and gazed at her.

She struggled to meet his eyes. "Can we talk?"

"Ah." His gaze flicked with understanding. "You mean about more than new clothes and the weather and all of those things?"

She nodded.

"I've been counting on it. Tell you what... let's go back to the hotel and drop off our packages. I don't want to wear you out on your feet. We'll pick up the buggy and go for a ride down by the bay."

"All right." Her throat constricted at his words. Yet she knew that until they cleared the air and settled all her questions, she would have no peace in her heart. Without knowing what was going on, she couldn't imagine returning to Hurley with him.

An hour later, they rode side by side in Paul's buggy. He'd waggled some fruit and a canteen of water from the hotel manager in case they were gone for a long time. Who knew what she would have to do to get answers from her husband? Apparently, he must've been thinking similar thoughts to have prepared so.

She noticed he had also tucked a blanket into the boot of the buggy.

"We aren't getting kicked out of our rooms, are we?"

"No." Paul's warm smile lit up his face. "But you never know when the wind might kick up off the lake. Best to be prepared."

They drove west on a road that ran parallel to the railroad line. The waters of Chequamegon Bay sparkled in the spring sunshine. Five miles across the bay, the shoreline swung back around and headed to the north and east, eventually running past the Apostle Islands far beyond Jesi's ability to gaze.

They rode quietly, both of them subdued. Jesi's heart beat faster as she tried to form her thoughts. The day had been so lovely thus far. Should she really say something now that could ruin it all?

"Paul." She blurted his name before she could think better of it. "It's nice to spend the day with you. I mean -- I love Marie, and it's been wonderful to see her again, just as I knew it would be. But I enjoy your company, too."

"I know." He reached over and gently took her fingers in his. "I like spending time with you, too."

"Do you?"

"I know it hasn't seemed like it lately. But I do." He turned his head to face her, and his look told her she could believe him.

"I wish I could tell you how sorry I am."

He glanced at her again, then snapped the reins lightly. His lips fell into a straight line and the color drained from his face as he watched the road ahead.

"You don't believe me."

"Yes, I do."

"I wish I could take that day back."

"That day?"

"That day in Hurley. I wish--"

He squeezed her hand and set his jaw. The joint in his cheek moved.

"Paul--"

"I'll let you go if that's what you want. I don't want to keep you tied to me, Jesi. If you're sorry you didn't go when you had the chance, then I'll give you the chance."

"I would *never* go back. Not to him." Her mouth went slack. She stared at Paul. A fire in her body pulled her to the edge of the seat. "I'd thought... I'd *hoped* you'd believe me when I told you I don't care for him."

"But now you're sorry."

"Yes." She gasped. "I'm sorry for what I did that day. Sorry for even speaking to Clay Dalton. Sorry I didn't slap him silly right there in the mercantile instead of stepping outside and giving him the time of day. I'm sorry for hurting you and embarrassing you. Paul, I'm not sorry about losing Clay. I'm sorry that I came so close to losing *you.*"

"I see." With one hand he clenched the reins, and with the other he tightened his grasp on her fist. "You... you mean it?"

"Of course I do. I don't deserve to be in your life. I never have. I don't deserve the kindness and caring I've gotten from you or Marie. But I don't want to go back. I don't want anything else."

His shoulders relaxed, and he didn't seem to notice the horse had slowed its pace.

"I misunderstood. Now *I'm* sorry." He finally glanced at her quickly, and then again with a more thorough perusal.

Jesi leaned closer. "Still, as much as I don't want to go back to that life, I'm afraid I'm keeping you from the one you want."

Paul pulled back on the reins and stopped the buggy. As the wheels creaked to stillness, the water lapping against the sand and swishing over the reeds along the shore filled the air around them. A seagull squawked overhead as it reeled over the bay.

He looked at her fully. "I thought I made it clear to you that this is the life I want. I chose you, and now *you* are the life I want."

"What about the letter you got from Miss Gillette?" Jesi glanced down and fidgeted with the button on her skirt. "Surely you must have some regrets about being saddled with me."

"I've planned to talk to you about her and that letter. Maybe I should say *those* letters."

"Marie told you I pried?"

"You didn't pry." He touched her chin and drew it upward so she had to look at him. His voice softened. "You didn't pry."

"Fine, but..." Her eyes burned, and suddenly he blurred before her. "You love her."

"No. I don't. Jesi, look at me." He nudged her chin again. "The letter was about a church position her father wanted me to know about. It bore nothing of a personal nature. I'll show you."

"What--" She gasped when he reached inside his coat and pulled out the bent, flimsy missive. "You don't have to--"

He stilled her with a touch to her lips.

"Dear Paul, My father asked me to write to you. I told him it would likely be of no use, but as usual, he has some idea I may be able to prevail upon you. But I know you are called to the northern woods. Nevertheless, a position for a pastor has opened in a small but healthy church in Appleton. Father believes you would be just the man to fill it. Before I say anything more, I must assure you I have no schemes up my sleeve in writing to you. I am, as you must guess, a happily married woman, and I trust you are still content there within God's will among the lumberjacks and the wilderness.

"You know as well as I that things would never have worked well between us. I am called to remain in broader society, serving the Lord faithfully in whatever capacity he calls me. You could never have been happy to do so. I doubt you have changed in that regard, but I must fulfill my father's wishes. I pray for your abundant happiness as well as great fulfillment in your ministry. If I am wrong and you feel God nudging you toward the aforementioned position, by all means, please respond to tell us. Best wishes, as ever, *Mrs.* Imogene *Weinhert*."

Paul turned the letter toward her, proving Imogene had written nothing further.

"The letter doesn't make your heart ache?"

"My heart ceased aching for Imogene long, long ago. Even before you came to us. I just hadn't recognized it because I was so full of questions and uncertainties about the future. But then I asked God for just one soul." He smiled at her, his meaning clear.

"Well, you certainly did save me."

"Only God saves."

"You were his instrument."

"If I was, then I'm glad."

Jesi pondered him for a moment. God had used Paul to save her. But to save her from what, exactly? From sickness and possible starvation, maybe. From a life in Hurley's or some other town's brothels.

Surely. He'd saved her from the humiliation of going back to Superior and facing her family with her sin. Yet she knew that wasn't exactly what Paul meant. She hadn't forgotten the unspoken question in his statement about being glad. *He wonders if I've repented.*

"Paul... I almost don't know what to say. I am sorry. Truly. You deserve someone like Imogene, if not Imogene herself. Someone who loves God and is pure..." Her eyes blurred again.

Paul jumped out of the buggy and reached for her hand. She placed it in his, and he lifted her to the ground. All the while, he studied her. "Do you know how beautiful you are?"

She jerked up her head. His eyes held steady on her. She shrugged and moved away from him, uncomfortable with his compliment even while she hungered for it.

"You know, you've told me before -- on more than one occasion, I might add -- how dirty and shameful and undeserving you feel. Do you realize Satan wants you to feel that way? In fact, he is the one who tried to make you fall."

"He was successful."

"Not entirely. You didn't stay where you'd fallen. So he used his next avenue of attack. He told you how useless and dirty you are. And he isn't finished. He'll keep attacking you with thoughts like those to convince you you're unworthy of God's or anyone else's love."

Jesi moved her feet slowly in the thick sand along the shore. She pondered Paul's words as he ambled along beside her.

"You're a threat to Satan. That's why he does it. Your beauty gives you power over him because it is your unique way of carrying the glory of God into the world."

The Glory of God? In me? She frowned.

"God is the creator of beauty. Look at it." Paul swept his hand toward the expansive blue water and the deep blue sky. A pair of swans appeared along the western shore, gliding out of the reeds. They swam in and out. Perfect. Pure in their whiteness. Grace and enchantment in their movements.

Jesi bit her lip. She'd known all along that Satan enjoyed laughing at her, ever since she'd set out on her own course of self-destruction. She'd just never thought she had the power to make him stop.

Paul's voice fell to nearly a whisper. "The devil hates beauty."

"Thank you for telling me. I've never thought of anything like that before."

He turned to her and took her hand again. Then he stroked it and raised it to his lips, gently laying a kiss on the backs of her fingers.

"Please believe me when I tell you it's so," he said. "Your beauty comes from God, and I feel as blessed to bask in it as I do in viewing this great vista lying before us."

Chapter Twenty-Nine

"Good night, Jesi."

She returned Paul's smile and let herself inside her room. The sensation of his strong fingers lingered on hers. The door clicked shut, and she let out the breath she'd been holding almost all day. Had she really just spent such an intoxicating time with Paul?

They'd lived alone for weeks and weeks, and yet how many days had passed since she'd been so close to him? How long since she'd felt as if something true existed between them?

Jesi spun in a circle, collapsed onto her bed, and turned her gaze to the wall separating her from her husband. She reached out and touched it, wondering what he was doing, what he might be thinking on the other side.

He thinks I'm beautiful. Really, truly beautiful.

A slow smile curved her lips. Was he right? Did she really deserve God's love? Jesi curled on her side and thought about it. Just as quickly, memoires of her affair with Clay stabbed her conscience. She swallowed as the sharp reminder cut into her heart.

I was such a fool. Such an idiot. What if I hadn't done it? What if I had actually cared about what God wanted? I might not even have met Paul... but then again, I wouldn't know that. What would God have done?

She asked so many fruitless questions, and yet she couldn't help wondering. She *had* made terrible choices in her life, choices that had led her on a road to near destruction. She might have easily ended up spending her life -- body and soul -- at Maisey's. Yet if she hadn't chosen to give everything to a man like Clay who had never loved her, life *would* have been different. If she'd only acted differently.

Even so, God had sent her Paul.

Dear God, you sent Paul. I don't know why--

Yes, she did know why. Because God loved her. He'd seen how lost she was, and he'd loved her anyway. He'd scooped her up out of the mire of her life and loved her.

Jesi closed her eyes. Her nose tingled.

"I'll never feel as if I deserve him." She squeezed moisture from her eyes; not bitter tears, but sorrowful ones. Yet at the same time, she was thankful. "God, if you can forgive me for being so wrong, so foolish... I'm so sorry. Not only because of what happened to me and how much pain I've created for others, but also because I don't deserve it. I'm sorry. Please, please God, forgive me. I want to be a different woman. I want to make Paul happy. I want to know what else You can do. I want my life to be something better than the mess I've made it. I want to spend the rest of my life alive."

Dear God, if I'm really beautiful, if you made something in me that Paul sees, then please help me to never again let the devil have it.

A flush of strength infused her. She blinked her eyes open. Darkness had fallen, and the room lay in shadows. In her heart, however, a light shone.

I have to tell Paul I love him.

The thought burst through her like the roar of a train. She frowned, for a brief moment unsure if she had again listened to her own foolish inclinations. But... no, she was Paul's wife, and what she felt for him went beyond wanting and having him to call her own.

Paul had invaded her being almost as surely as God had. He'd shown her something more than passionate arousal merely pretending to be love.

That's what the Devil does. Right, God? He tricks people with counterfeits of love. Before we know it, we fall, and its weight crushes us. I understand that now.

She didn't know how she'd be able sleep tonight. More thoughts rolled over and through her, as though God conversed with her. Perhaps He did. Jesi smiled. She hadn't noticed the tears accumulating on her lashes. She dabbed the edge of her pillow cover against her eyes. She'd never experienced anything like this before.

Yes. She'd find the right time and the right place, and she'd tell Paul everything, beginning with her repentance, and ending with the love God had given her for her husband.

*****

Paul whistled as he stirred the lather in his cup with his shaving brush and then dabbed his face with white foam. As he laid the razor across his jaw, a small knick drew blood. He grinned and dabbed it away with a cloth.

Better to concentrate on what he was doing instead of on that gorgeous redhead in the next room.

Heeding Marie's advice about courting Jesi had been a good idea. He could hardly believe the transformation that had taken place in their relationship in just one day. What might have happened if he'd overcome his thick-headedness right after that brawl in Hurley? What if he'd taken her home and comforted her instead of reconstructing that wall between them? What if he'd assured her then that he trusted her?

Because for a short time, doubt bamboozled me.

Well, he wouldn't let Satan have another victory. Jesi needed him, whether she knew it or not, and he loved her, whether she knew it or not. He wouldn't let his wife slip away from him on account of getting duped by some outsider like Clay Dalton or Johnny Ray ever again

Let them make any claim they liked. Let them lie straight to his face. Let them even try to put a finger on her...

He cupped water in his palms and dashed it into his face three times. Then he wiped it off with a towel, wishing the water had cooled down his thoughts.

He had two more days with Jesi here in Ashland before he took her home again. By God's grace, she'd know by then just how he felt. He'd treat her like she'd never been treated before. Not by him, and surely not by the other men she'd known.

Conversation flowed from his heart to God while he dressed. *I'd like to have another go at Mr. Dalton, Father, but I rather doubt You'll let me. Fair enough. I will have a go at showing my wife that my feelings for her extend well beyond that of a missionary for a lost soul.*

A grin split his lips, and he asked aloud, "You can understand that, can't You?"

He whistled while he shoe-horned his boots onto his feet. His glance fell on the jar of flowers sitting on the small table by the window. He and Jesi had continued their stroll up the beach yesterday and had talked about other things. He'd decided to open up and tell her all about Imogene, hoping she'd feel a sort of mutual understanding about the blunders of his own youth. She'd seemed reassured that he didn't have feelings for Imogene, unless the sparkle he'd *thought* had filled her eyes was only his own hopeful wish.

He'd bid goodnight to Jesi last evening after their shared dinner, and he'd had to stop himself from taking her into his embrace and kissing her.

One thing at a time. Got to assure her of my sincerity first. She's known enough fickle-mindedness, even from me.

So after he'd seen her safely to her room, he set back out on a mission to get the flowers. Not many spring blooms had sprouted yet. Still, he'd noticed some sprigs on the branches of a wild plum tree near the road on their return, and he had gone back for them.

Not exactly roses, but their scent was nearly as intoxicating as Jesi's beauty was to him.

He straightened his collar, picked up the jar, and inhaled their sweet aroma.

Jesi's blue eyes widened in her sun-kissed face when he held the flowers out to her a few moments later.

"Put them on your windowsill. The breeze will carry the scent around the room."

"Th-Thank you. I--" She stumbled for words, then smiled, filling him with pleasure. "They're so pretty. Mmm..."

She closed her eyes and then opened them again. She turned away to set the flowers on the sill, swishing across the room and making him smile."Did you ever smell anything so good?"

Swinging back around to face him, she lifted her shoulders and laced her fingers in a posture of anticipation. "Well? Are we off to find Marie?"

"We are."

This time, she came to him and slipped her arm through his as if it were the most natural thing in the world. He tucked her close as they left the hotel.

She seemed so willing to trust him as long as he made the path smooth. Why hadn't he noticed that before?

The day stretched out before them like an unopened gift. They picked up Marie and then rode on to the bay. A ship came in as they talked about the turning of the seasons in the lumber camp, his ministry, and Marie's hopes for the future. His sister's heart had truly settled on her labors for others away from him.

Maybe that's why God brought me Jesi.

In the afternoon, they went back to Marie's boarding house and enjoyed a meal with her, Mrs. Berg, and the other residents. All through the day, Jesi had been relaxed and more at ease with him than he remembered her being in a long time. While the three of them were outdoors together, her face, dotted with freckles, glowed in the sunshine. At dinner in the boarding house, she quickly stepped up to help serve the meal and clean up afterward, her eyes alight with laughter; her bearing, filled with contentment.

Paul longed to be alone with her again, to speak even more closely, more intimately. She had warmed up to him, and maybe by the time they returned to Hurley, she would have fallen in love with him. He just had to remain gentle, move slowly, and give her enough time for her confidence to grow.

During their respite in the parlor after dinner, he caught her stifling a yawn.

She gave him the most becoming blush. "I'm sorry. I didn't mean to do that."

"Are you worn out? We've done a lot the past few days."

Jesi nodded. "I guess I am. I don't know why. I got to bed early last night."

Yes, they both had. But Paul hadn't slept well. He'd been too busy thinking of her. Perhaps she'd stayed awake thinking of their day, too.

"Maybe we should head back soon. Marie has the morning free, then she has to work at the hospital, isn't that right?"

"I'm afraid so." Marie leaned forward. "You two will have to entertain yourselves again, but we'll have brunch together here first."

Paul rose, stretched, and held out his hand to Jesi. "Want to call it a day?"

"I might have a nap." She slipped her fingers into his. A perfect fit. "Then maybe I'll write a letter to my family."

"I'll go get the buggy." Paul released her fingers.

*****

When Paul left the room, Jesi turned to find Marie watching her with an appraising eye.

"I see you're considering it."

"What?"

"You're considering how you feel about Paul."

"What's there to consider? I've already told you--"

"He's considering, too."

She was afraid to hope, but a spark leapt to flame in her breast. "He's acted differently the past two days."

Marie smiled knowingly. "I told you he'd come around."

"Marie," Jesi stepped toward her. "Do you think -- I mean -- has Paul said..." She shook her head. "I feel ridiculous asking."

"You just enjoy your evening." Marie touched her shoulders. The corners of her eyes crinkled. "I see the change in him, too. Take advantage of it." She gave Jesi's shoulders a gentle squeeze. "Let down your guard."

Jesi allowed her words to wind into her as she hugged Marie. Such a true sister she was. "Thank you. I will."

Paul came through the door. "Are you all set?"

Jesi and Marie broke apart, and Marie patted her back. "I'll see you both tomorrow around eleven, all right? Rest up now, and have a lovely evening."

Jesi nodded. Something special resonated in her sister-in-law's smile. Without acknowledging it, Jesi turned to Paul. "All set."

A short while later, they were on their way. Peace descended on Jesi, and she let a quiet sigh slip out.

"You must be worn out."

"Not too bad. I was just thinking."

"Care to share your thoughts?"

"Marie is quite a woman, and quite a friend."

His hand stole across the seat and found hers, sending a tingle through her. "I'm glad you like her. That means a lot to me."

"Yes, well... Marie deserves a lot of respect and admiration." She allowed a hint of laughter to creep into her voice. "She must have had her hands full with you."

"Hey, now. Be careful. You've inherited her job of taking care of me, you know."

She smiled at his wry glance until he looked back at the road and swerved to avoid a rut. She gave his hand the slightest squeeze. "I'll try to do a good job."

He didn't say anything, but moved his fingers softly in hers. Her heart picked up its rhythm.

The sun still remained high in the sky as they reached their hotel. Paul jumped out of the buggy and came around to help Jesi down. His hands lingered on her waist, and his eyes settled on hers, his gaze unreadable but steady.

She needed to say something. "Well... I suppose I'll take a nap before I write that letter."

"I'll walk you to your room." He grinned. Since his room was right next door, she knew he was attempting levity.

But he didn't let go of her hand.

She thought her heart might burst. The words she longed to say came to her lips, but died away. She remembered the night she'd given them to Clay. Oh, how foolish she'd been. She didn't know love then. This was something so different. So heart-churning. So *wonderful*. The words this time meant so much more. They were like an eternal gift, and she wouldn't offer them haphazardly.

Yet she *would* offer them. She must. Paul needed to know.

He unlocked her door and held it open for her. She hesitated.

"We can eat something together later," he said.

She nodded, daring to look at him. He leaned forward and grazed her cheek with his lips. Then he whispered in her ear, "Rest well."

She backed into her room and closed the door. Her heart raced, chasing thoughts of sleep away.

Chapter Thirty

Jesi sat on the edge of the bed and raised her fingertips to her cheek. The kiss Paul had left her with felt ghostly and surreal, yet her body tingled as though imprinted by its feathery softness. She glanced at the wall separating their rooms and vibrated with the urgency to declare her feelings. Almost as though a hand pushed her along, and a voice prodded, "*Tell him. Tell him, before it is too late.*"

Could it be too late? If she let this time go by and they went home to Hurley without saying the words, would she have missed her opportunity? Who knew what the next day, the next week, the next month might hold?

You want me to tell him, don't You?

A warmth as holy as she'd ever known invaded her. She didn't know why God had chosen now to push her, but she knew with sudden clarity that He had. She hugged herself.

I don't know what to do next.

Her gaze roamed the room and landed on the small desk by the window. No longer sleepy, she remembered her intention to write a letter to her family. Perhaps that would help her bide her time until she saw Paul again.

She pulled a sheet of hotel stationery from the drawer while she thought of what to tell her parents. Her heart was full to overflowing. She would have an easy time writing about the trip to Ashland, about Marie's work, and about the days she'd spent with Paul. Mostly about Paul.

He's been offered a church in Appleton, but has decided to stay where he is, doing the work God called him to do.

She searched for a pen while she rehearsed the lines she wanted to write. She would tell her family she had asked God's forgiveness. That much was also certain.

Jesi found a half bottle of ink, but no pen in the desk. She bent and looked behind it in case it had rolled onto the floor.

No pen. She searched through the armoire, knowing she hadn't seen a pen inside with her few clothes, but for lack of any other place to look, she hunted there anyway.

"Well, how am I supposed to write it now?" she asked herself aloud. "I suppose I could go ask the clerk at the front desk."

She turned to go and stopped. Again Paul invaded her thoughts, and her heart leapt. *What if I ask him?*

Jesi picked up her hairbrush and loosened the thick knot of hair at her neck until it fell around her shoulders, tumbling to her waist. Her thoughts raced as she brushed it. She looked in the mirror and pinched her cheeks. Then she ran her hands over her skirt to smooth out the wrinkles, let herself out of her room, and closed the door with barely a click. She stepped up to Paul's door and lifted her fist. Breathing once, twice, she pushed a strand of hair over her shoulder and gave a quick knock.

She'd barely lowered her hand when the door swung open and Paul stood before her. He had removed his suspenders from his shoulders, and they now drooped from the sides of his pants. He'd also taken off his shoes. His white shirt lay partially unbuttoned and open at the top, and he had rolled up the sleeves to just below his elbows. He looked as if he'd pushed a hand through his uncombed hair on his way to the door.

"Jesi."

Was he pleased, or just surprised? "Did I wake you?"

"Ah, no. No, not at all. I was just reading." He glanced back to his bed.

Jesi peered past him to where his Bible lay open. "I'm sorry to interrupt."

"You're not interrupting. Is everything okay?"

She nodded. "I was going to write a letter, but I couldn't find a pen."

Her words sounded exactly like the excuse to see him that they were. Had Paul noticed?

He stepped back. "I'll find you one."

"Thank you." She folded her hands.

He turned halfway and stopped to look at her again as she stood inside the doorway. "Better yet, why don't you just sit here and write it? I'm used to having you around doing things while I'm studying." He gave her a smile.

Jesi thought about all the hundreds of hours she'd cooked or mended or did her own reading while he studied his Bible. Why should doing so feel different now?

Because I'm in love with him, and he doesn't know it.

Then again, the voice inside her prodded her. "That sounds fine. Truth be told, I was tired when we left Marie's, but when I got to my room I grew a bit restless. I guess I'm not used to being alone, either."

She stepped all the way inside and shut the door. When she faced him again, his smile had broadened and relaxed. Heat rose into her cheeks.

"You are beautiful, Jesi. I so seldom see you with your hair down."

She shrugged and came further into the room. "It gets in the way when I work, and it wouldn't be proper for a woman my age to go about town with it loose like this."

He stepped closer. She pulled in her breath and tried to let it out slowly. "It can be an awful lot to manage sometimes. My mama wanted to cut it off more than once, but Pa said it was a glory."

Now she really did blush. Heat infused her skin, drawing an even wider grin from Paul. How had he closed the gap between them so quickly?

"Your pa is right. I knew I liked him." Paul reached up and fingered a strand of her hair. "Do you mind?"

She shook her head, her breath more tenuous than a single strand of her hair stretched taut. Slowly he stroked it with the back of his hand, from the side of her face all the way down its length, pausing to rub it between his fingers at the end.

She closed her eyes, then forced them open again before she was lost. Yet never had she so wanted to be lost to a man's touch. Never.

Paul cleared his throat and stepped back. "Forgive me. I nearly forgot myself."

"Nothing to forgive." She blinked. "You're my husband, after all."

His eyes had grown darker. They'd deepened with some pent up emotion, some... longing.

Now. Tell him now. "Have you paper?"

He nodded and stepped even further away. He pulled a sheet of hotel stationery from his desk drawer and gave it a wave, then laid it on the desk. She cleared her throat and tried to lighten her voice as she brushed past him. "Maybe I'll write you a letter, too."

"Will you?"

She nodded and sat at the desk, her back to him. She dipped her pen into the ink bottle and blotted off the excess.

"Dear Paul," she said, poising the pen in the air. Her voice turned soft and thoughtful as she continued, "Thank you for the loveliest time I can remember. The trip to Ashland has been like no other vacation I've ever had. I'm ever so grateful you've taken me along. I'm ever so grateful you've--"

Her voice caught as his hand lay against her hair again. No, *both* hands. They caressed the sides of her neck and shoulders, smoothing her wild tangles.

"Nothing could make me happier than to read such a letter." His voice was rich and thick.

Her heart thudded against her rib cage. She went on, "Then I'd say... I'd say, Paul, you have made me so very happy. You have no idea how much I love you."

His hands stilled, and her heart stopped. The branches of a tree brushed across the window in front of her. A bird hopped from limb to limb. She imagined it chirping, but all that echoed in the room was the throb of her heart rushing blood through her head.

Her chest rose and fell. She thought she might faint. Then he gave the slightest tug on her shoulders and turned her to face him. She spun in her chair and looked up into his eyes to find him staring at her, his gaze full and searching and still not telling her if she'd been wrong. Only one way would she find out.

"I love you." She didn't blink, didn't turn away, didn't feel anything but certainty as she said those three words. "I love you, Paul. *So* much."

He cupped her fingers in his and tugged her to her feet, allowing only the tiniest space to breathe between them.

"Jesilyn."

She had to explain before he stopped her. "I asked God if He would forgive me for hurting you so -- you and everyone."

He blinked and studied her.

She scrambled to explain, to ward off any rebuttal. "Then I just knew I had to tell you." His expression was so fathomless, she didn't know how to read it. "Are you angry?"

"Jesilyn." He lifted his brows, and his eyes filled.

She shook her head. "I'm sorry. I only meant--"

"Jesi--" He pulled her against him, and his body shuddered. He buried his face in her hair. An aching murmur rose from his throat. "You love me."

She nodded.

He held her tighter. "How I've longed for it."

"Truly?"

"I love you, Jesilyn. I love you more dearly than my life."

Now she pulled back and looked into his eyes again. Is that what had been in his gaze all this time? Love? His eyes were red and wet. Was he truly so moved by these feelings she'd never expected to hear him express?

"Do you believe me, darling Jesilyn?"

A huff escaped her, and she didn't know whether to laugh or cry with joy. Her lips quivered, and then she lifted them in a smile. His own bent like a bow.

She nodded. "You make me believe."

"I do?"

She nodded again.

"And what if I do this?" He moved his hand beneath the mass of her hair, curved it around her neck as he drew her closer, and then lowered his lips to hers.

*****

The kiss Paul gave Jesi was one he'd been saving -- holding it for one special woman, and he had finally found her. She'd been his all along, only now, they both knew it.

She clung to his waist as he held her face in his hands and lost himself in kissing her. Beneath his shirt, the pressure of her long fingers left their imprint on his body as surely as if she had branded him. Part of him wondered if he should release her, but the main part knew the time had come for him to never let her go.

His passion grew as he sensed her response. As though she'd been waiting just as anxiously as he.

He pressed her to him, caressed her, loved her. At last, she gasped.

He touched his forehead to hers, and with all the strength he could summon, released the words that had crawled up his throat. "Do you wish me to stop?"

She traced his neck with her delicate fingers and stroked his chin until he looked into her eyes. Deep blue swirled against the gray of her irises like the waters of Lake Superior, beckoning him to swim forever in their depths.

"I want to be your wife, Paul. Completely."

"Are you sure?"

She nodded. "Very sure."

He held her fast and kissed her again. The pen and paper lay on the desk, the letter unwritten. Forgotten. Yet the pages of his heart lay open, filling with a lifetime of promises that would only be read by her.

Chapter Thirty-One

Mid-morning arrived too quickly for Jesi. She knew it was important they keep their brunch date with Marie, but she would have gladly nestled longer next to Paul. His tenderness had nearly made her weep with joy, and she was determined to make him equally as happy.

But for some reason, in the midst of all her happiness, Corianne invaded her thoughts. Jesi stood in front of Paul's desk near the window and glanced down at the paper lying next to the unused pen.

Cori, I'm sorry I ruined everything for you.

A shiver ran through her.

Paul whistled a tune as he pulled up his suspenders and reached for his coat. Just hearing his voice charmed her, but she couldn't stop thinking about her sister. She would certainly have to write to her parents, as well. That would be easy with her now so blissfully content.

Or almost content.

Paul slipped his hands around her waist and tucked his face into the curve of her neck.

"Happy?"

She nodded.

"Everything all right?"

Jesi blinked, then turned in his arms to face him. "Everything is wonderful."

"What is it, then?" He kissed her fully, and she reveled in his embrace. As he drew back, however, he puckered his brows. "Something is troubling you."

She shrugged. "Nothing really. I just can't seem to stop thinking of Corianne. How terribly I hurt her. I really do need to write to my family, and I suppose it's time I address one to her."

"You are wonderful, do you know that?"

She smiled, chagrined. "You just love me."

"I do." He brushed a strand of hair back from her face and kissed her brow. "It's more than that, though. You are a remarkable woman. And you're sensitive. More sensitive than you think you are."

"I don't think Cori would agree."

"She doesn't know how you really feel or how you've begun to let the Holy Spirit guide you. But..." He stepped back, holding her hands. A pensive light came into his eyes. "I have an idea."

"What is it?"

"We need a honeymoon."

She gasped. "We're already on a vacation, and when we return we'll have the whole woods practically to ourselves."

"No. It's not the same." He maneuvered her over to the desk. "Write a brief note to your parents, and we'll drop it by the telegraph office on the way to Marie's. Tell them we're coming to see them. We'll be there on the train tomorrow."

"But--" She swiveled to look at him.

His lips were set in a determined line. "It's time, Jesi. We told them we'd come, and now we must. You'll never be fully released from your guilt until you talk to Cori."

He was right. They'd told her family she and Paul would come when the weather warmed. Now would be the best time. She could go to her family without fear -- without lies.

And beg Corianne to forgive me.

"My sister may not look forward to my coming."

Paul's voice softened even more. "God is prodding you. He'll prepare the way with her."

"Are you promising me she'll accept my apology, just because God is pushing me to give it? Don't you know better?"

"No." He covered her hand and bent to kiss her forehead. "He doesn't promise us success, but faithfulness has its own rewards."

Her heart swelled. She reached up and pushed his bangs out of his face. "Yes, my love. You're right. It does."

*****

Cori shut the door and turned to look at the telegram just as her mother stepped into the hall from the kitchen.

"Who is it from?"

"Oh, um..." Cori offered the paper to her mother.

Lainey opened the note and scanned it. A smile spread across her face, lifting the creases at the corners of her eyes. "Jesi's coming!"

She hurried down the hall to the study where Papa worked. Her buoyant tones echoed back to Cori as she shared the news. A stone weight rolled into Cori's chest. She crossed her arms to steady it. Mama fluttered back into the hall.

"When?" That one word was all Cori could say.

"Tomorrow. It doesn't say which train, but she'll be arriving straight from Ashland so we should expect her by midday."

"And Mr. Winter?"

"Oh, yes, of course. Paul, too." Mama stopped and grasped Cori's shoulders gently. "It's time, don't you think?"

"I suppose so." Cori shrugged free. "For your sake. And for the others."

"Wait until your grandma and grandpa hear. Would you like to give them the news?"

"I'd rather not, if it's all the same." Cori shook her head. "I have some things to do. Jamie will be here on Monday."

She lifted her chin a little, as though to remind Mama that he was a *real* guest -- more so than Jesi would ever be. Of course, she did have a husband, but what kind of pushover must he be? Cori preferred to push them both from her thoughts and think instead about Jamie's coming. He would stay all week. Then they wouldn't see each other again until the Independence Day holiday.

She started to walk away, but paused by the parlor door. "Any idea how long she intends to stay?"

"No. I hope for the week, at least."

For the week -- at least.

Cori had plenty to do. First and foremost, she'd have to figure out how best to keep Jamie away from her soiled sister's clutches.

*****

The parlor clock ticked away the hours on Saturday morning, making Jesilyn's arrival imminent. Wishing she didn't have to see her sister, Cori knotted her hands. Correction. Wishing she wouldn't have to see *them*. Yet she couldn't help wondering about the man Jesi had wed. Papa had said he was a young camp preacher. He must come from money. Or maybe not. Maybe Jesi really did marry him just to slake her lust.

However, her marrying him for security was more likely.

Jesi had run away with little in her pocket, and she'd never spoken of having found a job to earn her keep. She must have turned up at the camp like a wastrel and not wasted any time before pouring her charm over the poor, misguided preacher. That was it.

He must be fair looking. Jesi wouldn't have likely married a slouch unless he really did have money.

Cori paced her room at the corner of the house. From her view, she could see the intersection of the two roads converging below and all the way up to the lake a mere three blocks away. Mama's roses hadn't budded yet, but the dull ache of early spring had given way to the lush promise of summer. The seasons had changed so suddenly.

If only she could recapture the burst of that wonderful feeling inside. The feeling that had resided in her heart until the telegram came.

Tomorrow she'd likely have to sit with them in church. Oh, how she wished Jamie were already here. She felt so defenseless. And yet she was glad he wasn't here. What wiles would Jesi have up her sleeve this time? Why, one look at Jamie's handsome face, and who knew what intentions she might develop? Especially if her marriage was a fraud, and Cori figured it was.

A rattle of harness and wheels drew her attention to the window once again.

Jesi and Paul had arrived.

Cori couldn't see her sister's face past the wide brim of her hat. The fullness of a beautiful blue-striped gown fell around her as a man, also unidentifiable in a hat, ushered her out of their father's carriage. Papa gathered their luggage out of the boot as Jesi linked her arm through her husband's and paused on the walk. Her hand went to the top of her head to steady her hat as she swept her gaze upward, over the house. A smile swelled on her face, and Cori decided she looked far more peaceful than she should.

The prodigal returns like she's royalty.

The murmur of exclamations came from below. Evie's voice carried the loudest. Gran would be there, and before long the whole troop would come upstairs to see Gramp. He was feeling a lot better, and their hope for his full recovery had been ever on the rise. Now with Jesi coming home, maybe he'd get the extra boost he needed to be on his feet again.

Well, so be it. Jesi was his granddaughter, after all. He'd good reason to worry. Still, that didn't change how Cori felt or what she feared.

Jesi could just knock on Cori's door if she wanted to see her. Cori wasn't about to go out of her way to greet her sister. As it was, they'd probably have to face each other over dinner.

Before long, they swooshed along the hallway outside her door. Cori pressed her ear to one of the panels. Only two soft voices met her ears. She recognized Jesi's, and decided the lower, more resonant voice must be Paul's. They knocked on Gramp's door, and with the greatest of care, Cori turned her knob. She only wanted to peek at them because she was curious about Paul. She didn't want a single surprise at dinner time.

Unfortunately, he swept into her grandparents' room behind Jesi, leaving Cori to catch only a glimpse of his build and the back of his head where straight, brown hair brushed his collar. She closed the door and chewed on the skin next to her fingernail. The wait would be long and miserable until Jamie arrived. Then he could sweep Cori away and keep her occupied as much as possible until Jesi went away.

Cori wandered over to the mirror and planted her hands on her hips. "I'll try to be civil while she's here, but no one had better expect me to be friendly."

Two hours later, her grandmother dropped by to tell her to come down for supper. Cori refused to acknowledge her raised brows and expectant manner. She found everyone seated in the dining room and took her own chair without acknowledging anyone.

"Corianne, have you met your new brother-in-law?" Leave it to Papa to force her to break the ice.

Cori gave lip service to a smile and nodded in Paul's direction, her quick glance taking him in more thoroughly than anyone might suspect.

"I guess I would have recognized Corianne anywhere," Paul said in an obvious attempt at humor.

"I suppose you would," she replied. "Hello, Jesi."

"Hello, Corianne."

Jesi seemed nervous. Well, that was a relief. She should be. She should be scared stiff about coming back after her horrid behavior and the way she'd left. Cori found it bad enough that her sister sat there looking regal next to such a handsome husband.

And he's a preacher, no less. Humph.

Cori wanted to let her thoughts ooze out, but she reined them back. The man was much more than she had expected, or was he? Wasn't Clay handsome? And hadn't Jesi set her sights high? Another glimpse caught the fact that Paul held Jesi's hand. An obvious warmth exuded between them. She could fathom that much in just a brief look.

"So you've decided to come home for a spell. I'm a bit surprised."

"I believe Paul told Papa in a letter that we'd come."

"Yes, well... that was the expected thing to do, I suppose. I didn't really think you would."

Mama eyed Cori with a frown, but she ignored it.

She poured a cup of coffee, sloshing a bit over the edge of her cup. "So we're all dying to know how you met Paul. Aren't you going to tell us?"

"I mentioned it in a letter. I--"

Cori set down a coffee pot and waved her sister silent. "Posh. We know about the long walk to Mellen. Really, Jesi, there must be more to it than that. I mean, for Paul's sister to up and leave and then the two of you to just decide to marry? Really. One can't help but think how contrived it seems."

Paul cleared his throat, but Papa jumped in. "Cori, I think you're being just a bit ungracious to your sister, not to mention her husband. They'll tell us all about it in good time."

Though he had spoken calmly, Cori sensed her papa was curious, too, even though he'd already been acquainted with Paul.

"Paul and Marie did rescue me," Jesi said. Everyone stilled. Plates of food sat steaming on the table. "I'm ashamed to admit that my plans to make it on my own fared with even less success than I'd imagined they could. I was flat broke."

"*Humph.* I bet."

"I found myself destitute, and I might not have ever made it to Mellen. I'd collapsed when Paul found me along the rail line."

Mama's brow furrowed and Gran's fingers crept up to her chin.

"There is more to the story, but--"

Paul's fingers squeezed around his wife's. "It's not important," he said. "The important thing is that I found her. She and my sister took to one another right away." His gaze fell directly into Cori's. "They became close friends." He glanced to Mama. "My sister's an intelligent woman. She could see I was beginning to feel strongly for Jesi."

"I didn't encourage it," Jesi whispered, her words clearly for Cori's benefit.

"No, she didn't. But in the end, we both knew it was God's answer for our lives. I asked Jesi to marry me, and she honored me by accepting." Now he looked at Papa. "I love your daughter very much."

"Glad to hear it. Now can we get on with dinner?"

Papa's gaze bore down the table at Cori. She nodded and settled back in her chair, her eyes focused on her plate though she felt like eating little.

So Jesi had smoothed things over with a story. She'd given them enough truth to satisfy her parents. Well, more would be forthcoming if Cori had anything to say about it. Apparently her husband really did care for her. That wasn't so hard to imagine. Yet she still had to question whether or not Jesi returned his affection.

Then again, who knew? Jesi's affections were fickle. Perhaps they'd stay with Paul, at least until someone else came along. Someone like Jamie.

Cori returned to her room after dinner and allowed her regular chore of helping with the dishes to fall to Jesi. They'd make short work of cleaning up as they talked about Paul and Jesi's life in Hurley's backwoods. Frankly, there wasn't much more Cori wanted to hear.

She started when someone knocked on her door. Instinctively she knew it was Jesi. Her sister's particular one-fingered tap on the door was burned like a brand in her memory. She wasn't ready for this.

"What is it?"

"May I come in? Please?"

If she opened the door, they would have to talk. Maybe that was for the best. Better to face each other now, out of earshot of the others.

"It's not locked."

Jesi entered the room, closed the door behind her, and leaned against it. Neither of them spoke at first. Cori sat on the bed, her arms crossed at her waist.

Finally, Jesi drew her hands together in front of her. Her mouth trembled.

"Cori, I..." She bit her lip. "I know you're still angry. You have every right." She hurried to add, "What I did was..." She pinched her eyes closed and shook her head.

"Despicable." Cori couldn't help supplying the word, filling it with a powerful amount of venom.

"Yes. Yes, it was."

Cori hadn't expected Jesi's nod, or such compliance. "You ruined my future."

"I know. I did, and it was wrong. I was so confused."

"Confused? You call it confusing to steal your sister's fiancé and *have relations* with him?"

"I'm not excusing--"

"There is no excuse for what you did!"

"No, there isn't. That's why I'm here to apologize and to beg your forgiveness."

Jesi straightened her shoulders and looked Cori directly in the eye. To humble herself must have taken courage, but at the moment Cori didn't care.

"How am I supposed to believe that? You've always deceived me."

"Not always."

"You broke my trust. Clay's trust. *Everyone's* trust."

"I know." Jesi hung her head and wiped her eyes. "I know."

"Then you had the gall to run off -- who knows what you did to get Paul to marry you -- and now you return here like nothing could be better."

Jesi's eyes took on the look of a stormy gale over the lake. She stepped closer. "Nothing *is* better. That's true. I did come back, and it's good that I did because I have a lot to make right."

"How do you propose to do that?" Cori spat.

"First, like this. By giving you my apology. By asking you to forgive me. I don't expect you to do it, or at least to give me an answer right away. But I am sorry, Cori. Truly, I am."

"I suppose you are." Cori shifted on the bed. A niggling discomfort wormed through her. Jesi sounded sincere. More facts rolled through Cori's thoughts, and she took a reinforcing breath. "After all, being deceptive didn't work out very well for you, did it? Clay still rejected you. And then you turned to someone else."

"Yes, Clay did reject me. Only, that's not why I'm sorry. I'm sorry because of what I did, and that it hurt you. I'm sorry because it hurt me more than I thought it could. I didn't care, Cori. I didn't care if I was hurt. Not then. But I care now. I care that the repercussions of my choice were more than I ever dreamed they could be."

Cori shrugged. "So what do you expect me to do, sympathize?"

"No. Not at all. Just listen to my apology. I'll only stay here for the week. Paul will have to get back to his obligations by then, and I have some of my own. But if we can manage to fix the breach--"

"Don't count on it."

Jesilyn stared at Cori until Cori looked away. Let Jesi wonder. Let her suffer with her remorse. When she finally glanced back, Jesilyn nodded and reached for the door.

"Paul is a good man, Cori," she said, her back to her. "I love him very much. I'm grateful that he's helped me find my way back home -- to my family, and to God." She opened the door. "I just thought you should know."

Chapter Thirty-Two

Jesilyn stood among the roses bushes and wept. Cori was right. She didn't deserve anyone's trust or forgiveness.

Forgiving someone isn't about their deserving it.

Paul had said that many times when he'd preached. Now the words came back to her. Here she stood in a garden ready to bloom with new splendor. She was like the new buds. The old petals had fallen away from her heart, and inside something new and lovely had burst forth. Wasn't that what repentance was? A change of mind? The letting go of the old so the new and beautiful could grow in its place?

Still, tears rolled down her face.

Warm hands startled her, tugging at her shoulders until she fell against Paul's solid chest and into his embrace. "Ssh... It'll be all right."

"I don't think it ever can be." She heaved a sob and crumbled in his arms. "She hates me. I want to be faithful, but it hasn't solved anything."

"It might take time -- and you're wrong. Your faithfulness *has* solved something. It's made you stronger and braver, and has kept you in step with God's will."

"I don't feel very strong."

"Look at me." Paul tugged at her chin. His eyes glowed with love. "You're so strong, Jesi. It's part of your beauty, your grace. But you don't have to be strong all alone. I'm here with you."

She closed her eyes and allowed him to kiss her, filling her with strength and greater courage.

"There. Is that better?" he murmured. "You have God, and you have me… and you have everyone else in your family rooting for you."

She nodded. "I guess they are. Did you see grandfather trying to get out of bed to hug me?"

"Yes. Did you see how your grandmother scolded him?"

Jesi laughed and wiped her nose. "Yes."

"I suppose that's how it'll be with you and me before long. You'll tell me what to do, and I'll do just as I'm told."

Jesi giggled and sniffed. "I don't know if Gramp truly does what he's told. I expect he'll be out of that bed as soon as he can, with or without Gran's permission." She sighed as the realization stole over her that she might never have seen her grandparents again had she stayed on her course of flight. "I'm so glad he's doing better. Mama says the doctor is hopeful. The tumor is gone. Now we have to pray it doesn't return."

"Yes." Paul draped his arm across her shoulders, and they strolled back toward the house. "We will."

"I have to remember that God doesn't promise us success."

"That's right." Paul tugged her into the crook of his arm and kissed her temple. "Sometimes, though, He gives it."

"We could do a lot worse than to turn out like my grandparents... or my parents."

"Well, I'll have to talk with your grandfather, then, and see if I can learn a few things."

Jesi didn't see Cori again that day. On Sunday, she and Paul attended church with her parents, her grandmother, and Evie. Cori stayed behind to attend Gramp. Though it seemed a kindness to Gran, Jesi couldn't help feeling her sister did it simply as a convenience to keep apart from her.

She prayed for her relationship with Cori. Yet even doing so in church didn't reassure her. Jesi wondered if everyone took turns staying with Gramp on Sundays, or if she was right about Cori using it as an excuse to avoid her.

At first she'd been nervous about attending the service, afraid people she'd known all her life would look at her disapprovingly. Most of them welcomed her back, however, and they were very gracious to Paul.

On Monday morning, she woke lazily. She rolled onto her side to trace the side of her husband's jaw with her finger. He was handsome even in sleep. Stubble tickled the soft skin under her fingernail. His hair fell down across his brow, and she wanted to tuck it back but knew it wouldn't stay. The certainty that he loved her and that she had fallen so deeply in love with him made her head spin. *This is my honeymoon.* The reality struck her again, just as it had each of the past four mornings. And the nights, well... they proved it.

She smiled and gazed at him, hardly aware of discovering he gazed back until his hands moved over her waist and drew her to him. A long, intoxicating kiss followed.

"Good morning, my love," she murmured against his lips.

He kissed her again in answer. When he finally drew back, she melted into the pillow, her shoulders curved against his chest. She never could have imagined such oneness.

His lips played against the skin of her neck, earlobes, and eyelids. His whisper tickled her ears. "Are you enjoying your honeymoon?"

"Yes. And you?"

He moaned. "I don't want you to go on errands for your father. I want to keep you here."

She laughed as he growled and kissed her neck more fervently.

She gasped with a giggle. "Remember, you're my pastor."

Peering at her, he waggled his eyebrows. "Pastor and husband. Dual authority. Hmm... I like the sound of that. Although--" He flipped back the covers, creating a breeze that had her reaching for them. "You did promise your father you'd pick up your grandfather's medicine so your mother wouldn't have to do it, and as much as I don't want you to leave me even for an instant, I have a game of chess waiting for me with said grandfather after breakfast. A breakfast that may have already come and gone, I might add."

"It isn't that late, surely."

"Indeed it is." He gave her another quick kiss, and though the look in his eyes told her he wanted more, he swung his legs over the side of the bed. "I'm afraid we've created a household scandal."

"One my family would approve of, I'm sure. Except for Cori."

"Don't let her bother you." His grin fell. "You're forgiven. Remember that. And you've done your part to reconcile. You can't force her to accept your apology. It's my guess she didn't expect it, and now she needs time to consider what it means."

"Yes, I know." She rose and reached for her chemise and stockings. "I think, between you and God, I'm finally convinced. I just wish He'd answer my prayers about it a bit quicker."

"All in His time."

Jesi sighed in agreement.

Half an hour later, she left the house to drive the buggy to the doctor's office. Doc Niemi had spoken to her parents at church the day before, reminding them he'd be out to check on his patient in a few days, but that he'd be happy to send more pain medication if Gramp needed it. When Jesi mentioned her willingness to run the errand, she'd hoped for a quiet drive with Paul so she could show him her hometown. Her father had given them some money for a belated wedding gift, and she hoped to take him to buy a new suit and to get herself some new shoes. Only after her grandfather's eyes glinted and he challenged Paul to a chess game did she discover she'd have to go alone, and that they'd have to take their outing another day.

Driving through Superior again felt strange and almost foreign. Her life had changed so much during the nine months she'd been away, almost as quickly as the city itself had. She looked at her hometown now with different eyes. She waved a hand at the old gentleman walking his dog down the road leading into the east end business district. He'd taken that walk daily for most of her life, but she'd never actually met him.

Contentment surged through her. She turned the corner to head across town toward the west end and Dr. Niemi's office near the hospital. Admiring the many stately homes she'd forgotten about, she realized she appreciated the city so much more now that she lived in a small cabin in the woods.

Yet the thought of returning to that cabin filled her with warmth and pleasure. How fine it would be to wake morning after morning next to Paul, to rise and make his breakfast, to bake bread for Charlie and the men while Paul studied, to rock his children by the fire.

Joy bubbled through her so she didn't see the pothole in the road, and she hit it with a lurch. Regaining her balance on the buggy seat, she laughed.

She was happy to have made peace with her family. Mama and Papa and even her grandparents had accepted her apology with tears and embraces. She hadn't told them of the full descent she'd made into Hurley's brothel society, but she knew they suspected she'd dealt with harsh realities. *They are so much more gracious and loving than I expected. They would never have rejected me. I was wrong to flee, and wrong to fear returning.*

If only Cori, too, could forgive me.

Having shared treasured camaraderie with Marie, Jesi missed her sister. They'd been close once. Growing older had sent them in different directions, and they'd had their adolescent sibling spats. Yet never before had she so desired a relationship with her twin. A string pulled on her heart, drawing her toward Cori. Love had ripped it open and laid it wide.

Oh, Cori... If only we can repair the breach.

During her four mile drive to Dr. Niemi's, Superior bustled with activity. Jesi sensed a new hope in its citizens since last year's panic, or maybe her own outlook on life had made the difference.

Superior had several driving parks, and as she passed by one of them, the scent of lilacs wafted on the breeze. She decided she'd take a detour on the way home and see if she could find enough to make a bouquet for the dinner table, and a small one to bring to her grandfather's bedside. Last but not least, she'd save a few sprigs to set on the nightstand in her and Paul's room. Their heavenly fragrance conjured images of romance as she approached her destination.

"Ah, you've come for your grandfather's prescription," Dr. Niemi's nurse said as Jesi entered the doctor's waiting room. "The doctor mentioned you'd be arriving. I'll let him know you're here."

Dr. Niemi came out from his examination room with the nurse a few moments later. "Good to see you again. Here's the bottle. Now, make sure he doesn't take more than he needs. How is he feeling today?"

"He has a lot of pain, as you know, but he's doing better than when my husband and I first saw him Friday evening. Gramp has challenged Paul to a game of chess. You can be sure he won't let Gramp overdo it."

"Good. Glad to hear it."

"Doctor, I'm afraid I've caused a large share of stress on my grandfather as well as the rest of my family. Do you think there's reason to fear long term results? I guess what I'm really asking is whether or not you believe my grandfather will recover." Jesi shrugged and glanced at her toes. "Oh, I know everyone has such high hopes and is positive, but I guess I've become something of a realist over the past year. I don't do well with false hopes. Will the growth on Gramp's shoulder return, or is there cause to think it may have spread elsewhere?" She looked at him squarely, demanding nothing less than the truth.

Doc Niemi tucked his fingers into his vest pocket and nodded. "Young lady, I wouldn't want to give anyone false hope. Yet I find myself in the peculiar situation of having to be forthright with my patients while at the same propping them up with as much emotional support as I can so they'll find the will to heal. Patients without hope and the will to heal tend to do much worse than those who have a good dose of that peculiar psychological medication. Do you understand?"

She nodded.

"That said, I also understand the need to speak frankly about such matters to a straight-forward thinker such as yourself. Your grandfather has a very good chance. We caught the tumor before it had grown very large. But these things can sometimes sprout up again elsewhere. The lungs are a concern. We will have to monitor his progress very closely. If he lives another five years, then I believe we will have a good prognosis."

"My grandfather is already in his seventies, Dr. Niemi."

"And why shouldn't he live to be in his nineties?" The doctor offered her an encouraging smile, patted her shoulder, and turned her gently toward the door.

"That is what we'll pray for, then." She turned back to him one last time. Emotion crept up her throat. "Thank you, doctor. You've no idea what you've done for our family -- or for me."

"Now, now--"

"Truly, you've given me time I've needed to recapture. Thank you."

"In that case, you're welcome. Although, such things are really in the Lord's hands. I am only a tool."

Yes. God uses us all like that.

Jesi took a deep breath as she climbed into her buggy. She brushed moisture from her eyes and settled the bottle of medicine beside her on the seat. With a shake of the reins, she headed up Tower Avenue, drawing back at the next intersection to give way to a passing street car. She'd turned up the street about to follow its progress and move around it when someone shouted from the car. "Cori!"

Her gaze jerked up to see a young man leaning out of the street car waving at her. He was dark, with curly hair and a lively smile. Jesi didn't recognize him.

Must be someone Cori knows. She offered a polite wave but stayed back while he kept looking at her.

"Cori, I'm getting off!" he shouted.

Jesi reined her buggy as the fellow jumped from the streetcar, suitcase in hand, and ran in front of her. Without any effort at all, he came about and hoisted himself into the buggy.

"Stop!" she cried.

He paused while the horse stamped its front feet and other traffic moved around her.

"I-I'm sorry," she said. "I'm not Cori."

His expression jarred in confusion.

"I'm Cori's--"

"No, wait." Suitcase in one hand, he held up the other. "You must be Jesi."

"Yes..." She glanced about, certain she had distressed the other drivers on the street, and the gentleman seemed to realize it.

He gave a quick nod at the seat. "May I? I really am a friend of Cori's."

"Yes. Come on."

He climbed with light feet into the buggy and sat beside her. She quickly scooted the bottle of medicine out of the way.

"Sorry to accost you this way."

He was a handsome man; his brown eyes deep, his face broad and friendly. Yet sitting so close to a stranger, no matter how nice looking or even how good he smelled, didn't feel right. Thankfully, he explained who he was the moment she moved the buggy forward.

"I'm James Gilbert, a nephew of your great aunt Jean's. I'm on my way to stay with your family. I knew Cori had a twin, but I didn't expect to see her."

"Oh." Her breath rushed out. "You must be the one they call Jamie."

"Yes. That's me. It's good to meet you, despite the awkward timing."

"Yes, it is," she said. Jamie held out his hand to her, and she loosened her hold on the reins to shake it. Then she blinked. "Does Cori know you're coming?"

"Oh, yes. She knows."

Jesi's thoughts squirreled about. Of course Cori knew, and she certainly wouldn't say anything about it to Jesi. Their parents must have forgotten to mention it.

"I've hoped to meet you," Jamie said. "As you may have heard, I'm quite taken with your sister, but it didn't seem right to know everyone in the whole family except the one most like her."

"Does she say we're most alike?"

He chuckled. "I guess I was thinking about your outward appearance. No. She actually says quite the opposite."

Jesi tried with a quick glance to gauge his meaning, even though she felt pretty certain Cori had been adamant about their differences. Jesi was the shameful sister, after all.

"Yes. Well, it's too bad I left when I did. That probably did nothing to improve my first impression."

Now she did look at him more directly and found him studying her with an open face and honest smile. "I try not to let the opinions of others sway me until I've had a chance to judge for myself, not even if those other people are dear to me."

"Well, thank you for that." Jesi relaxed. Jamie seemed sincere. Suddenly the aroma of lilacs taunted her senses again. "I hope you don't mind, but I'm on a bit of a mission. I'd like to take a drive through the park and find some lilacs before we go home."

"I don't mind at all. It'll give us more time to talk with the added benefit of stretching our legs for a minute or two. I've just come from the Union Depot. I've been on the train since dawn."

Jesi turned into the park and soon spotted the lilacs. They were only just opening, but their perfume already thickened the air. Jamie helped her down from the buggy, and between the two of them, gathered an armload of lilacs in only a few minutes.

"Thank you for your help," Jesi said as they got on their way again. "I love flowers."

Jamie laughed. "Then you and Cori are an awful lot alike."

"These are for my grandfather and the rest of the family." She cast him a small grin. "With a few for my husband Paul."

"That's right. You're married. Tell me about your husband. I'm anxious to meet him."

"Paul is..." Jesi had written to her family mentioning Paul in several letters, describing him or his ministry in different ways. She'd never had to describe him to another person face to face. Her heart filled.

"Paul is the man who came to my rescue along a railroad line in Hurley. After he rescued me from sickness, he proceeded to rescue my spirit and my heart." She knew she had blushed by the warm flush coming over her, but she didn't care. She smiled at Jamie. "We had an unusual start, but he's a very good man, and he has put up with me beyond anyone else's endurance. Even Cori's."

Jamie smiled in return. "Cori doesn't so much put up with you as much as she defends her own pride."

Jesi gave a little shake of the reins and turned to look at Jamie again. She hadn't expected such a statement -- not from anyone. Cori had always been *good*. Yet here was this man who clearly cared about her, pointing out a flaw.

"James--"

"Jamie."

"Jamie, do you hope to marry my sister?"

A gasp half-filled with humor rushed out of him. His two black eyebrows arched. "You are forthright."

"Do you love her?"

"Yes, I do. That is the answer to both of your questions. None of us are perfect, not even Cori, though I love her dearly. You aren't the only one who's sinned."

"I assume you know all about... what happened."

"You mean Clay Dalton? Yes, I know. I know more than what Cori told me."

Jesi veered as another streetcar passed through the intersection in front of them. She tightened her grip on the reins. "What do you mean?"

"I didn't tell Cori, because I didn't think it would help her to work through her anger. I met Mr. Dalton at your home once. He came shortly after you'd gone, when I was visiting your family for the first time. Dalton arrived to plead his case with Cori, but she sent him on his way." Jamie smiled thoughtfully. "I was quite impressed and not a little intrigued. I'd already found her lovely and interesting and caring. To see her send the man packing like she did with nothing less than a verbal slap in the face… why, it made her even more alluring."

"So you were attracted by her temper?" Jesi laughed. Cori didn't often display her temper to anyone outside her family the way Jesi might. Perhaps her sister had been a bit chagrined at being found a little more like Jesi than she cared to be.

"Yes. My father's family is Irish, and my mother's is Indian. I'm acquainted with a quick tongue." He smiled again.

The sun had risen to nearly noon, and the day had grown warm. Superior's commerce seemed to have picked up, as shoppers hurried in and out of shops along the boardwalk. Horses and carriages clattered by on the cedar block pavement and occasionally bumped over sandstone curbs. Jamie leaned back deeper into the horsehair seat beneath the buggy's canopy.

"I ran into Dalton again recently, on my last trip to Superior, downtown by the station. He looked at me strangely, and I knew he recognized me but couldn't place where he'd seen me before. I thought about speaking to him, but didn't. Then he approached me and asked me where we'd met." Jamie gave a mirthless laugh. "He's a businessman, I take it. He doesn't want to offend a possible contact that might be someone important."

"That sounds like Clay."

"Yes, well… when I pointed out our mutual acquaintance, he turned sour. He seemed to think I would be open to the kinds of things he might say to his friends. He congratulated me on winning Cori. I'm not sure how he knew I had."

"He wanted her back. He must have kept track of her life and heard she was seeing you."

"Yes, probably. Anyway, he asked me if we'd seen or heard from you."

Jesi's heart skipped a beat.

"Then he went on to say he'd found you in Hurley. Your family already knew of your whereabouts by then, of course. But he wanted to make trouble."

Jesi wasn't sure if she should ask, but she had to know. "He told you about the encounter in town?"

"He said you would probably leave your husband someday. He

expected he'd meet you again, eventually."

"Meaning?" Her pulse throbbed in her throat, and the warm sunshine suddenly overwhelmed her. Jesi followed the line of Jamie's intent gaze to a saloon as they passed by.

He answered softly. "He told us about the work you'd been doing before meeting Paul."

She clenched her teeth. After breathing deeply for several moments, she released her breath in a hiss.

"He's wrong." She glanced at Jamie. She wanted to plead her case, but gathered her courage instead. "Not entirely, of course. I did find myself living among Maisey's *soiled doves*. But I ran away before -- well, you understand -- before anything happened. Anything too terrible..."

"I'm not condemning you, Mrs. Winter. Is it all right if I call you Jesi? I won't if it seems too familiar."

Her shoulders slumped. "After this conversation, you wonder about familiarity?"

"I just want you to know I haven't judged you. I hope to call you my sister sometime. But I don't want to presume."

She would have wept if her emotions hadn't been so tangled. She blinked, shook her head, and tried to concentrate on the road.

"Thank you, Jamie. I can see why Cori cares about you. Thank you for telling me. I'm sure my parents suspect my misdeeds, but they haven't asked me to divulge the hideous truth. The business with Clay was bad enough. I don't know if Cori would ever forgive me if she knew. But really, that part of my life has been settled between me and God. I don't think she needs to know."

"Those are my thoughts, as well. But I didn't want to get off on the wrong foot by not being frank with you."

Jesi reached over to pat his hand. He grasped hers in his and squeezed, offering her a reassurance she both appreciated and respected. She glanced his way again. She didn't see the wagon coming.

It charged from the side street next to them. They were in the center of the intersection when it struck, colliding with the buggy and pitching it over. The horses reared, their front hooves raking the air while Jesi's nag stumbled over with the buggy. The buggy's tongue twisted, rending the air with a squeal and the crash of wheels and wood.

Lumber and brick loaded on the wagon clattered and smashed in a loud cacophony combined with horses' neighs, a teamster's shout, and Jesi's shriek.

The horses continued to flail, causing the buggy to jerk and mash its occupants about while the wheels spun over Jesi's head. Jamie's body smashed against hers, and he groaned deeply. The smells of mud and dung and blood mingled with the odd intensity of lilacs.

Pain shot up Jesi's leg and arms, and fear overcame her. Jamie's groan fell silent and he went limp, his body pressing against her and the slippery feel of his blood running down her neck.

"Jame… Jamie. Jamie." She gasped. Her free shoulder shook with a tremble and a sob. Voices rose, and the jangle of the streetcar bell joined the discordant chaos ringing in her ears.

Feet hurried around the buggy, and the occasional face peered in on them. Boards and bricks and dust settled, and then pain wrenched through Jesi again.

Jamie didn't move.

Chapter Thirty-Three

A boy who couldn't have been more than twelve or thirteen stood at the door turning his cap over in his hands. Mama squeezed her eyes shut and pinched her forehead between her fingers. Cori's knees went weak, and she nearly swooned.

Papa stood in front of the boy. "Thank you for bringing us the message."

He glanced at Paul, whose Adam's apple moved up and down, but otherwise he remained calm.

"I'm coming." Mama hurried out of the hall and returned a moment later with her bonnet. "Cori, we have to hurry."

Cori shook her head. Numbed, she couldn't find the words for the fear wrapped like a fist around her throat. *Jesilyn and Jamie? Together?*

She'd paid little attention to Jesi's activities since coming home. Her sister had mentioned running an errand, but Cori didn't know what it was or when Jesi had planned to go, only that she was gone and Paul was here with them.

Hideous memories flowered like iron rust in her mind, eating away at her sense of calmness. Jesi had used errands as an excuse to meet with Clay. Yet this was much worse. Cori loved Jamie with all of her soul. If Jesi had corrupted that love...

Papa frowned. "Cori?"

Tears of fear and anger made twin pools across her vision. "I can't..."

They looked at one another, but Cori dropped her gaze and squeezed her fists.

"Come on, Paul."

Her parents and brother-in-law left. As the door closed behind them, a weight sank like an anchor inside her chest. She broke into a sob and cried out, crossing one arm over the other and pounding her shoulders.

"*God!*" She covered her face and wailed.

"What on earth?" Evie burst around the corner at the sound of the commotion.

Cori shook her head.

"Cori." The housekeeper grabbed her forearms and pulled her hands from her eyes. "Cori, what's wrong?"

"She killed him."

The woman's eyes grew even wider. "What?"

"Jesi, she..." Cori gulped and sobbed again. She clenched her jaw. "She k-killed Jamie. There's been an accident."

"What on earth... You come and sit down here with me."

Evie directed her into the parlor and sat with her on the settee. Their knees touched, and Evie kept Cori's hands clenched in her own. Cori could have broken free. Part of her wanted to run out the door and not stop until she'd thrown herself into Lake Superior. Part of her wanted to go upstairs and destroy every last shred of Jesi's belongings that acknowledged her sister's existence. Part of her wanted to go to the hospital, and if Jesi were conscious, tear out her hair and...

Part of her just wanted to sit and weep.

Evie handed her a hankie and waited for Cori's crying to abate. "Tell me now. What happened?"

"A boy came just a little while ago. He said there'd been a terrible accident and that both of them were taken to the hospital. There was blood and..." Tears oozed from her eyes again, and she could hardly breathe.

Evie tucked Cori's head onto her soft shoulder. "Dear girl..."

She rocked Cori just like she had when Cori was a child, and probably didn't even know she'd spoken when she said, "Jamie was with Jesi?"

The impact of her words, like the draw of a sharp knife across Cori's veins, underscored her deepest suspicions.

*****

Paul said little on the trip to the hospital. Jesi's parents whispered back and forth, words of comfort and mutual reassurance. They included him from time to time, but mostly he remained locked alone inside his worry and prayers.

Let her be all right, Lord. Please don't take her from me now.

He knew he should pray for Cori's friend Jamie, too, and he uttered a few words in his heart toward God for Jamie's deliverance, but his heart twisted for his wife. *Please give the doctor wisdom and add strength to Jesi's body.*

He hardly realized Zane had spoken.

"I'm sorry?"

"I said I want to apologize for Cori. I'd have thought that hearing Jesilyn was in an accident would have moved her. I don't know what could be going through her mind, or why she'd stay away without knowing Jamie's condition."

Paul thought he knew why, but with Mrs. Beaumont so on edge, he wasn't sure if he should say. Besides, maybe he was wrong. Maybe Cori was merely in a state of shock -- like they all were.

They found Jesi sitting up in bed in a room between two other patients at St. Francis's Hospital. Jamie was in another room, and the doctor was still with him.

She sat straighter as they walked into the room, and her eyes searched for Paul's. He hurried to her side.

"Jesi." He breathed her name. A rush of relief washed over him to see that she was all right. A large bruise on her cheek seemed to be her only visible injury. He stroked the underside of her chin and examined her further. "Are you hurt anyplace else?"

She shook her head. "Only some more bruises, mainly on my hip and right leg. Jamie Gilbert spared me by taking the brunt of the impact."

Tears filled her eyes and he longed to kiss them away, but he didn't want to hurt her.

"Is he going to be all right?"

Zane stepped forward and caressed his daughter's hand. "I'm going to see him now and will find out. I'll be back shortly."

Lainey stepped forward and sat beside Jesi. "Can you tell us how it happened?"

"It was so sudden. We were driving home, and a wagon came through the intersection and struck us. I've heard the other man is fine, but they haven't told me anything about Jamie."

"How did you come to be with him?" Paul wanted to know now, before anyone else asked questions.

"I was driving home from Dr. Niemi's, and he passed by on the streetcar. He thought I was Cori." Her eyes lit suddenly and darted between him and her mother. "I explained who I was, then brought him along. We were on our way to the house. He was so anxious to see her."

Lainey patted her hand. "That's what I thought."

"Where is Cori?" Jesi frowned.

Paul raised her other hand to his lips and pressed a soft kiss to the back of it, noticing some small abrasions on her knuckles as he did so. "She stayed behind. She was afraid to come, afraid to find out the worst, I think."

Jesi's gaze steadied, conveying that she wondered otherwise.

A doctor entered the room and addressed them. "How are you feeling, Mrs. Winter? Any other pain? Dizziness of any kind?"

"No. Just what I told you before, and a headache."

"I'd like to keep you here tonight, just to keep an eye on you. By morning, if you're feeling all right, I'll send you home to your family's care."

"Please, Doctor. This is my husband, Paul, and my mother, Elaina Beaumont. They'll give me the best of care if I can go home with them now."

The doctor glanced between the three of them, his brow bent in consideration. "Well, as it appears you don't have any severe injuries, I'll agree to that arrangement, but if your headache worsens or you feel unusually dizzy -- if anything else troubles you, anything at all -- then you should send for your regular doctor right away, understand?" He glanced down at his notes. "You said you normally see Dr. Niemi?"

"Yes. That's right. He'll be stopping by in a day or two to see my grandfather anyway, so I'll be sure and tell him if I have any trouble."

Lainey smiled. "We'll tuck her in and make sure she rests."

Paul shook the doctor's hand. "Do I need to sign anything for her release?"

"Yes, the nurse will be right in. Take care, now."

They murmured their thanks. The doctor left just as Zane returned. He tucked his hands against his armpits. "Jamie won't be going home for a few days. He's got a gash across the back of his head, and the doctors say he's suffered a fracture to his skull. He's also got some strained ligaments in his leg and will limp for a while once he's on his feet. Praise God it's nothing worse."

"Is he awake?"

"He is, but he's not very lucid." Zane took Lainey's hand. "He doesn't quite remember what happened yet. He'll need close watching."

"I'm so relieved," Jesi said, shaking her head, her voice choked, raspy. "Of all the awful things to have happen."

"But you're both going to be all right," Lainey said.

They tucked Jesi gently into the buggy for the ride home. She rested her head against Paul's shoulders until they arrived. Evie met them at the door and quickly arranged a place on the settee in the parlor for their patient. Paul would have liked to take her upstairs to their room and take care of her himself, but realized they all needed to be able to express comfort to Jesilyn and thus themselves that no serious harm had, indeed, come to her.

For James Gilbert, they could do little. Lainey and Zane assured Cori he would be right as rain before too many days, but that his injuries had been serious enough to become dangerous if not carefully monitored, and thus he'd need to remain hospitalized for a time.

To Paul's astonishment, she seemed shaken, yet asked little else. And she didn't seem ready to go to the hospital to see Jamie. Paul couldn't do much about it in any case, as his priority was to take care of his wife.

"I'm going to sit here and read to you later, but for now I'm going to let you rest."

"No. Please, don't go." She laid a hand on his arm and stopped him. "For a moment when the accident first happened, the world flew by, and all my memories were suddenly before me, all jumbled together at once, and I saw them in an instant. In the midst of them all was you, and how I thought for that one split second I might never see you again."

"Jesi." He bent and kissed her on the lips. "Now you see that God was watching over you, just as he was watching over me, because He knew how much I need you."

Her face was close to his, and her gray eyes swirled with questions.

"Oh, Paul, I feel so terrible about it. If I had been only a minute sooner or a minute later, I never would have met him. He wouldn't have gotten off the trolley. Or if we hadn't stopped to pick the flowers..."

Paul cocked his head. "Flowers?"

"Yes. I stopped in the park for lilacs. Jamie helped me pick them."

"You stopped in the park for lilacs."

"Yes, a big bunch of them. After the accident, while I lay there, I could smell the lilacs and horses and... Jamie." She shook her head again and closed her eyes.

Paul kissed the top of her head and pulled her close. "It must have been very frightening. I'm sorry I wasn't there with you. I should have been driving."

She sighed, her breath warm against his neck. So many times she'd been in peril, and he hadn't been there. God willing, he would never let it happen again. Yet Paul had no way to always protect, always provide. At times, God alone would be a refuge for each of them.

Thank you, Lord God, for covering her.

Paul tried to imagine the scene of the accident with Jamie's body guarding Jesi's and knew that somehow God had orchestrated it. If Jamie had injured his head, what might have happened to Jesilyn without the cushion of his protection?

But why him?

As if on cue to the direction of his thoughts, Cori stood in the doorway looking at them.

Paul came to his feet, but she didn't acknowledge him with more than a cursory glance. Her gaze penetrated her twin's, and a strange surrealism hovered about them, an undercurrent of unspoken animosity from Cori colliding with expectation and even acceptance from Jesi. Cori's chin lifted only an inch, but Paul recognized the rod of iron and fierce determination in her small movement.

So like Jesi's could be at times.

"Well." Cori's single word, spoken without expression, turned her lips into a straight line parallel to her arms crossed over her midsection, and set the tone of her intentions.

Paul stepped forward, prepared to make sure she didn't upset Jesi. But his wife spoke first.

"Come in, Cori. I've been expecting you."

"I guess you should." Cori's lashes moved, only hinting at her momentary surprise. "Do you mind if I have a private word with my sister, Paul?"

"If you don't take long." Paul glanced at his wife, but she hadn't wavered from Cori's stare. "Jesi needs to rest."

"I won't be long."

Paul reached for Jesi's hand and squeezed it. He gave her a feathery kiss on the cheek. "Don't tax yourself."

Her glance softened, and she gave him a small smile. So only he could hear, she whispered one word. "Pray."

*****

Jesi's eyes felt heavy. Her head pounded. Yet she could plainly see why Cori had come. She'd wondered if the entire week would pass without Cori speaking to her again, but now the opportunity had presented itself and Jesi wouldn't miss it, no matter how ragged and beaten her body felt. Unfortunately, the accident with Jamie had made it certain that Cori would berate her for getting him hurt.

Or so she thought.

"You haven't changed. You can't fool me by batting eyes at your husband and acting like a preacher's wife. That's all it is. An act. You're still the same hussy you were when you pursued Clay. What's the matter, Jesi? Isn't Paul enough for you? Or are you only satisfied when you can have any man who wants me?"

Jesi's blood ran cold. Was that what Cori thought -- that she had *planned* to be with Jamie? She hadn't even known he was coming to town. Clearly, Cori had figured otherwise.

"I heard about the flowers strewn about the street," Cori continued, stepping closer to hover over Jesi, forcing her gaze upward. "How romantic. And wasn't it convenient to fix it so that your husband would be engrossed with Gramp all morning long? You... you tramp."

Jesi shook her head, and it pounded all the more. "No, Cori."

"Ha." Cori paced back and forth beside the settee. "I can't believe you're still up to such games. Did you make him think you were me? I thought Jamie would know better than to fall for your false charm. He's different than Clay, you know. He's respectful. He's..."

Her eyes, glassy and full, spilled over. Her lips trembled, whether with sorrow or rage or both, Jesi couldn't say for sure.

"You're right. He is. I could see that the moment I met him."

"So you're ready to make another confession. Afraid being caught will ruin your position with Paul, perhaps?"

"No. Not at all. Cori, do you hear yourself? I've never met or spoken to James Gilbert before this morning, and only just a short while before the accident."

"That makes it all the worse. I'm sure he thought you were me, and you let him think it, playing him false like you've always done." Suddenly Cori's expression changed. Her eyes widened and then narrowed. "I've just remembered. You went by a false name in Hurley. Why was that, Jesilyn? To hide from your family... or for some other reason? So men wouldn't know your real name?"

"Something like that."

Cori clamped her lips together. She obviously didn't know what to think. Still, she acted so sure...

"I was hiding, and I was ashamed. I found the only room I could afford. When I ran out of money to pay the rent, the proprietor offered me a job." Jesi let her words sink in. Cori seemed to process them and come to a conclusion well enough. "I couldn't do the work they asked of me, so eventually I left."

"You couldn't? You shouldn't have had any trouble at all if the work was what I think it was."

"You're probably right. But I couldn't. It wasn't remotely the same, Cori. Something you don't understand is that I really cared for Clay. I thought I loved him. I know better now."

"Do you? How could that be?"

"I have Paul. And I do love him. Paul is... he's everything to me. You must know something about that. Or at least, I thought you must. You care for Jamie more than you cared for Clay, or so I thought."

Cori's mask fell for a second, but she quickly put it back in place. "If he has been false with me, how can I love him?"

If...

That was only a small crack in her certainty, but Jesilyn grasped it. "Jamie wouldn't do such a thing. I've known him for less than a day and spoken with him for less than an hour, but I can see that much. He would be true to you, Cori, if you wouldn't doubt him."

Cori faltered. She gazed again at Jesi, and this time Jesi could see the uncertainty in the blue of her irises. She wanted to believe Jesi, and she wanted to hope in Jamie.

Jesi took advantage of it. "I'm through carrying shame, Cori. I deserved it, I won't argue that. But try as I might, I couldn't live that life. I gave it away. I gave it to God and now it's gone. Forever. I don't have to shoulder it any longer."

"But you were with him."

"Jamie did think I was you, but only for a moment. I explained to him who I really was. Do you suppose, Cori, that I don't know what sort of things you've told him about me? Don't worry. I'm not angry at you for it. Jamie cares a great deal for you. I'm glad he does."

Cori's eyes flashed. "How do you know that?"

"He told me. And I encouraged him in that regard. He couldn't wait to get here to see you. Are you sure you want to throw that away based on unfounded misgivings?"

"Unfounded?"

"I'm sorry, Cori." Jesi flushed. Pressure squeezed her temples. "I hope I never hurt you again. Please believe me. Please trust Jamie."

Cori stared hard at her, but Jesi recognized by the way her chest rose and fell that she was about to cry. She turned and fled the room, her skirts swirling behind her and her feet pummeling the stairs as she sought sanctuary.

Jesi dropped her arm over her eyes and closed them against the light. *I hope I did right. God, please make it right. I know nothing else to say.*

*****

Corianne paced her room, her thoughts running to and fro, impossible to keep up with. For the first time in over a year, she longed to believe her sister. She longed to trust her words. *I'm sorry. I hope I never hurt you again.*

Over and over she heard them. *I'm sorry. I'm sorry. I love Paul. I'm sorry.*

She pictured Jamie, crushed beneath the buggy on the street, horses stamping and rearing, blood pouring from the wound to his head -- while he'd been hurrying to see her. And now he lay in pain in the hospital with no one there beside him, no one in this whole city who knew him, while bitterness and resentment kept her away.

She squeezed the sides of her dress, clenching and unclenching the material until she'd wrinkled it beyond repair, and she finally made a decision.

The following morning, with only the barest attention to her toilet, Cori donned her bonnet and left the house early, scurrying past the parlor where Jesi sat propped against pillows with a coffee tray on a small table between herself and her husband's chair.

Cori couldn't seem to harness the horse to the buggy quickly enough and barely noticed the chilly wind off the lake as she drove the interminable distance across the city to the hospital.

"Please, I need to find a patient," she told the first nurse she saw.

Minutes later, the nurse took her to Jamie's room.

She hesitated and took a breath, praying he'd want to see her and hoping that what Jesi had said was true. He lay awake, his head swathed in bandages, his gaze toward the window. A lump filled her throat, and she cleared it softly.

His head swiveled slowly, and he stared back at her.

Had someone told him she hadn't wanted to come? Was he angry she'd stayed away? She took slow steps to his bedside. He turned his palm up and gave her the edges of a smile.

Her fears melted away, and she took his hand.

"Thank you for coming."

"Jamie." Her breath caught, and she had to look away for a moment as guilt sailed through her. "I'm sorry I didn't come yesterday."

"It's all right. I was confused then. I remember your father was here."

"Yes. He told me about your condition when he arrived home."

"You're here now."

Tears edged her eyelids. She nodded and sniffed. "Are you in a terrible amount of pain?"

"No, not if I'm still. My head hurts if I move it too quickly, and my leg when I shift it."

"I should have come before now."

"It's all right--"

"No. I stayed away because... because..."

He frowned, but the gentle tug on her fingers told her he was willing to listen. She looked around for a chair, letting go of his hand to pull one closer. She sat on the edge of the hard seat near him and took his hand again.

"I was afraid, but not for reasons you may think. I'd found out you were with Jesi, and I was afraid--" Shame stole her voice. "Afraid she'd stolen you from me."

No dimples pressed into his cheeks. His white smile didn't shine. His eyes remained dull with pain, likely from her words as much as his injury. "How could you think such a thing?"

"I couldn't help it, not then."

"Cori..." He, too, seemed at a loss for words. Shocked, almost.

How could she have thought such a thing of him? Of Jesi, yes. But not Jamie.

She corrected herself. No, she shouldn't have even thought it of Jesi. Cori was so confused. Jesi had apologized for her actions with Clay the day she'd arrived. She'd seemed genuinely changed, despite Cori's best effort to reject it.

"What did your sister tell you?"

"She told me you were anxious to see me." Cori sniffed again. "My father said you saved her life."

Furrows lined his brow. Likely, he still didn't remember much about the accident.

"I was very anxious, Cori. When I first saw your sister, I thought she was you, but of course she corrected me right away, almost the minute I'd realized my mistake."

"She did?"

He smiled a little now.

"Wait. You... you realized I wasn't in the buggy?"

"You aren't the same people." He traced his thumb across her knuckles. "I know you, Corianne."

The tension binding her shoulders slid away. No one had ever been able to tell her and Jesi apart except their parents. She searched Jamie's face, saw the swelling and bruising beneath his eyes, longed to caress away his pain.

Yet he continued to soothe her, his voice like balm. "Your eyes are such a bright blue. If she had been you, I would have wondered what had taken their light away. And your skin is so fine and smooth. Your hands are like those of the porcelain dolls my sister Ginny keeps in a trunk at my da's house. Your lips..." He looked at her mouth in such a way that she momentarily forgot he was in pain. "Your lips are like the pinkest of your mother's roses."

He lifted his fingertip and brushed it across her lower lip. "I want to touch them."

His hand caressed her chin, drawing her to him. Cori leaned close, allowing him to coax her nearer until their lips gently touched.

Muddled by the joy that seemed bent on dissolving her confusion, she blinked and sat back in the chair.

"You look very different from your sister, at least to me."

"I do?"

"Yes, you do."

The truth poured over her, and she saw herself clearly. Her bitterness toward Jesilyn had so clouded her vision that she'd almost let it destroy her chance with Jamie. As if she'd been drowning, she suddenly reached the surface. Cold, fresh air, sharp and filling, bit into her lungs. She opened her eyes, and the sun shone on her soul. She gasped.

"What is it? What's wrong?"

"Nothing." She shook her head. "Nothing is wrong. I feel as though things are finally right. Oh, Jamie, how have you borne with me?"

He reached for her hands with both of his and held them fast. "Don't you know how?"

"No. No, I really don't. I've been so wrong. You've urged me to forgive Jesilyn, and I just couldn't do it. Not even when she did exactly what I wanted her to do. She asked me for my forgiveness. Instead of believing her, I wanted to punish her."

"But not anymore?"

She shook her head and laughed a little through the moisture gathering in her eyes.

Jamie laid his head back. He still held her hand, but he'd grown weak and would probably need to sleep again soon.

"I spoke with her today before I came. I wasn't very pleasant. But when I go home I'll go to her and tell her I'm sorry for not listening. I'll forgive her. I promise."

"You don't have to tell me."

"Yes, I do. I have to tell you because for a lunatic moment, I judged you to be like Clay, even though I knew you weren't."

"Thank you for that." His eyes, hooded with weariness, opened a bit wider, and he gave her a soft smile. "But do you know why you truly can believe both your sister and me?"

"Why?" she asked, as his pulse ran from his fingertips into hers.

"Because she truly loves her husband Paul, just as I love you."

She squeezed his hand, longing to have him kiss her again, but he closed his eyes and drifted into sleep.

Chapter Thirty-Four

Jesi planted her hands on her hips and gazed around her old room. A trunk lay open on the bed, waiting to be filled with things she wished to take along to her new home in Hurley, as well as with some of the household goods Mama, Gran, and Evie insisted she take. Dear Evie. She'd given Jesi and Paul a beautiful quilt, one she'd admitted making long ago and tucking away for a wedding present. Another awaited Cori should she marry. Mama passed along some special dishes, and Gran had supplied her with some pretty linens for her table and bedroom. She truly felt like a bride.

She pressed her cheeks between her hands and spun about, pausing to glance in the mirror. She'd never thought herself so pretty. Not nearly so much as she did now with the glow of Paul's love shining on her face.

Well, she'd better get on with the task. They'd be leaving in a few days, and there was still so much to do. Paul had gone to the church to visit with her family's pastor and wouldn't be back for a while.

She'd only packed a few books and wrapped a music box in one of Gran's linens when a tap on her door pulled her away from the task. "Come right in."

Her heart lurched when Cori stepped into the doorway, an unsettled look on her face.

"Cori." Catching herself, Jesi stepped back, allowing her sister plenty of space. "Come in. Please."

Cori knotted her hands against her waist as she hesitantly entered the room.

"I'm sorry for interrupting. You're packing?"

"Yes." Jesi gestured limply at the open trunk. "Just some things I've been missing."

Cori gave a nod. "I suppose you've been living primitively over there."

"It's not so bad. It's peaceful, actually."

Cori gazed downward. "I'd miss the liveliness of a city like Superior."

"Oh, Hurley has plenty of liveliness, I can assure you." She laced her voice with all the chagrin she felt. "I'd just as soon stay clear of it."

"You have changed."

Jesi lifted her head, and Cori looked directly at her as though seeing her for the first time since she'd returned.

"I didn't really believe it before. I didn't *want* to believe it before."

Unsure of where Cori's observations might lead her, Jesi was afraid to speak. She decided to just be quiet and let her sister say whatever she'd come to say... or to ask what she wanted to find out.

"I went to see Jamie." Cori's eyes turned glassy, and she fidgeted. "I know now that you didn't do anything wrong." She shrugged. "But *I* did. Jesi, I'm sorry. I'm sorry I didn't accept your apology. I'm sorry for resenting you."

Jesi wanted to rush forward and hug Corianne, but she held back. She wasn't sure if she dared.

Cori glanced at her and hurried on. "You were right. If I'd cared two cents about Jamie, I'd have rushed straight to the hospital. And I do care. But I was so blinded by my own distrust and fear, I let it drown me. I was wrong."

Tears leaked out and trickled down her face. Her glance drifted to the window, where her vision was obscured by a heavy fog off Lake Superior. "I feel as if I've been living under a fog for so long, enshrouded in a mist of my own making."

"Not your own entirely." Jesi stepped forward and slowly lifted her hand, letting it hover without touching Cori.

Cori suddenly clutched Jesi, and they intertwined their forearms. "But too much."

The distance between them collapsed, and they embraced. Tears came to Jesi, too, and Cori sobbed softly.

"I'm sorry, Cori."

"I know. I forgive you. I'm sorry, too."

"I let my foolishness ruin so many things." Jesi squeezed her sister more tightly. "I ruined your future, and I ruined myself. I didn't deserve to find Paul. I know that."

"Nor I, Jamie."

They stepped back, their arms still outstretched, holding on to one another.

Cori sniffed. "I find myself wondering what would have happened the first time Jamie came here, if I'd still been so silly over Clay. I would have missed him entirely."

"Well, Clay is gone from our lives, and we can both be thankful for that."

"Do you ever worry about seeing him?"

Jesi's heart jumped. She considered Cori's innocent question and knew that for them to have a new start, she must be honest. "I saw him once, not long ago. It did not go well." She scrunched up her nose. "Paul knocked him into the street."

"He did? Tell me about it."

"Paul and I had gone to town, and he left me at the mercantile while he did another errand."

Cori turned and sat on the bed next to the trunk, scooting over to make room for Jesi.

Jesi tucked her skirt around her legs and sat down. "Suddenly Clay was there."

"He did go after you, then. I thought he might."

Jesi didn't want to speculate about that. If Clay had really tried to find her, she was certain he'd done it for less than honorable reasons. He'd made that clear with his invitation. And even if he hadn't, she knew now what kind of man he was, and that a relationship between the two of them would have never worked out -- nor contained the kind of love she had for Paul, or the commitment he offered.

"I think Clay is a very confused man. He was sorry he threw away what he had with you. He hated me, Cori. You were right about that. I was foolish to think otherwise."

"And?"

"But he was there in Hurley. At first he acted pleasant, and I became curious about him. I wondered if he really had cared for me. Then he made accusations and caused a scene. When Paul arrived, Clay said some horrible things. A man named Big John was also there, and he only made matters worse."

Cori's eyes widened, but she didn't ask about Big John.

Jesi went on, "Paul hit Big John, and Big John hit Paul. Then -- oh... it's all a blur, really -- Clay said something Paul wouldn't let go by, and he sent Clay flying into the dirt, right there in front of the whole town."

"Wait a minute..." Cori frowned. "You said this happened not long ago. You and Paul were married. But you wondered about Clay, even then?"

Jesi's collar felt as if it might choke her. She rose and opened the window, letting in a rush of damp, chilly air. She couldn't stop now. If she didn't tell Cori the truth, it would always be hidden just behind a curtain of shame, ready to pop out and surprise them both.

"Yes. We were married. Cori, I'm so thankful we're having this conversation, so thankful you've forgiven me. But the truth, Cori, is that I'm afraid you'll change your mind. Yet I want to tell you everything."

Cori reached for Jesi and pulled her back beside her. "I never want to go into that place of bitterness again. Tell me."

"All right." She studied Cori's face, like looking in a reflection. Then she cleared her voice. "I didn't love Paul when we first married, but neither did I try to trap him. We'd come to the decision together. Paul and I lived together for a number of months as man and wife, but we didn't behave as man and wife." She let that sink in.

"You didn't..."

"Sleep in the same bed? No, not even in the same room. Our marriage was one of convenience only... for both of us. But Paul respected me, and I was not over my past. Slowly that changed, however. I eventually saw Paul for the man he is, and I fell in love with him."

"And he with you."

Jesi nodded, a pleasant warmth filling her, a small smile tugging at her lips. "Recently."

"How recently?"

She blushed. "Just last week."

Cori leapt to her feet. "You've been together all that time, but just last week you--"

"I love him so much, Cori."

Cori bent and hugged her. "Then I'd say you *didn't* trap him."

Jesi laughed, and Cori joined in. The laughter felt good, as if they were children again, sharing secrets.

Finally, sobering, Cori walked over and closed the window. "It's cold in here. What happened to springtime?"

"It's here."

Cori looked at Jesi, who pointed at her heart. It bloomed like a rose when Cori smiled and nodded.

*****

Dr. Niemi snapped his bag shut and tucked his spectacles into the pocket of his vest. Then he addressed Jesi's grandfather.

"I'm optimistic, Mr. Kade. I have no way of knowing with absolute certainty, of course, that a tumor won't reappear in another location, but you've withstood the ordeal well for a patient of your mature years. I see no sign of infection at the surgical site. We'll continue to monitor your recovery closely. I don't see any reason at all why you shouldn't have hope. Your family is certainly rooting for you, and that is perhaps the greatest asset in such a situation."

Mama clasped her hands together. "You aren't going to be leaving us for a long time, Pa, if I have anything to say about it."

Gramp huffed. "And we all know how stubborn you are."

"That's why I keep praying."

Gran squeezed his hand and gave it a small shake.

Jesilyn limped over and bent to kiss his cheek. "You'll never know how sorry I am that I ran off when you needed me here."

"Well, that all worked out though, didn't it?" His eyes twinkled at her beneath his bushy brows, then he flashed a glance at Paul.

She straightened and returned to Paul's side, the muscles of her sore leg contracting against her bruises.

Gramp looked at her pa. "What about the other patient? How's he doing today?"

After three days in the hospital, Jamie had been released to their care. He now occupied the settee in the parlor Jesi had first claimed.

Pa gave a nod. "He's feeling much better, though I think that has less to do with medical attention than it does to the attention of my other daughter."

"Those Gilbert men were never ones to waste a good courtin' opportunity," Gramp said. He and Dr. Niemi exchanged wry smiles.

Gran rolled her eyes and patted his hand. "You'd better keep that in mind. Maybe it'll get you back on your feet before Joe comes back for a visit."

They all laughed, then left Gramp with Gran to rest.

Downstairs, they found Cori stitching away on a piece of embroidery while she sat with Jamie. He looked better. His color had returned, and they had to expend more effort keeping him abed. He glanced at them all as they strode into the parlor.

"The sunshine is calling. I sure would like to get out for a while."

"No reason why you shouldn't take a stroll on the lawn," Dr. Niemi said. "Just walk slowly and rest often."

Jamie grinned at Cori. "I told you he'd approve."

"Are you certain, Doctor?"

"Give him a chair to rest in. Fresh air will do him wonders."

"Maybe we'll join you," Paul said.

Every time Jesi thought she'd appreciated her husband as much as she could, he found another door into her heart. She and Cori were no longer at odds, and Paul always found ways to give them more time together. A stab of melancholy pierced Jesi's heart. What a shame she and Paul were leaving the next morning, now that she'd finally made amends with her sister. And yet, a sort of thrill settled into her core, too, to think about the new life waiting for them back in the woods camp below Hurley.

"I suppose you're anxious to get back to your work," Jamie said to Paul a short time later. The doctor had gone, and Jesi's parents and Evie had left the room to tend tasks in other parts of the house. Paul helped Jamie to his feet and then adjusted the sling on his shoulder so it was comfortable before the four of them went out into the garden.

Paul winked. "I am a bit anxious, to tell you the truth. And that makes me rather glad. It's more proof it's where God wants me. You have more recuperating to do before you can work with your father and uncles again, though, don't you?"

"I plan to be here for a while, so I should be fine by the time I have to go back."

They walked out into the garden and found the bench Jamie and Cori had shared many times before.

"Look, Paul, a bloom."

"It's a bit early," Cori said as Jesi examined it.

"It's like a gift," Paul said, capturing Jesi's hand.

"You should take a bush back to Hurley with you."

Jesi turned to Cori. "That would be a wonderful idea. I wonder if Mama would mind."

"I'll ask her for you." Cori squinted at her against the bright sun.

"I'm sure she'd love it. It would be like taking part of her along with you. You know how terribly she's going to miss you being here."

"A rose would look lovely by the doorstep," Paul said. "What do you say we stroll about and find a likely candidate, my love?"

"Stay a moment, will you?" Jamie's unexpected request stopped them both.

Jesi took in his serious expression and glanced at Paul, but a glint in his eye told her he knew what Jamie was about to say.

"I couldn't wait to get back up north." He reached for Cori's hand and clasped it in his. "The adventure started off on a different foot than I'd expected, to be sure. I'd planned to see Corianne and to take her out about the town. More picnics in the park, more carriage rides and boat rides, perhaps. Quiet dinners with her family. I certainly didn't expect to wind up in a hospital, and then spend the better part of the week abed. Yet she has nursed me to a fine robustness."

Cori blushed and flitted an embarrassed glance at Jesi and Paul. Jamie went on as Paul slid his arm around Jesi and tugged her close.

"Truly, to have such devoted attention from my girl has been nothing to complain about. Not even a head injury can ruin such delight."

Cori continued to blush and looked as if she were about to speak, but Jamie laid a finger against her lips and hushed her before the words could escape. He looked at her as though the two of them were alone in the garden, or maybe all the world.

"I came here to spend time with you, and I have. I came here to admire you, and I have. I came here to enjoy the presence of your family." He glanced briefly at Jesi and Paul. "But mostly, I came to do one thing, and I won't let even an accident deter me.

"Corianne Beaumont, I came to ask you to be my wife."

He held out his hand, and Paul stepped forward. He reached into his pocket and handed something to Jamie.

Shock and even greater love for Paul rolled over Jesi.

Jamie opened his fingers and extended a small, shining band to Cori, whose blush had drained away, leaving her face pale, her eyes bright. Jamie's dark good looks contrasted sharply with hers, but Jesi could not imagine a more beautiful couple.

He smiled, and dimples etched grooves in his cheeks. "Will you?"

Cori suddenly seemed to realize their presence. But her eyelids drooped, her shoulders relaxed, and she found her tongue. "Yes, Jamie Gilbert. I'll marry you."

Paul cleared his throat softly so only Jesi noticed. He turned her away and pressed her hand with his, a smile of secret delight lighting his face. Jesi could still hardly believe he'd been in on Jamie's secret, and she cast her sister a momentary backward glance. Cori's hand was on her fiancé's shoulder, and he cupped her face. The moment now belonged only to them.

Jesi looked forward to the moments to come with Paul. For now, only God knew the secrets and surprises they'd share, the moments of bliss or pain.

They belonged to each other, and to no one else. As He had ordained.

Epilogue

Leaves lay thick and dry upon the forest floor. Jesi and Paul's feet swished through them, and her senses livened at the pungency of leaf mold and pine resin filling each breath as her long skirt brushed past the boughs and low brush. Paul paused in his step ahead of her, and with a quick glance over his shoulder, pressed his finger to his lips.

Jesi stilled. Slowly they both crouched low. Paul rested the stock of his gun on the ground and pointed up ahead. Jesi peered along his arm. A grouse danced beneath the halo of a spruce tree, picking at seeds and fluffing its feathers. Suddenly it crouched and vibrated the air with the haunting sound of drumming wings.

Paul turned slowly and handed her the gun. Its weight pulled her forward, and she tried to steady it on the strutting bird. Her arms shook and her heart beat as loudly in her ears as the bird's wings pounding the earth. She pinched one eye closed and squeezed the trigger.

Leaves and dirt flew up around the bird, but it jumped and flew off into the woods, dipping and arcing until it disappeared completely.

Jesi slumped, and Paul laughed.

"You'll get better. I promise."

"I can't believe I missed."

"Don't worry. We won't starve." He patted the bag of fowl resting on the ground beside them.

"It'll be entirely up to you and this little fellow to provide for us, I'm sure." Jesi patted her small rounded stomach, and Paul's gaze fell on her hand.

A smile stretched across his face, and he slid one arm around her while he used the other to relieve her of the heavy gun. "What if it's a girl?"

"She'll probably be a better hunter than her mother."

"You just need more practice."

"As in everything, it seems."

He kissed her lightly on the lips and took her hand in his.

As they walked ahead, the cabin not far off, Jesi stroked Paul's strong hand with her thumb. She couldn't believe so much had happened since that awful day a year ago when she'd first stepped off the train in Hurley. She doubted Paul had any idea that today was the anniversary of that date. She'd come into town with such haughty expectations. She'd fully believed in her ability to conquer the world and somehow make a future that excluded her family, yet would include a man like Clay.

How differently things had turned out. How merciful God's grace had been.

Now she and Paul would soon be blessed with this little one cradled inside her.

They walked along, each in their own thoughts, Jesi's on the days and years ahead and the kind of contentment she'd never dreamed to possess. She glanced at Paul. He would continue his work among the logging camps until God directed him elsewhere. She would listen to his sermons and encourage him in any way she could. She'd never stop showing him how much she loved him. They'd be happier than anyone else in the world.

The rest of her time she'd spend baking bread and pies for Cookee and the fellows in camp and teaching whatever skills she could to Charlie Hanke's girls. And she would raise her and Paul's child, loving him or her as fiercely as she loved the child's daddy.

That's what the future held. Jesi intended to rush into it gladly.

Reaching the cabin, they stopped at the doorstep. Paul settled the bag of game on the ground and leaned the gun against the wall. Then he turned and took Jesilyn into his arms. His kiss was cool and soft on her lips, filling her with delight in a way she'd thought already complete, taking her to a place of joy that spoke of promises and belonging. She wrapped her arms around his neck and returned his love, his passion.

In some ways, today was like that day a year ago. A new future stretched out before her, the dowry of a changed life, filled with fullness and purpose and love.

The End

Acknowledgements

I hope readers have enjoyed the fifty-year saga of the Kade/Beaumont/Winter family as much as I have enjoyed writing it. I would like to thank every reader who has taken time to be carried away on my tales of romance, adventure, and faith in the Northwoods. Each time I complete another generation's story set in the larger framework of Wisconsin's great lumber and railroad era, I begin imagining what will happen next. I think of all the real adventures bound in Wisconsin's marvelous history. I'm so appreciative of the true-life stories that fill the research books. They light my imagination on fire.

Special thanks go to those whose resources gave me ideas for story themes. They often come in small places: a sermon, a personal struggle, a song. For themes in *The Black Rose,* I'd like to identify a couple of those sources. One was from the book *Captivating: Unveiling the Mystery of a Woman's Soul* by Stasi and John Eldredge, a husband and wife writing team. They wrote about the concept that Satan hates beauty because beauty displays unique evidence of God's glory. Therefore, Satan will try to find the means to destroy it or twist it. That spoke to me. I believe this is one of the ways he attacks young women who seem to have everything going for them. He either destroys their beauty outright, or mangles it by tricking them into giving it away, along with their self-respect. I implied this truth when Paul said to Jesilyn, "You're a threat to Satan... Your beauty gives you power over him because it is your unique way of carrying the glory of God into the world." Thank you, John and Stasi, for unveiling such an important truth.

I am also appreciative of the message in the song *Mess of Me* by the band Switchfoot. When Jesilyn finally prays to God, confessing the mess she'd made of her life, she reveals how dead she'd felt and that she now has a new longing."I want to spend the rest of my life alive," she says. That line is directly from the song. Thank you, Switchfoot, for such powerful lyrics.

As I finished *The Black Rose*, I realized that Paul and Jesi's child will reach adulthood just before The Great War. Not only that, but he or she will ride the tide of the Roaring Twenties. A time when bootlegging and outlawing was commonplace in Wisconsin, and names like Capone and Dillinger rose to infamy for their notorious hideouts and profiteering rackets in the Northwoods.

I leave it to readers to imagine the next step in the story. By the turn of the twentieth century, Jamie's prediction of the logs playing out had come to pass, and the logging era began a swift decline in Wisconsin.

Mining, farming, and factories soon became the main source of industry. Logging lives on, even now, but much of its lore and romance has faded into history, along with the scream of a thousand buzz saws in a thousand mills along the rivers, the clang of the cookee's dinner bell ringing the men to supper, and the bark of the camp boss rousing, "Time to get up! It's daylight in the swamp!"

About Naomi Musch

Naomi loves women's fiction and romance submerged in American history, but enjoys writing contemporary fiction as well. Whatever the venue, her aim is to surprise and entertain readers while telling stories about imperfect people who are finding hope and faith to overcome their struggles.

For that reason, she also serves as a staff writer for the award-winning publication *Living Stones News* in which she writes feature stories of real lives changed through faith in Christ. Her articles of encouragement for homeschooling families have appeared in a number of magazines and websites, and she mentors young and developing writers through A Novel Writing Site and via her own blog Write Reason.

Naomi and husband Jeff enjoy epic adventures around their home in the Wisconsin woods with their five grown children and three grandchildren (so far). She invites readers to say hello and find out more about her stories, passions, and other writing venues at http://www.naomimusch.com or look her up on Facebook: Naomi Musch - Author, Twitter: NMusch and Goodreads: Naomi Musch.

Made in the USA
Lexington, KY
20 March 2017